The Berenstain Bears

Save Christmas

The Berenstain Bears Save Christmas

Stan & Jan Berenstain
with Mike Berenstain

◆ HARPERCOLLINS*PUBLISHERS*

The Berenstain Bears Save Christmas Copyright © 2003 by Berenstain Enterprises Printed in the U.S.A. All rights reserved. www.harperchildrens.com
Library of Congress Cataloging-in-Publication Data Berenstain, Stan, 1923– The Berenstain bears save Christmas / Stan & Jan Berenstain ; with Mike Berenstain.
p.   cm.   Summary: Thinking that the spirit of Christmas has been lost, Santa Bear disappears, until the Berenstain Bears show him that it still exists. ISBN 0-06-052670-X
— ISBN 0-06-052671-8 (lib. bdg.)   [1. Christmas—Fiction.   2. Bears—Fiction.   3. Stories in rhyme.]   I. Berenstain, Jan, 1923–   II. Berenstain, Michael.   III. Title.
PZ8.3.B4493 Bhim 2003   [E]—dc21   2002151782   Typography by Matt Adamec   1 2 3 4 5 6 7 8 9 10   ❖   First Edition

'Twas the month before Christmas,
and all round the mall
the pre-Christmas traffic
had slowed to a crawl.
The stores were a-selling,
the horns were a-blowing,
the shoppers were
busily to-ing and fro-ing.

Even the family that lived
down the sunny dirt road
(for directions just ask
any chipmunk or toad)
and were usually full of
calm Christmas cheer—
they too were going
Christmas-crazy this year!

Mama Bear missed
how it all used to be,
when all Christmas needed
was a small Christmas tree.
Christmastime once was
a time just for caring,
a time for all families
to be giving and sharing.

But now it seemed Christmas
no longer meant love.
Now it seemed Christmas
meant let's push and shove!
Let's fight for that
very last toy on the shelf!
Let's look out for that
fellow known as yourself!

But a watcher was watching
that Bear Country scene,
keeping close track of Christmas
on his scanner-machine.
And who was that watcher,
did I hear you ask?
Why, the person in charge
of the whole Christmas task!

It was Santa himself
who was watching this mess.
And what did he think?
You can probably guess.
What was happening to Christmas,
grown swollen and huge,
was turning old Santa
right into a *Scrooge!*

Santa, like Mama,
longed for Christmas of old,
when he flew through the night,
so bracingly cold,
in his magical sleigh
all laden with toys
for all the good
little cub girls and boys.
But now things had changed
and not for the better.
He used to enjoy
reading each little cub's letter.
Now Santa got e-mail,
which he read with alarm,
all asking for toys
fully lacking in charm.

Dear Santa,
I would like a doll and some skates. Love, Suzie

Santa:
Bring me —

"This cub wants a video game,
     and I hate to say it,
but this game is so complicated
it's easier not to play it!
And here is one that's even worse—
cubs simply do not need it—
a virtual pet that up and bites
if you fail to feed it.
And worst of all,
this cub wants this innovative cutie,
a miniature canine named
Little Doggie Dooty,
with an item purchased extra
that's positively super,
a high-tech battery-operated
electronic pooper-scooper."

Santa Bear was angry,
upset, and annoyed.
"If things don't change," he thundered,
"Christmas will be null and void!"
And depressed and discouraged,
he jumped into his bed,
turned out all the lights,
and pulled the covers over his head.

Meanwhile, look at what was happening
on the Bear family's street.
Christmas had become a chance
for all bears to compete!
You have never seen such gaggles
of winking blinking lights
or such a loud and rude display
of un-Christmasy sounds and sights:

Great big plastic Santas
that were roaring "Ho! Ho! Ho!,"
a whole entire house
that was wrapped with a bow,
gigantic candy canes
reaching for the sky,
speakers blaring Christmas hits
at neighbors passing by,

Reindeer whose red noses
would put Rudolph's nose to shame.
The bears, one and all,
had been caught up in the game.
All of them were trying
for the best Christmas display.
All of them were trying
to turn nighttime into day.

T he cubs were also caught up
in this nasty Christmas rage.
Their Christmas wish list
grew to cover page after page.
Mama Bear tried her best
to pull Pa from the brink.
She begged him, please,
to take a moment just to stop and think.
But Papa, like the cubs,
was still carried quite away.
There was no doubt the greedies
would spoil Christmas Day!

Now Mrs. Santa loved Christmas
just as much as her mate.
She especially liked the catalog
that came from Bearal and Crate.
But she too thought that Christmas
had gotten out of hand
and that the Christmas greedies
were spreading through the land.

She was worried about Christmas,
but worried more about her mate.
Hot tea usually cheered him up,
with fresh-baked cookies on a plate.
But Santa Bear was gone!
There was just a note on the bed.
It was pinned to Santa's pillow,
and this is what it said:

Subject: Christmas is Canceled!
To my dear and loving wife,
Christmas is my life,
and what I have to say
is that the true spirit of Christmas
has somehow lost its way.
I have gone to find it.
I will search until I do.
But better that there's none at all
than what it's turned into.

Your loving husband

Of course Santa's disappearance
made the network news.
Folks gathered round their TV screens
in fours and threes and twos.
They called up all the talk shows
and all said, "What a shame!"
But not a single bear thought
the bears were to blame.

Mama Bear knew better.
"Of course Santa Bear has quit!
And with all that's happened,
you can't blame him a bit!
We've blotted out the stars
with a million watts of light.
We have lost the Christmas spirit
and forgotten all that's right."

The bears knew in their heart of hearts
    that Mama Bear was right,
and that they had all contributed
to Christmas's sad plight.
The bear cubs got the message,
and Papa Bear did, too.
But what was done was done, they thought,
and what were they to do?

"Well," said Mama Bear,
"we could set a good example.
I think a few lights around the door
will be more than ample."
So Papa and the cubs saw
the error of their ways
and, working very quickly,
they took down the huge displays.
But Santa was still missing,
when all was said and done,
and the chance of saving Christmas
seemed clearly slim to none.

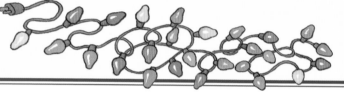

But Santa had a plan,
and he was really still about.
And with the fate of Christmas
still very much in doubt,
he went among the bears
very carefully disguised,
and traveling without his sleigh
he went unrecognized.

So in his tweedy cap and suit,
he traveled far and wide,
and looking for the Christmas spirit,
he searched the countryside.
He had to keep on searching;
he could not give up hope.
Hmm, this place looked familiar.
He had seen it on his scope!
Santa looked up at the stars
sparkling in the sky.
No longer did the lights below
outshine the lights on high.
Well, that's a start, thought Santa,
with a hopeful smile.
Maybe my long, lonely search
will finally prove worthwhile.

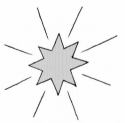

But Santa needed more than
just soft lights around the door.
He needed the true spirit of Christmas
back in place once more.
Santa still worried
about Christmas and its fate.
And then he checked his watch,
which showed the time, the day, the date.
And with alarm he cried out loud,
"Good grief! It's Christmas Eve!"
Was there still time enough
for Christmas's reprieve?

Santa knew full well
that it was about to snow.
He could always feel it coming
in his left big toe.
But suddenly it was snowing
with all of nature's might.
It whipped and whirled and swirled.
It whited out the night.
It crystallized the air.
It filled the very skies!
It was as if the air
were filled with icy fireflies.

Then at that very moment,
through the whirling, swirling snow,
far off in the distance,
he saw a gentle glow.
Despite the cold and blowing snow,
he could clearly see
that the light he saw before him
came from the Bears' big tree.
The very same Bear family
he had seen upon his scope.
The very same Bear family
who had made him give up hope.

Just then the door opened,
and there was Papa Bear
coming out into the cold
from his warm and cozy lair.
Out he came so bravely
through the deep and drifting snow,
even though the windchill
was eighty-six below.

Papa had a cup of birdseed
and a tiny holly wreath.
And he pressed forward further
into the blizzard's icy teeth.
Papa had come out to feed a tiny bird
no bigger than a mouse,
a tiny hungry bird
in a tiny cold birdhouse.
Pa hung the wreath
and placed the cup under the eaves,
safe beneath the shelter
of snow-laden leaves.

Santa said to Papa,
"What a nice thing to do."
"Not at all," said Papa.
"Little birdies gotta eat on Christmas, too.
But if you don't mind my asking,
who the heck are you?"
"Er—Yule's the name," said Santa.
"Just a stranger passing through."
"Well, whoever you are," said Papa,
"'tain't fit out for bear or beast.
So come in and get warm.
I can't offer you a feast,
but Mama's Christmas cocoa
is the best warmer-upper.
And we would be so tickled
if you would stay for supper."

So Santa Bear and Papa Bear
came in from the cold.
And then Santa saw Christmas
as it was in days of old.
There was a fresh-cut tree,
paper stars on the windowpanes,
and all around the room
were homemade paper chains.
Santa's search had ended,
and his spirit was more than buoyed.
Santa Bear was more than pleased.
He was overjoyed!

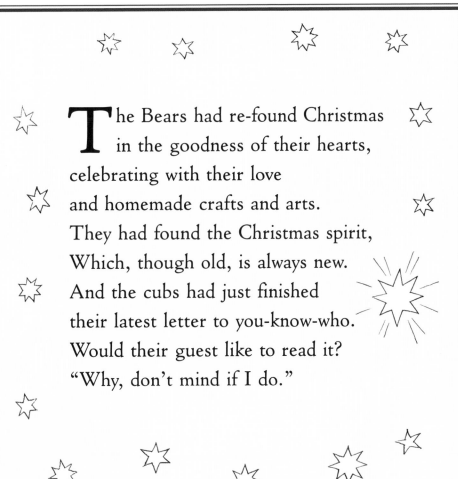

The Bears had re-found Christmas
in the goodness of their hearts,
celebrating with their love
and homemade crafts and arts.
They had found the Christmas spirit,
Which, though old, is always new.
And the cubs had just finished
their latest letter to you-know-who.
Would their guest like to read it?
"Why, don't mind if I do."

Santa quick put on his specs
and read the cubs' brief note.
As he read it, he got quite
a lump inside his throat.
The letter did not ask
for every greedy Christmas whim.
It left the matter of gifts
for them completely up to him.

It requested gifts for others:
a toy mouse for Miz McGrizz's cat,
a plant for Miz McGrizz herself,
and for Mailbear Bill, a hat,
something nice for Grizzly Gus,
who had had a fall.
As gifts for themselves—again,
that was Santa's call.
A great big smile spread slowly
across old Santa's face.
Yes, the true Christmas spirit
was alive in this warm place.

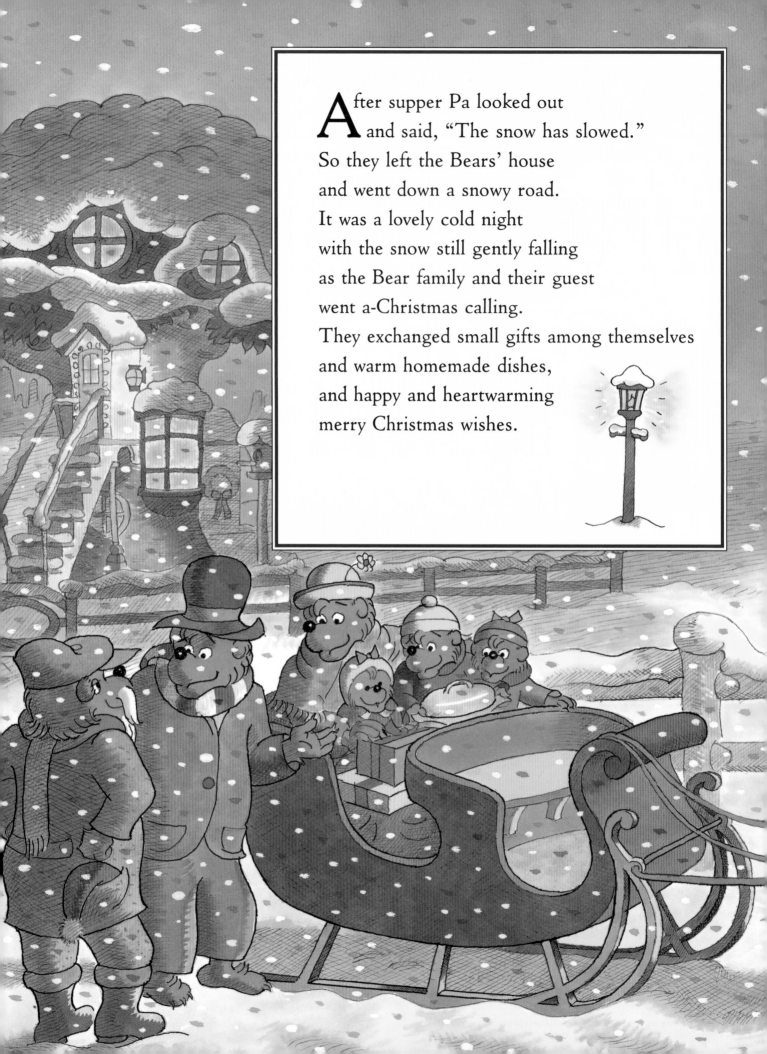

After supper Pa looked out
and said, "The snow has slowed."
So they left the Bears' house
and went down a snowy road.
It was a lovely cold night
with the snow still gently falling
as the Bear family and their guest
went a-Christmas calling.
They exchanged small gifts among themselves
and warm homemade dishes,
and happy and heartwarming
merry Christmas wishes.

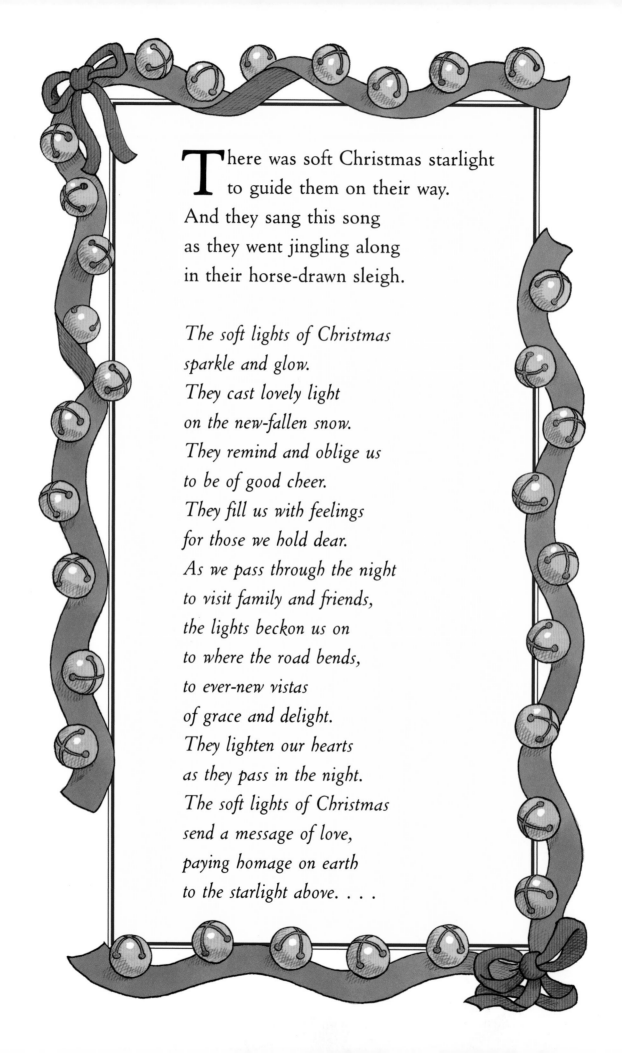

There was soft Christmas starlight
to guide them on their way.
And they sang this song
as they went jingling along
in their horse-drawn sleigh.

The soft lights of Christmas
sparkle and glow.
They cast lovely light
on the new-fallen snow.
They remind and oblige us
to be of good cheer.
They fill us with feelings
for those we hold dear.
As we pass through the night
to visit family and friends,
the lights beckon us on
to where the road bends,
to ever-new vistas
of grace and delight.
They lighten our hearts
as they pass in the night.
The soft lights of Christmas
send a message of love,
paying homage on earth
to the starlight above. . . .

"Thanks for the lift. Now I must leave,"
said old Santa Bear.
"Here's where you can let me off.
I'm staying over there."
And with a wink and a twinkle
he bid them all good-bye.
And then he was off like magic
through the Christmas Eve sky.
"I have searched for Christmas!" he cried.
"And found the Spirit True.
Now if you'll excuse me,
I have work to do."

North Pole

Merry Christmas!

INTRODUCTION

by Edward L. Ferman

The general obsession with youth in this country (and abroad) shows no signs of abating. Most people are still thinking young, dressing young, talking young, or, at the very least, talking about the young. Some of the artificial highs of the under-twenty-five generation will probably be followed by a comedown, complete with shakes and nausea. But the basic youthful attributes of energy and extremism are natural ones, and they are exactly the sort of qualities which are essential to a magazine if it is to retain its editorial vigor. The *Magazine of Fantasy and Science Fiction* is now eighteen years old, which, considering the mortality rate in the business, is something like ripe old age for a magazine. We like to think that we retain a youthful state of mind, and, as important, that we do so in a continuous and natural manner.

In this collection of stories from the magazine's seventeenth year of publication, we considered all the usual editorial balances: short with long, SF with fantasy, light with heavy. When the collection was completed, we realized that we had been handed another sort of balance which was not planned: a balance of respected and familiar names with talented young writers. Avram Davidson, Ron Goulart, Fritz Leiber and Brian Aldiss have appeared many times in these collections and have written with distinction in the SF and fantasy field for some years. Victor Contoski, Jean Cox, Robert Nathan, and Russell Kirk are, of course, prominent and proven authors whose work is primarily outside the genre. Monica Sterba, George Collyn, Samuel R. Delany, and Thomas M. Disch are all young writers who are relatively new to this field and brand new to these annual collections, yet at least two of them—Delany and Disch —have already made a considerable mark in the field.

This youthful balance is as cheering as it is unplanned. It promises well for the future vitality of the magazine and of the literature of science fantasy; and, we think it may, in a subtle fashion, add to your enjoyment of this collection.

The Best from Fantasy and Science Fiction

17th Series

ACE BOOKS

A Division of Charter Communications Inc.
1120 Avenue of the Americas
New York, N.Y. 10036

ACKNOWLEDGMENTS

The editor hereby makes grateful acknowledgment to the following authors and authors' representatives for giving permission to reprint the material in this volume:

William Morris Agency for *Cyprian's Room* by Monica Sterba

George Collyn for *Out of Time, Out of Place*

Victor Contoski for *Von Goom's Gambit*

Scott Meredith Literary Agency, Inc. for *Bumberboom* by Avram Davidson, *Randy's Syndrome* by Brian W. Aldiss

Collins-Knowlton-Wing, Inc. for *Fill In the Blank* by Ron Goulart

Russell Kirk for *Balgrummo's Hell*

Henry Morrison, Inc. for *Corona* by Samuel R. Delany

Robert P. Mills for *The Inner Circles* by Fritz Leiber, *Problems of Creativeness* by Thomas M. Disch

Curtis Brown Ltd. for *Encounter in the Past* by Robert Nathan

Jean Cox for *The Sea Change*

Littauer and Wilkinson for *The Devil and Democracy* by Brian Cleeve

CONTENTS

Our usual search for information about authors new to these pages has this time yielded only these spare details: Monica Sterba is young; she is now living in Turkey with her husband; she has had stories in Harper's *and* The Reporter. *And that is all. We are not, however, inclined to press our search further. There is a certain richness in mystery, as this superior story so rewardingly demonstrates.*

CYPRIAN'S ROOM

by Monica Sterba

HILDA WENDEL

The house I lived in looked so right from the outside. It had the proper aura of faded elegance; it had quizzical gables and tall brooding windows. Besides being all I could afford, it seemed a house where extraordinary people might live. There should have been, I thought, an eccentric, elegantly faded landlady, writing interminable memoirs, who would fill the house with other eccentrics; her charming disreputable nephew, letting dazzling aphorisms fall like pearls in his aunt's moth-eaten salon; other clever young men, aspiring poets and painters; a gifted musician whose flutings or fiddlings would drift up deliciously through the cold radiators; a silver-haired, beautifully dressed gentleman of reduced circumstances and venerable age, who in the bloom of his youth had been the subject of a famous portrait or a famous scandal and perhaps one of our landlady's distinguished lovers . . .

But for me there was merely greasy upholstery and tattered carpeting. No delightful eccentric landlady but a landlord whose only saving grace was that he appeared so seldom, a squat little man with reeking cigars and the harassed air of someone stuck at the lowest end of the real estate business. As for the other tenants, they seemed mostly to be poor but hearty Irish waitresses. They were out most of the time, working furiously to save money for a better life back home. Sometimes, late at night or on Sunday, they had male friends in, and then beery harmonica music drifted up through the cold radiators.

In other respects as well, the city I had dreamt of through my small-town student years was eluding me. My job was routine and dull. Among the few people I had met was not one I really wanted to know. The poems I wrote secretly, in painstaking elation, were rejected by every little and littler magazine to which I sent them.

But the city had compensations. I wandered happily through the museums and art galleries. I joined a private library and spent whole Saturdays among the stacks of dusty books, enjoying not only the odd things I found to read but, though I never spoke to them, the presence of the frail distinguished old men who haunted the place, silver-haired and beautifully dressed. Sometimes, of course, I made efforts to break out of all this and live in the present. It was after one of them, a noisy party where I had spent an hour miserably sandwiched on a couch between people who talked across me, that I came home to find all the Irish girls on the staircase, terribly agitated. I asked what was wrong. It was Isabel Kelly, the one below me, they said, suddenly gone awfully bad and started coughing up blood. She had been taken to the hospital for an operation and would then be sent away to the country; they did not know if she would come back to the house at all.

Two weeks went by. Sorry as I was about Isabel, I could not help thinking how peaceful it was without the harmonica music. Then, one evening, another sound came up through the radiator, a sound unlike anything I had ever heard in the house. I thought at first there must be something wrong with the pipes, and then I realized it was someone playing a flute. Schoenberg, perhaps, I thought, but who on earth could be playing Schoenberg downstairs? Then suddenly the atonal music stopped and my radiator rang with a melody so fresh, gay and wild that I put down my book and sat breathless until it was over.

I heard the flute again the next two evenings, but the soaring melody was not repeated. The flute slurred and sputtered and wailed, producing sounds like the mating songs of cats, and other sounds that were more bizarre still. I began to wonder if this was Schoenberg or any composer, and if in fact the instrument that produced such odd notes was a flute, or any instrument I knew.

On the fourth evening, I decided that I must find out who was playing. I could say—which was quite true—that the music was disturbing me. I went down the stairs and knocked hesitantly on the door that had been Isabel's.

"Come in, the door's not locked," said a young man's voice.

I opened the door, and was greeted by another blast of unharmonious sound. Then the flutist, who was seated on the bed, took the flute out of his mouth, wiped it reflectively on his trouser leg, and looked at me.

And I looked at him. I remember thinking that he had fine hands, that he was very thin, and that he looked sleepy and not well. As if to confirm this he coughed. A dry, elegant little cough. Then he pointed with his flute to a chair near the bed, and said, "I can't get up at the moment. But please come in and sit down."

"Are you ill?" I asked politely, having seen that he was fully dressed and the bed was made.

"No, I'm not ill. It's just weakness."

"You can't be very weak if you play your flute like that."

"Not physical weakness. Moral." He put the flute to his mouth and played the delicious melody I had heard before. Without thinking, I closed the door and went over to the chair.

"Is it very rude of me not to get up?"

"Yes, if there's nothing wrong with you. And to have made so much noise the last few nights. I was trying to concentrate on—"

"No. You were not trying to concentrate on anything. You have been perishing to come down here and find out who was playing Schoenberg."

"I was—I was not—I did wonder—"

"Well anyway, it is not Schoenberg. These are my own compositions."

"I'm afraid they're just noise to me," I said, recovering myself and determined to be rude back.

"Do you understand the twelve-tone system?"

"No. I'm afraid I know very little about atonal music."

"It doesn't matter. My compositions have nothing to do with the twelve-tone system," he said in a tone of great satisfaction.

"What have they to do with?"

"They are based on a system worked out from the pattern of lunar phases, from wave patterns—ocean waves, not sound—and other organic movements and structures. They are also, to some extent, derived from certain obscure Eastern tonal systems. And then again, they are not. For art, which little scrubbed schoolgirls think of as reaching toward the light, is really"—he lowered his voice—"a grotesque fumbling, a furtive groping in dark corners."

"Well, your music does sound like that."

He laughed. "We could have a drink," he said. "Somewhere in that cupboard"—he pointed vaguely with the flute—"is a bottle of cheap whiskey. Would you mind getting it? The glasses are there too."

When I came back from the cupboard, he was chewing thoughtfully on the flute. I stood holding the bottle and glasses, wondering where I should put them down. At the last possible moment, he reached out his hands.

"Do people usually do things for you?" I asked.

"Yes," he said innocently. "In fact, rather too much. It's one of the reasons I have come to this terrible room. No one knows where I am now; no one but you, of course."

"That means, I suppose, you are here to escape your devoted admirers and devote yourself to your composing."

He ignored the edge in this. "Not really to compose," he said musingly. "I am not at all sure about composing. Like all art, music is only a meaningless order which one tries to pretend has some relevance to the chaos of the external world."

"But you said just now that art was groping and fumbling."

"That is what it should be. We have had enough feeble

12

microcosms, fuddled abstractions. Art must get back to being representational. And there is nothing to represent except disorder."

"But music isn't representational anyhow. And all of that is just Dada, or its latest imitations—"

"Nonsense. Dada was only a false disorder, as are its modern counterparts. It is the true disorder that one must capture. Think of an unwashed man in baggy pajamas, groggy from drink or drugs, crawling about under the bed on his stomach looking for a shoe that is not there, under the illusion that it is morning when it is really the middle of the night, and that he must get up to go to an office from which he has been dismissed long ago. There is a creature subject to the divine frenzy. That is the essence of true art."

"And that is what you want to put into your music?"

"Not put. It should simply be there, as the unwashed man under the bed is there. Listen."

He took the flute and began to play, blowing out and drawing in his breath on each note, so the effect was rather like the braying of a desperate donkey. After a minute, I had to put my hands over my ears, at which he stopped playing and smiled at me. There was something bright under their sleepy lids. I wondered with an unexpected rush of concern if it was really only what he called moral weakness that kept him from getting up.

"You are looking at me," he said at once, "with that horrible feminine look, the gimlet eye of the latent nurse. Most women are like that, full of depraved maternalism. Every bed to them is a potential sickbed; they come to be debauched with the air of ministering angels approaching a patient. Lurking inside the nymphomaniac is a creature in a starched cap, smelling of antiseptic, with a thermometer and an enema tube. You must promise never to look at me like that again."

"I wasn't looking at you like that," I said, furious. "I hate sickness. I wouldn't nurse you if you were dying. And all that about nurses and nymphomaniacs I think I've read somewhere—"

"Stop making aggressive protestations, and have your drink."

"It's you who's aggressive. In fact you're damned rude. And as for the drinks, you haven't touched yours."

He picked up his glass, made a wry face at it, and put it down again. "This was hardly my choice," he said.

"You don't mean it's Isabel's?"

"I don't know. Who is Isabel?"

"Isabel Kelly, who used to live here, and was sent away with t.b. I'm surprised they haven't taken all her things out. But we can't drink the whiskey if it's hers."

"I wasn't going to. I only wanted to offer it to you. To be hospitable."

"Do you always behave like this?" I said, distractedly taking a sip from my glass.

"Yes. And I doubt you object. If you did, you wouldn't still be here, drinking Isabel's awful whiskey."

"Then it is Isabel's. And I won't go on sitting here drinking her whiskey, especially since you assume it means I don't object to your behaviour, which I do."

"All right then. Would you like an apology? I am sorry to have offended you. I intend to have no other visitors, and I hope you will come again."

"Thank you. But I'm going."

"But you will come again. And now I have said that, you will be still more offended, and think out of pride that you must not. But why should we go through these silly prevarications? Why can't you simply come down to see me when it is obvious that you want to, and I want you to come?"

Three days went by before I knocked again on the door downstairs. This time my excuse was not sound but silence, and when the same voice said, "Come in," I found it difficult to hide my relief.

"I was wondering," I said defensively from the doorway, "I know you despise the latent nurse and all that, but I did wonder, since I hadn't heard any music, whether your moral weakness, or whatever it is, is worse."

"No, I'm perfectly well. The reason you haven't heard any music is that I have given the music up."

"Why?" I asked, wondering if I could, or should express regret.

"As I told you, I was never quite sure about music. Music, even my sort, is far too orderly. It allows no scope for those random, subterranean movements of mind to which I should like to give expression. Besides, music is regressive. It appeals, through its rhythm, to primitive motor mechanisms."

"But if you want subterranean movements—"

"Yes, but of the mind, not the body. The mind must be free to contemplate chaos. No, I have given up music. Instead, I am writing a play. Would you like to see it?"

"Yes," I said. He reached under the cushion behind his back and held out a sheaf of papers. I took them, and saw with a shock that the play was written in a peculiar foreign alphabet.

"I'm afraid," I said stiffly, "that I can't read Sanskrit, or whatever that is."

He sighed. "It's not Sanskrit. Look at it again."

I looked. The minute, beautiful squiggles danced before my eyes.

"It is no known alphabet," he said wearily, and without smiling. "The play is in abstract calligraphy."

"I think you will have a little difficulty getting it performed."

"It is not written to be acted. It is written to be read."

"Do you yourself know what it says then?"

"I know what it might say. To read my play, one must try to imagine the unimaginable. One must put out of one's mind all the normal subjects of the theatre, both the tragic theatre of the past, which concerned itself with the downfall of the great, and the pathetic theatre of the present, which concerns itself with the downfall of the little. Mine is the theatre of the three disunities, in which everything is possible but nothing happens, and time, place and action are irrevocably divorced."

"Look, are you really serious about this?"

"Of course I am." Then suddenly he began to cough, and bent over, holding one of the sheets of paper to his mouth. When he had finished coughing, he crumpled it up and threw it under the bed.

"But that's part of your play!"

"It doesn't matter. Once written, it exists. And were I

to attach value to the pieces of paper which are only its most trivial form of existence, I could not have conceived of such a play."

I could think of nothing to say to this. He began to cough again, and so disposed of another page of the play. At last, noticing that the glasses we had used three days ago were still standing beside the bed, I picked them up and went to the sink to wash them.

There was a silence. Then I said, bent over the sink, "But if you really are serious, you must want an audience, even if only the littlest of little cliques. I can't believe anyone wants to express something without having it reach anyone else."

"And if I were to write for an audience," said a voice almost in my ear, "who would the audience be?" Startled, I turned around, dropping one of the glasses into the sink. He had crossed the room without a sound and was standing behind me. He looked at the broken glass and smiled.

"I'm sorry I frightened you. You see, you would rather have me reclining on the bed, enabling you to play ministering angel. I disturb people when I'm up and about."

He took the pieces of glass deftly out of the sink, and dropped them into the garbage pail underneath. He was quite right, it was disturbing. I realized how tall he was, and his quick controlled way of moving did not fit at all with his mannered speech, or the perpetual sleepiness of his face.

"An audience," he went on, "wants only a reflection of itself, and persists in regarding this reflection as flattering. Even satire is a form of praise. The satirized come flocking to laugh at themselves, and leave more complacent than before, feeling they have added humour and tolerance to their other virtues. You forget that an audience is made of people."

"Then why do you do these things? Write, I mean. Or compose."

"It passes the time. And has other uses." He smiled in a way which made me slightly uncomfortable. Then he had another long spell of coughing. At the end of it he walked over to the bed and lay down. I went timidly up to look at him, wondering if I dared show my concern. Perhaps it was really his cough, I thought, that had made him give up the music. In fact, with such a cough it was uncanny he had been able to play at all. He lay quite still, with his eyes closed; I saw that his forehead was damp.

"Look," I said at last, "do you ever do anything about that cough?"

"It's amazing how authoritative you sound the moment I am flat on my back."

"I know you don't want to talk about it, but it is an awful cough. Have you ever been to a doctor about it?"

He opened his eyes, smiled at me, and sat up. "If you really dislike the cough, I will change it for you." He leaned forward and produced behind his hand the terrible deep wheezing sound that sometimes comes out of ragged old men on street corners.

"And now, here is another one, more delicate but quite effective, very good for the moment's hush just before the cadenza. It sounds merely querulous when muted, like the bark of a rheumatic Papillon. But to our friends the doctors, it indicates, so they think, the last stages of—"

"Please. I won't ask again about your cough."

"Good. I was afraid your nursing instinct was getting the better of you. And now I think I will let you talk about yourself." He coughed once more and lay back on the bed. "We could start with your name."

"Heavens, how strange. We've never asked each other that. I can't understand why."

"Well, what is your name?"

"Hilda. Hilda Wendel. It's an awful name."

"No more than most. Mine is Cyprian—" he hesitated for a second. "Cyprian Meyerbeer."

"It isn't really!"

"Why not? I'm sure you don't doubt other people's names. Why must you doubt mine?"

"I just don't believe anyone nowadays would really be named Cyprian. Especially by parents called Meyerbeer. And it's the sort of name you would make up for yourself. It has that quality of incongruity you seem to find so valuable."

"Quite true. But is it not possible that my love for incongruity comes from the very fact of having been baptized

17

Cyprian Meyerbeer? However, we've had enough of this. I want to hear about Hilda Wendel."

"What? The story of my life?"

"Everything." He settled himself more comfortably and closed his eyes.

"It's all very ordinary, really. I come from a small town not far away. I've been here a year now, and I have a dull job in a publishing house, in the sales department. I try to write poetry, but it doesn't seem to get anywhere. But maybe one day it will. Unlike you, I do still believe in communication . . ." I looked over at the bed and saw that Cyprian was sound asleep.

I got up at once and went out, banging the door, hoping desperately that Cyprian would wake up and come after me to apologize. But he did not.

Four miserable days went by, during which I began to think how hypersensitive I had been. After all, he might have fallen asleep exhausted by his illness; the cough was probably genuine, and all the business about changing it at will so much bravado. But I could not bring myself to knock on his door again, although my eagerness to see him was whetted by the sound of a typewriter below, which clicked rapidly at all hours. Surely the typewriter could not be used for plays in abstract calligraphy?

The fourth evening, I found a note on my door. "Dear H.," it said, in the alphabet I could read, "I'm sorry if you're offended again. Please forgive me and come down."

We spent another evening much like the last one. During the next few weeks, we spent many such evenings. I asked him once to come up to my room instead; he said rather gruffly, "I never go out." I did not ask again, but I did suggest that I might bring some food and cook a meal for us. This too Cyprian refused. He would say that he never ate anyhow, or that he could not bear anyone's cooking except his own. We did not even have coffee together. But whenever the smell of frying meat or onions came through from another room, Cyprian would go to stand near his door and sniff eagerly. I found this very odd, but I was learning not to remark on oddities.

After we had talked a few hours, Cyprian's cough would get worse, or he would look especially sleepy; or I would find his theories too wild, his arrogance too oppressive, and would go. But offended or not, I would be back again an evening or two later. "Why can't you simply come down and see me?" he had said. And baffled, infuriated, even frightened by him as I was, the thought of spending a few evenings without him was more painful than any loneliness I had known before.

I never saw him during the day. "I must have my day to myself," he said. What he actually did during the day, apart from odd bouts of typing, I never discovered. In fact, I still knew nothing about him at all. My few questions were rebuffed, at first jocularly, then with a certain sharpness.

"Whatever I told you, you would think was lying, as you think I lie about my name. So I would have to spend boundless amounts of energy inventing for you a Cyprian Meyerbeer you could believe, when the real one is here, all the time, in this room. If you can't accept me as I appear, if you must have a past or future Cyprian, you will have to forego the company of this one."

After this warning I asked no more questions, though I was dying to know, at the very least, for what he was using his old rattling typewriter. My curiosity about this was more than idle. I still thought his ideas chaotic and destructive, even mad. But perversely, the more he lectured me on the futility of things, the emptiness of art, form and order, the metaphysical beauty of the unwashed man under the bed, the more I felt that in Cyprian himself the disorder was only apparent, the superficiality only superficial. I had become convinced that there lurked in Cyprian a little flame of pure genius, like the perfect melody among the atonalities, a seed that wanted only tactful encouragement, intelligent devotion, to grow and bring forth its strange marvellous fruit.

So I wanted anxiously to see his new manuscript, and found myself more and more under his influence. I would go up to bed with my head reeling, doubting everything I had ever valued, but with burning certainty that in Cyprian's frenzied mind some extraordinary form or concept was struggling to be born. I no longer cared about anything else. And when I saw in the mirror my haggard face and shadowed eyes, more proper to nights of debauchery than a few hours of conversation, I wondered if my hope of regenerating Cyprian would not end with his poisoning and exhausting me.

The strange thing was, at the thought of our evenings becoming what my constancy and wasted appearance implied, my imagination simply reared back and stopped dead. Cyprian, for his part, made no move to initiate a physical relationship; perhaps his illness made it impossible. His occasional small endearments to me seemed the more spontaneous for sounding so careless. But he had never even shaken my hand.

But anyhow, I would tell myself firmly, my main concern was not with the physical Cyprian. And so I persevered. I listened; I asked no questions; I laughed when I was horrified. I tried encouragement, carefully disguised. "Think how it would upset people to read what you're saying!"

Then, one evening, my knock was not answered, although Cyprian's door had been left slightly ajar. Puzzled, I pushed it open and walked in. He was not there, nor was the typewriter, but a manuscript lay on the bed. I closed the door and, unable to resist, went and picked up the manuscript. It was headed *The Breed Apart,* by Cyprian Meyerbeer."

"If there is such a thing as savage urbanity—or urbane savagery—then this is the way to describe Mr. Meyerbeer's new novel. If indeed it can be described at all. For this is not only another chronicle of decadence in the 20th-century gothic vein. Its strange somber characters, moving through an endless tapestried twilight, under obscene frescoes they emulate in debauches detailed with an acrid clinical frankness rare even today, are more than they seem. At the end of 900 pages there is an impression of suppressed violence, of moribund grandeur, not likely to be forgotten.

"Gogo Loewenzahn, the antihero, is the last scion of a brief unsavoury dynasty of fascist magnates entrenched somewhere in South America. Gogo is a hunchback and the most passionate of philatelists, his 'grotesque little figure and ardent bespectacled rabbit face' are known to stamp shops and beloved by auctioneers all over the world. He lives in an enormous cluttered house with his younger sister, 'a long plain woman secretly in love with him,' whose only joy is occasional fornication with her favourite Alsatian dog, also named Gogo.

"In a few pungent pages we are introduced to this strange pair and the bizarre collection of sycophants, stamp-finders and suitors who camp in obscure corners of the house, 'with the tacit consent of Mathilda the sister, some of them unknown to Gogo the hunchback but all of them known, by scent and sound, to Gogo the Alsatian, who hated them.'

"The rest of the book is devoted to a catalogue of Gogo's stamp collection, with an occasional aside describing the goings-on in a nearby room or 'a pathetic rumble from the ulcerated stomach of Gogo' (the hunchback) who sits poring over his stamps. At the end, just before Gogo meets his death at the teeth of his namesake, we are told of the miraculous epithalamic frescoes on the ceiling of his study, under which, unseeing, he has lived and is to die. For what destroys Gogo is his rejection of the lank-haired dank-skinned Mathilda his sister, which is his rejection of Life."

So Cyprian had written a book. And the reviewer seemed impressed. But what reviewer? And why had Cyprian typed a copy of the review?

"At first glance, it seems strange that almost 800 pages should be devoted to the stamp catalogue. But as the book progresses, we see that the catalogue and the 'asides' form a dazzling disturbing whole, that the pattern of the asides within the catalogue is deliberate and meaningful, so the reader is alternately carried forward and jolted back in a compelling rhythm, a verbal pattern of great beauty . . ."

In the midst of this eulogy of the stamp catalogue, I myself was jolted by a suspicion I should have had at once if my eagerness to see Cyprian's genius fulfilled had not carried me away. I leafed quickly on. Another review, this time of a book called *Emmerdé*.

"The entire action of this remarkable little novel takes place in twenty minutes in the middle of the night, in the miserable basement flat of an obscure tenement. Zed, surely the last word in antiheroes, awakens and begins to search for his shoes, thinking it is morning, and we are given a minute account of all his sensations and thoughts while on his stomach under the bed . . .

"Mr. Meyerbeer, whose previous book, *The Sodomite*, told with daring and unexpected lyricism of the passion of a man for his mare, here shows he can deal with far more than the vagaries of sensual experience. Mr. Meyerbeer has been accused of writing pornography thinly disguised as literature; it would have been more just to accuse him of writing literature thinly disguised as pornography. This book should be adequate proof that he is a young writer of great scope and sincerity. But *Emmerdé*, like *The Sodomite*, is not a book for the squeamish . . ."

"I see you have found my reviews," said Cyprian behind me. I turned around; he stood with his air of being half-awake and smiled down at me. Not knowing what to say, I bent to put the manuscript back, and saw there were still a few pages on the bed. The top one was headed *"The Still Untempered Heart,* by Hilda Wendel." I picked it up and read aloud, my voice screechy with anger:

"Miss Wendel's, to be sure, is a minor talent. But her work has that keenness of perception, that sharply faceted luminosity as of finely cut crystal, which makes such minor poets a relief and a joy. They are poems of feeling rather than experience; like the young girl in *Birthdays*, one of her best poems, Miss Wendel moves falteringly from the yearnings and fears of secluded adolescence toward the coarser world outside, and leaves us with the most delicate of records, a gossamer trail marking a spiritual journey . . ."

I tore the page in half. "You shouldn't have," Cyprian said, smiling. "That was rather a nice one. And just what I thought you would like."

"It was one of the most cruel things you could have done to me. Have you really nothing better to do with your time? Reviews of books by yourself and myself which have never been written—just something to make fun of me and upset me?"

"Like all the injured, you see yourself as the center of things. I had my own reasons for writing those reviews. But I did do them partly for you. Don't think, Hilda, that I haven't noticed what you've been up to."

"What do you mean?"

"You have been swaying on the brink of a dangerous mission, Hilda. You have taken it into your head to reclaim me. You suspect I might be—don't deny it—what sensitive young women hope to find in shoddy furnished rooms, the undiscovered genius. And if I were, the end of it all, of years of humble self-sacrifice you can't wait to begin, would be a few hare-brained reviews. So I've written them for you."

I sat down on the bed and began to cry. Cyprian sat down beside me, and watched.

"But you can't," I spluttered between sobs, "you can't go on doing nothing. I don't believe you do nothing. I don't believe you don't want to do anything. I don't believe you, Cyprian."

"Would you believe me more if I never told you the truth? Give me your hand."

Without thinking, I did, and he slid his fingers through mine. I pulled back at once, but Cyprian did not let go. His hand was as cold as ice, so cold I had thought, at the first touch, that something was burning me. I sat tearless now and rigid, not daring to look at him, filled with an unreasoning fear. I wanted to get up and run out. But I could not. I was as afraid of getting up as I was of staying. After a few moments his other hand began to stroke, very lightly, the inside of my wrist. I still sat helpless and paralyzed, feeling as if my blood, pulsing under his fingers, was mixing with ice water. For his hands grew no warmer at all.

"Cyprian," I said at last, getting back my powers of speech and determined to break this dubious enchantment, "You—I—you're so *cold*, Cyprian."

"It passes," said Cyprian, very softly. But after another few moments he released my hand. And in spite of my fear I was perversely, immediately sorry.

"You see," said Cyprian, "you don't know what you want. And you're afraid. As I expect you to be."

I got up from the bed. "Afraid of what?" I said, furious again. "Afraid of you? I'm not at all afraid of you. And if you're not ill, as you keep insisting, why are your hands so cold?"

Cyprian smiled up at me, quite unperturbed. "Now you would like me to discuss the intricacies of my circulatory system. Which I won't. The cold, I told you passes. But this will do for a beginning. Come back tomorrow, when you're not so upset." He swung his legs up onto the bed, scattering the reviews, turned over on his stomach, and began to cough loudly into his pillow.

"Oh, to hell with you," I said, and rushed out.

The next day, and the next, and the next, I did not go back down. At the end of three days, I was sick with misery. Tomorrow, I thought, I will go down, but not today. I must have that much pride.

That night, I dreamt Cyprian was playing again. The music began with a pure clear melody, but after a few notes turned atonal with a vengeance, and trailed off in a high-pitched, nerve-shattering scream. Not even Cyprian could get such sounds out of his flute. It was a real scream that woke me. I turned on the light and ran to the door.

MOLLY O'LEARY

I'm not the sort who couldn't move in where someone had just died. That poor Isabel. Of course she didn't die in there, she died in the hospital. It happened a week before I took the room. I wouldn't really have thought about it, as I say I'm not the sort, but I noticed right away how close it was and sort of musty and those great heavy curtains that hadn't been cleaned in years, moving in that funny way when the wind blew.

It started the very first night. I went to bed about ten after getting the place tidied up. I put on my new woolly nightgown brushed nylon it is really and I had all the blankets on me and the hot water bottle for my feet but I was still cold and couldn't sleep for ages and when I did I woke up again with this awful feeling I was choking. I turned the light on and looked all over the room and under the bed and there wasn't anything but I couldn't get back to sleep and I kept the light on until morning.

The next day some of the girls helped me move the furniture around so it would be more comfy and when they went I had a cup of tea and I thought how silly I was because the room looked quite nice now. And I went to bed quite happy thinking it was all just a bad dream. But now comes the part you will never believe it must have been around midnight I woke up again and there was a Thing sitting on my chest it was all damp and clammy I could feel its feet through my woolly nightgown horrible little feet like a frog's they were it was just sitting there heavy as a rock on my chest a sort of toad thing how did I know I could see it well enough besides you couldn't mistake the feel of that thing if you've ever seen those awful squishy toads only big as a dog ouagh so horrible it makes me crawl all over just to talk about it and two yellow eyes looking two awful eyes I was frozen with terror but thank heaven I've got a good pair of lungs not like that poor Isabel and at last I got my voice and no I shrieked no and I screamed and screamed and that awful thing plopped off the bed then I couldn't hear it any more I just lay there screaming.

Then they came running from all over the house and people were saying help murder and at last I got the light on and got to the door and there was Mary and the others I just fell into their arms all hysterical they had to get me a sedative they couldn't quiet me down. And then there was that young girl upstairs came down and got all hysterical too said she couldn't understand why I was in that room because a Mr. Meyer was supposed to be in there well of course I got a bit offish at that having just had such a horrible experience and now her thinking I had a Mr. Meyer with me well there never was any Mr. Meyer the landlord said so too told her she was crazy there never was any Mr. Meyer in that room. Then she said we must have heard him typing and playing the flute and Mary and Rose and all the others said no they never heard anybody so then I knew the room was haunted so I said quietly to Rose there's only one man can handle this that Father Gavin who does exorcisms if we don't get Father Gavin I'll never sleep in that room again. So the next day off we went to get Father Gavin and he came with his book and started reciting all in Latin it was and we watched and waited and Father Gavin said there would be a smell of sulphur when the demon appeared but we couldn't smell

anything only Father Gavin's incense and Father Gavin
went on reciting for a while and then he said he thought it
was already gone and then he said maybe we imagined
it after all but then that girl came down again with her
hair all wild and started screaming at us get out of Cyprian's
room or something like that all hysterical she was and
Father Gavin rang his bell at her and you wouldn't ever
believe it she fainted dead away at his feet.

HILDA WENDEL

When I awoke it was in the room next door, and there
were people all around me fussing and clucking, which
was the last thing I wanted. I wanted to be left alone, and
most of all I wanted Cyprian. "Cyprian," I said, and began
to cry.

They all hovered around the bed, one of them kneeling,
and Miss O'Leary sighing heavily. I felt like the corpse at
a wake.

"Tell us about him, dear. Might be good for you to talk
about it."

"Father Gavin said it's not the first time he's been called
in like this. They can start off like a young man, those
devils, ever so handsome, and then they go all horrible."

"It was a toad it was sat on me. A great cold thing
with sticky feet. Oh, I can feel it now. Cold as ice it was,"
Miss O'Leary said.

"For God's sake," I said. "What is all this about?"

"You see," explained Miss O'Leary gravely. "You and
me, we've both been in the hands of an unholy creature
that was haunting that room. Possessed by an evil spirit.
But we'll be all right now, Father Gavin said. He knew
when you fainted. He's driven it away."

Dear God, I thought, they really believe all this. Then
they got up to make tea. I was gathering my forces to
escape when a girl I had not noticed before bent over me.

"Would you ever tell me," she whispered shyly, "did
he . . . Terrible, it must be. So cold, they say, and as big
as a bull's."

This was more than I could stand. "Get away from me,"
I said.

"Now Mona, you've been on at her. Never you mind Mona, dear. Nice cup of tea for you."

"I don't want any tea. You're all crazy. The young man who was here—and I swear he was—had nothing to do with your delusions about toads. He used to show his plays to me. He was not some sort of sex fiend. He had t.b. or something. He never even touched me." I began to cry again; the absurdity of having been visited by—or visited—what they thought an incubus, and not even to have slept with him!

One of them began, quite kindly, "Here now, we were only trying to help you," but I managed to get up, and dizzy as I was, escaped upstairs.

For several frantic days, I made the rounds of the neighborhood shops, questioned the landlord, and cross-examined, when I could face them again, my bewildered neighbours. I was determined to prove there had been a real person in that room. But my search was fruitless. The landlord was quite certain the room had not been occupied until Miss O'Leary took it, and did not see how anyone, even with an illicit key, could have camped in it for six weeks without his knowing. He said he had been into the room once or twice during that time and found it just as Isabel Kelly had left it. The Irish girls were adamant about never having heard the typewriter or the flute; one had seen me coming out of the room once and wondered about it; another had heard footsteps, but these could have been mine. As for Miss O'Leary's toad, it had gone as mysteriously as Cyprian, whether because of the exorcism or because, as the landlord said, there were better beds to visit than Miss O'Leary's.

As time went by and I was unable to turn up a single trace of Cyprian, I began to consider the ignominious possibility that Miss O'Leary and I had both been subject to a spinsterish delusion. But could one visit a delusion night after night, drink whiskey it poured, read things it had written? Perhaps Miss O'Leary's fantastic superstitions were true, and we had been haunted after all, by the same predatory ghost. What exactly he had wanted, I did not know. But now that Cyprian had disappeared into thin air, I longed no more for his unfulfilled talents but for the body that had seemed insubstantial enough before and which now I was not certain existed at all. I discovered that my imagination had been inflamed by his one icy touch and by Mona's whispering, and now ran on unbridled. Had he appeared as Miss O'Leary's toad, or colder than ice and trailing cerements, whatever he was, delusion or demon, I wanted him. And if an incubus could "start off like a young man and go all horrible," might not the reverse be true—might he not, like the frog prince, turn back to a young man in the morning?

So I waited, night after night, torn between terror and desire. But nothing appeared. No notes on the door, no distant Arcadian melody. No ghosts, no toad. Nothing. And Miss O'Leary, delivered of her evil, snored peacefully downstairs; I could hear her through the radiator.

When I had investigated everything I could, I decided to leave pending the question of the real Cyprian and pursue the unreal one. First I tried to find out if anyone like Cyprian had ever lived in the room, and possibly died there. This too led nowhere. Then I contacted physical research societies and mediums. Some of the people I met were obvious fakes, some silly; some were intelligent, friendly and helpful. But none were able to produce either the spirit of Cyprian or a satisfactory theory to explain his appearance and disappearance.

Then, as a last resort, I began to pick my way through the dusty books on the Demonology shelf in my library. They were mostly accounts of possession, one very like the next. I waded impatiently through pages and pages describing the torments of young women who had convulsions, swallowed pins, screamed curses and obscenities, wrestled with unseen forces, denied God and their parents and were eventually exorcised—usually by the clerical author of the account.

And then I found a little red book entitled "*Demoniality, or Incubi and Succubi, a Treatise*, by the Reverend Father Sinistrari of Ameno (17th century), published from the original Latin manuscript discovered in London in 1872, now translated into English with the Latin text."

Father Sinistrari attempted to prove the existence of "rational creatures having spirit and body distinct from man, but actually of a higher order," i.e., the incubi and succubi. What followed was a very strange doctrine indeed:

"As for intercourse with an Incubus, wherein is to be found no element, not even the least, of an offence against Religion, it is hard to discover a reason why it should be more grievous than Bestiality and Sodomy . . . man degrades the dignity of his kind by mixing with a beast, of a kind much inferior to his own. But with an Incubus, it is quite the reverse . . . man does not degrade, but rather dignifies his nature; and taking that into consideration, Demoniality cannot be more grievous than Bestiality."

However, Father Sinistrari concluded, with a neat theological twist, "men and women, by mixing with Incubi, whom they do not know to be animals but believe to be devils, sin through intention, ex conscientia erronea, and their sin is intentionally the same . . . in consequence, the grievousness of their crime is exactly the same."

This reasoning struck me as very peculiar. However, I read Sinistrari's description of his incubi more carefully. They were "subtile and slender" and more learned than men; they were born and died, and were divided into males and females, even as men. "Their food, however, instead of being gross and indelicate like that required by the human body, must be delicate and vapoury, emanating through spirituous effluvia from whatever in the physical world abounds with highly volatile corpuscles, such as the flavour of meat, especial of roasts . . ." I remembered suddenly how Cyprian, who never ate anything, had stood by the door sniffing eagerly when anyone was cooking nearby.

Father Sinistrari thought it quite possible that the incubi behaved as humans do, "Cultivating the arts and sciences, exercising functions, maintaining armies . . ." Their sexual tastes, it seemed, sometimes ran to still other beings than human. "It happens not merely with women but also with mares; if they readily comply with his desire, he pets them, and plaits their mane in elaborate and inextricable tresses . . ." The thought of an incubus plaiting his beloved's mane in elaborate tresses made me giggle. Then I remembered Cyprian's unwritten book about "the passion

29

of a man for his mare," and the dog of Mathilda Loewen-zahn.

Absurd as Father Sinistrari's theories were, they fitted Cyprian better than any I had come across. The tubercular artist appearance he had chosen for me might be like his real self; even the cough might have been genuine, produced by a foreign atmosphere unhealthy for him, or the germs of poor Isabel Kelly. And the toad appearance might have been a joke to frighten Miss O'Leary out of his room. A joke which had rebounded; I wondered sadly if the exorcism had worked after all.

In other respects, the Sinistrari theories were most unpleasant. The thought of being the rival of the nearest horse was a painful one. But if Cyprian would have faced degradation in seducing a human being, it might explain his restraint. Though Sinistrari's incubi, I found on reading further, seemed to have no such scruples. They were impassioned lovers. And their flesh was not cold at all.

But Cyprian had said of the cold, "It passes," and one could hardly expect Sinistrari to be correct in all details. In any event, this strange little book had convinced me Cyprian was more than a private delusion. I wanted badly to discuss it with someone who knew more Latin and more about theology—or demonology—than I.

On the way out, I passed one of the distinguished old scholars I had always admired. He looked up and smiled. On impulse I stopped, smiled back, and said breathlessly, "Please, I don't know what your field is, but I wonder if you could help me. I've come across this very odd little book, and I'd like someone's opinion—"

He took the book and looked at the title. "Are you doing a thesis on this subject, my dear?" he asked, kindly but with amusement.

"No, I'm just interested. But if you don't have time—or if—"

"It won't take any time. I am already acquainted with Father Sinistrari. He was an eminent demonologist, although somewhat heretical. Another of his works was in fact put on the Index of prohibited books until it was posthumously corrected. This particular manuscript, *Demoniality*, did not appear at all in Sinistrari's lifetime; it was apparently discovered much later, by a French publisher who bought it for sixpence in a London bookshop. I myself find this book utterly fantastic, even of its kind. One expects demonologists to have a perverted turn of mind. But a treatise of this sort, only come to light in the 19th century, and which reads like a satire—one wonders if even that good Father could have been guilty of its authorship. Mind you, this is a purely private opinion."

"You mean you think this book might be a forgery—written as anti-clerical propaganda, or something like that."

"I would hardly commit myself so far. I would only say that I find its content, and the circumstances of its publication, peculiar. Of course, there is no accounting for the fantasies of an overworked inquisitor."

This opinion, instead of disappointing me, filled me with joy. It seemed to me suddenly crystal clear that if a book which might apply to Cyprian was possibly fake and certainly fantastic even of its kind, then Cyprian or some form of him was real. My logic, I knew, was as obscure as Cyprian's, but I felt I was right.

"It's like the unwashed man under the bed," I said eagerly. "Everything takes place in the realm of the absurd." Then I turned embarrassedly to the silver-haired man who was still holding Sinistrari. "I'm sorry, I don't really know what I'm saying. But thank you very much. You've been very kind."

"Not at all," he said. Then, slowly, he got up. I saw with a start how tall he was, and then he was not as old as I had first supposed. He smiled down at me in a way that was oddly familiar, then he handed me the book. I wanted to say something else to him, to ask why he too had apparently read much of this esoteric subject; but that looming figure between the bookshelves had become obscurely frightening, and I did not. It was only after he had disappeared, his feet oddly soundless on the metal flooring, that I, perhaps condemned—and this may have been my tormentor's devious gratification—to be always too late, like the man under the bed, for what it was too late to be late for, began to suspect who he was.

George Collyn is a young writer who has been published frequently in the British SF magazines. This is his first story to appear in the U.S.; it's an admirably strong and concise account of an astronaut with a fifty-year handicap, and his attempt to adjust to a society which has moved in unforeseen directions.

OUT OF TIME, OUT OF PLACE

by George Collyn

If I had stayed with the others and we had stuck together as a team, it probably need never have happened—we could have formed a mutual defense against our individual insecurity. As it was, our nerves were rubbed red-raw with the sight of one another.

Of the fifty years we had spent together, all but ten had been spent in stasis. That is true. But ten years in an enclosed environment is quite enough for a man to become intolerably aware of every fault in his companions. Mannerisms which are quite innocuous in themselves become emotional dynamite when one sees them repeated year in and year out. This is especially true when one's living conditions preclude any form of privacy and every single function of one's waking life has to be carried out in the sight of your fellows; and theirs in yours.

At first we were forced to remain as a group in order to justify the official junketings which celebrated the return of the first ship to journey beyond the solar system. As soon as the festivities were over, we heaved a collective sigh of relief and went our separate ways; seeking our own

32

individual adjustments to the world which had aged fifty years to our ten.

Reactions were as varied as we were individuals. Peter, our captain, relished his role as our representative at the banquets, receptions and audiences which were given in our name. He could enjoy his share of the limelight—and the best of luck to him.

Without that prop the rest of us fell into three distinct schools. There were those who did not give a damn- and who plunged into their renewed lives with the insensitivity to their surroundings of a drunk in a low dive. There were others who set out to explore this strange new world, with the same zest for the unknown that explorers have always exhibited. The majority—and I was one of them—could not make the psychological adjustment to a world which was all the more strange for being hauntingly familiar. Out of our crew of twenty-eight there were four suicides within a year of our return. Of the rest, most turned inwards on themselves and shut out the world.

When one is twenty-three, the thought of the problems inherent in returning at the age of thirty-three, to find that the world has progressed through fifty years of social and technological change, seems unimportant. To the young, progress must remain an abstract concept simply because they do not possess the retrospective breadth of vision to see how a cumulation of minor changes can, over the years, revolutionize a way of life.

I had, of course, been aware of an older generation which criticised the world their juniors were creating. But my elders had at least had the chance to shape the world. They had seen "changes" but, because they had lived through them and not had to assimilate them in one go, they were less aware of "Change."

No one, least of all my twenty-three-year-old self, could foresee the emotional impact of our return from Space to a world which had changed out of all recognition. It was like being born again, but with all our ideas and prejudices already formed and at variance with the accepted social norm.

Certain things one could steel oneself to meet—only to have one's ideas overset by the unexpected. I had told myself that my father would be dead when I returned; that my step-mother—his second wife and a girl of my own age—would be an old woman; that my baby step-sister, whom I had last seen squalling in her cot, would be fifty-odd and could well have grandchildren as old as my memory of her. All this I was prepared for—I was not prepared for the advances in geriatric drugs and treatment. I was met at the airport by my centenarian father. Not only was he still alive, he looked younger than I did with the strain of a decade telling on my thirty-three years. The meeting made me sick to my stomach, as if I had had to watch some obscene perversion.

More than these very personal upsets, it was the general greyness of life which revolted me. Not the greyness in color though—with the massive, concrete slabs that passed as architecture and the drab, dungaree-like garments which passed as clothing for both sexes—that was depressing enough. Rather it was greyness as a quality of life which obsessed me. These people might have abolished old-age, but they had destroyed the joy of youth in the process. People walked the ugly streets in their ugly clothes and their faces were the ugliest of all. Blank, vacant, lack-lustre, they seemed to see but not feel.

Add to all this the technological advances of a half-century and guess at my perplexity. There was a driverless vehicle they called a robo-cab; some new entertainment medium they called the altrigo and various other weirdly named gadgets whose names I never did understand. In fact I knew the workings and purpose of none of the new inventions, though there were people enough willing to explain them to me. I just shut my ears and, as soon as I had permission to go, fled to an apartment the Space Agency rented on my behalf.

The apartment consisted of five rooms perched, in glorious isolation, on top of one of their man-made mountains. It possessed only one modern invention: an automatic food-dispensing machine. For this at least I was grateful, since it removed any need for contact with the outside world. For the rest I had my books and my records to pass my time. At first I persisted with the video in the hopes that through it I could come to know, and accept, the world. But for

34

some reason the video had lost its popularity, and all I could receive were two part-time channels. Since almost everything they talked about was incomprehensible to me, I fell back on the written word and the music of Bartok and Schoenberg. And I spent a lot of time in half-sleep, half depressed reverie.

If I tried to forget the world, the world refused to forget me. Mail poured through my door and the phone never stopped its summons. At one point I burnt all the former and disconnected the latter. As a result I was nearly court-martialled for failing to attend a presidential reception, the invitation to which I either destroyed or did not receive. In the end I employed a man to intercept all calls and open all letters, gauging their merit before he passed them on to me. The same man acted as my agent for all external transactions.

What merit Barbara Fellin possessed in this man's eyes I cannot say. She claimed to be my sister-in-law, having married a brother who was born after my departure and who died, by accident, before my return. Our relationship should not have given her the automatic right to speak to me; my relations were under the ban. Yet my censor saw fit to put her through to me—to my eternal regret.

She wanted to invite me to a party. I gathered it was to be one of the come-and-stare-at-the-famous types of affairs, and I was to be one of the stared-at-celebrities. That I should go was unthinkable to me and alien to my frame of mind at that time. And yet, when she rang off, I found that I had in fact agreed to attend; and in such a way as made it impossible for me to retract later.

That entire sequence of events was enough to convince me of the inevitability of Fate. So much happened that should not have happened; from Barbara Fellin contacting me to my agreeing to go to her party. I can hardly think I was defeated by her arguments. Rather I must have suffered a revulsion of feeling as complete as the one that had led to my seclusion.

That party re-introduced me to a world I thought had ceased to exist. If the world at large was drab and uniformly grey, that party was a riot of color. I had been reluctant to attend, but I had not known then that these gay and vivacious people still existed. When the gaiety and color washed over me, I felt the tensions drain away and, for the first time in over a year, I began to think that life was worth pursuing.

My hostess was a momentary deterrent who gushed like the adolescent her petrified looks falsely proclaimed her to be. I do not know how old she really was; I was too disgusted by the idea of artificial preservation to want to know. But she looked to be no more than nineteen and she dressed and acted accordingly; hanging on my arm and gazing into my eyes with all the fervour of a teenager with a crush on a hero-figure.

She noticed my limp and immediately referred to it—to my great embarrassment. I tried to gloss over the accident which caused it, but she exclaimed loudly that I must not mind because she thought it was so romantic and how brave we spacemen were. The entire company must have heard her and, certain that all eyes must be on me, I trailed self-consciously after her, feeling like a Byronic figure of tragedy in a nineteenth century salon.

For a time I was content again. I wandered among the guests, eating, drinking and exchanging commonplace talk about commonplace subjects which, in their capacity for being discussed at length without involving serious content, had not changed in fifty years.

The girl was standing alone in one of the inner rooms. I caught myself staring at her, and involuntarily I smiled. One could not help smiling at this girl; she radiated so much that was calm, warm and friendly. She was aware of and part of the party and yet not quite part of it, so that she formed a still center of the storm around which so much frenetic energy eddied; leaving her untouched. She was alone but not aloof, smiling on the guests with a gentle benediction in her luminous eyes.

I had bewailed the lack of color in this world, but this girl, in blacks and whites, was more striking than the gaudiest scarlet. The skin of her face and shoulders was the pure, glowing white of pearl, while her flowing hair was so deeply black as to appear to have blue-purple highlights. Her dress was of the same glossy black and was austerely and classically draped, falling to her ankles in utter simplicity.

She drew me like a magnet, the other guests parting momentarily to form a corridor between us, as if two poles of attraction were repelling all extraneous matter.

"Good evening," I remember saying, "my name is David Fellin."

"I know and I'm very pleased to meet you," she said, quite simply.

I was completely at a loss for something to say. I felt I had to say something or appear a moonstruck idiot. Yet, everything which came readily to my tongue seemed either too trite or too flippant for the impression I wanted to make on her. I was rescued from my dilemma by my hostess.

"Oh, you've met," cried Barbara. "I'm so glad— She's Marion Watkins, you know."

She hissed the last into my ear in a stage whisper that half the room must have overheard. I was confused partly because I did not know the name which was obviously meant to convey something to me; partly because I could not resist Marion's obvious amusement at Barbara's awe-struck tone. I regret to say that I laughed aloud—to the discomfiture of my hostess.

Barbara moved off again, her butterfly mind flitting from task to task and rapidly forgetting my slip in the delight at being the nucleus of so many people's attention. Marion and I were left in companionable silence.

"When can I see you again?" I said at last.

"We've only just met," she said and her eyes danced, her nose twitched, her mouth curved, every mobile feature of her face partook of and communicated her amusement. "Why ask to see me for a second time when you're still seeing me for the first time?"

"I mean away from all these people. I know I want to meet you and talk to you. But I don't like people."

"I know."

"That's the second time you've said 'I know.' How can you know so much about me when I know nothing about you?"

"But you are the nation's favorite mystery man at the moment, didn't you know? David Fellin, the spaceman recluse; the hermit of Tower Block C; the man who has been to the stars but will not cross the street. What does he look like? Don't you realise that Barbara only got so many people here because they hoped to meet you?"

I was lost for a second and it was then, with so much more left to say, that Barbara pounced, like a persistent dog who cannot leave go of a bone.

"David, I'm most annoyed with you. Those people who didn't come to meet you, came to meet Marion. I can't have my two main attractions monopolizing one another. Now come and meet some people."

I was dragged away unwillingly and put to the purgatory of meeting more people. I lost sight of Marion and my misery soon became so acute that I made a hurried and early departure, without seeing her again.

I did see her again, however. Simply because, having got her phone number from Barbara, I bombarded her with calls until she agreed to see me. How I would have overcome my revulsion for the outside world if Marion had asked me to face it I do not know; although, for her, I think I would have made the effort. As it was, Marion, like myself, and like a mere handful of others, had a taste for a way of life that had died with the previous century. She introduced me to an entire sub-world which existed to cater for tastes not attuned to the contemporary greyness. We went together to places where we ate meat that had lived and vegetables that had been plucked from the earth rather than from some chemical tank: places where the food was served by human waiters and waitresses; places where we were entertained by live singers and dancers.

Such a way of life was expensive of course. The food, the clothes Marion wore, all these things—things and habits which were commonplace in my youth, were now the perquisite of only the rich and few. Luckily my state-given pension was large enough to cover such expenditure and Marion too seemed to be moderately wealthy.

"What do you do?" I once asked her. "You seem to be very well-paid. Are you an actress?"

"Yes," she said. "I suppose you could call me an actress."

"But act at what? There's no stage, no movies, no video . . ."

"I act at life," she said. "I live to the full for people who are only half-alive."

I did not understand her and thought she was speaking metaphorically. As if I already knew that full knowledge would only distress me, I shied away from the topic and switched to some safer subject.

I do not think that I ever asked Marion to marry me. Somehow and at some point in our relationship, it simply became understood that we would marry.

The ceremony was a compromise. Marion, as was natural in a woman, wanted as gay and as splendid an affair as was possible. Still anti-social, I wanted as quick and as secretive a wedding as was possible. In the end we were married in one of the city's ancient churches and with all due pomp and circumstance. But only a few of Marion's close friends were present. For myself, I had no guests—not even relatives.

I had succeeded in buying a private flier. It cost a small fortune because such a machine was a rare antique at that time. But as soon as the ceremony was over and I was alone in the air with Marion, I felt that the cost was worthwhile. Having tasted the freedom of the air, I left my cares with the world on the ground. My joy in the flight, in my bride, in having my hands on the controls, was briefly marred by the sight from the air of the grey amorphous mass of buildings which stretched from horizon to horizon. But Nature is too old, too strong and too wily to be ever totally defeated by Man. The city finally ended and the pristine green of grass and trees succeeded the grey of concrete.

In the early evening we descended to the hideaway that the Space Agency had found for us—a stone lodge crouching where a tree-filled valley debauched onto silver sands, within sight, sound and scent of the sea. We were quite alone. No roads led to the valley and it was never overflown. For a week we were totally given over to each other and to nothing else.

I can find no words for my feelings during that time. Perhaps any two people in love feel the same, but the feelings are so personal that it seems a unique experience that could never be shared by anyone else. We did things that week that would seem laughable or shameful if written down or spoken of—and yet, because of our mutual trust they were natural and beautiful actions.

All the fears, the distaste, the unease with which I had faced that strange world disappeared in the joy of our marriage and union.

I had been soured by my first contact with the world and became bitter in the process, but living with Marion was slowly melting the barrier of ice I had erected around myself.

Marion made no demand that I change my way of life. All she asked was that I should not seek to impose it on her. She came and went as she had always done, but gradually I grew accustomed to accompanying her to restaurants and on shopping expeditions. And, as Marion broke down my reserve, these expeditions became more frequent. I became almost tolerant of all the strange customs of the world; except for the almost hysterical curiosity with which my appearance on the street was greeted by certain people. This I assumed to be the result of my brief fame as an astronaut. For a time I was tolerant and happy.

Then the nightmare began. It was a fine spring morning and I was alone in the apartment, Marion having gone to an appointment with her dressmaker. The phone warbled its call-note.

I had retained my agent to intercept all incoming calls. I therefore felt safe in answering.

"My name is Sheldon Walker," said the man with the good-living, smooth face, "and I'm a vice-president of the Altrigo Corporation."

"I'm afraid my wife is not here," I said, assuming that he wished to speak to Marion. I knew now that Marion was employed and extremely well paid by the Altrigo Corporation, engaged by them as an actress in whatever form of entertainment they purveyed. About what form that took, I was not too clear.

"I didn't want to speak to Marion, Mr. Fellin," he said. "It was you I wished to speak to. Do you think that you could come round to our office for an hour or so? I have a proposition to put to you."

And I agreed, may the Lord help me.

The offices of the Altrigo Corporation were, by the addition of a little chrome strip and stainless-steel panelling, a little less drab than their neighbors in the commercial quarter. The building was also singled out from its fellows by the knots of people who congregated in the street to stare at it as if it were some shrine or national monument. As I climbed out of the robo-cab which had brought me, I felt their eyes turn to me, and I fled from their gaze like a nocturnal animal fleeing from the blaze of the sun.

I was received like visiting royalty. Doors opened at my approach and an army of deferential heralds bowed or scraped me through the corridors which led to Walker's door.

Sheldon Walker in life was as smooth, plump and ingratiating as his image on my phone screen. Like myself and Marion and the rest of our circle, he was dressed in a brightly-hued suit quite at variance with the grey commonalty. His office was luxuriously appointed, and he obviously belonged to this world's anachronistic elite.

He made a command performance out of seating me, of providing me with food and drink. He showed a startling reluctance to get down to the business in hand. When it came, he blurted it out without preliminary.

"We want you to work for us. In fact we need you as an emitter so much that you can virtually state your own terms. Marion has always been popular but since the marriage her ratings have rocketed way over the top of the chart. Now we're being besieged by the menfolk who, because we won't accept cross-sex subscribers, feel they're being deprived of something."

"I'm afraid I don't know what you're talking about, Mr. Walker."

"I'm asking you to become an emitter for Altrigo, Mr. Fellin—a full twenty-four-hour, unshared channel on the Altrigo network. Just like your wife."

"But what would it involve?" I asked—I had no acting skill.

"Well, there's the operation of course. But it's very simple and quite painless I assure you. If you want to know more, I'm sure that one of the technical staff can . . ."

"You don't understand, Mr. Walker. I don't mean I want to know *how* your system works. I don't know what it *is;* what it *does.*"

He looked at me with all the astonishment he would have shown had I pleaded ignorance of the facts of life. "But surely Marion has . . ."

"She began to explain. But you must understand that I am like a man who has been resurrected from the dead. The world I knew and grew up in is the world of fifty years ago. Perhaps I should try and understand your world, but there is so much in it that is repugnant or incomprehensible, that I do not want to understand. And Altrigo, as far as I can tell, is so much a part of the world that I would much rather know nothing about it."

"Mr. Fellin . . . Dave . . . You cannot begin to understand the world until you know something about the Altrigo system. It may have started as entertainment, but nowadays it's one of the primary bases of our civilization. I must show you."

He pressed a switch on his desk intercom and, when his secretary answered, said, "Miss Matthews, will you tune in my desk set to the Marion Fellin channel please."

From his desk he picked up a dark tangle of filaments and held it out to me, telling me to slip it over my head. It was like a net of fibrous strands with nodules of metal shining in the mesh. I pulled it over my head where it clung limpet-like. I wanted to protest at the discomfort—it was tight and the metal tags dug at my scalp. Yet, even as I opened my mouth, I was no longer aware of it. For that matter, I was no longer aware of myself, the room, of Walker.

I was standing, it seemed, in a dress-shop, adjusting a dress which an assistant had just slipped over my head, an assistant who said, "I think madam will be pleased, if madam would care to look in the mirror . . ." The illusion of being this other person was overwhelming. It was not just that I could see and hear with this person's eyes and ears—I could feel the cool silk on my body and the touch of the assistant as she smoothed a crease from the material; I could smell the delicate odor of the perfume I—this other person—was wearing. Even the thoughts and consciousness of that person were fighting to dispossess my own but were held back for a moment by the tumult in my mind as the certainty grew that when this person looked in the mirror I would see—and I did—my wife.

I admire myself in the mirror. The dress is perfect. It looks right; it feels right; it is right. I run my hands down my body, feeling the sheen of the material and give a little twist to see the hem flare.

"Madam likes it?"

"Oh yes," I say. "It's beautiful. I'll take it."

"It is a little expensive but I'm sure it is worth it. I'm certain Mr. Fellin will admire it."

I'm sure he will too, and blush a little at the thought. And blush a little deeper at my own weakness. One year married and I still act like an innocent bride when I think of David.

There was a flash of violent color and a voice in my head said, "This is channel fifteen of the Altrigo Corporation. Your alter ego is Marion Fellin. Under statute number twenty-eight of the authority constituting the Corporation we must now give you sixty seconds in which to orientate yourself and switch off your receiver if you so desire. These breaks will follow at quarter hour intervals and this warning is emitted every hour, on the hour."

I was back in Walker's office. I looked across at him, and he stretched out his hand towards the switch to which the headpiece was joined by a thin cord. Bemused, but wanting to know more, I shook my head.

I am walking down the street, delighting in the warm spring breeze and admiring glances of the people I pass. Should I go back to the apartment, I think. No, I decide. I'll have a cup of coffee with the crowd at Magrit's.

Over a dozen of them are there in the darkened room with the scent of coffee and chocolate, pastry and cream. My new dress is the center of attention, drawing looks of envy from the women and of admiration from the men.

This time Walker cut it off without asking me.

"That will be enough I think," he said. "In a way I'm breaking the rules in letting you see that—female channels are strictly for women only. But I felt that your wife was your best introduction to . . ."

"How long has this been going on?" I broke in.

"With Marion you mean? Since shortly after her twelfth birthday, I believe. Her father signed the contract with us as soon as she was legally of age to become an emitter. That means she's been with us for nearly twenty years. That's why she's so popular—half our audience have watched her grow from a girl to womanhood."

"But how . . . ?"

"As I told you, I'm no technician but, basically, there is a tiny emitter buried in the brain of our emitter subjects. This picks up and transmits the brain patterns of that subject. We receive the signals, amplify them and send them over the wire to our subscribers. Twenty-eight channels, fourteen for men and fourteen for women, eighteen of them nationally networked."

"And how often do you transmit? I mean, how many hours a day can these people . . . how do you put it? . . . tune in on my wife?"

"Oh, it never stops. We can't switch off the emitters, you know. They transmit twenty-four hours a day. Of course, a subscriber won't be tuned in on one emitter all the time; there are competing channels. Then a subscriber has to eat, sleep and go to work. That's why we have the breaks—it's very easy for subscribers to become so immersed in an emitter's life that they forget about their own existence."

"And how many people are there spying on my wife?"

"You shouldn't say spying, you know." He was bluff, trying to laugh off my choice of words. "It's very seldom that a subscriber is with Marion all the time but, since the interest created by the marriage, I suppose between ninety and a hundred million subscribers tune in to channel fifteen at some time during the day."

I could hear Marion's voice saying, "I act at life. I live to the full for people who are only half alive." So much was explained. Particularly the lack-lustre absence of vitality in the community. Why live yourself when someone else can do it for you so much better, so much more richly, so much more vividly?

"You sicken me," I said suddenly.

"What do you mean?" yelled Walker with that shrillness of a man who knows he is defending something which is, at root, indefensible. "Don't you see the benefits this brings? There have always been the rich and the poor, the haves and the have-nots. How much truer that is today when the world's population is growing out-of-hand. Who can afford to live above subsistence level except a very few? But, thanks to Altrigo, the people who have the riches are the people who can share the good things with the masses, and share them in full. In reality the masses eat stodge, wear rags, live in hutches. But through Marion and the people like her, they can eat in luxury restaurants, wear silk and worsted, sleep between linen sheets . . ."

His argument sounded moral and just. But I was remembering an incident from our honeymoon.

It was night, and the rolling breakers were foaming white against the black, glass-like surface of the sea. Marion and I had bathed in the light of the full moon and then lain, naked and wet, on the beach in the warm, evening air. We did not even make love but just lay there, peacefully content. Our bodies were apart but close enough for each to feel the presence of the other and we linked hands. We said nothing but shared the peace and silence of that moment. I had thought then that if anyone had seen us they would have thought us at best laughable, if not mad. And yet, in a strange way, that was one of the most perfect moments of my life—simply because we were alone together and sharing our pleasure. Now it burst upon me that I might well have been sharing that moment with untold millions of women.

I felt utterly debased. I felt unclean inside. I felt an utter hatred for the entire parasitic system as personified by Walker and my wife. Without another word I ran from that room.

I was pursued from the building and along the streets by the cries of Walker and his minions, but I did not hear them because I was also pursued by my own self-created phantoms. Every woman I passed in the street could have been the recipient of words and actions which I could only have said or done to a person I loved. Every alley seemed to be full of hidden eyes and the air seemed full of scandalised whispers.

I slammed the door of the apartment against them but, this time, I could not shut out the world.

She came out of the bedroom, as lovely and desirable as ever, wearing the dress I now knew only too well. If I could have seen her then through the all-accepting eyes of courtship, perhaps I might have understood and accepted things as they were. I did not, could not, hate Marion, but behind her eyes lived millions of creeping things—parasites who fed on her emotions.

"I'll teach you to stare at me," I yelled at them. "So you want to know how to live? Well learn what it's like to die."

And I took Marion's throat in my hands.

They tell me I killed Marion. What is harder to believe is that, since the emitter never ceased to function as she died, I killed more than two million other women as well. That there were not more, I am told, is due to the pure coincidence that one of the statutory breaks occurred before Marion's life was quite extinct.

Their figures mean nothing to me; I find it hard enough to grasp the one simple fact of my murder of Marion. I do not believe I intended to do more than frighten her and them. But I can only remember what I have told you; everything else is buried in a haze which persisted until I came round, here in prison. I know only what other people tell me about my trial and the feelings of anger which swept the world.

I hear the rioters and lynch-mobs have been out on the streets, calling for my blood. Well, for their sakes, I wish I could die. I am so sorry—not for those two million; I knew nothing of them—but for killing my lovely Marion. How could she be guilty when what she did was regarded as commonplace in her world?

My own crime was not in killing her but in marrying her. However much I thought I knew her, I could not in fact know anyone in her world any more than she could have known anyone in mine. There is no geographical gap which is as great as the gap between the ages. My own age died fifty years ago, and I should have died with it. I can never have any sympathy with the present. Over and over I tell myself that I have deprived two million human beings of their lives. And time and again my true self answers, saying, those same people had deprived the entire human race of its dignity.

*The author of this very funny story about chess writes that
he is "thirty years old, a graduate student in English at the
University of Wisconsin, married, fat and happy. I have
published poetry, translations of modern Polish poetry, and
book reviews in a variety of little magazines," and adds, "by
the way, I'm a lousy chess player." But a first-rate writer.*

VON GOOM'S GAMBIT

by Victor Contoski

You won't find Von Goom's Gambit in any of the books on
chess openings. Ludvik Pachman's *Moderne Schachtheorie*
simply ignores it. Paul Keres' authoritative work *Teoria
Debiutow Szachowych* mentions it only in passing in a foot-
note on page 239, advising the reader never to try it under
any circumstances and makes sure the advice is followed
by giving no further information. Dr. Max Euwe's *Archives*
lists the gambit in the index under the initials V. G. (Gambit), but fortunately gives no page number. The twenty-
volume *Chess Encyclopedia* (fourth edition) states that Von
Goom is a myth and classifies him with werewolves and
vampires. His Gambit is not mentioned. Vassily Nikolayevitch
Kryllov heartily recommends Von Goom's Gambit in the
English edition of his book, *Russian Theory of the Opening*; the Russian edition makes no mention of it. Fortunately Kryllov himself did not—and does not yet—know the
moves, so he did not recommend them to his American
readers. If he had, the cold war would be finished. In
fact, America would be finished, and possibly the world.

Von Goom was an inconspicuous man, as most discoverers
usually are; and he probably made his discovery by ac-

cident, as most discoverers usually do. He was the illegitimate son of a well-known actress and a prominent political figure. The scandal of his birth haunted his early years, and as soon as he could legally do so he changed his name to Von Goom. He refused to take a Christian name because he claimed he was no Christian, a fact which seemed trivial at the time but was to explain much about this strange man. He grew fast early in life and attained a height of five feet, four inches, by the time he was ten years old. He seemed to think this height was sufficient, for he stopped growing. When his corpse was measured after his sudden demise, it proved to be exactly five feet, four inches. Soon after he stopped growing, he also stopped talking. He never stopped working because he never started. The fortunes of his parents proved sufficient for all his needs. At the first opportunity, he quit school and spent the next twenty years of his life reading science fiction and growing a mustache on one side of his face. Apparently, sometime during this period, he learned to play chess.

On April 5, 1997, he entered his first chess tournament, the Minnesota State Championship. At first, the players thought he was a deaf mute because he refused to speak. Then the tournament director, announcing the pairings for the round, made a mistake and announced, "Curt Brasket—White; Van Goon—Black." A smell, cutting voice filled with infinite sarcasm said, "Von Goom." It was the first time Von Goom had spoken in twenty years. He was to speak once more before his death.

Von Goom did not win the Minnesota State Championship. He lost to Brasket in twenty-nine moves. Then he lost to George Barnes in twenty-three moves, to K. N. Pedersen in nineteen, Frederick G. Galvin in seven, James Seifert in thirty-nine. Dr. Milton Otteson in three and Baby George Jackson (who was five years old at the time) in one hundred and two. Thereupon, he retired from tournament chess for two years.

His next appearance was December 12, 1999, in the Greater Birmingham Open, where he also lost all his games. During the remainder of the year, he played in the Fresno Chess Festival, the Eastern States Chess Congress, the Peach State Invitational and the Alaska Championship. His

score for the year was: opponents forty-one; Von Goom
zero.

Von Goom, however, was determined. For a period of
two and one-half years thereafter he entered every tournament he could. Money was no obstacle and distance was
no barrier. He bought his own private plane and learned
to fly so that he could travel across the continent playing
chess at every possible occasion. At the end of the two-
and-one-half-year period, he was still looking for his first
win.

Then he discovered his Gambit. The discovery must surely have been by accident, but the credit—or rather the
infamy—of working out the variations must be attributed
to Von Goom. His unholy studies convinced him that the
Gambit could be played with either the White or the Black
pieces. There was no defense against it. He must have
spent many a terrible night over the chessboard analyzing
things man was not meant to analyze. The discovery of the
Gambit and its implications turned his hair snow white, although his half mustache remained a dirty brown to his
dying day, which was not far off.

His first opportunity to play the Gambit came in the
Greater New York Open. The pre-tournament favorite was
the wily defending Champion, grandmaster Miroslav Terminsky, although sentiment favored John George Bateman,
the Intercollegiate Champion, who was also all-American
quarterback for Notre Dame, Phi Beta Kappa and the
youngest member of the Atomic Energy Commission. By
this time, Von Goom had become a familiar, almost comic,
figure in the chess world. People came to accept his silence,
his withdrawal, even his half mustache. As Von Goom
signed his entry card, a few players remarked that his hair
had turned white; but most people ignored him. Fifteen
minutes after the first round began, Von Goom won his
first game of chess. His opponent had died of a heart attack.

He won his second game too when his opponent became
violently sick to his stomach after the first six moves. His
third opponent got up from the table and left the tournament hall in disgust, never to play again. His fourth broke
down in tears, begging Von Goom to desist from playing

the Gambit. The tournament director had to lead the poor man from the hall. The next opponent simply sat and stared at Von Goom's opening position until he lost the game by forfeit.

His string of victories had placed Von Goom among the leaders of the tournament, and his next opponent was the Intercollegiate Champion John George Bateman, a hot-tempered, attacking player. Von Goom played his Gambit, or, if you prefer to be technical, his Counter Gambit, since he played the Black pieces. John George's attempted refutation was as unconventional as it was ineffective. He jumped to his feet, reached across the table, grabbed Von Goom by the collar of his shirt and hit him in the mouth. But it did no good. Even as Von Goom fell, *he made his next move.* John George Bateman, who had never been sick a day in his life, collapsed in an epileptic fit.

Thus, Von Goom, who had never won a game of chess in his life before, was to play the wily grandmaster, Miroslav Terminsky, for the championship. Unfortunately, the game was shown to a crowd of spectators on a huge demonstration board mounted at one end of the hall. The tension mounted as the two contestants sat down to play. The crowd gasped in shock and horror when they saw the opening moves of Von Goom's Gambit. Then silence descended, a long, unbroken silence. A reporter who dropped by at the end of the day to interview the winner found to his amazement that the crowd and players alike had turned to stone. Only Terminsky had escaped the holocaust. The lucky man had gone insane.

A few more like results in tournaments and Von Goom became, by default, the chess champion of America. As such he received an invitation to play in the Challengers Tournament, the winner of which would play a match for the world championship with the current champion, Dr. Vladislaw Feorintoshkin, author, humanitarian and winner of the Nobel Peace Prize. Some officials of the International Chess Federation talked of banning the Gambit from play, but Von Goom took midnight journeys to their houses and *showed them the Gambit.* They disappeared from the face of the earth. Thus it appeared that the way to the world championship stood open to him.

Unknown to Von Goom, however, the night before he arrived in Portoroz, Yugoslavia, the site of the tournament, the International Chess Federation held a secret meeting. The finest brains in the world gathered together seeking a refutation to Von Goom's Gambit—and they found it. The following night, the most intelligent men in their generation, the leading grandmasters of the world, took Von Goom out in the woods and shot him. The great humanitarian Dr. Feorintoshkin looked down at the body and said, "A merciful end for Van Goon." A small, cutting voice filled with infinite sarcasm said, "Von Goom." Then the leading grandmasters shot him again and cleverly concealed his body in a shallow grave, which has not been found to this day. After all, they have the finest brains in the world.

And what of Von Goom's Gambit? Chess is a game of logic. Thirty-two pieces move on a board of sixty-four squares, colored alternately dark and light. As they move they form patterns. Some of these patterns are pleasing to the logical mind of man, and some are not. They show what man is capable of and what is beyond his reach. Take any position of the pieces on the chessboard. Usually it tells of the logical or semi-logical plans of the players, their strategy in playing for a win or a draw, and their personalities. If you see a pattern from the King's Gambit Accepted, you know that both players are tacticians, that the fight will be brief but fierce. A pattern from the Queen's Gambit Declined, however, tells that the players are strategists playing for minute advantages, the weakening of one square or the placing of a Rook on a half-opened file. From such patterns, pleasing or displeasing, you can tell much not only about the game and the players but also about man in general, and perhaps even about the order of the universe.

Now suppose someone discovers by accident or design a pattern on the chessboard that is more than displeasing, an alien pattern that tells unspeakable things about the mind of the player, man in general and the order of the universe. Suppose no normal man can look at such a pattern and remain normal. Surely such a pattern must have been formed by Von Goom's Gambit.

I wish the story could end here, but I fear it will not

end for a long time. History has shown that discoveries cannot be unmade. Two months ago in Camden, New Jersey, a forty-three-year-old man was found turned to stone staring at a position on a chessboard. In Salt Lake City, the Utah State champion suddenly went screaming mad. And, last week in Minneapolis, a woman studying chess suddenly gave birth to twins—although she was not pregnant at the time.

Myself, I'm giving up the game.

Cannon or, more precisely, bombards have an exciting and colorful history, going back to the 13th Century in China. (Chinese records called them "the heaven-shaking thunder bombs.") That there have been few if any SF stories based on cannon-lore is perhaps no great surprise; that when one came along it would be from the imaginative and far-ranging pen of Avram Davidson should be not much greater a surprise. Here then, with all the sweep and thunder you might expect (along with more than a bit of humor; Mr. Davidson's wit is not easily muzzled) is the story of that gigantic engine of destruction . . .

BUMBERBOOM

by Avram Davidson

Along the narrow road, marked a few times with cairns of white-washed stones, a young man came by with a careful look and a deliberate gait and a something in his budget which went drip-a-drip red. The land showed gardens and fenced fields and flowering fruit trees. The bleating of sheep sounded faintly. The young man's somewhat large mouth became somewhat smaller as he reflected how well such a land might yield . . . and as he wondered who might hold the yield of it.

Around the road's bend he came upon a small house of wood with an old man peering from the door with weepy eyes that gave a sudden start on seeing who it was whose feet-sounds on the road had brought him from his fusty bed. And his scrannel legs shook.

Around the road's bend he came upon a small house of wood with an old man peering from the door with weepy

54

eyes that gave a sudden start on seeing who it was whose feet-sounds on the road had brought him from his fusty bed. And his scrannel legs shook.

"Fortune favor you, senior," the young man said, showing his empty palms. "I do but seek a chance and place to build a fire to broil the pair of leverets which fortune has sent my way for breakfast."

The old man shook his head and stubble beard. "Leverets, my young, should not be seared on a naked fire. Leverets should be stewed gently in a proper pot with carrots, onions, and a leek and a leaf of laurel, to say the least."

With a sigh and a smile and a shrug, the young man said, "You speak as much to the wit as would my own father, who (I will conceal nothing) is High Man to the Hereditor of Land Qanaras, a land not totally without Fortune's favor, though not the puissant realm it was before the Great Gene Shift. Woe!—and my own name, it is Mallian, son Hazelip."

The old man nodded and bobbled his throat. "This place, to which I make you free, though poor in all but such mere things as pot and fire and garden herbs—this place, I say, is mine. Ronan, it is called, and I am by salutary custom called only 'Ronan's.' To be sure, I have another name, but in view of my age and ill health you will excuse my not pronouncing it, lest some ill-disposed person overhear and use the knowledge to work a malevolence upon me . . . Yonder is the well at which you may fill the pot. So. So. And who can be ignorant—ahem-hum-hem—of the past and present fame of Land Qanaras, that diligent and canny country in which doubtless flourishes a mastery of medicine of geography, medicine of art and craft, and medicine of magic as well as other forms of healing; who? Enough, enough. Water, my young. The leverets are already dead and need not be drowned."

The stew of young hares was sweet and savory, and Ronan's put his crusts to soak in the juice, remarking that they would do him well for his noonmeal. "Ah ahah!" he said, with a pleasurable eructation. "How much better are hares in the pot with carrots than in the garden with them! And what brings you here, my young," he sought for a fragment of flesh caught by a rotting tush, "to the small enclave which is this Section, not properly termable a Land, and under the beneficent protection of Themselves, the Kings of the Dwerfs; what? eh? um ahum . . ." He rolled his rufous and watery eyes swiftly to his guest, then ostentatiously away.

Mallian gave a start, and his hand twitched towards his sling and pouch, none of which totally escaped rheumy old Ronan's, for all his silly miming. "I should have known!" Mallian growled, bringing his thick brown brows together in a scowl. "Those cairns of whited stones . . . It is a Bandy sign, isn't it?"

Now how the old senior rolled his watery eyes up and down and shook his head! "*We* make no use of that pejorative expression, my young! *We* do not call Them 'Bandies,' *No! We* call Them, the Kings of the Dwerfs, so." He winked, pouching up one cheek, squeezing out a tear. "And we are grateful for Their benevolences, yes we are." He drew down the corners of his cavernous and hound-lip mouth in a mocking expression. "*Let* the Dwerfs humorously call us 'Stickpins!' But—'Bandy?' Hem! Hem! No sir, that word is not to be used." And he rambled on and on about the Dwerfymen and his loyalty, meanwhile drawing his face into all sorts of mimes and mows which mocked of his words, when there came in from the distance a confused noise, at which he fell silent and harkened, his mouth drooping open and nasty.

It was not until they were outside in the clear day that they could hear the noise resolve into a shouting or a howling and a continuous rumbling and rattling. Old Ronan's began to shake and mumble, keeping very close to his visitor, as though having observed again that this one had large hands and shoulders and was young and seemingly strong. "Fortune forfend that there should be foreign troops in the Section," he quavered. "An outrage not to be born, do I not pay my tax and levy, for all that I'm a Stickpin? Go up a bit, my young, on that hill where I point, and see what is the cause and source of all this unseemly riot— not exposing yourself unduly, but taking pains to spy out everything."

So up Mallian went, spiraling along the hill through the fragrant acacias and the stinking reptilian sumacs, and so to the top, where, through the coppice peering, he could see all these good fenced fat lands and the deep wide grasslands.

But more immediately below and along the road he saw a most unprecedented sight, stood open-mouthed and tugged the coarse bottoms of his bifurcated beard, grunting in astonishment. He turned and, through cupped hands, called once, *"Come up—!"* and turned again to watch further, paying no wit to the querulous pipings and pantings of the ancient.

Up from around the concealing curve of another hill and along what Mallian conceived must be the famed Broad Road which led to and through the whole length of the Erst Marshes came a procession in some ways reminiscent of pilgrim throngs of decimated tribes fleeing famine or pestilence or plunder—men and women and children clad in rags when clad at all, some few afree afoot, some fewer riding, but most of them attached in one way or other to the thing ridden: a thing, immense, of great length, tubular, rather like the most gigantic blow-gun the most inflamed imagination might conceive of, trundling and rumbling along on enormous and metal-shod wheels, the spokes and rims as thick as a man—some of them in harness to which they bent so low that they were horizontal, squatting as though for greater traction—some bowing as though at huge oars, pushing against beams thrust through the spokes—some straining their arms against the rims of the wheels or against the body or butt of the monstrous engine—others pushing with their backs—

This tremendous contrivance rocked and rumbled and shook and rolled on, and all the while its attendance roared and shouted and howled, and the wind shifted and flung the stink of them into Mallian's face. "In Fortune's name, what is it?" he demanded of old Ronan's, extending an arm to pull him up. The senior looked and shrieked and moaned and pressed his cheeks with his palms.

"What is it?" cried Mallian, shaking him.

Ronan's threw out his arms. "Juggernaut!" he screamed. "Juggernaut! Bumberboom!"

All that frightened old Ronan's had to do—indeed, was able to do—was skitter back to his little house and release

the pigeon whose arrival in the proper belled cage of its
home dove-cote would not only inform the local confederate
Dwerf King that something was wrong in his realm but
would inform him a fairly close approximation of *where.*
Yet the old man refused utterly to perform this small task
by himself, would not unhand Mallian at all, and pulled
along with him until they were back at the senior's place
and the bird released.

"Remain, remain with me, my young," he pleaded, loose
tears coursing down his twitching face. "At least until the
Sectional Constabulary shall have arrived and set things
aright."

But the last thing which Mallian wanted was an interview
with a Bandy border-guardsman. He arose and shook his
head.

"Stay, stay, do. I have smoked pullets and both black
beer and white, strained comb-honey, dried fruits," he began
to enumerate the attractions of abiding, but was interrupted
in a way he had not fancied to be.

A smile full of teeth parted Mallian's light brown beard.
"Good, good. Not bad for one of your priorly announced
poverty; well may one envy the rich of this Section. Now—
as a reward for my accompanying you back here, to say
nothing of the work of topping that mountainous hill to
obtain intelligence for you—let you replenish, and quickly!
my budget here with as many such smokelings as will fit.
Then you may fill the chinks and interstices with the aforesaid dried fruits. No, no, another word not. I am too modest
to appreciate the compliments you would pay me by a
continued solicitation of my presence. One jug of black beer
I may be persuaded to take; the honey I must forego until
another occasion. So.

"Fortune favor you, senior Ronan's. One further deed we
may do each other. You will not need to inform your
Dwerfymen of my presence or passage; I, in turn, will not
need to inform them—unless I am stopped by them, of
course—hem! hem!—of your treasonous grimaces and repeti-
tions of the fell name of *Bandy.* Sun shine upon you, and
forfend the shadow of the Juggernaut Bumberboom!"

Thus, laughing loudly, he left the ancient as he had
first found him, weeping and alarmed, and went on his way.

Indeed, he had fully retraced his way to the top of the hill before he realized that he had not asked *the* question. He scowled and fingered his long moustaches, deliberating a return, but finally decided against it. "Such an old queery man would know no medicine of any sort," he assured himself. "Let alone wit of this most vital matter. But I will keep in mind his words about the vaporous device which pumps and drains the Erst Marshes, for—if, indeed, it is not a mere vapor of the senior himself (and how he cozened me out of half a hare; shame!)—for such medicine may well imply the presence of more. Hem, hem, we will see."

The road was riddled and griddled with great ruts from the gigantic gunwheels. Amidst clots of filth lay a man who had unjudiciously interposed his neck between wheel and road, and a child who mewed and yippered at Mallian but made no attempt to walk. Man and child, quick and dead, looked as like as the spit of their mouths—blond hair so pale as to be almost as white as that of the People of the Moon—equally pale, but pale, pale blue of small, small eyes—a sort of squinting blankness of expression— and slack, silly mouths. Idiot father and idiot son, was Mallian's impression. And he wondered how they had come to be with the gun crew. And he went on.

Warm was the day and the beer soon went down swift. Mallian was about to hoist the jug for the last time when he heard a too-well-remembered thudding on the road and looked, quickly, from one to another side for cover. But the land was flat for many arms' lengths on either side of the road. "Curse!" he muttered and reached with a sigh for sling and stones, when he bethought that he might hide —did he trot fast—behind a certain maple tree.

Mallian trotted, saw the ditch behind the tree, tumbled into it cod over cap, and had just time to right himself and peer out as the *thudthud-thudthud* of hooves came by, and he saw the mounts.

There were two of them, fat and hairy barrel-bodied Bandy ponies—a description which would as well have fit the two squat Dwerfymen riders whose short legs fit the curves of their mounts' sides as though steamed and bent thereto. Large heads, broad backs, beards which would reach to their protruding navels if not whipped away by wind, faces neither grim nor alarmed but intent and determined, the Bandies came at the gallop. The scabbards of their slashers were on their backs, within quick reach of their hands. They looked to neither side nor did they speak; in a moment more they were gone.

But the crossroads, when he came to them, swarmed with people.

"They have taken everything, everything eatable in my house!" a woman wailed, gesturing to the empty shelves revealed by the open doors.

But another cried, " 'Take?' I did not wait for them to *take*—I *gave* them all there was to eat in mine!"

"Wisely done, wisely done!" a man agreed, wiping from his red face a sweat which came from agitation rather than heat. "Food can always be purchased, food is even now growing and grazing—food, in short, can be replaced. But how can one replace that destroyed by the destruction sure to be caused if the Crew of Bumberboom were to fire even one shot from their enormous cannon? Surely it would shatter bodies and houses alike!"

And a fourth person, by his look and manner probably someone of some stature in the community, said in a sober tone of voice as he patted the middle front of his well-filled tunic, "All this is very true, but since the community and property of the Section as a whole is threatened, it is not a problem to be entirely dealt with by individuals. Fortunately, as we have seen, our protectors have been alerted. Two of their constables have already passed by and, by now, are doubtless making arrangements with the cannon's Crew. It is equally fortunate," he pointed out, looking around and gathering in the approval of the crowd, "that the demands of the Crew of Bumberboom are so modest . . . that it is only food they seek and not women or power or dominion. Eh ahem? For who could resist in the face of that tremendous and destructive engine!"

Someone else muttered that it might be better for the Crew if their needs were not limited to food alone but included water, soap, and a change of clothing. There were scattered laughs at this. The magnate, however, pursed his lips and drew his face into lines of disproval. "That is as it may be," he said, severely. "The educated person knows that customs differ among different people, and it is not for us to risk offending the Crew of Bumberboom by making gauche comments on such matters. For my part, so long as they withdraw satisfied from the Section, I care not if they ever or never bathe again, eh ahem?"

Clearly he spoke for the majority and the majority slowly began to disperse to go about their other business, confident that the Dwerf agents would deal with the matter which had so excited and upset them. Mallian approached the magnate and saluted him, the latter returning the gesture with an air of mildly surprised condescension. "Whence and whither, strange my young?" he enquired. "And for why?"

Mal sighed. "Ah, senior, your question not only sums up the matter, it places a finger upon the sore center of it. The whence is easily answered: Land Qanaras, a Land afflicted and perplexed. As to whither, I do not yet know, and can say only that I am wandering in search of a medicine which will supply an answer. Which last, I perceive you have already realized, comprsises the why. But before I speak of that I would enquire of you concerning a current matter. Sympathize with my ignorance and inform me as to what is Bumberboom, or Juggernaut, as I have heard it also denominated, and who its Crew may be."

The magnate's face had shown a conflict between flattery at Mal's compliments and unease at the prospect of being involved in his problems. But the gathering round of a few gaping loungers eager for free diversion decided his mind. "Important matters," he said, importantly, holding up his chin so that his jowls withdrew, "are not to be discussed where every lack-work may gawp and crane at an inoffensive visitor. Come along with me, my young, and I will not scruple to take time away from my many important affairs and inform you."

And, as they walked slowly through the crossroads hamlet, he related to him that Bumberboom was an engine or contrivance of both great size and potency, founded upon the principles of a medicine known only to its Crew. It had the capacity of casting great shots over great distances accompanied (so it was said) by hideous and deadly fires and deadly and hideous noises. Whence it had been derived, when and by whom made, only the Crew itself could say, and they—perhaps naturally enough—would not. "Suffice it that they have the secret of this medicine and that they use it to go whither they will, depending for sustenance upon the inevitable desire of those among whom they wander that they immediately wander elsewhere without giving an exhibition of their powers, which would prove painful in the extreme. Thus, my young, is your question answered.

"As for your problems, hem hem, I greatly regret that my civic and commercial duties do not permit me to indulge in hearing them. I must content myself reluctantly with saying that no Land under the beneficent protection of the Kings of the Dwerfs can be either afflicted or perplexed, and on this note I, alas, must take my leave. Fortune favor you!"

He waddled off briskly towards a showy dwelling-place from which came kitchen smells indicative that at least one household had left the supply of food of the Crew of Bumberboom for the governing powers to deal with.

"Sun shine upon you," Mal said, somewhat glumly, for he had learned very little from the man which he had not already been able to deduce by himself. But as he reflected on the possible uses of Bumberboom it occurred to him that therein it was conceivable lay an answer to his quest and question, though not in any way which he had previously considered.

The hamlet fell away behind him, and as he continued along the famed Broad Road he saw upon its dusty surface the hoofprints of the Dwerfish ponies, and the grooves made by the great wheels of Bumberboom. Slowly he began to smile, and then he quickened his steps and strode briskly along.

The situation at the border was perhaps brittle rather than tense; so occupied with their affairs were those gathered there that they did not observe Mallian approaching. He heard a hoarse babble of voices from farther away and saw the huge muzzle of Bumberboom lifted up from behind a rise of ground. The whitewashed stone cairns marking the dominion of the Dwerfs stood on each side of the road, and beyond them on each side of the road was another symbol consisting of two long wooden beams painted red. Their ends were planted in the ground and they inclined towards each other until for a short space they crisscrossed. The sight of the two Dwerfs brought him to pause a moment and to consider concealment . . . but they were on foot, and their mounts were tethered off at a distance, and moreover their territory clearly came to an end here, although he was not familiar with what new territory might be symbolized by the red beams.

Neither had he before ever seen men like those who stood conversing with the Bandies. They wore not the breeches, shirt and tunic so common elsewhere, but close-fitting upper garments extending as a sort of hood or cap closely over the scalp and to which a sort of curious simulated ears were attached. And tights of cloth they wore about their loins. These garments had not the rough look of wool nor (it suddenly seemed) the dull look of linen, but they had a mightily attractive smoothness and sheen and glow, and they rippled when even a muscle was moved.

"Oh, we are so infinitely obliged to the Kings of the Dwerfs," one was saying, in a tone which seemed to indicate very little sense of true obligation. Rays of sunlight slanted through the bowering branches of the trees and picked out the emblematics embroidered upon the red tunics of the Dwerfymen. "We are so obliged to them—through their constables of course—" he bowed and put more expression into the salute than was in his face, "for having sent us this number of greatly desirable guests. And such guests as they are, too!"

And a second said, with a dull and lowering look, "Our appreciation will be conveyed from our Masters to yours, very shortly, have no fears."

One of the Dwerfs said with a shrug, "They would away, as we have told you, and who can hold what will away? Furthermore, who can argue with Bumberboom?"

The other Dwerf, hearing or perhaps subtly feeling the approach of someone behind, glanced back and saw Mal coming. He took his comrade's arm and turned him around. "Hold, Raflin. Do you remember that report?"

Raflin puckered his caterpillar brows and nodded. "I do.

And I do believe, Gorlin, that this is one with whom we would speak. Halt, fellow, in the names of the Kings!"

But Mal, skipping nimbly, said, "It is a false report, to begin with, and a case of erroneous identification to continue with. Furthermore, the names of your Kings are as nothing to me for I was never their subject, and lastly—"

"Hold! Hold!"

"—lastly," Mal said, lining up beside the stranger-men, "I am not at the present moment any longer in your Section or your Land at all, and accordingly I defy you, Bandy rogues that you are!" And he spraddled his legs in contempt at them.

The Dwerfs grunted their rage and simultaneously began to reach for their slashers and to move forward upon their crook legs, but the guards from the other side of the border took several paces toward them and regarded them with extreme disfavor. They stopped.

"So be it, then," said Raflin, after a moment. "We will not invoke the doctrine of close pursuit. But be assured, Stickpin," he flung the term at unflinching Mallian, "and be assured, you other Stickpins, that we will complain upon you for harboring a malignant, an enemy, a ruffian, fugitive, and recusant, a rapiner and an otherwise offender against our Kings, their Crowns and Staves; and we will demand and, I do not doubt, will obtain his return."

Mallian bracked his tongue and again spraddled his legs.

Said one of the other guards, "Demand, then. It may be you will secure his return—and with him, too, the return of Bumberboom and all its Crew."

The Dwerfs made no reply to this but turned and proceeded to their ponies. One of them, however, whirled around and flung out his hand and forefinger at Mal. "As for you, fellow!" he declared roundly, "were you at all instructed in any wise of medicine of history, you would understand—you would *know*—that the bodily form of the Dwerfs is the original bodily form of all mankind. We have only pity for you who descend out of those misshapen sufferers from the Great Gene Shift." He swung himself about once more and neither of them spoke again. The two stout ponies went trot-a-trot down the road, dust motes rising to dance in the sunbeams.

Mallian turned his head to see the stranger-men regarding him without expression. He thrust his hand into his bosom and withdrew the letter of statements in its pouch. He handed it out . . . to the air, as it were, for none reached to take it. After a moment and in some perplexity he asked, "Does none desire to examine the well-phrased let-pass with which my natal territory—or, to be more precise, its governance—has supplied me?"

With a slight yawn one of them said, and he shook his head, "None of whom I know . . . Such ceremonies are reserved for those arrived on official purposes, and not for mere proletaries or profugitives."

Stung by such belittling indifference, Mallian exlaimed to the effect that he was indeed on just such purposes arrived. The strangers smiled at him a trifle scornfully. "These pretensions are at the moment and under the circumstances amusing," they said, "but they will not do, barbado; a-no-no, they will not do at all. Those arrived on official purposes unto this Land of Elver State, of which we of the corps of guards are both the internal and the external defense, arrive with proper pomp. They, for one thing, are dressed in garments of serrycloth, as indeed are we, ahem hum. For another, they ride upon smooth-haired horses adorned with many trappings of broideries and burnishments, and so do all their party—which, by definition, is numerous. And for another and the last, though this by no means the least, they come provided with a multitude of rich donatives of which distribution is made to the members of the corps of guards."

Mallian cast down his eyes and gnawed upon his lips. "Nonetheless," he declared, "I have been issued with this letter of statements directing all to let me pass, and the fact of your having made no gesture to prevent my passage at all would not altogether seem to justify my failing to present it. And inasmuch as you desire not to trouble to read it, it would be a pretty courtesy on my part to read it to you. I have oftentimes been commended for my reading voice, and I doubt not but that you gallants of the Elver Guards will desire to do the same, and furthermore, the problem set down herein, which is the high purpose of my journeyings, may so move you as to search among your minds to see if per-adventure you know of a medicine which may shed both light and hope thereon."

And he read them the let-pass, or letter of statements, as he had done to the pseudomorphs, and to the People of the Moon.

"Ah, well," said one with a sniffle of his nose, "interesting and absorbing as the beardy one's problem is, and while I doubt not that the medicines of our Masters contains an answer to it—it is no more than a speck of a fly compared to the problem lying over the rise there. Anent which, let us move and consider, for an action of some sort will assuredly be required of our hands."

They proceeded upward and then paused, considering, Mal with them. There had evidently been a house of some sort there below, but it had been unstrategically situated in terms of the attempts of the Crew of Bumberboom to pass with their weapon along the road above it. It had gone off the road, and the marks of its going were eaten into the berm, and before it had either been brought to rest or come to rest of its own accord, it had thoroughly crushed the house—the fragments of which were being now unskillfully transformed into cook-fires. The harnesses hung empty, the guide-ropes lay ignored upon the ground. The Crew was both at rest and at meat. And, it became at once apparent, at other occupations as well.

"Scandalous!" exclaimed Mallian. "Shocking!"

One of the Elver Guards shrugged. "As well be scandalized or shocked at cats and dogs," he said.

Mal protested. "But dogs and cats are not human—"

The upper lip of the Elver Guard went up further. "Are *those?*" he demanded.

Not overmuch regarding this remark, Mal allowed his mind to run still more over a notion which, in seedling form, had occurred to him before. Cautiously, tentatively, he began to broach the matter. "I have been in some measure too overwhelmed by your kindliness in offering me refuge," he explained, "from those hangmen Dwerfs to express my gratification fully. But—"

"No need, no need," the Elver murmured, scratching his armhole—then, as though only then becoming aware of what he was doing, he stepped back from the berm with a curse and a scowl. "A tetanty upon those wittol swine! They must have fleas as large as mice—if indeed no worse. I am for going away and constructing a steam-lodge and boiling self and habit."

"Do, Naccanath," murmured another Elver. "And when asked how you proceeded to rid the State of this lumbering menace, be prepared to answer, 'I bathed me.' But for praise or commendation, do not be prepared."

The guard Naccanath hesitated, muttered, scratched.

Mallian moved his mouth against the sudden fretful silence. "But now that I am able to take two consecutive breathes free from fear of Bandymen pursuit and am made aware not only of my safety and refuge but of the wisdom of those whose—"

A fight broke out among the Crew below, but was soon settled.

An Elver said, in a faintly dissatisfied tone, "Ah . . . he did but club him. I had thought he might well eat him; it would surprise me not a wit."

And another said, a peevish note in his voice, bruising a blossom under his nose to counteract the noisome taint now rising from below, "Why need they eat each other when all the world rushes to supply them with far less gamy food? In fact," his face became a sight brighter, "may this not be a possible solution?—videlicet, simply to supply them with a steady ration of victual, thus depriving them of incentive to leave their present location. Denizened right here, they remain under supervision and do no further damage and post no further threat."

Musing a moment, the others then shook their heads. Another said, "They would breed, Durraneth, at a rate which would soon enough make their maintenance a cost not to be considered. Further, experience has shown that nomads do not easily take to denization."

They sighed and sucked their lips and their unhappy breaths caused their smooth garments to ripple and shimmer in a marvelous manner, for which Mallian, nevertheless, had but small eyes.

"—whose tolerance has undoubtedly saved my life," he continued resolutely—and a shade more loudly. The Elver Guards now turned to consider him and his words. "What is the point of your narration, profugitive?" demanded the one called Durraneth, in his voice a coolness only to be expected in one whose own proposal had just now been considered and dismissed. Barely had he finished asking his question when a head appeared above the berm, its countenance vacant and filthy, and looked at them open-mouthed as they stepped backwards with fastidious precaution. "Cappin?" it inquired. "Cappin Mog?" A bellow from below diverted it so that it turned, released its hold, slid down and away and did not return.

"The point of my narration, gallant Guards Elver, is just this: that I would ask of you a consideration for which I offer to perform a service, thus and thus, inform me kindly where I may inquire of your Masters a medicine to solve the problems of my own Land Qanaras, and in return I will rid you and all the Land of Elver State forever of Bumberboom and its Crew."

The green shade flashed blue as a jay noisily chased another through the trees. Narrowly the guards regarded him. Then Naccanath said, "Seemingly such an agreement would be of benefit to all and of detriment to none. Still, I am moved to inquire—not from suspicion, fie upon such a thought, hem hem, but out of mere curiosity and interest—how do you propose to do this?"

Mallian's fingers stroked the left and then the right tip of his short beard, through which a slight smile peeped deprecatingly. "To reveal this before an agreement has been reached would perhaps be out of keeping with the traditions of negotiating. I point this out, not from suspicion, fie upon the thought, hem hem, but simply because I have been very traditionally reared and do not desire to cast reflection upon my upbringing by departing therefrom even in trifles."

After another silence, Durraneth said, with something like a frown, "Would it be untraditional for you to indicate by which route you intend for yourself and them to depart, and your destination as well?"

Mallian said it would not. Logic, he pointed out, would indicate a departure by the shortest route (other than the one back into the near-lying Section of the Dwerf Kings' dominions) out of Elver State, and to show his perfect good will and trust in the matter he would entreat the advice of the company as to a good route to achieve this purpose—accompanied, perhaps, by a map—and, as for his destination, well:

"I am a hill man by origin, and lonely therefore. Nevertheless there is nought of the hermit in my background or makeup; I admire also the proximity of fair lowlands and goodly towns to which one may conveniently descend to purchase merchandise with the modest yield of the hills. And therefore—"

Durraneth cleared his throat and cast a slant glance at his fellows. "And therefore—inform me if I understand you arightly, Mallian son Hazelip—and therefore you desire information about a place lying outside of Elver State and situated upon a hill overlooking fair lowlands and goodly towns, or perhaps at least one goodly town. Is it so?"

Mal frankly admitted that the conjecture was correct. "At least one goodly town," he murmured, "although two or even three would be better."

The guard-lodge had a stark neatness about it which Mallian, familiar with the companionable disorder of Qanaras and the opulent show of the Dwerfs, found a bit chilling. There were, to be sure, many contrivances visible which seemed both curious and interesting, as well as an entire shelf bearing nought but books, which much impressed him. " 'Where are much books is much medicine,' " he quoted, reverently.

The Elver Guards gave but a nod or two at this and began to spread a table with maps and to converse in low tones among themselves, paying to Mal's thoughtfully-pointed-out observation that it was now high noon and mealtime, inattention to which the very best of wills could only call coarse. He therefore did not feel a compunction at devoting himself forthwith to the smoked pullets and dried fruits with which his budget had thoughtfully been filled by old Ronan's. And when the guard Naccanath said, over his shoulder, "Attend hither, profugitive," he replied that he in no wise feared that Elver folk would work him a malignancy via use and medicine of his own and proper name, and therefore he would cheerfully respond to it, which was Mallian, son Hazelip High Man to the Hereditor of

Land Qanaras. "But at the moment I eat," he pointed out.
He raised his brows and bit and chewed.

The Crewmen's supply had all been eaten to a fare-
theewell, and they sat or lay about snoring or scratching
or simply staring about them as Mal approached. He had
come quite near before it occurred to them to stare at him.
He was already among them before any of them had made
up their minds that he perhaps ought not to be. But it was
not until he had begun to make a circuit of the ponderous
engine that anything like concern began to make itself
evident. The sight of Bumberboom at close up proved interesting enough even to banish the train of thought caused
by the sight of the Crew close up. The same near-idiot face
repeated over and over again in varying stages of grime,
the same snaggle and snarl of pale hair and small, vacant,
pale blue eyes—what did it mean?

It scarcely could mean that the same moron Crew
which was now attached to Bumberboom had created it in
the first place. They could never have fashioned those immense and massy wheels of stout wood reinforced with iron
and rimmed with broad iron tires. Never could they have
founded that gigantic tube whereon, in the casting, figures
of beasts and monsters had been fixed, never have devised
that ornate breech in the shape of a bearded face with lips
puckered as though whistling, nor the even more ornate
and in fact rather frightening face which terminated the
great tube's other end, mouth distended into an enormous
shout—mouth silent now, but threatening of anything but
silence . . .

Anything but silence now among the Crew, whose disturbance bore more resemblance to a poultry-yard than
an anthill, running and squawking—thrice in succession
people fell full-tilt against Mallian, but it was certain from
their great alarm that it had not been their aim to do so.

And as they trotted about they set up a cry and howl
which presently resolved itself in Mallian's ears into the
same words, meaningless as yet, which he had heard before from one of them . . . now, however, not as a question, but as an appeal for aid. "Cappin Mog! Cappin Mog!
Cappin Mog!"

And Mal meanwhile continued his perambulation and

examination. The carriage was fitted with large boxes, but these were locked. He was about to make a closer inspection when someone bellowed close by, and at the same moment, something struck him between the shoulder blades. He took a quick step sideways before spinning around, and the sight of his face acted as instant deterrent to the one who had evidently flung the clod and was now doing a sort of angry dance with another clod in his hand. His arms were inordinately long and thickly thewed; chest and trunk were barrel-thick; neck there was none visible, and the broadnosed face was alive with fury.

"Gid 'way!" it shouted, though perhaps with a shade more caution than in its previous bellow. "Gid 'way! Gid oud! Don' touch-a! Killya! Cutcha-troat!"

And the others of the Crew, male and female, taking courage from this couthless champion, began to draw in behind him, shaking their fists.

"Cutcha-troat, tellya! Gid oud! Don't touch-a! Bumberboom! Bumberboom!"

The rabble highly approving these sentiments, at once began to shout the word most familiar to them: "Bumberboom! Bumberboom! *Bumberboom! Bumberboom!*"

Mallian stood where he was and let them howl, and by and by they began to tire of it. He had by now become a familiar object to them and, as he neither moved nor spoke nor did anything of further interest, they grew bored with him, and—one by one—he could see some emotion too faint to be wonder, perplexity of a low order, perhaps, begin to overtake them. They did not really know any more why they were there or why they were so loudly engaged. And so, first one by one, and then, as regarded those who were left, all of a sudden, they ceased their commotion and wandered off.

Not so the one who had thrown both turf and threats at Mal. Highly intelligent he was not, but neither was he an utter idiot. He knew that Mal had no business near the great weapon, and he was determined to get him away from it. Regardless of the defection of his Crew he now came a step nearer, hitched up his dissolving breeches, and menaced with his hands.

"Toll ya, gid oud!" he bellowed. "Trow ya down and kill-ya, ya don' gid oud!"

Mal asked, "Who are you?"

A look of astonishment came upon the man's face. He had evidently never been asked the question before, and it was not any doubt as to his identity but a shock that his identity was not universally known which made him go slack.

After a moment he said, "Who my? My Cappin Mog! Is who." And for emphasis shouted, "Mog! Mog! Cappin Mog! Cappin of Bumberboom and alla Crew! Is who—"

Mallian allowed his own face to register an extreme mixture of enlightenment, astonishment, impressment, and self-deprecation: "Oh, *you* are Captain Mog!"

The captain gave an emphatic nod and grunt, patted his stomach, clearly quite pleased with the effect. "My Cappin Mog," he affirmed. "Is who."

"Pardon, senior . . . pardon, Captain . . ." He bowed and showed his palms. "I did not know, you see . . ." The man nodded and came close to smirking and in fact emitted a pleased sound which came close enough to being a giggle to be identified as such, grotesque as the sound seemed coming from him. He gazed from side to side and wiped his loose mouth with the back of his bristly paw. And at that, Mallian gave a bound and a jump and sailed forward and upward and kicked him in the side of the head and felled him like a tree.

Some of the Crew observed what happened and their hoots of astonishment brought others back from casual wandering about the vicinity. They formed a rough circle about the two, though it was without either intention of doing so or awareness of the utility thereof. Several of them growled and even shouted at Mallian and bared their dirty teeth and spat. One or two even went so far as to look about for a weapon—but what immediately came to view was an overlooked loaf of bread, and in a moment they were too concerned with an idiot quarrel about it to pursue the audacious gesture.

Mog lay awhile on his side, his eyes opened, he frowned, he rolled over on his elbows and gazed at Mallian and at the Crewmen. He smacked his lips tentatively. "Cutcha-troat," he said, but without real passion. Then he raised his rump and so in stages got to his feet. "Gid oud," he repeated. "Killya . . ." He looked around for some means of accomplishing this, saw nothing save his slack-mouthed followers and the great gun. Toward this he flung up his arms. "*Bumberboom!*" he cried, warningly. "*Bumberboom!* Goddamn sunamabitchen big noise! *Drop-down-dead!*"

His small pale eyes observed approvingly that Mal, apparently convinced by this fearsome threat, had begun to walk away, and he drew back a trifle to let him pass. Whereat Mal repeated his spring and his sally and knocked him down again. This time he remained down a much longer time, and when he next arose, it was not to address himself to Mal at all. He put his hands at his hips and threw back his head and shouted. The words meant nothing of themselves to Mal, but the effect was immediate. The Crewmen left their places in the circle and bent to their positions in the harness and elsewhere. Mog took a deep breath. He cried, "Forehead . . . *harsh!*" They bent, dug in their feet, groaned.

"Bumber*boom!*" they cried.

"Bumber*boom!*" The limber lifted.

"*Bumber*boom!*" The trail lifted.

"*Bum . . . ber . . . boom!*" The ponderous equipage trembled, shifted. The great wheels shivered, dropped dirt and turf. Turned. Turned slowly. But turned.

Bumberboom began to move forward.

"You may stop her here, Captain Mog," Mal said, presently. The man looked at him. "Stop? *Here?*" Mog's face moved, uncertainly. Mal gestured, pointed. Then he gave a slight teeter or two, as though readying himself to jump. Mog crouched, cried out, covered his head with his arms. He shouted, walking backwards. And the cannon's wheels ceased to turn and the crew promptly slipped its harness and lay down in the road like dogs.

Elver Guard Naccanath asked, coming forward with his compeers, "You do not propose to leave them there, I trust?"

"Not for any longer than is required for us to settle

our indentures. You have an information to give me—or, rather, two; likewise, a map."

Naccanath's thin lips parted in his thin, smooth-shaven face. He unrolled something in his hands. "Attend, then pro—hem—Mallian son Hazelip High Man to the Hereditor of Land Qanaras. Here is a carto or map which is limned upon strong linen, and we have marked with red a few serveral places which bear upon this present business. Thus: this border station. This road. Follow my finger, now . . . This road forks *here* and *here* and *here*. The right of this last one leads to our capital community, wherein our Masters of a surety can medicate your question—but thither you go not now, for instead you are to follow via the left fork of this first furcation, and this leads, as is clearly delineated, to the Great Rift and all the Land Nor.

"And concerning this same, observe how we have reddled for you a choice of hills, few of which overlook less than a league of fine fat flatland nor fewer than two prosperous trading towns."

Mallian's pursed lips thrust out in concentration between his beard and his moustachioes, he nodded, traced the lines with his brown and furry fingers, so different from the thin pale digit of his present informer, who, asked what sundry of produce and people Land Nor afforded, replied that it was a good yielder of hogs and hides and horses, as well as grain and small timber, but that its people were of a sullen and willful disposition. "Though I do not doubt," he concluded, "that they will be willing enough to trade with you."

"Nor do I," Mallian said, well enough pleased. He reached his hand for the map, but it was not forthcoming. "Come, come, Elver senior," he said, reproachfully; "surely you do not think that even my own keen mind can have committed the carto to memory? Why, unless you relinquish it, neither I nor my newly-gained companions can be sure of finding our way out of Elver State as expeditiously as all of us might wish."

Naccanath rolled the map up and thrust it into a tube of worked leather. "You may be well sure of it," he said, "for guard Durraneth and I will accompany you as far as the Rift. We would think it but ill hospitality," he said, "to do other."

Mallian cleared his throat and avoided eyes. "I am like to be overwhelmed by such high courtesy. But so be it . . . Captain Mog! *On!*"

He took his seat, with some sullenness, upon the cases fixed by the gun-carriage, and, the procession underway, diverted himself by picking the locks. He found in one nothing but some handsful of a mouldy-powdery substance, and in the other nothing but an ill-made book. With a shrug of his shoulders, he began to turn the dusty pages and to read. Presently he cast a glance, swiftly and suspiciously, at the Elver pair. But they, absorbed in moody thought, spared him no look but rode silently along on their lean horses. He grunted and turned a leaf.

The pothecary in the first town wherein they paused threw up his hands as Mallian entered. "I have no victualry at all to supply you with," he cried, in a trembling and petulant voice. "By reason of lacking either wife or servant-woman, I eat in the cookshops. Moreover, such treacles and comfits as my shelves afford are of a highly bitter and aperient sort, though a measured quantity may never harm you if you are of a costive disposition. . . . But what can these terms mean to him," he added, in a lower tone, as though to himself; "is it not known to me, if to none other, that all these cannoneers are as dull of wits as dogs, by virtue of having neither bred nor gendered outside their number for generations? Still, they have the medicine of the deadly noise, and it behooves me to speak dulcetly," he sighed. "What would you, senior?"

"Sixteen and one-half measures of crushed charcoal," said Mallian, "to begin with . . . large measures, the largest you have."

The pothecary's lower lip drooped. "Hem, hem, this would suffice to rid of wind the stomachs of a small army, though to be sure it is a small army which . . ." The apple of his throat bobbed in sudden perceptive terror. "Pay no heed to my previous comments, Master!" he pleaded. "I perceive with utter conviction the falsity of my conjectures. Charcoal—sixteen and one-half large measures. Immediately, Master! Immediately!"

He scurried about from keg to ladle to scales, darting looks of bewilderment at Mallian. Presently he inquired, "And what next is your design, lordling? You say fourteen and a half large measures of sulphur? It will be my delight —nonetheless, may I not point out that sulphur is not in current favor for fumations? Asafoedita is much preferred nowadays as an ingredient to banish the daemons and miasmas, as well—hem! Observe how I fawn contritely for having made the suggestion! Sulphur it shall be . . ."

The third substance caused him no little concern; he nibbled his mouth and frowned and snuvvled. "Snowy nitrum, Master? Forgive both the poverty of my mind and shop alike, but—Hold! I adjure but myself, Master-Lord! Is not 'snowy nitrum' another name for what is also termed the saline stone, or saltpeter? In one moment I shall have looked into my lexicon. Thus, thus. And my conjecture was correct! Sixty-nine large measures of saltpeter, more correctly denominated 'snowy nitrum' . . . it may well exhaust my supply, but of that, nothing. The drysalters must wait their pickled meats upon a fresh supply, whenever.

"I know not the use nor preparation of this triune of charcoal, sulphur, and saltpeter. Shall I triturate it for you with mortar and pestle?"

"By no means," Mallian said, hastily. "That is . . . hem. Reflection seems demanded here." He pulled a bit on his beard and peeped from under his lashes at the pothecary, a small and bony-browed man of no particular age. There were things which this one was accustomed to doing which Mallian had never done himself; furthermore, he had said a thing which Mallian wished to hear be said again and at more length. The more he considered the more he favored the notion. At last cleared his throat and spoke.

"Senior pothecary, is yours a trade which might be swiftly sold for a profit?"

The drugsman looked out the open door in a quick and fearful look. He put his dry lips up to Mallian's sunbrowned ear. "There is no business to be sold for a profit in Elver State," he hissed. "The taxers lurk like beasts of prey . . . Why do you ask? There is no business even to be *held* for a profit. Why, lordling mine, do you ask? What is stational commerce to you? You pass through, Master, with your giant thundermaker and you are supplied and you pass on and you pass on. Neither profits nor taxes nor stocks nor sales are matters you need review . . . *Why do you ask?*"

Indeed, the shop did have a decidedly well-taxed look to it and its meager shelves. Mal was fortunate in having obtained the things he wanted. "The Free Company of Cannoneers" he caught the open mouth, blank look—"Bumberboom, that is—" "Oh, aye, Master. Bumberboom." "—The Free Company of Cannoneers is in need of the services of a responsible and learned man, versed in such medicines as history and, for another example, pothecation. And it thus befalls me to wonder—"

The pothecary genuflected and kissed Mallian's hands and knees. He locked his shop and deposited the keys with the local chirurgeon. And that night whilst the Crew lay deep in snoring and the Elver Guards camped disdainfully apart with heads upon saddles, he and the pothecary spoke long and low together beside a guttering fire, and the coldly indifferent stars pulsed overhead.

"No," said the chymist, whose name was Zembac Pix. "No, Master-Lord, I have made no especial study of the matter. All of my life, Bumberboom—or, as some call it, Juggernaut—has been a byword. Bad mothers frighten bad children with it. One comes across references to it in chronicles. Whence it first came, neither do I nor anyone else know. Nor who first devised it. I was a younger man when first I saw it; most fled in terror or hasted to bring out food, but I tarried as near as I dared. So it was, or so it seemed, that none but I noticed that these fearsome fellows were little better, if better at all, than idiots. This one Mog was not then their captain. I know not what he was named, 'twas long ago and my mind has been crammed overfull ever since of drug receipts and tax-demands. Well, hem a hum. But he was not quite an idiot; indeed, I think he was a wit wittier than this one. Let us say a moron, then. And off they trundled, I wondering as they went. Twice more before today have I seen them. And heard of them more than twice. It has been counted a cause for thanks that, unlike other wandering armsmen, they never ravished nor rapted away any women. They took no recruits, either.

"The reason for this gensual clannishness, I cannot say. But its results are plain: No fresh genes have come their way since, aye, hem, who knows when? And whatsoever flaws they had amongst them to start with, such have been multiplied and squared and cubed, to use the tongue of the medicine called mathematic. And thus only idiot habit keeps them going and coming and passing to and fro. And only equally idiot habit keeps the rest of the world afearing them and yielding to them. I cannot say how old this olden book you've found may be—a century at least, I venture. It is not by the gun alone, then, nor by medicine alone, then, that the great noise and destruction comes . . . No . . . But by these three substances, mixed and moisted and dried and cracked and sieved. By my cod and cullions, this is no small thing you have discovered!"

Mallian spat into the fire. Then he reached out in the dimness and gently took Zembac Pix, the pothecary, by the throat. "You must remember that pronoun," he said softly. He felt the apple of the throat bob up and down. "Not you. *I.* Not we. *I* . . . Fortunately Mallian son Hazelip is of a trusting nature." He released his grasp.

"*Fortunately . . .*" said Pix, in a tremulous whisper.

"I have great plans. Great needs. I can offer great rewards. You, potionman, may become the councillor of the councillors of kings. Therefore be exceedingly virtuous. And exceedingly cautious."

He gazed into the other's eyes, glinted by a single dull-red spot of fire-glow in each. And watched them move as the other nodded.

They stood upon the lip of the cliff. There down beyond lay the Rift, wide and uneven and hummocked here and there; and beyond on the other side the ruins huddled haggardly. Mallian spat stoutly. "It will be no easy crossing," he observed. "Still, I perceive there is a road of sorts, and cross we must. Nevertheless . . ."

He paused so long that Durraneth and Naccanath stirred somewhat restlessly, and the unease communicated itself to the other Elvers who had ridden out from their near-adjacent city to witness both arrival and departure,

"What mean you by *nevertheless?*" Naccanath asked—perhaps still recollecting his flea-bite, he reined his horse up a way apart from Bumberboom and its Crew. The way hither had followed no rigid schedule. The Crew waked to the day when it felt the day full upon it, was by no means immediately prepared for toil, and made up for its swiftness at eating by its almost pythonic requirements for post-digestive rests. Naccanath had urgently hinted for more speed; Mal had—rather less urgently—passed it on to Captain Mog, and Captain Mog had cursed and kicked and cudgeled . . . and gotten a short burst of increased pace . . . for a moment or so. At intervals.

"By *nevertheless*," Mallian said, rather slowly, "I mean that there is something which we must do before we begin to cross." He issued a loud order to Mog, who issued a louder one. Mog knew nothing of Mallian's quest, nothing of the problem behind Mallian's question. All he knew to the point was that if Mal asked him to do something and he did not do it, he would be kicked in the head. He had tried a number of ways to avoid this, but the only one which ever worked was to obey orders. Quickly.

Slowly, therefore, erratically, Bumberboom began to move around until its great muzzle was pointing toward the Rift. Another order, and the massive gun was unlimbered. Its trail now rested on the ground. Naccanath cleared his throat, looked at Durraneth. Durraneth returned the look.

"What—and I point out the extreme civility with which the question is asked—what is it your intention to have done now, son Hazelip?"

Mal stroked the points of his beard. "It is my intention to fire the gun," he said.

The horsemen backed up a pace or two or three as though they had practiced the movement. "Fire—fire *Bumberboom?*"

"So some call it. Others, I understand, prefer the name of Juggernaut."

One of the Elvers said, "I have not heard that this has been done at all of late." He cleared his throat twice.

"So much the better for doing it now. The Crew wants

79

practice, and no one can object to whatever damage may be done the Rift."

Naccanath said, rather sharply, "The Rift! It is not the Rift which concerns us—we are still on Elver soil, and I consider the possible great damage which may be done thereto . . . including, and this is no small consideration, to us—It would be much better for you to wait until you are already in the Rift."

"No it would not. I desire to calculate a matter called range . . . a matter of arcane medicine which it will henceforth be important for me to know . . . and in particular the trajectory as calculated from an eminence of land, as it might be a cliff or hill."

The Elvers consulted hurriedly together and then requested that Mallian might delay his calculations until they were able to get well away from the site. He frowned, gave a short and slightly impatient nod, and they were off even faster than the two Dwerfymen had gone, the time Mallian had hidden in the ditch.

"They fear the fatal noise," he said to Zembac Pix, with a twisted grin. "It is as well. The less they see, the better so. Well. Down goes the large-grained powder as the book directs. Hold firm the ladle, Zembac Pix. So. So. Smoothly. So." Mallian took the ram and tried to follow the directions so that the powder was securely back where it should be but not so firmly packed that it would not properly ignite. Then, satisfied, he ordered the shot brought forward. Mog and his mates came up with the great round stone, hoisted it . . . dropped it. The man responsible howled for his toes and then howled for his ribs as Mog beat upon them. But it was done at last.

Next the fine powder was laid in a train along the groove to the touch-hole. "What next?" asked Mallian. Pix looked into the book. "Next is fire," he said. "Captain Mog! A brand of fire!"

The Crewmen seemed unsure of how they should seem. What memories they might hold of actual gunfire must be at many removes and quite dim, muted not by time alone but by the thick membranes of their sluggish minds. They had been bred to the gun, lived by and for the gun, had nought but the great gun at all. Yet they had never fired it, had forgotten how to make its fuel, forgotten perhaps all save some dim glints of recollections of old mumblings and mutterings which served them for history. They were excited. They were uneasy. Something new had come into their brute lives. One of them, who had watched the loading, perhaps spoke for all. "Bumberboom . . . Bumberboom *eat*," he said.

Zembac Pix received the burning stick and said, before handing it to Mal, "Stand carefully as the handbook directs, lest the cannon crush you by its—" But Mallian, impatient, seized the fire and thrust it at the train of powder. It hissed, vanished. Then, with a roar like thunder waging war on thunder, the hideous muzzle-mouth spewed flame and smoke. The gun leaped as though wounded, fell back, subsided. Darkness, thick darkness, evil stench surrounded them. Gradually, it cleared away. They looked at each other. ". . . recoil," Zembac Pix finished his sentence.

The Crew rose slowly from the ground, idiot faces round with awe and terror and joy. The occasion required words. They found them—or, at least, *it*. "*Bumberboom! Bumberboom! Bumberboom!*" They leaped and lurched and shouted and roared.

"Bumberboom!

"Bumberboom!

"Bumberboom!"

Zembac Pix pointed far out into the Rift. "The shot seems to have scored a trench along that hillock. Ha! Ahem hum-hum!"

"So I see . . . yes. Suppose that were a row of houses. Ha! Ha-ha!"

"Elver houses!"

"Bandy houses!"

"Ha *ha!*"

Something caught their eye. Something gleamed there in the trench now as clouds drifted away and the sun came through—a something which seemed to have slightly deflected the path of the stone shot. They discussed what it might be, agreed that whatever it might be could well go on waiting. "Captain Mog! On!"

"Forehead . . . *harsh!*"

It was a while later that they saw the Elvers descending

81

by another road which allowed them to steer far clear of the great gun and its Crew—a line of Elver horsemen and behind each guard and riding on the crupper, a man with a spade. "Curious," said Mal. "Very curious, Master-Lord," agreed Zembac Pix. But by the time they themselves had gotten close enough to leave the toiling, chanting Crew and go and see, the sight was more than merely curious.

"Observe, Mallian son Hazelip," said Naccanath, in an odd tone and a gesture. "See what sight the monstrous voice of Bumberboom has uncovered."

It was a sight indeed. The hillock had been shoveled and the ground excavated a good way beneath the surface of the general ground-level. There lay revealed the immense figure of an image with upraised arm and with a crown or coronet upon its head from which radiated a series of great spikes at least twice the length of a man. As far as they could see, it was clad in a flowing garment of some strange sort. It was an unfamiliar shade of blue-green which was almost black.

"What is it?" asked Mallian, voice low with awe.

The Elvers shrugged. "Who can say . . . it seems to be hollow." Thus Naccanath. Durraneth had something else to say.

"Do you recall, Prince of Qanaras," he began—Mallian noted his own promotion in rank but showed nothing on his face—"Do you recall what said the Dwerfy constable? . . . as say they all, of course . . . that before the Great Gene Shift all men were of their dwerfish size?"

Mallian said, "I do recall. What of it?"

Slowly Durraneth said, "This great image is hollow. There are passages within. But the spaces seem exceedingly small. Do you suppose—"

"Do I suppose that this evidences a possible truth to the absurd Bandy boast? Never! As well declare that the gigantic statue demonstrates that the original form of mankind was that of the race of the gigants!"

Durraneth nodded slowly. Then his eyes moved from gigantic statue to gigantic gun and back once more. "I wish . . ." he began. "I wish I knew what it had held in its hand . . ." he said. "Oh, I do not know, of course, that it had held anything in its hand. It has an arm, it must have had a hand. . . . No consequence; it was a mere sudden fancy, of no rational importance."

But Mallian had now a question of his own. He pointed down into the pit, past a fallen tree, to where four Elvers stood regarding the newly-found wonder and a fifth stood upon its face. On the brim stood a box of strange sort, from which wires led down to the body of the statue. "What is that?" he asked.

Durraneth shrugged. "An engine . . . a toy, really. It simulates a magnetical current. Really, it tells us nothing—save only that the entire figure seems to be made of metal. All of it! Incredible. No, I suppose you are correct. About the original stature of man. The matter, I must suppose, remains as before . . ." For yet another moment he stood there, musing. Then he said, "When you are ready, Prince, to pose your question, we will be ready to serve you in seeking its answer. Do not tarry too long among the morose and barbarous folk of Nor. Fare you well. Fare you well."

The morose and barbarous folk of Nor had for the most part, forewarned by the echoing roar of Bumberboom's sole shot and, further, by the sight of it being toiled across the Trans-Rift Road, fled into the raddled ruins where it was hardly practicable to follow them. They had taken much of their substance with them, but the Crew were experienced foragers; noses keen as dogs', they soon sniffed out food and even sooner devoured it.

Mallian had no desire to go groping about in the ruins after anyone. He consulted the map—Naccanath still held the leathern tube, but Mal held the map, whether Naccanath knew it or not—and consulted Zembac Pix as well. "I would that I had reflected to demand, hem a hum, to request horses of the Elvers. Doubtless they could be trained to pull the gun."

The pothecary's eyes narrowed beneath their bony brows, and he smiled a knowing smile. "Horses will come later," he said. "Horses . . . and many other things . . ."

Getting Bumberboom up a hill had to come first. After that would come supplies—not hastily proffered or hastily seized to be hastily gobbled, but efficiently levied, to be efficiently distributed. And efficiently consumed? Not all of them. The key word was *surplus*. Surplus of commodity meant trade, which meant wealth and power. One area of farms and towns to start with. Power firmly established there meant a fulcrum firmly established there. And with a fulcrum once established, what might not leverage do?

But haste was not to be indulged in. Leaving Zembac Pix in charge of gun and Crew, Mal set off to scout out the land, with a particular emphasis on hills. The first one he came to overlooked, to be sure, fine fat fields and no less than four towns, all of them prosperous, but the roads leading up the hill were too narrow by far to admit of Bumberboom's huge carriage being taken up. Widening would be a matter of months. Not to be thought of. The second hill was easy to access but looked down on one small town only, and that none too favorsome in its appearance. He sighed, pressed on. A third hill was well-located but culminated in a peak of rocky scarps such as could afford abiding-place only to birds. A fourth . . . A fifth . . .

Perhaps it was the seventh hill which seemed so ideal in every way but one. There was a slope of mountable angle, the top was both flat and wide, with enough trees to provide shade when desired and yet without interfering with the maneuverability of the great gun. From the summit Mal could see widespread and fruitful fields, and the rooftops of several towns. He had passed by two of them and observed with approbation the signs of good care and productivity, and a third appeared to be large enough to justify an assumption of the same. It was as tempting, as inviting from above as it had seemed from below; therefore, he had surmounted it despite a difficulty exemplified in the mud even now drying on his feet and shanks. There was definitely a current; one could not exactly say that a swamp lay at the foot of the hill athwart the only possible approach, but there was no gravel-bottomed shallow ford, though carefully he looked for one. Mud, sticky, catchy mud—and Bumberboom mired securely was as good as no Bumberboom at all. Mallian sighed and retraced his steps.

There was a man in the water when he came through it again, breeches slung around his shoulder and shirt tucked up shamelessly around his ribs, and he was spearing small fish with a trident. "Fortune favor you," said Mal.

The man said, "Mm."

"Fortune favor you," repeated Mal, a trifle louder, a trifle annoyed.

"We don't say, 'Fortune favor you' in these parts."

"Oh? What do you say, then?"

"We say, 'Mm.' "

"Oh. Well, then—Mm."

"Mm." And the man speared another small fish, and another, gutted them and strung them. He had set up a small makeshift smokehouse ashore, and now proceeded to deposit his catch therein before returning to securing more.

"You prefer smoked fish to fresh fish?"

"No, I don't," the man said decidedly. "But they keep and fresh ones don't. Be you purblind? Look-see that dried mud yonder side. And nigh side. I catch fish while there be water. Soon there'll be none till the rains."

Mallian wondered that he had not observed this before. "Senior, I thank you," he said sincerely. "Now indulgently inform me what you say in these parts for farewell."

The man peered into the water. "We say, 'Mm,' " he answered.

Mal sighed. "Mm."

"Mm," said the fisherman. He scratched his navel and speared another fish.

"What governance have you in these parts," he inquired of a man leading a pack-horse as he passed through the next town.

"None," said the man. "And wants none. The Land Nor is nongovernanced, by definition."

"I see. I thank you. Mm," said Mal.

"Mm," said the packman.

He accompanied the great gun all the way, but sent Zembac Pix ahead and aside to spread the word that other lands and their rulers—as it might be the Kings of the Dwerfs or the Masters of Elver State—envying the ungovernanced condition of Land Nor, had determined to send armies, troops, spies, and other means of assault thereto, with the intention of establishing a governance over it and over its people. But that the Free Company of Cannoneers, hearing of the daemonical plan, had come unsolicited to the defense of Land Nor with a weapon more utile than a thousand swords, videlicet, the great cannon BUMBER-BOOM. Zembac Pix went forth and fro and by and by caught up with Mal and Mog and Crew where they were encamped on a threshing-floor.

"Spread you the word?"

"Most diligently, Master-Lord."

"And with what countenance and comments did they receive it?"

The pothecary seemed to hesitate. "For the most part," he said, "without change of countenance and with no other comment than the labial consonant, Mm."

Mal pondered. Then he raised his eyes. "You say, 'For the most part—' "

"A true relation of my statement, Master-Lord. There was an exception, a tiresome and philosophizing man who keeps an hostelry for the distribution of liquor of malt"—here Zembac Pix wet his lips very slightly and made a small smile—"and his comment was to the effect that Land Nor is nongovernanced by definition and it thus follows that Land Nor cannot be governanced inasmuch as according to the laws of logic, a thing is not what it is not but is what it is, and to speak of the governancing of Land Nor is to speak of the moving of the immovable which is to speak nonsense. And much other words he spoke, but only to recapitulate what he had already spoken."

Mal said nothing, but after a moment he shook his head. Then he rose from the threshing-floor. "Captain Mog! *On!*"

Captain Mog rose from the threshing-floor. "Forehead—*harsh!*"

The crew rose from the threshing-floor and fell to in its sundry posts and places. "Bumberboom! *Bum*berboom! Bum-ber*boom!*"

"*Bumberboom!*"

The great wheels trembled.

"*Bumberboom!*"

The great wheels moved.

"*Bumberboom!*"

The great wheels turned.

Along the dusty roads it trundled and rumbled. Not in one

day did it reach the base of the hill, nor in two, nor three. But by the time it reached it, most of the marshy stream had vanished away, leaving a foundation of good hard, sun-baked mud. Fallen trees were selected and trimmed to act as brakes and props. And when the now-dwindled stream had dwindled to a mere trickle, they began the ascent. They shouted, they chanted, they grunted rhythmically, they howled. They pushed, they pulled, they levered. Now and then they turned a rope around a stout tree; now and then they rested the gun upon the logs and panted and drew breath, then fell to once again. "Bumber*boom!* Bumber*boom!* Bumber*boom!*"

And at last they dragged it up upon the very crown and summit of the hill, wheeled it into the best place of vantage, and unlimbered it. "Now," said Mal, "to compose and distribute a proclamation." Zembac Pix assisted him in the wording of it, which was to the effect that the Free Company of Cannoneers had now commenced the arduous duty of defending Land Nor against alien and hostile forces intent upon establishing a governance over the Land aforesaid. And that in order to compensate the previously denominated Free Company and in order to sustain it subsequently and to guarantee its defensive postures, voluntary contributions according to the schedule subappended would be received. Each town was held responsible for collecting the donatives of its citizens and should any town fail to collect and transport the voluntaries assessed it, this would reveal that it was secretly supporting the tyrannical alien pro-governance plan Whereat, it would be necessary for the Free Company to bombard the town aforesaid. And herein fail not.

"How shall we sign it?" asked Mal, mightily pleased by the several crisp turns of phrase.

"Might I suggest, Master-Lord, a succint: *Mallian, General-Commandanting?*"

"Hem a hum . . . Very good. But . . . do you not recollect how the Elver Guard referred to me as 'Prince'? I do not wish to appear high-flown or much-given to elaborate titles. What think you, then, of a simple *Mallian, Prince;* what?"

Zembac Pix nibbled the end of his quill. "Beautifully sug-

87

gested, Lordling. Subsequently. When they are ready. One must not seem over-humble to commence with."

A breeze wafted up from the terrain below and it conveyed in it a hint of hogs, hides, horses, and others of the rich usufructs of the land. A faint smile played upon Mallian's features. "I allow myself to be persuaded," he said. "So be it. Go now, have copies made, post them in the public places and proclaim it at the crossroads. You may accompany the first train of tribute, a hum hum, of donative . . . if you wish."

Zembac Pix declared it would be his pleasure. He descended. He ascended. Time had elapsed. "Canting and poxy pothecary!" Mal cried, raging. "Where have you been? And why so long? Where are the voluntaries of food and drink and staples, of steeds and trade-goods and manufactured articlery? From what knacker's yard did you steal that wretched beast which mocks the name of horse? Answer! Reply! And give good account, else I will spread you to the off-wheel of Juggernaut and flog you with the traces!"

Zembac Pix descended delicately from the scrap of rug bound with a rope cinch which served him for saddle, and was momentarily seized with a spasmodic contraction of the glottis which impeded his speech and may possibly have been responsible as well for the slight instability of his gait. And in his arms he tenderly cuddled a firkin containing some sort of liqueous matter.

"Master-Lord," he began, "with the utmost diligence have I carried out every word of your instructions, whether plainly expressed or merely implied. I purchased writing materials, I made clear copies in the most exquisite calligraphy, and I long retained in my possession a specimen the mere sight of which would instantly persuade you; alas, that on returning hither I was with infinite reluctance constrained to employ it for a usage too gross to be named between us—hem hem— though even kings must live by nature.

"Furthermore I posted them in the public places and I proclaimed their message at the cross-roads. Moreover I entered into all places of resort and refreshment in order the more thoroughly to disseminate the matter. Conceive, then, with what incredulous and tearful regret I must report that, far from hastening to contribute to the meritorious support of the Free Company, they merely hastened to confect pellets of wool and wax to stuff into their ears 'to save them,' as they said, 'from the horrid noise and torturesome sound' of Bumberboom . . . The steed and this firkin of liquor of malt do not represent, Lordling, even one single poor contributor but only my success in a game of skill at which I was constrained to participate, they threatening me with many mischiefs and malignancies should I refuse."

There was a long, long silence. Then Zembac Pix, sighing deeply, drew from the firkin of liquor a quantity in a leather cup and offered it to Mallian. And in truth it did not smell ill. The breeze played upon the hill; the Crewmen dozed or picked for lice; the sun was warm. "To think of such ingratitude," Mal said, after a while. Zembac Pix wept afresh to think of it. They were mildly surprised to find themselves holding to the wheels of the cannon and gazing down upon the reprobate lands below.

"I owe it to my father not to disgrace his name and station by a breach of my word, would you not agree?"

"Utterly, Master-Lord."

"I said that contumacy would merit bombardment." He belched slightly upon the vowels of the last word. "And so it must be."

In this they were in perfect accord, but a slight difference of opinion now arose as to whether the town nearest below lay at a distance of two hundred lengths or at one nearer to three hundred lengths—and also whether the demonstrated distance of Bumberboom's range was as much as three hundred lengths or as little as two hundred lengths. They concluded that it was better to use more force than necessary rather than less than necessary, and they accordingly loaded a charge a third heavier than that used before. Further more, on the same principle, they rammed a double shot down the barrel.

"And now for to prime her," said Zembac Pix, giggling slightly.

"Hold," said Mal. "Last time we were too close to witness the moment of ejection. I would witness this act and not have my vision clouded with smoke."

The pothecary nodded and chuckled. "Perfectly do I understand and take your meaning. I shall lay a long powder-trail

. . . let me use this length of wood as a gently inclined plane. Excellent, excellent; the powder stays in place and does not slide off! . . . and thus and thus and thus . . . Ahem hem, I seem to have used up the last of the powder."

His face was so woebegone that Mallian was constrained to laugh. "No matter. No matter. We will make more. Is not the recipe contained in the formulary book? Where is the fire-stick? Here. Ha! Hear it sizzle! So—'morose and barbarous' you have been termed, folk of Nor, and now here is your requition for—"

All the thunders of the sky and lightnings thereof burst upon them in rolling flashes of fire and smoke. The earth shook like a dying man, and they were instantly thrown upon the quaking ground. Things flew screaming over their heads. They lay deafened and stunned for long moments.

Mallian, presently seeing Zembac Pix's mouth moving, said, with a groan, "I cannot hear. I cannot hear."

"I had not spoken. Woe! Mercy! Malignant fates! Where is Bumberboom?"

And the Crew, now picking themselves up from the dirt, with shrieks and wails, began the same question. "Bumberboom? Bumber*boom*? *Bumberboom*?" But a few fragments of twisted metal and a shattered wheel were all that remained of that great cannon and weapon more utile than a thousand swords . . .

Mallian felt a sob shake his throat. All his plans, all his efforts, wasted and shattered in a single moment! He fought for and found control. "Age and disuse," he said, "must have corroded the barrel. Never mind. We will somehow contrive to cast another."

Zembac Pix agreed, and said through his tears, "And to prepare more powder. Four and one-half measures of sulphur to thirty-one and a third of—"

"You err. It was of a certainty twenty-five and a fifth of sulfur to six and one eighth of snowy . . . Or was it eleven and one tenth of . . . We must consult the formulary." But of that sole book wherein alone the arcane and secret art of gunnery was delineated, only one scorched bit of page remained, and on it was inscribed the single word *overload*. There was another silence, the longest yet, disturbed only by the idiotic and inconsolable ululations of the Crew.

In a different voice Mallian said, "It is just as well. Clearly the engine represented a mere theorizing, and, as we have plainly seen, is of no practical value whatsoever. What is perhaps more to the point, I observe that the horse is uninjured, and I propose we mount him immediately and proceed by way of the woods to the northern and nearest border of this land of morose and barbarous folk, for I trust not their humors at all."

"Oh, agreed! Agreed, Master-Lord!" declared Zembac Pix, scrambling up behind him. "Only one question more: What of the erstwhile Crew? Should we try to persuade them to follow?"

Mal wheeled the horse around. "I think not," he said. "Soon enough their bellies will bring them down to where the pantries and the bake-ovens of the Nor-folk are. But we will not tarry to witness this droll confrontation. We will, however, think about it. I am of the firm opinion that they deserve one another."

He kicked his heels into the horse's sides and Zembac Pix smote it on the rump. They rode down the hill.

Regular readers of the magazine will be familiar with Ron Goulart's stories about Max Kearny, occult investigator. Max has been faced with some truly bizarre situations in the past, but nothing quite like this frightening confrontation with the zeitgeist of the sixties. Will Max lose his cool when faced with the apparently inscrutable spirits of these times? Read on.

FILL IN THE BLANK

by Ron Goulart

The calico cat yowled and came somersaulting down the shadowy attic stairs. It skittered into Ollie's high darkwood bedroom and dived under the bunk bed. Thunder rolled and hard rain battered the stained glass skylight. The heavy wooden window shutters creaked and fought the hard pull of the night wind.

"Why can't I stay up and see the ghost?" asked Ollie from the upper bunk.

At the doorway Patricia Lewin said, "It's past your bedtime, Ollie."

"You could make an exception when there's a ghost roaming around the halls."

"There's no ghosts here, Ollie," said Patricia. "The thunder scared the cat."

"My stomach hurts," said Ollie. "I have to get up."

"No," the slender blonde girl told the boy. "Now I'm letting you sleep in the upper tonight. Don't push things too far."

"Uncle Ogden bought me a bunk bed just for me so I could have variety," said Ollie. "He doesn't care if I sleep high or low. I forgot to put the cap back on the tooth-paste. I'd better get up."

"Stay where you are, Ollie. It's after nine, go to sleep."

Lightning flashed and the window glass rattled with the thunder that followed. The calico cat slipped out from under the bed, rolled on its back and punched a paw at a flap of blanket. "See," said the seven-year-old, "Oscar isn't even ascared of thunder. It takes a real authentic ghost to make a cat's hair stand up like it was. Why does a cat's fur do that, Patricia?"

"We'll look it up in the morning, Ollie." Patricia narrowed her eyes, watching the long thickly rugged hallway of the mansion.

"My ears hurt when I lay down."

"I'm going to put your lights out now," said the girl. She put her back to the doorway and walked toward the boy's bureau.

"When you lay with your head down probably the whole insides of your head could run out of your ear," said the dark-haired boy.

"We'll look up ears in the morning, Ollie." Patricia glanced at the oval mirror above Ollie's lamp. It gave her a view of the hall. Floating there now, three feet from the floor, was a dusty sheaf of papers. Old, age wrinkled yellow sheets of note paper. As Patricia watched, the small bundle gradually disappeared, like a moon waning in a speeded up film.

The cat let its head loll back and its wide eyes darted a look at the hallway. Yowling again, the cat shinnied up a bedpost and jumped on Ollie's back. "Probably a whole parade of ghosts going by," said the boy, handing Oscar out to Patricia.

The girl tucked the cat against her left breast and turned off the lights in the bedroom. "Night, Ollie," she said. "Don't let anything scare you."

"I don't want to get scared by the ghosts. I just want to get a look at them."

Patricia stepped carefully into the hallway. Thunder rolled again, fainter. Oscar arched his tail and brushed at her cheek. Patricia inhaled deeply, then pressed her lips together. Nearly a month now. She couldn't admit it to Ollie.

But it must be ghosts, or one of those poltergeists. They were supposed to like children.

She had been governess for Ollie Boothrod for three months and she liked the job. She'd have to tell Ogden Boothrod, Ollie's uncle and her employer, about the things happening nights up on the third floor of his Presidio Heights mansion. The floating objects, the odd creakings, the footsteps.

Boothrod was in the beamed white kitchen, under the hanging pots and skillets, squinting into a copper kettle on the iron stove. In his long fingered left hand he had a wooden spoon. He was a tall, narrow man, bald with a round polite face. He was just forty and his brown rimmed glasses were steamed. After dipping the spoon carefully into the kettle, Boothrod stepped back. "I can't remember about the carrot."

Patricia dropped Oscar on the parquet and the cat jumped for a sliver of chicken that had fallen off the big wood butcher's table. "Mr. Boothrod," began the girl.

"The veal knuckle is in," said Boothrod, sniffing the spoon. "I can't see the carrot or detect its flavor. Still, if I add one now and there's already a carrot that'll make two. Which will blow the stock for sure."

"Mr. Boothrod. Is there anything in the traditions of this house to indicate, well, unnatural phenomena?"

Boothrod scratched the chest of his striped chef's apron. "You taste this, Patricia. See if you can sense the presence or absence of one large sliced carrot." He held the wooden spoon to her. "Boothrod Manor was built in 1876. My great-grandfather, Omer Boothrod, was a typical San Francisco banker and land pirate. There was Uncle Oscar. Uncle Oscar. How does that taste?"

"It tastes like hot water, Mr. Boothrod."

"My impression, too." He shook his head. "After three hours of simmering with a four to five pound washed and trussed fowl in there, not to mention ten whole peppercorns, you'd expect more than a warm tap water flavor. I can't move on to anything else without good stock to work with. Stock is everything in cooking, to paraphrase Escoffier."

"Was your Uncle Oscar murdered, violently done in up in the attic maybe?"

"No, he fell off the gazebo just before the quake," said Boothrod. "He was always dabbling."

"Dabbling?"

"On the borders of science and medicine," said her employer. "Don't you have a friend who's an expert on cooking matters?"

"Jillian Kearny," said Patricia, brightening. "She's a professional food consultant, works for advertising agencies here in San Francisco. And her husband is . . ."

"Is what?"

"Oh," said the girl, "he's an art director with an agency. Why don't I invite them over. Tomorrow night?"

Boothrod nodded. "That's swell, Patricia. Ask them for dinner. They won't object to the fact that I believe Ollie's governess should be treated as one of the family and share the family table? No, fine. I'll prepare one of my full course awful dinners, and Mrs. Kearny can criticize each terrible part of it as we dine. As to dinner this evening—"

"I'll pop down to that little French place on Laurel. I can stop by the Kearny's flat afterwards; it's near there."

"I suppose I can salvage enough fowl out of the stock to fix myself a chicken sandwich," said Boothrod. "Are you certain the thunder and lightning and rain won't make going out too much of a hazard?"

"I like to walk in the rain," the girl said. She smiled and left the kitchen. Maybe Max Kearny was exactly the right person to invite to Boothrod Manor.

The man with the shoulder length red hair slapped down into the theater seat next to Max Kearny. He reached across Max and shook hands with Max's slim, auburn-haired wife. "Hi, Jill, Max. Welcome to my premiere."

"How'd you get your hair to grow so fast, Misch?" said Max.

Misch McBernie dutch rubbed Max's crewcut. "It's a wig. The moustache is authentic. I'm in a transition period, Max, Jill. From $25,000 a year junior account executive on Doob's Cottage Cheese to psychedelic playwright in just two brief months. A difficult life period. Rebecca's left me."

Jillian Kearny said, "We didn't know that, Misch."

Misch shot the cuffs of his orange shirt out beyond the sleeves of his paisley suit. "I'm not one to broadcast self-pity, Max, Jill. Rebecca simply didn't comprehend the point that if I don't get in on the youthquake now, I won't ever have another chance. My god, I'm twenty-eight."

Max, who was thirty-four said, "With that wig you could pass for twenty-two."

The big man chuckled. "I get real charismatic when I'm around these kids, these beautiful young people. So when the Fatal Glass Of Beer offered to produce my second play with some of their money, I hopped right in. I'm expanding."

"We're looking forward to seeing the play," said Jillian.

Misch tapped the Mickey Mouse watch on his wrist. "Curtain is going to be delayed," he said, gesturing at the fifty or so young people in the small North Beach theater. "These kids aren't time bound. Curtain at eight-thirty, that's a tradition meaning nothing to them."

"Why is it late?" asked Max.

"See, you've got the over thirty establishment mind," grinned Misch. "The cops are backstage frisking the Washington Merry-Go-Round. They think the electric sitar player is holding grass."

"Are the folk rock groups going to be in your play?" asked Jillian, as a girl in a yellow and lavender mother hubbard sat down in front of her.

"Yes, they form the Greek chorus," said Misch. "The Washington Merry-Go-Round and the Fatal Glass Of Beer will both be on stage. Except for Lupo, Fatal's electric tambourine man, because he got busted for selling a book of pornographic Chinese love lyrics."

"Been several down with pornography raids lately," said Max.

"Not only the fuzz," said Misch. "All kinds of dingbat groups. Especially a bunch who call themselves Comstock:2. They've even been phoning me and telling me not to put on *The Lightbulb*, my play tonight. Comstock:2, they're against everything. Fill in the blank. They're against it."

"They really think your play is lewd?" said Jillian.

"Well, they got word that Joan of Arc isn't going to wear any clothes and it unsettled them," said Misch. "Actually, *The Lightbulb* isn't dirty in any traditional sense.

Whatever so-called dirty words are in the dialogue are drowned out when the folk rock kids play their electric blues anyway."

The theater lights went out and the art nouveau rolled up. The audience murmured, grew quiet. On the bare stage three people stood next to a darkened phonebooth.

"Joan of Arc, Secretary Rusk and Humphrey Bogart," explained Misch in a whisper.

"Bogart in the trenchcoat," said Max. "I guessed him."

The actor playing Secretary of State Rusk pointed at the phonebooth and said, "Crap."

Joan of Arc, in a violet swimsuit, started to reply. Instead, she rose four feet in the air, floated toward the phonebooth. She screamed and waved her arms. Humphrey Bogart's trenchcoat jumped up, bunching around his head, and Dean Rusk yelled and sailed off the stage and into the front row seats. Joan of Arc, still floating, knocked over the phonebooth.

"Great special effects," said Max.

"Holy moley," yelled Misch. He leaped up and went running for the stage. "Where are you dingbat establishment bastards? Stop tampering with the mood of my play."

Joan of Arc flew straight into him, the lights snapped out and the audience began roaming.

"Another fuzz stunt," said the girl in the mother hubbard.

Jillian caught Max's hand. "Max, what did that?"

Max shrugged. "I more or less gave up occult investigation when we got married. I'm just an over thirty AD now."

"Unless Misch is putting us on," said his wife, "something occult caused all the frumus up there. Ghosts or magic spells?"

The lights blossomed on and Max took Jillian by the arm. "You know, there have been several odd things like this happening lately. Two hundred copies of that book of anti-Vietnam limericks that set themselves on fire in the window of the Modern Times bookshop, that psychedelic blues singer who floated out the window of the Yardbird Suite and the Love & Freedom Brigade girl who was apparently attacked by a bunch of her own lapel pins."

"Where'd you hear about those?"

"In Herb Caen's column," said Max. "A ghost patrol, some conservative warlocks. Who, I'm not sure yet."

Misch had himself untangled from Joan of Arc and was jumping up and down on the stage. Three uniformed policemen were peeking out of the wings.

"Let's wait in the lobby for Misch," said Max.

"Too bad the play got spoiled. I wanted to find out what was wrong with the phonebooth."

"Lightbulb didn't work. Like society."

They moved for the lobby and Max was pushed against a door jamb by two blond boys in checkered suits. He side-looked at his elbow as it scraped against a protruding nail head. Max took three steps, halted, stopped Jillian. He waited until the last of the audience, three Negro girls in red leather pants suits, exited.

"Huh," said Max. He reached out and touched the nail. He had felt a round head, but the nail he saw seemed headless. Gingerly he pinched it. The tip of his finger disappeared.

"What are you doing with your finger, Max?"

Max felt rough cloth where his finger end had vanished. "It's a piece of cloth."

Reaching out, Jillian asked, "It makes things invisible?" She touched his unseen finger tip. "Feels like monk's cloth, some rough cloth."

Max took the swatch and dropped it in his pocket. "With a whole suit of this stuff, or a cloak—"

"You'd be invisible."

"And if you lifted up Joan of Arc and tossed," said Max, "you'd give the impression she was floating."

"Good thing she wasn't in armor," said Jillian. "So whoever disrupted *The Lightbulb* came by here, snagged himself on the nail either sneaking in or getting away."

Max shook out a filter cigarette and fitted it into a filter holder. "The occult detection thing has always been just a hobby with me. My real profession should be advertising. No reason to get involved in tracking down a bunch of invisible men."

"Come on," said his wife. "Advertising isn't a real profession. Besides, putting on an invisible suit and throwing three actors and a phonebooth off a stage, that's a violation of civil rights. Not to mention those attacks on other people."

Max said, "Yeah, I'll get involved."

Patricia Lewin was sitting on their Victorian doorstep, hands in pockets and knees tight together. Max helped her up, digging out the door keys.

"I decided to wait," said the girl. "Hello, Jillian."

"It's nearly midnight," said Jillian. "Is there trouble over at that mansion where you work?"

"The place is haunted," said Patricia.

"No," said Max, pushing the thick door open and standing aside. "No, I'm not going to listen."

"Max already has an occult case to work on," said Jillian when they were in the Kearny flat.

"Not being much up on the occult business," said Patricia, "I don't know if you can handle two occult problems at once or not."

"It's not a business," said Max. "A hobby."

"Tell him anyway," said Jillian. "Coffee?"

"Fine," said Patricia. She sat in a yellow wicker armchair. "You have a new rug, Jill?"

"Three hundred dollars worth of Bokhara," said Max. "Bought behind my back from a couple of Armenians in an alley."

"The problem," said Jillian.

Patricia said, "As you know, Max, I work as a governess in a gloomy Victorian mansion up hill from here. I look after a bright seven-year-old boy and help him with his lessons. For the past month a series of odd things has been happening."

"Your boss is a mysterious dark man and he never lets you go into the north wing?" said Max.

"He's bald and affable, works in a brokerage firm. He's an amateur gourmet chef, Jill. The only place I can't go is the basement, because that's been converted into an apartment and Mr. Boothrod's nephew and two of his friends live there. Richard C. Karno is his name and I think he's sort of a conservative."

Max had picked the brandy bottle from the mantle. He set it back. "What?"

"Mr. Boothrod is an amateur gourmet."

Max shook his head. "Richard C. Karno lives in your basement?"

"In Mr. Boothrod's gloomy Victorian basement."

"Karno," said Jillian, bringing in the china coffee pot. "We saw him interviewed on Channel Nine."

"Yeah," said Max, "he's the head of Comstock:2, the group that's been hounding Misch." He frowned at Patricia. "Exactly what's happening at the Boothrod place?"

"Things float," said the blonde.

"And?"

"Or vanish. Sometimes I hear footsteps and don't see anybody. The attic. Lots in the attic I hear scraping noises. My notion is that Ollie, he's the one I governess for, he probably attracts ghosts. The way children do. Don't they?"

"Teenage girls," said Max. "Not six-year-old boys."

"Ollie is seven."

"Still," said Max. "Pat, I'd like to get inside that mansion."

Patricia smiled from Max to Jillian. "Mr. Boothrod wants you to come to dinner tomorrow night, around eight-thirty. He's an awful cook."

"We'll be there," Max said.

"Maybe Richard D. Karno was wearing the trick suit," said Jillian while she poured the coffee.

"You married people," said Patricia. "You have all kinds of personal slang outsiders can't fathom."

From the rainy street sprang the sound of a guitar. Max crossed to the bow window. "Seems to be Misch McBernie and the Washington Merry-Go-Round." A Volkswagen bus with violet roses painted on its sides was parking in the driveway of the Kearnys' building.

At his side Jillian said, "That's not the Washington Merry-Go-Round, it's the Fatal Glass Of Beer."

"That's right," said Max. "I recognize the guy with the paisley tattoos."

"Are you having a party?" asked Patricia.

"Nope," said Max, his hand closing over the small piece of invisible cloth in his coat pocket. "Just another one of my clients.

On the way to work the next morning, Max stopped in at Pedway's Book Store. W. R. Pedway was a small, tense man with straight standing white hair. He had talked Max into buying a remaindered occult encyclopedia six years back and shortly after started him on his career as an amateur ghost breaker and occult investigator. Max still came to Pedway for advice.

Pedway was pulling up the big shades in the secondhand shop windows, grimacing at the misty rain. "I hear that in Los Angeles they held a drive-in black mass last week," he said to Max.

"You can't do anything in LA without a car." From his pocket Max took the invisible swatch. "Can you identify this for me?"

Pedway took the sample and wrapped it around his thumb, which disappeared down to the first joint. "Piece of home woven cloth torn from a cloak of invisibility. Where'd you come by it?"

Max told him, and about Misch's play and Richard C. Karno's group and the rest. Then he asked, "Anything in the history of the old Boothrod mansion to tie it in with magic? Our friend, Pat Lewin, mentioned an Oscar Boothrod who fooled around with alchemy in the 1890s."

Pedway unwound the cloak fragment and this thumb came back. He set the sample on his counter and shifted a stack of air pulps. Underneath was a dime store scrapbook. "I'm considering putting a lot of my files into a computer," he said, flipping the book open. "I can't get the style computer I want."

"Which is it?"

"Black Forest." Pedway flicked pages. "Here. Oscar Boothrod was a pioneer in steam aerodynamics."

"You mean he made an airplane back in 1890 that flew on steam?"

"No, he was a bird fancier, too. He invented a steam-driven seagull. Got a patent on it," said Pedway. "He also leaned in the direction of alchemy. Signed a pact with the devil."

"How do you know that?"

"He had the pact notarized. I got a copy of the records." Pedway dropped the open scrapbook. "There were rumors in the '90's that Oscar had cracked the invisibility barrier. Even a story in the *Examiner*, in the fashion section, hinting he'd loomed a couple of cloaks of invisibility. Only rumors."

"Oscar Boothrod's files, maybe even the cloaks," said Max, leaning against a table of girls' series books, "the stuff could have been stored in the attic at the mansion."

"Exactly," replied Pedway. "Oscar was still tinkering with invisibility when he fell off a gazebo. He was up there waiting for his steam gull to home."

"How can you counter this kind of magic invisibility?"

"Boothrod's solution to the problem may have been magic and it may have been alchemical. I'll give you something for both angles," said Pedway. "You planning to go up against this Richard C. Karno and his Comstock:2?"

"If he's using the stuff, yes. We're going over to the Boothrod mansion for dinner tonight and Karno lives in the basement."

Pedway lifted the invisible cloth. "I saw a play by your friend, McBernie. They put it on in an all night cafeteria out in Potero Hills. Called *The Towelrack*. Lyndon Johnson, James Dean and Bo Diddley are in a wash room trying to get the towelrack to work."

"Yeah, well," said Max. "Somebody has to defend the right to be lousy."

"Makes a nice crusade," Pedway bobbed, reached under the counter. "I'll give you two spells and some powder I got from an alchemist over in Oakland who went backrupt. Should turn the cloak visible, probably permanently. We can try it out on this little piece first." He had fetched up a leatherbound book and a plastic pill bottle filled with yellow grains of powder. "I'll read the spells and you shake some of this powder on the cloth. Okay?"

Max snapped the lid off the powder container. "This says take one spoonful in an ounce of water four times a day."

"Not the bottle it came in." Pedway began muttering and Max shook the yellow powder.

There was a faint sizzling sound and a square of brown cloth appeared atop the counter.

"Not much of a shade," said Pedway.

When Max left the store he had the two spells and the powder in his briefcase.

Max stood under a striped sandwich shop awning on Montgomery Street, trying not to watch a pale man with rimless glasses chewing a baloney sandwich. Two lunch hour secretaries walked by, one saying, "If you like chicken I know a place."

Across the wet street was a small store front office labeled Comstock:2. A poster on the door said, "Clean Mind, Clean Body, Clean Air, Clean Water, Clean Streets."

Max sprinted over, went into the Comstock:2 office. There was nothing in the low rugless room but a card table piled with pamphlets and broadsides, next to it a straight-standing young man in a navy blue suit. Three air conditioners hummed, one in each wall.

"Refreshing in here, isn't it?" said the man. He talked like a ventriloquist, lips stiff. He was Richard C. Karno.

"Feels clean."

"Comstock:2 is against pollution," said Karno. "We've successfully cleaned up the air in two major California's cities. We've unpolluted the water in an important river's tributary. Closed down three lithographers who specialized in girl calendars and caused the picketing of four hundred and three newsstands."

"I guess I can't smoke in here?"

"No, it would pollute," said Karno. "How can I help you?"

"I thought I'd pick up some of your literature."

"Here you have our newest. Entitled *Four Hundred And Sixty-Two Pounds of Smut*."

"Your own title?"

"Yes. It refers to the amount of smut the average blue-eyed blonde-haired little seven-year-old girl passes on her way to Sunday school."

"How did you figure that?"

"We bought some smut and weighed it." Karno touched the tip of his chin, bent over the card table. "I think I'll give you one each of our booklets and a Comstock:2 bumper sticker, which says, 'Don't let your blue-eyed blonde-haired little girl be ruined by smut.'"

"Won't fit on the average bumper."

"I have to admit to a slight overlap," said Karno as he made Max a bundle of Comstock:2 literature.

"Would you have anything on magic?" asked Max, raking the material off the table and into his briefcase. "Spells, transmutation, invisibility, dowsing?"

Karno had a Comstock:2 lapel button in his hand. He jabbed the pin into his thumb and said, "What was your name, sir?"

"I'm just an average blue-eyed blond average citizen."

"You don't have blue eyes or blond hair," said Karno, who had both. "Please return my reading matter and leave."

Max jammed the briefcase under his arm and backed quietly out. Across the street the pale man was still at his sandwich.

Black, three stories high, at the top of a zigzag flagstone path, was the Victorian Boothrod mansion. The rain had stopped. Thin fog was tumbling down over the tree tops and gliding across the brush thick grounds.

Max took his hand from Jillian's and rang the bell. The two spells were in his coat pocket wrapped around the yellow powder.

Jillian sniffed. "I think I can smell dinner going awry."

"People don't use the word awry in real life. Only in Misch McBernie plays."

"By the way, did you see Misch this morning?" asked his wife. "I forgot to tell you."

"When? No, I didn't."

"Right after you left for Pedway's. He came by in a pastel bus with a group called The Bayshore Freeway. Misch said a lightbulb had gone off over his head and he wanted to see you. I told him where you were headed."

"No," said Max, poking the bell again. "He must have missed me."

The carved door swung in and a dark-haired little boy looked out. "Are you the ghost breaker?"

"Yeah," said Max. "You Ollie?"

"Uncle Ogden is out in the kitchen with a flat soufflé and he won't listen to me but Cousin Richard caught Patricia exploring the attic, which she said your wife told her was loaded probably with arcane lore, and they've got her, I bet all tied up by now, in their rooms downstairs."

"Did you call the cops?"

"On occult matters I thought I might as well wait for a specialist," Ollie told them.

"How do I get to Richard's flat?"

"Go around the house, through the arbor and then there's an orange door down some stone steps. Better sneak, though."

Behind the boy Ogden Boothrod appeared. "Mrs. Kearny, I've got a really terrible halibut mousse inside. Can you come in and inspect it and tell me where I went astray?"

"Awry," said Jillian. "Shall I stick with you, Max?"

"No. Get inside."

"I lost control of the dill weed," Boothrod explained, ushering Jillian in. Ollie started out but Jillian caught him back.

Max moved into the tall, wet grass along the gravel path which circled the house, then nudged into the high bushes. Leaves suddenly spattered him, and a bus engine roared in the fog. Max jumped, and a violet and crimson bus shot by and braked, stopping against the mansion's gingerbread side. Lettered on the bus was The Fatal Glass Of Beer.

A scarlet motor scooter and three lemon yellow motorcycles came fast in the wake of the bus. One of the cycles had a sidecar and in it, his red hair flying, was Misch McBernie. "Max, I've been dogging your footsteps and I know all," shouted Misch. "I got a lightbulb over the head when I got to thinking about what your friend, Patricia, was telling me at your place last night." He leaped to the dark lawn. "When I missed you at Pedway's I had a chat with him and confirmed my hunch that the plot against me centered here. I got my kids rounded together and decided to coincide my invasion with yours. It should be beautiful."

"Quiet," said Max. "How the hell do you think you're going to sneak up on anybody in yellow motorcycles?"

"Blitzkriegs don't have to be subtle."

The door of the bus hissed open and the Fatal Glass Of Beer jumped out, each in bellbottom pants, leather vests and Indian headbands. "Crap," said the lead man and Max recognized him as the actor who'd played Dean Rusk.

The driver of Misch's motorcycle was dressed General Custer style, except for a hand-painted hula-girl necktie. The other cycles held the rhythm section of the Washington Merry-Go-Round. Three Negro girls in red leather pants suits climbed out of the bus. A young man in an orange levi suit began unloading amplifiers from the luggage bin.

Max said to Misch, "Back off. They've got Pat in their apartment."

Misch flew into the air, arms flapping, and landed against the scooter.

An invisible fist punched Max in the nose. He ducked, twisted sideways and yanked out the spells and powder. He read the backwards Latin and scattered yellow grains. No one appeared. Then a karate chop caught Max from behind and he slammed to his knees.

"It's the invisible guy," said one of the Fatal Glass of Beer. They all jumped.

Somebody expelled breath. Max shook his head clear and palmed himself upright. He threw powder at the stack of folk rock singers and repeated the spells. The wet grass sizzled and in a moment Richard C. Karno materialized beneath the Fatal Glass Of Beer, wearing a full length brown robe.

"I like his gear," said the tallest Negro girl.

"Where's Pat?" Max said, down next to the pile on.

"Not a clean mind or body in the lot," said Karno, after a stiff-necked survey.

"Where is she?"

"Well," said the Comstock:2 leader, "she's in the den with two of my lieutenants."

"Invisible ones?"

"You find out, said Karno.

Max ran for the orange door, followed by Misch.

Misch pushed ahead of Max and galloped halfway down a buff hallway before he tripped over nothing and spread-eagled. Max said the spells and tossed powder and the round man who'd tripped Misch appeared. Max knocked him out.

The guard with Patricia was visible, tall and straight standing.

"They've only got two cloaks," said Patricia, who was tied in a claw-footed chair. "They found them up in the attic when Richard was snooping around last month. Since then they've been smuggling Oscar Boothrod's notes and papers down here, hoping to get the formula for making more cloaks."

"All we've unearthed so far," admitted the unarmed guard, "is nearly nineteen volumes of old Oscar's pornographic memoirs."

Max said, "Your cloaks are neutralized for good, meaning no more invisible vigilante raids. I think you better spend the rest of tonight moving out."

"Dick's got a lease."

"Or maybe Patricia will come up with a kidnapping charge."

"She was poking in the attic and Dick brought her here to see how much she knew about us, and about old Oscar."

"Move," said Max. He untied Pat, helped her get her arms and legs working.

Misch had gone back outside, after trussing up the other Comstock:2 member with three hand painted ties and a paisley belt. Ogden Boothrod was talking to him near the bus. The Fatal Glass Of Beer were tuning instruments in the arbor. Jillian and Ollie were examining the motorcycles.

"Mr. Boothrod has invited us all to dinner," announced Misch. "He says the food will be really terrible."

Max led Patricia over to Jillian and Ollie. Putting his arm around his wife's shoulders, he asked, "Want to stay?"

"No," said Jillian. "As a cook he's beyond help."

They said goodnight and walked away from the spires and towers of the mansion.

Russell Kirk's THE CONSERVATIVE MIND *was published in 1953, and since then he has been regarded as the chief philosopher of the new American conservatism. Also in 1953, Dr. Kirk left the faculty of Michigan State College, noting with some misgivings the majority of students who "resent the minority who read books" as well as the administrators who "would establish colleges of necromancy if they thought anyone would enroll." Since then, Dr. Kirk has written widely on conservative thought and educational theory. He had also written fiction: primarily Gothick fantasy, "tales more of the outer darkness than of the twilight zone." Dr. Kirk's favorite recreation is walking; he says of this latest story that "it has more than a grain of true narration at the core of it, and the setting is genuine." He has indeed walked in some haunted places.*

BALGRUMMO'S HELL

by Russell Kirk

The moment that Horgan had slipped through the pend, Jock Jamieson had glanced up, grunted, and run for his shotgun at the gate cottage. But Horgan, having long legs, had contrived to cosh Jock right on the threshold. Now Horgan had most of the night to lift the pictures out of Balgrummo Lodging.

Before Jock could close those rusty iron gates, Nan Stennis —in her improbable role of new night nurse to Lord Balgrummo—had stalled her car in the pend. In the rain, Jock couldn't possibly have made out Nan's face, and now Horgan pulled off the silk stocking of Nan's that he had worn over his own head. With Nan's help, he trussed and gagged Jock, the tough old nut breathing convulsively, and dragged him into a kitchen cupboard of the gate-cottage, and turned the key on him. Jock's morning mate, and the morning nurse, wouldn't come to relieve him until seven o'clock. That left no one between Horgan and those paintings except

108

Alexander Fillan Inchburn, tenth Baron Balgrummo, incredibly old, incredibly depraved, and incredibly decayed in Balgrummo Lodging, which he had not left for half a century.

In that nocturnal February drizzle, Nan shivered; perhaps she shuddered. Though there could have been no one within a quarter of a mile to hear them, she was whispering, "Rafe, can you really get through it without me? I hate to think of you going into that place all alone, darling."

Competent Rafe Horgan kissed her competently. She had left her husband for him, and she had been quite useful. He honestly meant to meet her at the Mayfair, by the end of the month, and take her to the Canaries; by that time, he should have disposed of the Romney portrait for a fat sum, to an assured Swiss collector with a Leeds agent, enabling Horgan to take his time in disposing of the other Balgrummo pictures. Nan could have lent him a hand inside Balgrummo Lodging, but it was important for her to establish an alibi; she would change automobiles with him now, drive into Edinburgh and show herself at a restaurant, and then take the midnight train to King's Cross. The principal trouble with operations like this was simply that too many people became involved, and some of them were given to bragging. But Nan was a close one, and Horgan had spent months planning.

The only real risk was that someone might discover his name wasn't Horgan. For that, however, a thorough investigation would be required. And who would think of investigating the past of Rafe Horgan, Esq., a South African gentleman of private means who now lived in a pleasant flat near Charlotte Square? Not Dr. Euphemia Inchburn, gray spinster who liked his smile and his talk; not T. M. Gillespie, Writer to the Signet, chairman of the trustees of Lord Balgrummo's Trust. With them, he had been patient and prudent, asking questions about Balgrummo Lodging only casually, in an antiquarian way. Besides, did he look as if he would carry the cosh? No, the police would be after every gang in Fossie housing estate, which sprawled almost to the policies of Balgrummo Lodging. Horgan's expenditure of charm, and even of money, would be repaid five thousand times over. The big obstacle had been Jock's shotgun, and that was overcome now.

"His high and mighty lordship's bedridden," Horgan told Nan, kissing her again, "and blind, too, they say. I'll finish here by three o'clock, girl. Ring me about teatime tomorrow, if you feel you must; but simply talk about the weather, Nan, when you do. You'll love Las Palmas."

He stood at the forgotten gate, watching Nan get into the car in which he had come and had parked in the shadow of the derelict linoleum-works that ran cheek by jowl with the north dyke of Balgrummo Lodging. When she had gone, he started up Nan's own inconspicuous black Ford, moving it far enough for him to shut the gates. He locked those gates with the big brass padlock that Jock had removed to admit "Nurse" Nan. Then, slowly and with only his dims showing, he drove up the avenue—rhododendron jungle pressing in from either side—that led to the seventeenth-century facade of Balgrummo Lodging.

"Uncle Alec and his house have everything," Dr. Effie Inchburn had said once: "Dry rot, wet rot, woodworm, deathwatch beetle." Also, among those few who remembered Lord Balgrummo and Balgrummo Lodging, the twain had a most nasty repute. It was a positive duty to take the pictures out of that foul house and convey them into the possession of collectors who, if they would keep them no less private, certainly would care for them better.

Sliding out of the car with his dispatch-case of tools, Rafe Horgan stood at the dark door of Balgrummo Lodging. The front was the work of Sir William Bruce, they said, although part of the house was older. It all looked solid enough by night, however rotten the timbers and the man within. Horgan had taken Jamieson's big ring of keys from the gate-cottage, but the heavy main door stood slightly ajar, anyway. No light showed anywhere. Before entering, Horgan took a brief complacent survey of the tall ashlar face of what T. M. Gillespie, that mordant stick of a solicitor, called "Balgrummo's Hell."

Living well enough by his wits, Horgan had come upon Balgrummo Lodging by good fortune, less than a month after he had found it convenient to roost in Edinburgh. In a car with false license-plates, he had driven out to Fossie housing estate in search of a certain rough customer who might do a job for him. Fossie, only seven years old but already slum, was the usual complex of crescents and terraces of drab council-houses. Horgan had taken a wrong turning and had found himself driving down a neglected and uninhabited old lane; behind the nasty brick wall on his right had been a derelict marshalling-yard for goods-waggons, declared redundant by Dr. Beeching of British Railways. On his left, he had passed the immense hulk of a disused linoleum-works, empty for several years, its every window-pane smashed by the lively bairns of Fossie.

Beyond the linoleum-factory, he had come upon a remarkably high old stone dyke, unpleasant shards of broken glass set thick in cement all along its top. Behind the wall he had made out the limbs and trunks of limes and beeches, a forest amidst suburbia. Abruptly, a formal ancient pend or vaulted gateway had loomed up. On either side, a seventeenth-century stone beast-effigy kept guard, life-size almost: a lion and a griffin, but so hacked and battered by young vandals as to be almost recognizable. The griffin's whole head was lacking.

So much Horgan had seen at a glance, taking it that these were the vacant policies of some demolished or ruined mansion-house. He had driven on to the end of the street, hoping to circle back to the housing-estate, but had found himself in a cul-de-sac, the Fettinch burn flowing through bogs beyond the brick wall at the end. This triangle of wooded policies, hemmed in by goods-yards, wrecked factory, and polluted streams, must be the last scrap of some laird's estate of yesteryear, swallowed but not yet digested by the city's fringe. Probably the squalor and unhealthiness of the low site had deterred Edinburgh or Midlothian—he wasn't sure within which boundary it lay—from building on it another clutch of council-houses for the Fossie scheme.

Swinging round the lane's terminal wall, Horgan had gone slowly back past the massive pend, where the harling was dropping from the rubble. To his surprise, he had noticed a gate-lodge, apparently habitable, just within the iron grille of the gates; and a little wood-smoke had been spiralling up from the chimney. Could there be anything worth liberating beyond those gates? He had stopped, and had found an iron bell-pull that functioned. When he had rung, a tall fellow, with the look of a retired constable, had emerged from the gate-cottage and had conversed with him, taciturnly, in broad Scots, through the locked grille.

Horgan had asked for directions to a certain crescent in the housing-scheme, and had got them. Then he had inquired the name of this place. "Balgrummo Lodgin', sir"—with a half-defensive frown. On impulse, Horgan had suggested that he would like to see the house (which, he gathered, must be standing, for he could make out beyond the trees some high dormers and roofs).

"Na, na; Himself's no receivin', ye ken." This had been uttered with a kind of incredulity at the question being put.

Growing interested, Horgan had professed himself to be something of a connoisseur of seventeenth-century domestic architecture. Where might he apply for permission to view the exterior, at any rate? He had been given to understand, surlily, that it would do no good: but everything was in the hands of Lord Balgrummo's Trust. The Trust's solicitor and chairman was a Mr. T. M. Gillespie, of Reid, Gillespie and MacIlwraith, Hanover Street.

Thus Balgrummo Lodging had been added to Rafe Horgan's list of divers projects. A few days later, he had scraped acquaintance with Gillespie, a dehydrated bachelor, Initially he had not mentioned Balgrummo Lodging, but had talked in Gillespie's chambers about a hypothetical Miss Horgan in Glasgow, allegedly an aunt of his, a spinster of large means, who was thinking of a family trust. Mr. Gillespie, he had heard it said, was experienced in the devising and management of such trusts. As venture-capital, a cheque from Horgan had even been made out to Mr. Gillespie, in payment for general advice upon getting up a conceivable Janet Horgan Estates, Ltd.

Gillespie, he had discovered, was a lonely solicitor who could be cultivated, and who had a dry relish for dry sherry. After a bottle, Gillespie might talk more freely than a solicitor ought to talk. They came to dine together fairly frequently—after Horgan had learnt, from a chance remark which he affected to receive casually, that some good pictures remained at the Lodging. As the weeks elapsed, they were joined for a meal, once and again, by Gillespie's old friend Dr. Euphemia Inchburn, Lord Balgrummo's niece, a superannuated gynecologist. Horgan had turned on all his charm, and Dr. Inchburn had slipped into garrulity.

Perceiving that he really might be on to a good thing, Horgan had poked into old gazeteers which might mention Balgrummo Lodging; and, as he obtained from his new friends some hint of the iniquities of the tenth Baron Balgrummo, he looked into old newspaper-files. He knew a little about pictures, as he did about a number of things; and by consulting the right books and catalogues, he ascertained that on the rotting walls of Balgrummo Lodging there still must hang some highly valuable family portraits—though not family portraits only—none of them exhibited anywhere since 1913. Gillespie was interested only in Scottish portrait-painters, and not passionately in them; Horgan judged it imprudent to question Dr. Effie Inchburn overmuch on the subject, lest his inquisitiveness be fixed in her memory. But he became reasonably well satisfied that Lord Balgrummo, senescent monster, must possess an Opie; a Raeburn; a Ramsay or two; perhaps even three Wilkies; a good Reynolds, possibly, and a Constable; a very good Romney; a Gainsborough, it appeared, and (happy prospect) a Hogarth; two small canvasses by William Etty; a whole row of reputed Knellers; once, and just conceivably still, a Cranach and a Holbein were to be seen at the Lodging. The tenth baron's especial acquisition, about 1911, had been an enormous Fuseli, perhaps unknown to compilers of catalogues, and (judging from one of Dr. Inchburn's grimaces) probably obscene. There were more pictures—the devil knew what.

Perhaps some rare books might be found in the library, but Horgan was too little of a bibliophile to pick them out in a hurry. The silver and that sort of thing presumably were in a bank—it would have been risky to inquire. Anyone but a glutton would be content with those pictures, for one night's work.

Lethargy, and the consequences of permanent confinement to his house, naturally had made Lord Balgrummo neglect his inheritance. As the decades had slipped by, he had permitted his trustees to sell nearly everything he owned, except Balgrummo Lodging—once a residence of convenience, near Edinburgh, for the Inchburns, later a dower-house—and those pictures. "After all, never going out, Alec has to look at *something*," Dr. Inchburn had murmured.

Sufficient intelligence obtained, still Horgan faced the difficulty of entering the house without the peril and expense of a gang-raid, and of getting out undetected with those pictures. An attempt had been made several years before. On that occasion, Jock Jamieson, the night porter—"warden" would have been a better style—had shot to death one burglar and wounded another while they were on a ladder. Jamieson and his day mates (one of them the constable-type with whom Horgan had talked at the gate) were hard, vigilant men—and, like Lord Balgrummo's nurses, excellently paid. Time had been when it seemed at least as important to keep Lord Balgrummo in (though he had given his word never to leave the policies) as to keep predators out. Gillespie had implied that the police indulged in the peculiar porters of Balgrummo Lodging a certain readiness in the use of firearms. So Horgan's expedition had been most painstakingly plotted, and it had been necessary to wait months for the coincidence of favorable circumstances, all things being held in readiness.

The presence of a nurse in the house all round the clock was a further vexation; Horgan had not relished the prospect of pursuing a frantic nurse through that crumbling warren of a place. Should she escape through some back door . . . So when, only yesterday, Gillespie had mentioned that the night nurse had quit ("Nerves, as usual, in that house—and his lordship a disagreeable patient"), and that they had not yet found a replacement, Horgan knew his moment had arrived.

For one night, Jamieson had been required to do double duty, watching the policies and looking in on Lord Balgrummo every hour. Jock Jamieson, for all his toughness, probably liked being inside the place at night no more than did the nurses. So doubtless Jock had rejoiced when a la-di-dah feminine voice (Nan Stennis', of course) had informed him late that evening that she was calling on behalf of Mr. Gillespie, and that a new night nurse would make her appearance, in an hour or so, in her own car.

It had gone smoothly enough. Jock had opened the gate at Nan's honk, and then it had been up to Horgan, in the shadows. Had Jock been ten years younger, and less given to beer, he might have got his hands on the shotgun before Horgan could have reached him. But though disliking unnecessary roughness, Horgan had coshed men before, and he coshed Jock swiftly and well. No one came down that obscure lane after dark—few, indeed, in daylight. Therefore the investment in drinks and dinners for Gillespie and the Inchburn old maid, and the expenditure of Horgan's hours, now would be compensated for at an hourly rate of return beyond the dreams of avarice. Swinging his handsome dispatch-case, Horgan entered Balgrummo Lodging.

Within the chilly entrance-hall, the first thing Horgan noticed was the pervasive odor of dry rot. With this stench of doom, what wonder they had to pay triple wages to any nurse! Condemned to solitude, neglectful of business, and latterly penurious, Lord Balgrummo had postponed repairs until the cost of restoring the Lodging would have been gigantic. Even could he have found the money without selling some of his pictures, old Balgrummo probably would not have saved the house; he had no heirs of his body, the entail had been broken long before, and his heir-presumptive—Dr. Effie—never would choose to live in this desolation screened by the tumbledown linoleum-works. There remained only the question as to which would first tumble into atoms—Lord Balgrummo or his prison-mansion.

Horgan sent the beam of his big electric torch round the hall. It flashed across the surface of what appeared to be a vast Canaletto—a prospect of Ravenna, perhaps. Was it the real article, or only from Canaletto's school? Horgan wished he knew whether it were worth the difficulty of taking and concealing, its size considered. Well, he would leave it to the last, securing the certified goods first.

He had known there was no electric light in Balgrummo Lodging: nothing had been improved there—or much repaired—since 1913. He found, however, elaborate bronze gas-brackets. After fumbling, he found also that he did not know how to light them; or perhaps the gas was turned off here in the hall. No matter: the torch would suffice, even if the black caverns beyond its ray were distressing.

Before he went to work, he must have a glance at old Balgrummo, to be quite sure that the crazy old creature couldn't totter out to do some feeble mischief. (In this house, more than fifty years before, he had done great mischief indeed.) Where would his bedroom be? On the second story, at the front, just above the library, likely enough, judging from the plan of the Lodging, at which Horgan had once managed a hasty glance in Gillespie's chambers. Hanging the torch about his neck, Horgan made his way up the broad oak staircase, at first leaning on the balustrade—but presently touching that rail only gingerly, since here and there, even though he wore gloves, it felt spongy to the touch, and trembled in its rottenness when he put too much weight upon it.

At the first-floor turning of the stairs, Horgan paused. Had anything scraped or shuffled down there, below, down in the black well of the ground floor? Of course it couldn't have, unless it were a rat. (Balgrummo kept no dogs: "The brutes don't live long at the Lodging," Gillespie had murmured in an obscure aside.) How had those night nurses endured this situation, at whatever wages? One reason why Balgrummo Lodging hadn't been pillaged before this, Horgan ruminated, was the ghastly reputation of the place, lingering over five decades. Few enterprising lads, even from Fossie housing estate, would be inclined to venture into the auld bogle nobleman's precincts. Well, that ghostly wind had blown him good. No one could be more effectively rational than Rafe Horgan, who wouldn't fret about blood spilt before the First World War. Still, indubitably this was an oppressive house—stagnant, stagnant.

"Haunted?" Dr. Effie had replied hesitantly to Horgan's jocular inquiry. "If you mean haunted by dead ancestors, Major Horgan—why, no more than most old houses here in Scotland, I suppose. Who would be troubled, after so many generations, by old General Sir Angus Inchburn in his Covenanting jackboots? Ghostly phenomena, or so I've read, seldom linger long after a man's or a woman's death and burial. But if you ask whether there's something fey at work in the house—oh, I certainly suppose so."

Having paused to polish her spectacles, Dr. Effie continued calmly enough: "That's Uncle Alec's fault. He's not present merely in one room, you know; he fills the house, every room, every hour. Presumably I seem silly to you, Major Horgan, but my impulses won't let me visit Balgrummo more than I must, even if Alec does mean to leave everything to me. Balgrummo Lodging is like a saturated sponge, dripping with the shame and the longing of Alexander Fillan Inchburn. Can you understand that my uncle loathes what he did, and yet might do it again—even the worst of it—if there were opportunity? The horror of Balgrummo Lodging isn't Lord Balgrummo nine-tenths dead; it's Balgrummo one-tenth alive, but in torment."

The tedious old girl-doctor was nearly as cracked as her noble uncle, Horgan thought. Actually he had learned from some interesting research the general character of Lord Balgrummo's offenses so long ago—acts which would have produced the hanging of anyone but a peer, in those days. Horgan nevertheless had amused himself by endeavoring, slyly and politely, to force Dr. Effie to tell him just why Balgrummo had been given the choice of standing trial for his life (by the Lords, of course, as a peer, which might have damaged the repute of that body) or of being kept in a kind of perpetual house-arrest, without sentence being passed by anyone. The latter choice would not have been offered—and accepted—even so, but for the general belief that he must be a maniac.

As he had anticipated, Dr. Euphemia had turned prude. "Poor Alec was very naughty when he was young. There were others as bad as himself, but he took the whole blame on his shoulders. He was told that if he would swear never to go out, all his life, and to receive no visitors except members of his family or his solicitors, no formal charges would be pressed against him. They required him to put everything he owned into trust; and the trustees were to engage the men to watch the policies of Balgrummo Lodging, and the servants. All the original set of trustees are dead and buried; Mr. Gillespie and I weren't much more than babies when Uncle Alec had his Trouble."

From Gillespie, later, Rafe Horgan had learned more about that Trouble. But what was he doing, pausing in the darkness of the second-floor corridor to reminisce? A hasty inspection by the torch showed him that the Knellers, all great noses, velvets and bosoms, were hung on this floor. And there was the Gainsborough, a good one, though it badly needed cleaning: Margaret, Lady Ross, second daughter of the fifth Lord Balgrummo. The worm had got into the picture-frame, but the canvas seemed to be in decent condition, he made out on closer examination. Well, Horgan meant to cut his pictures out of their frames, to save time and space. First, though, he must look in upon Himself.

The corridor was all dust and mildew. A single charwoman, Gillespie had mentioned, came a few hours daily. Monday through Friday, to keep Balgrummo's bedroom and small parlor neat, to clean the stairs and to wash dishes in the kitchen. Otherwise, the many rooms and passages of the Lodging were unceasingly shuttered against sun and moon, and the damask might fall in tatters from the walls, the ceiling drip with cobwebs, for all old Balgrummo cared. Nearly every room was left locked, though the keys, all but a few, were in the bunch (each with its metat tag) that Horgan had taken from unconscious Jock. Even Gillespie, who waited on his client four or five times a year, never had contrived to see the chapel. Balgrummo kept the chapel key in his own pocket, Gillespie fancied—and, over coffee and brandy, had mentioned this, together with other trivia, to Horgan. "It was in the chapel, you see, Rafe, that the worst of the Trouble happened."

Acquiring that chapel key was an additional reason why Horgan must pay his respects to Lord Balgrummo—though he relished that necessity less, somehow, with every minute that elapsed. Henry Fuseli's most indecorous painting might be in that chapel; for the tenth baron's liturgy and ritual, fifty years before, had been a synthesis of Benin witchrites with memories of Scots diabolism, and whatever might excite the frantic fancy had been employed—all gross images. So, at least, Horgan had surmised from what he had garnered from the old newspaper files, and what Gillespie had let drop.

Uncertain of quite where he was in the house, Horgan tried the knobs of three doors in that corridor. The first two were locked; and it was improbable that the trustees ever had gone so far, even when Balgrummo was stronger, as to have him locked into his rooms at night. But the third door opened creakingly. Flashing round his light, Horgan entered an old-fashioned parlor, with what appeared to be two bona-fide Wilkie landscapes on opposite walls. Across the parlor, which was scarcely bigger than a dressing-room, a mahogany door stood half open. How silent! Yet something scraped or ticked faintly—a morose death-watch beetle in the panelling, probably. Despite irrational misgivings, Horgan compelled himself to pass through the inner doorway.

The beam of his torch swept to a Queen Anne bed. In it lay, motionless and with eyes shut, an extremely old man, skin and bone under a single sheet and a single blanket. A coal fire smouldered in the grate, so the room was not altogether dark. Horgan's flesh crept perceptibly—but that would be the old rumors, and the old truths, about this enfeebled thing in the bed. "In his prime, we called him Ozymandias," Gillespie had put it. But Lord Balgrummo was past obscenities and atrocities now.

"Hello, Alec!" Horgan was loud and jocular. His right hand rested on the cosh in his coat pocket. "Alec, you old toad, I've come for your pictures." But Alexander Fillan Inchburn, the last of a line that went back to a bastard of William the Lion, did not stir or speak.

T. M. Gillespie was proud of Lord Balgrummo, as the most remarkable person whose business ever had come his way. "Our Scots Giles de Rais," Gillespie had chuckled aridly while enjoying a Jamaican cigar from Horgan's case, "probably would not be found insane by a board of medical examiners—not even after fifty years of restriction to his own private Hell. I don't think it was from malice that the procurator-fiscal of that day recommended Balgrummo Lodging—where the capital offenses had been committed —as the place of isolated residence: it merely happened that this particular house of Lord Balgrummo's was secluded enough to keep his lordship out of the public eye (for he might have been stoned), and yet near enough to the city for police surveillance, during the earlier decades. I take it that the police have forgotten his existence, or almost forgotten, by this time: for the past three or four years, he wouldn't have been able to walk unaided so far as the gate-cottage."

It was something of a relief to Horgan, finding that Lord Balgrummo was past giving coherent evidence in a court of law—and therefore need not be given the quietus. Even though they no longer hanged anybody for anything, and even though Balgrummo could have been eliminated in thirty seconds by a pillow over his face, the police pursued a homocide much more energetically than they did a picture-fancier.

But was this penny-dreadful monster of fifty years ago, with his white beard now making him sham-venerable in this four-poster, still among the living? Horgan almost could see the bones through his skin; Balgrummo might have come to his end during the hour or so since Jamieson had made his rounds. To be sure, Horgan took a mirror from the dressing-table and held it close to the pallid sunken face. Setting his torch on its base, he inspected the mirror's surface; yes, there was a faint moist film, so the tenth baron still breathed.

Balgrummo must be stone-deaf, or in coma. Dr. Effiie had said he had gone almost blind recently. Was it true? Horgan nearly yielded to a loathsome impulse to roll back those withered eyelids, but he reminded himself that somehow he wouldn't be able to endure seeing his own image in this dying man's malign pupils.

The coshing of Jock, the nervous partial exploration of this dismal house, the sight of loathsome old Balgrummo on the edge of dissolution—these trials had told on Horgan, old hand though he was at predatory ventures. With all the hours left to him, it would do no harm to sit for a few minutes in this easy chair, almost as if he were Balgrummo's nurse—keeping watch on the bed, surely, to make certain that Balgrummo wasn't (in reasons's spite) shamming in some way—and to review in his brain the pictures he ought to secure first, and the rooms in which he was likely to find them.

But it would be heartening to have more light than his torch. Never turning his back on the bed, Horgan contrived to light a gas-bracket near the door; either these gas-fittings were simpler than those below stairs, or he had got the trick of the operation. The interior shutters of this bedroom being closed, there wasn't the faintest danger of a glimmer of light being perceived by chance passers-by—not that anybody conceivably could pass by Balgrummo Lodging on a rainy midnight.

Lord Balgrummo seemed no less grisly in the flood of gaslight. However much exhausted by strain, you couldn't think of going to sleep, for the briefest nap, in a chair only six feet distant from this unspeaking and unspeakable thing in the bed; not when you knew just how "very naughty," in Dr. Euphemia's phrase, Balgrummo had been. The Trouble for which he had paid had been only the culmination of a series of arcane episodes, progressing from hocus-pocus to the ultimate horror.

"No, not lunatic, in any ordinary definition of the term," Gillespie had declared. "Balgrummo recognized the moral character of his acts—aye, more fully than does the average sensual man. Also he was, and is, quite rational, in the sense that he can transact some ordinary business of life when pressed. He fell into a devil of a temper when we proposed to sell some of his pictures to pay for putting the house and the policies in order; he knows his rights, and that the trustees can't dispose of his plenishings against his explicit disapproval. He's civil enough, in his mocking way, to his niece, Effie, when she calls—and to me, when I have to see him. He still reads a good deal—or did, until his sight began to fail—though only books in his own library; half the ceiling has fallen in the library, but he shuffles through the broken plaster on the shaky floor."

On the right of the bed-head there hung an indubitable Constable; on the left, a probable Etty. The two were fairly small, and Horgan could take them whenever he wished. But his throat was dry, this house being so damned dusty. A decanter stood on the dressing-table, a silver brandy label round its neck, and by it two cut-glass tumblers. "Not a drop for you, Alec?" inquired Horgan, grinning defiantly at the silent man on the bed. He seated himself in the velvet-upholstered armchair again and drank the brandy neat.

"No, one can't say," Gillespie had continued (in that

last conversation which now seemed so far away and long ago), "that his lordship is wholly incompetent to take a hand in the management of his affairs. It's rather that he's *distant*—preoccupied, in more senses than one. He has to exert his will to bring his consciousness back from wherever it drifts—and one can see that the effort isn't easy for him."

"He's in a brown study, you mean, Tom?" Horgan had inquired, not much interested at that time.

"It's not the phrase I would choose, Rafe. Dr. Effie talks about the 'astral body' and such rubbish, as if she half believed in it—you've heard her. That silliness was a principal subject of Balgrummo's 'researches' for two years before the Trouble, you understand; his Trouble was the culmination of those experiments. But of course . . ."

"Of course he's only living in the past," Horgan had put in.

"*Living?* Who really knows what that word means?" T. M. Gillespie, W.S., devoted to the memory of David Hume, professed a contempt for rationalism as profound as his contempt for superstition. "And why say *past?* Did you never think that a man might be ossified in time? What you call Balgrummo's past, Rafe, may be Balgrummo's own present, as much as this table-talk of ours is the present for you and me. The Trouble is his lordship's obsessive reality. Attaining to genuine evil requires strict application to the discipline, eh? Balgrummo is not merely remembering the events of what you and I call 1913, or even 'reliving' those events. No, I suspect it's this: he's embedded in those events, like a beetle in amber. For Balgrummo, one certain night in Balgrummo Lodging continues forever.

"When Dr. Effie and I distract him by raising the trivia of current business, he has to depart from *his* reality, and gropes briefly through a vexatious little dream-world in which his niece and his solicitor are insubstantial shadows. In Alexander Inchburn's consciousness, I mean, there is no remembrance and no anticipation. He's not 'living in the past,' not engaging in an exercise of retrospection; for him, Time is restricted to one certain night, and space is restricted to one certain house, or perhaps one certain room. Passionate experience has chained him to a fixed point in Time, so to speak. But Time, as so many have said, is a human convention, not an objective reality. Can you prove that your Time is more substantial than his?"

Horgan hadn't quite followed Gillespie, and said so.

"I put it this way, Rafe," Gillespie had gone on, didactically. "What's the time of day in Hell? Why, Hell is timeless—or so my grandfather told me, and he was minister at the Tron.- Hell knows no future and no past, but only the everlasting moment of damnation. Also Hell is spaceless; or, conceivably, it's a locked box, damnably confining. Here we have Lord Balgrummo shut up perpetually in his box called Balgrummo Lodging, where the fire is not quenched and the worm never dieth. One bloody and atrocious act, committed in that very box, literally is his enduring *reality*. He's not recollecting; he's experiencing, here and (for him) now. All the frightful excitement of that Trouble, the very act of profanation and terror, lifts him out of what we call Time. Between Dr. Effie and me on the one side, and distant Balgrummo on the other, a great gulf is fixed.

"If you like, you can call that gulf Time. For that gulf, I praise whatever gods there be. For if any man's or woman's consciousness should penetrate to Balgrummo's consciousness, to his time-scheme, to his world beyond the world—or if, through some vortex of mind and soul, anyone were sucked into that narrow place of torment—then the intruder would end like *this*." Gillespie, tapping his cigar upon an ash-tray, knocked into powder a long projection of gray ash. "Consumed, Rafe."

Scratch the canny Scot, Horgan had thought then, even the pedant of the law, and you find the bogle-dreading Pict. "I suppose you mean, really, Tom, that he's out of his head," Horgan had commented, bored with tipsy and unprofitable speculation.

"I mean precisely the contrary, Rafe. I mean that anyone who encounters Lord Balgrummo ought to be on his guard against being drawn into Balgrummo's head. In what you and I designate as 1913 (though, as I said, dates have no significance for Balgrummo), his lordship was a being of immense moral power, magnetic and seductive. I'm not being facetious. Moral power is a catalyst, and can work for good or evil. Even now, I'm acutely uneasy when I sit with Balgrummo, aware that this old man might absorb me. I shouldn't wish to stir those sleeping fires by touching his passions. That's why Balgrummo had to be confined, five decades ago—but not simply because he might be *physically* dangerous. Yet I can't explain to you; you've not watched Balgrummo in what you call his 'brown study,' and you never will, happy man." Their conversation then had shifted to Miss Janet Horgan's hypothetical trust.

Yet Gillespie had been a bad prophet. Here he was, clever Rafe Horgan, man of supple talents and slippery fingers, leisurely watching Lord Balgrummo in his brown study—or in his coma, more precisely—and finishing his lordship's decanter of praiseworthy brandy. You had to remember to keep watching that cadaverous face above the sheet, though; if you let your eyes close even for a second, *his* might open, for all you could tell. After all, you were only a guest in Balgrummo's very own little Hell. The host mustn't be permitted to forget his manners.

Now where would the expiring monster keep his privy effects—the key to that chapel on the floor above, for instance? Steady, Rafe boy: keep your eyes on his face as you open his bedside drawer. Right you are, Rafe, you always were lucky; the nurse had put old Alec's three keys on a chain, along with watch and pocket-comb and such effects, into this very drawer. One of these keys should let you into the chapel, Rafe. Get on with you; you've drunk all the brandy a reasonable man needs.

"Don't you mean to give me a guided tour, Alec? Stately homes of Scotia, and all that? Won't you show me your chapel, where you and your young chums played your dirty little games, and got your fingers burned? Cheerio, then; don't blame me if you can't be bothered to keep an eye on your goods and chattels."

Back away from him, toward the door, Rafe. Let him lie. How had Dr. Effie put it? "He fills the house, every room, every hour." Cheerless thought, that, fit for a scrawny old maid. The talkative Euphemia must have nearly as many screws loose as had her uncle; probably she envied him his revels.

"I really believe the others led Uncle Alec into the whole

business, gradually," Dr. Effie had droned on, the last time he had seen her. "But once in, he took command, as natural to him. He was out in Nigeria before people called it Nigeria, you know, and in Guinea, and all up and down that coast. He began collecting materials for a monograph on African magic—raising the dead, and summoning devils, and more. Presently he was dabbling in the spells, not merely collecting them—so my father told me, forty years ago. After Uncle Alec came home, he didn't stop dabbling. Some very reputable people dabbled when I was a girl. But the ones around Uncle Alec weren't in the least reputable.

"Charlatans? Not quite; I wish they had been. They fed Balgrummo's appetite. Yet he was after knowledge, at least in the beginning; and though he may have boggled, more than once, at the steps he had to descend toward the source of that knowledge, he grew more eager as he pressed down into the dark. Or so father guessed; father became one of Uncle Alec's original trustees, and felt it his duty to collect some evidence of what had happened—though it sickened father, the more he uncovered of his brother's queerness.

"Toward the end, Balgrummo may have forgotten about knowledge and have leaped into passion and power. One didn't *learn* what one had sought to apprehend; one *became* the mystery, possessing it and possessed by it.

"No, not charlatans—not altogether. They took a fortune out of Uncle Alec, one way or another; and he had to pay even more to keep people quiet in those years. They had told Balgrummo, in effect, that they could raise the Devil —though they didn't put it in quite that crude way. Yet they must have been astounded by their success, when it came at last. Balgrummo had paid before, and he has paid ever since. Those others paid, too—especially the man and the woman who died. They had thought they were raising the Devil for Lord Balgrummo. But as it turned out, they raised the Devil *through* Balgrummo and *in* Balgrummo. After that, everything fell to pieces."

But to hell with recollections of Euphemia Inchburn, Rafe. Dry rot, wet rot, woodworm, death-watch beetle: the Devil take them all, and Balgrummo Lodging besides. One thing the Devil shouldn't have—these pictures. Get on to the chapel, Rafe, and then give Nan the glad news. Thanks for the brandy, Alec: I mustn't have got through the business without it.

Yet one dram too many, possibly? Horgan was aware of a certain giddiness, but not fully aware of how he had got up those Stygian stairs, or of what he had done with his torch. Had he turned the key in the lock of the chapel door? He couldn't recall having done so. Still, here he was in the chapel.

No need for the torch; the room, a long gallery, was lit by all those candle-flames in the many-branched candlesticks. Who kept Lord Balgrummo's candles alight? The stench of decay was even stronger here than it had been down below. Under foot, the floorboards were almost oozing, and mushroom rot squashed beneath his shoes. Some of the panelling had fallen away altogether. High up in the shifting shadows, the moulded-plaster ceiling sagged and bulged as if the lightest touch would bring it all down in slimy little particles.

Back of the altar—the altar of the catastrophic act of Balgrummo's Trouble—hung the unknown Fuseli. It was no painting, but an immense cartoon, and the most uninhibited museum-director never would dare show it to the most broad-minded critics of art. Those naked and contorted forms, the instruments of torment fixed upon their flesh, were the inversion of the Agony. Even Horgan could not bear to look at them long.

Look at them? All those candles were guttering. Two winked out simultaneously; others failed. As the little flames sank toward extinction, Rafe Horgan became aware that he was not alone.

It was as if presences skulked in corners or behind the broken furniture. And there could be no retreat toward the door; for something approached from that end of the gallery. As if Horgan's extremity of terror fed it, the shape took on increasing clarity of outline, substance, strength.

Tall, arrogant, implacable, mindless, it drifted toward him. The face was Balgrummo's, or what Balgrummo's must have been fifty years before, but possessed: eager, eager,

eager; all appetite, passion, yearning after the abyss. In one hand glittered a long knife.

Horgan bleated and ran. He fell against the cobwebby altar. And in the final act of destruction, something strode across the great gulf of Time.

Young (25) and talented Samuel R. Delany was born and brought up in New York City and now lives there with his wife. "Some time back at the Bronx High School of Science, I won a handful of literary awards—writing seriously since. Wrote my first SF novel six years ago." [Delany's BABEL 17 *won last year's Nebula award for best novel.] "Hobbies? Music—the listening to and writing of—mathematics, and cooking. This story," continues Mr. Delany, "was drafted in a confusion of American impressions during my first month in the U.S. after a year abroad (mostly Greece and Turkey)."*

CORONA

by Samuel R. Delany

Pa ran off to Mars Colony before Buddy was born. Momma drank. At sixteen Buddy used to help out in a copter repair shop outside St. Gable below Baton Rouge. Once he decided it would be fun to take a copter, some bootleg, a girl named Dolores-jo, and sixty-three dollars and eighty-five cents to New Orleans. Nothing taken had ever, by any interpretation, been his. He was caught before they raised from the garage roof. He lied about his age at court to avoid the indignity of reform school. Momma, when they found her, wasn't too sure ("Buddy? Now, let me see, that's Laford. And James Robert Warren—I named him after my third husband who was not living with me at the time —now my little James, he came along in . . . two thousand and thirty-*two*, I believe. Or thirty-*four*—you sure now, it's Buddy?") when he was born. The constable was inclined to judge him younger than he was, but let him go to grown-up prison anyway. Some terrible things happened

128

How do your cigarette's tar and nicotine numbers compare with True?

20 CLASS A
CIGARETTES

TRUE

FILTER CIGARETTES

LATEST U.S. GOVERNMENT TESTS:
12 MGS. TAR. 0.6 MGS. NICOTINE

Place your pack here.

Compare
your cigarette's
tar and nicotine
numbers
with True.

20 CLASS A
CIGARETTES

TRUE

MENTHOL FILTER

LATEST U.S. GOVERNMENT TESTS:
13 MGS. TAR. 0.7 MGS. NICOTINE

No numbers on the front of your pack? True puts its numbers right out front. Because True, regular and menthol, is lower in both tar and nicotine than 99% of all other cigarettes sold. Think about it.

20 CLASS A CIGARETTES

TRUE

FILTER CIGARETTES

LATEST U.S. GOVERNMENT TESTS:
12 MGS. TAR, 0.6 MGS. NICOTINE

Warning: The Surgeon General Has Determined That Cigarette Smoking Is Dangerous to Your Health

© Lorillard 1971

Regular or menthol.
Doesn't it all add up to True?

Regular: 12 mg. "tar", 0.6 mg. nicotine,
Menthol: 13 mg. "tar", 0.7 mg. nicotine, av. per cigarette, FTC Report, Aug. '71.

there. When Buddy came out three years later he was a gentler person than before; still, when frightened, he became violent. Shortly he knocked up a waitress six years his senior. Chagrined, he applied for emigration to one of Uranus's moons. In twenty years, though, the colonial economy had stabilized. They were a lot more stringent with applicants than in his pa's day: colonies had become almost respectable. They'd started barring people with jail records and things like that. So he went to New York instead and eventually got a job as an assistant servicer at the Kennedy spaceport.

There was a nine-year-old girl in a hospital in New York at that time who could read minds and wanted to die. Her name was Lee.

Also there was a singer named Bryan Faust.

Slow, violent, blond Buddy had been at Kennedy a year when Faust's music came. The songs covered the city, sounded on every radio, filled the title selections on every jukebox and scopitone. They shouted and whispered and growled from the wall speaker in the spacehangar. Buddy ambled over the catwalk while the cross-rhythms, sudden silences, and moments of pure voice were picked up by jangling organ, whining oboe, bass and cymbals. Buddy's thoughts were small and slow. His hands, gloved in canvas, his feet, rubber booted, were big and quick.

Below him the spaceliner filled the hangar like a tuber an eighth of a mile long. The service crew swarmed the floor, moving over the cement like scattered ball bearings. And the music—

"Hey, kid."

Buddy turned.

Bim swaggered toward him, beating his thigh to the rhythms in the falls of sound. "I was just looking for you, kid." Buddy was twenty-four, but people would call him "kid" after he was thirty. He blinked a lot.

"You want to get over and help them haul down that solvent from upstairs? The damn lift's busted again. I swear, they're going to have a strike if they don't keep the equipment working right. Ain't safe. Say, what did you think of the crowd outside this morning?"

"Crowd?" Buddy's drawl snagged on a slight speech defect. "Yeah, there was a lot of people, huh. I been down in the maintenance shop since six o'clock, so I guess I must've missed most of it. What was they here for?"

Bim got a lot of what-are-you-kidding-me on his face. Then it turned to a tolerant smile. "For Faust." He nodded toward the speaker: the music halted, lurched, then Bryan Faust's voice roared out for love and the violent display that would prove it real. "Faust came in this morning, kid. You didn't know? He's been making it down from moon to moon through the outer planets. I hear he broke 'em up in the asteroids. He's been to Mars, and the last thing I heard, they love him on Luna as much as anywhere else. He arrived on Earth this morning, and he'll be up and down the Americas for twelve days." He thumbed toward the pit and shook his head. "That's his liner." Bim whistled. "And did we have a hell of a time! All them kids, thousands of 'em, I bet. And people old enough to know better, too. You should have seen the police! When we were trying to get the liner in here, a couple of hundred kids got through the police block. They wanted to pull his ship apart and take home the pieces. You like his music?"

Buddy squinted toward the speaker. The sounds jammed into his ears, pried around his mind, loosening things. Most were good things, touched on by a resolved cadence, a syncopation caught up again, feelings sounded on too quickly for him to hold, but good feelings. Still, a few of them . . .

Buddy shrugged, blinked. "I like it." And the beat of his heart, his lungs, and the music coincided. "Yeah, I like that." The music went faster; heart and breathing fell behind; Buddy felt a surge of disorder. "But it's . . . strange." Embarrassed, he smiled over his broken tooth.

"Yeah. I guess a lot of other people think so too. Well, get over with those solvent cans."

"Okay." Buddy turned off toward the spiral staircase. He was on the landing, about to go up, when someone yelled down, "Watch it—!"

A ten gallon drum slammed the walkway five feet from him. He whirled to see as the casing split—

(Faust's sonar drums slammed.)

—and solvent, oxidizing in the air, splattered.

Buddy screamed and clutched his eye. He had been working with the metal rasp that morning, and his gloves were impregnated with steel flakes and oil. He found his canvas palm against his face.

(Faust's electric bass ground against a suspended dissonance.)

As he staggered down the walk, hot solvent rained on his back. Then something inside went wild and he began to swing his arms.

(The last chorus of the song swung toward the close. And the announcer's voice, not waiting for the end, cut over, "All *right* all you little people *out* there in music land . . .")

"What in the—"

"Jesus, what's wrong with—"

"What happened? I told you the damn lift was broken!"

"Call the infirmary! Quick! Call the—"

Voices came from the level above, the level below. And footsteps. Buddy turned on the ramp and screamed and swung.

"Watch it! What's with that guy—"

"Here, help me hold . . . Owww!—"

"He's gone berserk! Get the doc up from the infirm—"

(" . . . *that* was Bryan Faust's mind-*twisting*, brain-*blowing*, brand new release, *Corona!* And you know it will be a *hit!* . . .")

Somebody tried to grab him, and Buddy hit out. Blind, rolling from the hips, he tried to apprehend the agony with flailing hands. And couldn't. A flash bulb had been jammed into his eye socket and detonated. He knocked somebody else against the rail, and staggered, and shrieked.

(". . . And he's come down to Earth at *last,* all you baby-mommas and baby-poppas! The little man from Ganymede who's been putting *the* music of *the* spheres through *so* many changes this past year arrived *in* New York this morning. And all *I* want to say, Bryan . . .")

Rage, pain, and music.

(". . . is, how do you *dig* our Earth!")

Buddy didn't even feel the needle stab his shoulder. He collapsed as the cymbals died.

Lee turned and turned the volume nob till it clicked.

In the trapezoid of sunlight over the desk from the high, small window, open now for August, lay her radio, a piece of graph paper with an incomplete integration for the area within the curve $X^4 + Y^4 = k^4$, and her brown fist. Smiling, she tried to release the tension the music had built.

Her shoulders lowered, her nostrils narrowed, and her fist fell over on its back. Still, her knuckles moved to the remembered rhythm of *Corona*.

The inside of her forearm was webbed raw pink. There were a few marks on her right arm too. But those were three years old; from when she had been six.

Corona!

She closed her eyes and pictured the rim of the sun. Centered in the flame, with the green eyes of his German father and the high cheekbones of his Arawak mother, was the impudent and insouciant, sensual and curious face of Bryan Faust. The brassy, four-color magazine with its endless hyperbolic prose was open on her bed behind her.

Lee closed her eyes tighter. If she could reach out, and perhaps touch—no, not him; that would be too much—but someone standing, sitting, walking near him, see what seeing him close was like, hear what hearing his voice was like, through air and light: she reached out her mind, reached for the music. And heard—

—your daughter getting along?

They keep telling me better and better every week when I go to visit her. But, oh, I swear, I just don't know. You have no idea how we hated to send her back to that place.

Of course I know! She's your daughter. And she's such a cute little thing. And so smart. Did they want to run some more tests?

She tried to kill herself. Again.

Oh, *no!*

She's got scars on her wrist halfway to her elbow! What am I doing wrong? The doctors can't tell me. She's not even ten. I can't keep her here with me. Her father's tried; he's about had it with the whole business. I know because of a divorce a child may have emotional problems, but that a little girl, as intelligent as Lee, can be so—confused! She had to go back, I know she had to go back. But what is it I'm doing wrong? I hate myself for it, and sometimes, just because she can't tell me, I hate her—

Lee's eyes opened; she smashed the table with her small, brown fists, tautening the muscles of her face to hold the tears. All musical beauty was gone. She breathed once more. For a while she looked up at the window, it's glass door swung wide. The bottom sill was seven feet from the floor.

Then she pressed the button for Dr. Gross, and went to the bookshelf. She ran her fingers over the spines: *Spinoza, The Bobbsey Twins at Spring Lake, The Decline of the West, The Wind in the Wil*—

She turned at the sound of the door unbolting. "You buzzed for me, Lee?"

"It happened. Again. Just about a minute ago."

"I noted the time as you rang."

"Duration, about forty-five seconds. It was my mother, and her friend who lives downstairs. Very ordinary. Nothing worth noting down."

"And how do you feel?"

She didn't say anything, but looked at the shelves.

Dr. Gross walked into the room and sat down on her desk. "Would you like to tell me what you were doing just before it happened?"

"Nothing. I'd just finished listening to the new record. On the radio."

"Which record?"

"The new Faust song, *Corona.*"

"Haven't heard that one." He glanced down at the graph paper and raised an eyebrow. "This yours, or is it from somebody else?"

"You told me to ring for you every time I . . . got an attack, didn't you?"

"Yes—"

"I'm doing what you want."

"Of course, Lee. I didn't mean to imply you hadn't been keeping your word. Want to tell me something about the record? What did you think of it?"

"The rhythm is very interesting. Five against seven when it's there. But a lot of the beats are left out, so you have to listen hard to get it."

"Was there anything, perhaps in the words, that may have set off the mind reading?"

"His colonial Ganymede accent is so thick that I missed most of the lyrics, even though it's basically English."

Dr. Gross smiled. "I've noticed the colonial expressions are slipping into a lot of young people's speech since Faust has become so popular. You hear them all the time."

"I don't." She glanced up at the doctor quickly, then back to the books.

Dr. Gross coughed; then he said, "Lee, we feel it's best to keep you away from the other children at the hospital. You tune in most frequently on the minds of people you know, or those who've had similar experiences and reactions to yours. All the children in the hospital are emotionally disturbed. If you were to suddenly pick up all their minds at once, you might be seriously hurt."

"I wouldn't!" she whispered.

"You remember you told us about what happened when you were four, in kindergarten, and you tuned into your whole class for six hours? Do you remember how upset you were?"

"I went home and tried to drink the iodine." She flung him a brutal glance. "I remember. But I hear mommy when she's all the way across the city. I hear strangers too, lots of times! I hear Mrs. Lowery, when she's teaching down in the classroom! I hear her! I've heard people on other planets!"

"About the song, Lee—"

"You want to keep me away from the other children because I'm smarter than they are! I know. I've heard you think too—"

"Lee, I want you to tell me more about how you felt about this new song—"

"You think I'll upset them because I'm so smart. You won't let me have any friends!"

"What did you feel about the song, Lee?"

She caught her breath, holding it in, her lids batting, the muscle in the back of her jaw leaping.

"What did you *feel* about the song; did you like it, or did you dislike it?"

She let the air hiss through her lips. "There are three melodic motifs," she began at last. "They appear in de-

scending order of rhythmic intensity. There are more silences in the last melodic line. His music is composed of
silence as much as sound."

"Again, what did you feel? I'm trying to get at your
emotional reaction, don't you see?"

She looked at the window. She looked at Dr. Gross. Then
she turned toward the shelves. "There's a book here, a part
in a book, that says it, I guess, better than I can." She
began working a volume from the half-shelf of Nietzsche.

"What book?"

"Come here." She began to turn the pages. "I'll show
you."

Dr. Gross got up from the desk. She met him beneath
the window.

Dr. Gross took it and, frowning, read the title heading:
"The Birth of Tragedy from the Spirit of Music . . . death
lies only in these dissonant tones—"

Lee's head struck the book from his hands. She had leapt
on him as though he were a piece of furniture and she a
small beast. When her hand was not clutching his belt, shirt
front, lapel, shoulder, it was straining upward. He managed to grab her just as she grabbed the window ledge.

Outside was a nine story drop.

He held her by the ankle as she reeled in the sunlit
frame. He yanked, and she fell into his arms, shrieking,
"Let me die! Oh, please! Let me die!"

They went down on the floor together, he shouting, "No!"
and the little girl crying. Dr. Gross stood up, now panting.

She lay on the green vinyl, curling around the sound of
her own sobs, pulling her hands over the floor to press
her stomach.

"Lee, isn't there *any* way you can understand this? Yes,
you've been exposed to more than any nine-year-old's mind
should be able to bear. But you've got to come to terms
with it, somehow! That isn't the answer, Lee. I wish I
could back it up with something. If you let me help, perhaps I can—"

She shouted, with her cheek pressed to the floor. "But
you can't help! Your thoughts, they're just as clumsy and
imprecise as the others! How can you—*you* help people
who're afraid and confused because their own minds have

formed the wrong associations? How? I don't want to have to stumble around in all your insecurities and fears as well! I'm not a child! I've lived more years and places than any ten of you! Just go away and let me alone—"

Rage, pain, and music.

"Lee—"

"Go away! Please!"

Dr. Gross upset, swung the window closed, locked it, left the room, and locked the door.

Rage, pain . . . below the chaos she was conscious of the infectious melody of *Corona*. Somebody—not her—somebody else was being carried into the hospital, drifting in the painful dark, dreaming over the same sounds. Exhausted, still crying, she let it come.

The man's thoughts, she realized through her exhaustion, to escape pain had taken refuge in the harmonies and cadences of *Corona*. She tried to hide her own mind there. And twisted violently away. There was something terrible there. She tried to pull back, but her mind followed the music down.

The terrible thing was that someone had once told him not to put his knee on the floor.

Fighting, she tried to push it aside to see if what was underneath was less terrible. "Buddy, stop that whining and let your momma alone. I don't feel good. Just get out of here and leave me *alone!*" The bottle shattered on the door jamb by his ear, and he fled. She winced. There couldn't be anything that bad about putting your knee on the floor. And so she gave up and let it swim toward her—

—Suds wound on the dirty water. The water was under his knees. Buddy leaned forward and scrubbed the wire brush across the wet stone. His canvas shoes were already soaked.

"Put your blessed knee on the floor, and I'll get you! Come on, move your . . ." Somebody, not Buddy, got kicked. "And don't let your knee touch that floor! Don't, I say." And got kicked again.

They waddled across the prison lobby, scrubbing. There was a sign over the elevator: Louisiana State Penal Correction Institute, but it was hard to make out because Buddy didn't read very well.

136

"Keep up with 'em, kid. Don't you let 'em get ahead'n you!" Bigfoot yelled. "Just 'cause you little, don't think you got no special privileges." Bigfoot slopped across the stone.

"When they gonna get an automatic scrubber unit in here?" somebody complained. "They got one in the county jail."

"This Institute"—Bigfoot lumbered up the line—"was built in nineteen hundred and forty-seven! We ain't had no escape in ninety-four years. We run it the same today as when it was builded back in nineteen hundred and *forty*-seven. The first time it don't do its job right of keepin' you all inside—then we'll think about running it different. Get on back to work. *Watch* your knee!"

Buddy's thighs were sore, his insteps cramped. The balls of his feet burned and his pants cuffs were sopping.

Bigfoot had taken off his slippers. As he patrolled the scrubbers, he slapped the soles together, first in front of his belly, then behind his heavy buttocks. *Slap* and *slap*. With each *slap*, one foot hit the soapy stone. "Don't bother looking up at me. You look at them stones! But don't let your knee touch the floor."

Once, in the yard latrine, someone had whispered, "Bigfoot? You watch him, kid! Was a preacher, with a revival meeting back in the swamp. Went down to the Emigration Office in town back when they was taking everyone they could get and demanded they make him Pope or something over the colony on Europa they was just setting up. They laughed him out of the office. Sunday, when everyone came to meeting, they found he'd sneaked into the town, busted the man at the Emigration Office over the head, dragged him out to the swamp, and nailed him up to a cross under the meeting tent. He tried to make everybody pray him down. After they prayed for about an hour, and nothing happened, they brought Bigfoot here. He's a trustee now."

Buddy rubbed harder with his wire brush.

"Let's see you rub a little of the devil out'n them stones. And don't let me see your knee touch the—"

Buddy straightened his shoulders. And slipped.

He went over on his backside, grabbed the pail; water

splashed over him, sluiced beneath. Soap stung his eyes. He lay there a moment.

Bare feet slapped toward him. "Come on, kid. Up you go, and back to work."

With eyes tight Buddy pushed himself up.

"You sure are one clums—"

Buddy rolled to his knees.

"I *told* you not to let your knee touch the floor!"

Wet canvas whammed his ear and cheek.

"Didn't I?"

A foot fell in the small of his back and struck him flat. His chin hit the floor and he bit his tongue. Holding him down with his foot, Bigfoot whopped Buddy's head back and forth, first with one shoe, then the other. Buddy, blinded, mouth filled with blood, swam on the wet stone, tried to duck away.

"Now don't let your knees touch the floor *again*. Come on, back to work, all of you." The feet slapped away.

Against the sting, Buddy opened his eyes. The brush lay just in front of his face. Beyond the bristles he saw a pink heel strike in suds.

His action took a long time to form. *Slap* and *slap*. On the third *slap* he gathered his feet, leapt. He landed on Bigfoot's back, pounding with the brush. He hit three times, then he tried to scrub off the side of Bigfoot's face.

The guards finally pulled him off. They took him into a room where there was an iron bed with no mattress and strapped him, ankles, wrist, neck, and stomach, to the frame. He yelled for them to let him up. They said they couldn't because he was still violent. "How'm I gonna eat!" he demanded. "You gonna let me up to eat?"

"Calm down a little. We'll send someone in to feed you."

A few minutes after the dinner bell rang that evening, Bigfoot looked into the room. Ear, cheek, neck, and left shoulder were bandaged. Blood had seeped through at the tip of his clavicle to the size of a quarter. In one hand Bigfoot held a tin plate of rice and fatback, in the other an iron spoon. He came over, sat on the edge of Buddy's bed, and kicked off one canvas shoe. "They told me I should come in and feed you, kid." He kicked off the other one. "You real hungry?"

When they unstrapped Buddy four days later, he couldn't talk. One tooth was badly broken, several others chipped. The roof of his mouth was raw; the prison doctor had to take five stitches in his tongue.

Lee gagged on the taste of iron.

Somewhere in the hospital, Buddy lay in the dark, terrified, his eyes stinging, his head filled with the beating rhythms of *Corona*.

Stop it! she whispered, and tried to wrench herself from the inarticulate terror which Buddy, cast back by pain and the rhythm of a song to a time when he was only twice her age, remembered. Oh, stop it! But no one could hear her, the way she could hear Buddy, her mother, Mrs. Lowery in the schoolroom.

She had to stop the fear.

Perhaps it was the music. Perhaps it was because she had exhausted every other way. Perhaps it was because the only place left to look for a way out was back inside Buddy's mind—

—When he wanted to sneak out of the cell at night to join a card game down in the digs where they played for cigarettes, he would take a piece of chewing gum and the bottle cap from a *Doctor Pepper* and stick it over the bolt in the top of the door. When they closed the doors after free-time, it still fitted into place, but the bolt couldn't slide in—

Lee looked at the locked door of her room. She could get the chewing gum in the afternoon period when they let her walk around her own floor. But the soft drink machine by the elevator only dispensed in cups. Suddenly she sat up and looked at the bottom of her shoe. On the toe and heel were the metal taps that her mother had made the shoe maker put there so they wouldn't wear so fast. She had to stop the fear. If they wouldn't let her do it by killing herself, she'd do it another way. She went to the cot, and began to work the tap loose on the frame.

Buddy lay on his back, afraid. After they had drugged him, they had brought him into the city. He didn't know where he was. But he couldn't see, and he was afraid.

Something fingered his face. He rocked his head to get away from the spoon—

"Shhhh! It's all right . . ."

Light struck one eye. There was still something wrong with the other. He blinked.

"You're all right," she—it was a *she* voice, though he still couldn't make out a face—told him again. "You're not in jail. You're not in the . . . the joint anymore. You're in New York. In a hospital. Something's happened to your eye. That's all."

"My eye . . . ?"

"Don't be afraid any more. Please. Because I can't stand it."

It was a kid's voice. He blinked again, reached up to rub his vision clear.

"Watch out," she said. "You'll get—"

His eye itched and he wanted to scratch it. So he shoved at the voice.

"Hey!"

Something stung him and he clutched at his thumb with his other hand.

"I'm sorry," she said. "I didn't mean to bite your finger. But you'll hurt the bandage. I've pulled the one away from your right eye. There's nothing wrong with that. Just a moment." Something cool swabbed his blurred vision.

It came away.

The cutest little colored girl was kneeling on the edge of the bed with a piece of wet cotton in her hand. The light was nowhere near as bright as it had seemed, just a nightlight glowing over the mirror above the basin. "You've got to stop being so frightened," she whispered. "You've *got* to."

Buddy had spent a good deal of his life doing what people told him, when he wasn't doing the opposite on purpose.

The girl sat back on her heels. "That's better."

He pushed himself up in the bed. There were no straps. Sheets hissed over his knees. He looked at his chest. Blue pajamas: the buttons were in the wrong holes by one. He reached down to fix them, and his fingers closed on air.

"You've only got one eye working so there's no parallax for depth perception."

"Huh?" He looked up again.

She wore shorts and a red and white polo shirt.

He frowned, "Who are you?"

"Dianne Lee Morris," she said. "And you're—" Then she frowned too. She scrambled from the bed, took the mirror from over the basin and brought it back to the bed. Now who are you?"

He reached up to touch with grease crested nails the bandage that sloped over his left eye. Short, yellow hair lapped the gauze. His forefinger went on to the familiar scar through the tow hedge of his right eyebrow.

"Who are you?"

"Buddy Magowan."

"Where do you live?"

"St. Gab—" He stopped. "A hun' ni'tee' stree' 'tween Se'on and Thir' A'nue."

"Say it again."

"A hundred an' nineteenth street between Second an' Third Avenue." The consonants his nightschool teacher at P.S. 125 had laboriously inserted into his speech this past year returned.

"Good. And you work?"

"Out at Kennedy. Service assistant."

"And there's nothing to be afraid of."

He shook his head. "Naw," and grinned. His broken tooth reflected in the mirror. "Naw. I was just having a bad . . . dream."

She put the mirror back. As she turned back, suddenly she closed her eyes and sighed.

"What'sa matter?"

She opened them again. "It's stopped. I can't hear inside your head any more. It's been going on all day."

"Huh? What do you mean?"

"Maybe you read about me in the magazine. There was a big article about me in *New Times* a couple of years ago. I'm in the hospital too. Over on the other side, in the psychiatric division. Did you read the article?"

"Didn't do much magazine reading back then. Don't do too much now either. What's they write about?"

"I can hear and see what other people are thinking. I'm one of the three they're studying. I do it best of all of them. But it only comes in spurts. The other one, Eddy, is an idiot. I met him when we were getting all the tests. He's older than you and even dumber. Then there's Mrs. Lowery. She doesn't hear. She just sees. And sometimes she can make other people hear her. She works in the school here at the hospital. She can come and go as she pleases. But I have to stay locked up."

Buddy squinted. "You can hear what's in my head?"

"Not now. But I could. And it was . . ." Her lip began to quiver; her brown eyes brightened. ". . . I mean, when that man tried to . . . with the . . ." And overflowed. She put her fingers on her chin and twisted. ". . . when he . . . cutting in your . . ."

Buddy saw her tears, wondered at them. "Aw, honey—" he said, reached to take her shoulder.

Her face struck his chest and she clutched his pajama jacket. "It hurt *so* much!"

Her grief at his agony shook her.

"I had to stop you from hurting! Yours was just a dream, so I could sneak out of my room, get down here, and wake you up. But the others, the girl in the fire, or the man in the flooded mine . . . those weren't dreams! I couldn't do anything about them. I couldn't stop the hurting there. I couldn't stop it at all, Buddy. I wanted to. But one was in Australia and the other in Costa Rica!" She sobbed against his chest. "And one was on Mars! And I couldn't get to Mars. I couldn't!"

"It's all right," he whispered, uncomprehending, and rubbed her rough hair. Then, as she shook in his arms, understanding swelled. "You came . . . down here to wake me up?" he asked.

She nodded against his pajama jacket.

"Why?"

She shrugged against his belly. "I . . . I don't . . . maybe the music."

After a moment he asked. "Is this the first time you ever done something about what you heard?"

"It's not the first time I ever tried. But it's the first time it ever . . . worked."

"Then why did you try again?"

"Because . . ." She was stiller now. ". . . I hoped maybe it would hurt less if I could get—through." He felt her jaw moving as she spoke. "It does." Something in her face began to quiver. "It does hurt less." He put his hand on her hand, and she took his thumb.

"You knew I was . . . was awful scared?"

She nodded. "I knew, so I was scared just the same."

Buddy remembered the dream. The back of his neck grew cold, and the flesh under his thighs began to tingle. He remembered the reality behind the dream—and held her more tightly and pressed his cheek to her hair. "Thank you." He couldn't say it any other way, but it didn't seem enough. So he said it again more slowly. "*Thank* you."

A little later she pushed away, and he watched her sniffling face with depthless vision.

"Do you like the song?"

He blinked. And realized the insistent music still worked through his head. "You can—hear what I'm thinking again?"

"No. But you were thinking about it before. I just wanted to find out."

Buddy thought awhile. "Yeah." He cocked his head. "Yeah. I like it a lot. It makes me feel . . . good."

She hesitated, then let out: "Me *too!* I think it's beautiful. I think Faust's music is so," and she whispered the next word as though it might offend, "*alive!* But with life the way it should be. Not without pain, but with pain contained, ordered, given form and meaning, so that it's almost all right again. Don't you feel that way?"

"I . . . don't know. I *like* it . . ."

"I suppose," Lee said a little sadly, "people like things for different reasons."

"You like it a lot." He looked down and tried to understand how she liked it. And failed. Tears had darkened his pajamas. Not wanting her to cry again, he grinned when he looked up. "You know, I almost saw him this morning."

"Faust? You mean you saw Bryan Faust?"

He nodded. "Almost. I'm on the service crew out at

Kennedy. We were working on his liner when . . ." He pointed to his eye.

"*His* ship? *You* were?" The wonder in her voice was perfectly childish, and enchanting.

"I'll probably see him when he leaves," Buddy boasted. "I can get in where they won't let anybody else go. Except people who work at the port."

"I'd give—" she remembered to take a breath, "—anything to see him. Just anything in the world!"

"There was a hell of a crowd out there this morning. They almost broke through the police. But I could've just walked up and stood at the bottom of the ramp when he came down. If I'd thought about it."

Her hands made little fists on the edge of the bed as she gazed at him.

"Course I'll probably see him when he goes." This time he found his buttons and began to put them into the proper holes.

"I wish I could see him too!"

"I suppose Bim—he's foreman of the service crew—he'd let us through the gate, if I said you were my sister." He looked back up at her brown face. "Well, my cousin."

"Would you take me? Would you really take me?"

"Sure." Buddy reached out to tweak her nose, missed. "You did something for me. I don't see why not, if they'd let you leave—"

"Mrs. Lowery!" Lee whispered and stepped back from the bed.

"—the hospital. Huh?"

"They know I'm gone! Mrs. Lowery is calling for me. She says she's seen me, and Dr. Gross is on his way. They want to take me back to my room." She ran to the door.

"Lee, there you are! Are you all right?" In the doorway Dr. Gross grabbed her arm as she tried to twist away.

"Lemme *go!*"

"Hey!" bellowed Buddy. "What are you doin' with that little girl!" Suddenly he stood up in the middle of the bed, shedding sheets.

Dr. Gross's eyes widened. "I'm taking her back to her room. She's a patient in the hospital. She should be in another wing."

"She wanna go?" Buddy demanded, swaying over the blankets.

"She's very disturbed," Dr. Gross countered at Buddy, towering on the bed. "We're trying to help her, don't you understand? I don't know who you are, but we're trying to keep her alive. She has to go back!"

Lee shook her head against the doctor's hip. "Oh, Buddy . . ."

He leapt over the foot of the bed, swinging. Or at any rate, he swung once. He missed widely because of the parallax. Also because he pulled the punch in, half completed, to make it seem a floundering gesture. He was not in the Louisiana State Penal Correction Institute: the realization had come the way one only realizes the tune playing in the back of the mind when it stops. "Wait!" Buddy said.

Outside the door the doctor was saying, "Mrs. Lowery, take Lee back up to her room. The night nurse knows the medication she should have."

"Yes, doctor."

"Wait!" Buddy called. "Please!"

"Excuse me," Dr. Gross said, stepping back through the door. Without Lee. "But we have to get her upstairs under a sedative, immediately. Believe me, I'm sorry for this inconvenience."

Buddy sat down on the bed and twisted his face. "What's . . . the matter with her?"

Dr. Gross was silent a moment. "I suppose I do have to give you an explanation. That's difficult, because I don't know exactly. Of the three proven telepaths that have been discovered since a concerted effort has been made to study them, Lee is the most powerful. She's a brilliant, incredibly creative child. But her mind has suffered so much trauma —from all the lives telepathy exposes her to—she's become hopelessly suicidal. We're trying to help her. But if she's left alone for any length of time, sometimes weeks, sometimes hours, she'll try to kill herself."

"Then when's she gonna be better?"

Dr. Gross put his hands in his pockets and looked at his sandals. "I'm afraid to cure someone of a mental disturbance, the first thing you have to do is isolate them from the trauma. With Lee that's impossible. We don't even know which part of the brain controls the telepathy, so we couldn't even try lobotomy. We haven't found a drug that affects it yet." He shrugged. "I wish we could help her. But when I'm being objective, I can't see her ever getting better. She'll be like this the rest of her life. The quicker you can forget about her, the less likely you are to hurt her. Goodnight. Again, I'm very sorry this had to happen."

"G'night." Buddy sat in his bed a little while. Finally he turned off the light and lay down. He had to masturbate three times before he finally fell asleep. In the morning, though, he still had not forgotten the dark little girl who had come to him and awakened—so much in him.

The doctors were very upset about the bandage and talked of sympathetic opthalmia. They searched his left cornea for any last bits of metal dust. They kept him in the hospital three more days, adjusting the pressure between his vitreous and aqueous humors to prevent his till now undiscovered tendency toward glaucoma. They told him that the thing that had occasionally blurred the vision in his left eye was a vitreous floater and not to worry about it. Stay home at least two weeks, they said. And wear your eyepatch until two days before you go back to work. They gave him a hassle with his workmen's compensation papers too. But he got it straightened out—he'd filled in a date wrong. He never saw the little girl again.

And the radios and jukeboxes and scopitones in New York and Buenos Aires, Paris and Istanbul, in Melbourne and Bangkok, played the music of Bryan Faust.

The day Faust was supposed to leave Earth for Venus, Buddy went back to the spaceport. It was three days before he was supposed to report to work, and he still wore the flesh colored eyepatch.

"Jesus," he said to Bim as they leaned at the railing of the observation deck on the roof of the hangar, "just look at all them people."

Bim spat down at the hot macadam. The liner stood on the take-off pad under the August sun.

146

"He's going to sing before he goes," Bim said. "I hope they don't have a riot."

"Sing?"

"See that wooden platform out there and all them loud-speakers? With all those kids, I sure hope they don't have a riot."

"Bim, can I get down onto the field, up near the platform?"

"What for?"

"So I can see him up real close."

"You were the one talking about all the people."

Buddy, holding the rail, worked his thumb on the brass. The muscles in his forearm rolled beneath the tattoo: *To Mars I Would Go for Dolores-jo,* inscribed on Saturn's rings. "But I got to!"

"I don't see why the hell—"

"There's this little nigger girl, Bim—"

"Huh?"

"*Bim!*"

"Okay. Okay. Get into a coverall and go down with the clocker crew. You'll be right up with the reporters. But don't tell anybody I sent you. You know how many people want to get up there. Why you want to get so close for anyway?"

"For a . . ." He turned in the doorway. "For a friend." He ran down the stairs to the lockers.

Bryan Faust walked across the platform to the microphones. Comets soared over his shoulders and disappeared under his arms. Suns novaed on his chest. Meteors flashed around his elbows. Shirts of polarized cloth with incandescent, shifting designs were now being called *Fausts.* Others flashed in the crowd. He pushed back his hair, grinned, and behind the police-block hundreds of children screamed. He laughed into the microphone; they quieted. Behind him a bank of electronic instruments glittered. The controls were in the many jeweled rings hanging bright and heavy on his fingers. He raised his hands, flicked his thumbs across the gems, and the instruments, programmed to respond, began the cascading introduction to *Corona.*

Bryan Faust sang. Across Kennedy, thousands—Buddy among them—heard.

On her cot in the hospital, Lee listened. "Thank you, Buddy," she whispered. "Thank you." And felt a little less like dying.

The life of Fritz Leiber has been every bit as varied and dramatic as his fiction: Born Chicago 1910; son of Fritz and Virginia (Bronson) Leiber, Shakespearean actors. Educated University of Chicago, Ph.D. in Psychology; actor in his father's Shakespearean company, Episcopalian lay-reader, dramatics teacher, editor, full-time writer since 1956. His last book was the first authorized Tarzan novel written by anyone except Edgar Rice Burroughs, which information will not in any way prepare you for the story below, but will illustrate the variety of Leiber's work. It's a long way indeed from the jungle of South America to the living room of Gottfried Helmuth Adler, the scene of this powerful psychology drama.

THE INNER CIRCLES

by Fritz Leiber

After the supper dishes were done there was a general movement from the Adler kitchen to the Adler living room.

It was led by Gottfried Helmuth Adler, commonly known as Gott. He was thinking how they should be coming from a dining room, yes, with colored maids, not from a kitchen. In a large brandy snifter he was carrying what had been left in the shaker from the martinis, a colorless elixir weakened by melted ice yet somewhat stronger than his wife was supposed to know. This monster drink was a regular part of Gott's carefully thought-out program for getting safely through the end of the day.

"After the seventeenth hour of creation God got sneaky," Gott Adler once put it to himself.

He sat down in his leather-upholstered easy chair, flipped

149

open Plutarch's *Lives* left-handed, glanced down through the lower halves of his executive bifocals at the paragraph in the biography of Caesar he'd been reading before dinner, then, without moving his head, looked through the upper half back toward the kitchen

After Gott came Jane Adler, his wife. She sat down at her drawing table, where pad, pencils, knife, art gum, distemper paints, water, brushes, and rags were laid out neatly.

Then came little Heinie Adler, wearing a spaceman's transparent helmet with a large hole in the top for ventilation. He went and stood beside this arrangement of objects: first a long wooden box about knee-high with a smaller box on top and propped against the latter a toy control panel of blue and silver plastic, on which only one lever moved at all; next, facing the panel, a child's wooden chair; then back of the chair another long wooden box lined up with the first.

"Good-by Mama, good-by Papa," Heinie called. "I'm going to take a trip in my spaceship."

"Be back in time for bed," his mother said.

"Hot jets!" murmured his father.

Heinie got in, touched the control panel twice, and then sat motionless in the little wooden chair, looking straight ahead.

A fourth person came into the living room from the kitchen —the Man in the Black Flannel Suit. He moved with the sick jerkiness and had the slack putty-gray features of a figure of the imagination that hasn't been fully developed. (There was a fifth person in the house, but even Gott didn't know about him yet.)

The Man in the Black Flannel Suit made a stiff gesture at Gott and gaped his mouth to talk to him, but the latter silently writhed his lips in a "Not yet, you fool!" and nodded curtly toward the sofa opposite his easy chair.

"Gott," Jane said, hovering a pencil over the pad, "you've lately taken to acting as if you were talking to someone who isn't there."

"I have, my dear?" her husband replied with a smile as he turned a page, but not lifting his face from his book. "Well, talking to oneself is the sovereign guard against madness."

"I thought it worked the other way," Jane said.

"No," Gott informed her.

Jane wondered what she should draw and saw she had very faintly sketched on a small scale the outlines of a child, done in sticks-and-blobs like Paul Klee or kindergarten art. She could do another "Children's Clubhouse," she supposed, but where should she put it this time?

The old electric clock with brass fittings that stood on the mantel began to wheeze shrilly, "Mystery, mystery, mystery, mystery." It struck Jane as a good omen for her picture. She smiled.

Gott took a slow pull from his goblet and felt the scentless vodka bite just enough and his skin shiver and the room waver pleasantly for a moment with shadows chasing across it. Then he swung the pupils of his eyes upward and looked across at the Man in the Black Flannel Suit, noting with approval that he was sitting rigidly on the sofa. Gott conducted his side of the following conversation without making a sound or parting his lips more than a quarter of an inch, just flaring his nostrils from time to time.

BLACK FLANNEL: Now if I may have your attention for a space, Mr. Adler—

GOTT: Speak when you're spoken to! Remember, I created you.

BLACK FLANNEL: I respect your belief. Have you been getting any messages?

GOTT: The number 6669 turned up three times today in orders and estimates. I received an airmail advertisement beginning "Are you ready for big success?" though the rest of the ad didn't signify. As I opened the envelope the minute hand of my desk clock was pointing at the faceless statue of Mercury on the Commerce Building. When I was leaving the office my secretary droned at me, "A representative of the Inner Circle will call on you tonight," though when I questioned her, she claimed that she'd said, "Was the letter to Innes-Burkel and Company all right?" Because she is aware of my deafness, I could hardly challenge her. In any case she sounded sincere. If those were messages from the Inner Circle, I received them. But seriously I doubt the existence of that clandestine organization. Other explanations seem to me more likely—for instance, that I am developing a psychosis. I do not believe in the Inner Circle.

BLACK FLANNEL (*smiling shrewdly—his features have grown tightly handsome though his complexion is still putty gray*): Psychosis is for weak minds. Look, Mr. Adler, you believe in upper-echelon control groups in unions and business and fraternal organizations. You know the workings of big companies. You are familiar with industrial and political espionage. You are not wholly unacquainted with the secret fellowships of munitions manufacturers, financiers, dope addicts and procurers and pornography connoisseurs and the brotherhoods and sisterhoods of sexual deviates and enthusiasts. Why do you boggle at the Inner Circle?

GOTT (*coolly*): I do not wholly believe in all of those other organizations. And the Inner Circle still seems to me more of a wish-dream than the rest. Besides, you may want me to believe in the Inner Circle in order at a later date to convict me of insanity.

BLACK FLANNEL (*drawing a black briefcase from behind his legs and unzipping it on his knees*): Then you do not wish to hear about the Inner Circle?

GOTT (*inscrutably*): I will listen for the present. Hush!

Heinie was calling out excitedly, "I'm in the stars, Papa! They're so close they burn!" He said nothing more and continued to stare straight ahead.

"Don't touch them," Jane warned without looking around. Her pencil made a few faint five-pointed stars. The Children's Clubhouse would be on a boundary of space, she decided—put it in a tree on the edge of the Old Ravine. She said, "Gott, what do you suppose Heinie sees out there besides stars?"

"Bug-eyed angels, probably," her husband answered, smiling again but still not taking his head out of his book.

BLACK FLANNEL (*consulting a sheet of crackling black paper he has slipped from his briefcase, though as far as Gott can see there is no printing, typing, writing, or symbols of any sort in any color ink on the black bond*): The Inner Circle is the world's secret elite, operating behind and above all figureheads, workhorses, wealthy dolts, and those talented exhibitionists we name genius. The Inner Circle has existed *sub rose niger* for thousands of years. It controls human life. It is the repository of all great abilities, and the key to all ultimate delights.

GOTT (*tolerantly*): You make it sound plausible enough. Everyone half believes in such a cryptic power gang, going back to Sumeria.

BLACK FLANNEL: The membership is small and very select. As you are aware, I am a kind of talent scout for the group. Qualifications for admission (*he slips a second sheet of black bond from his briefcase*) include a proven great skill in achieving and wielding power over men and women, an amoral zest for all of life, a seasoned blend of ruthlessness and reliability, plus wide knowledge and lightning wit.

GOTT (*contemptuously*): Is that all?

BLACK FLANNEL (*flatly*): Yes. Initiation is binding for life—and for the afterlife: one of our mottos is Ferdinand's dying cry in *The Duchess of Malfi*. "I will vault credit and affect high pleasures after death." The penalty for revealing organizational secrets is not death alone but extinction—all memory of the person is erased from public and private history; his name is removed from records; all knowledge of and feeling for him is deleted from the minds of his wives, mistresses, and children: it is as if he had never existed. That, by the by, is a good example of the powers of the Inner Circle. It may interest you to know, Mr. Adler, that as a result of the retaliatory activities of the Inner Circle, the names of three British kings have been expunged from history. Those who have suffered a like fate include two popes, seven movie stars, a brilliant Flemish artist superior to Rembrandt . . . (*As he spins out an apparently interminable listing, the Fifth Person creeps in on hands and knees from the kitchen. Gott cannot see him at first, as the sofa is between Gott's chair and the kitchen door. The Fifth Person is the Black Jester, who looks rather like a caricature of Gott but has the same putty complexion as the Man in the Black Flannel Suit. The Black Jester wears skin-tight clothing of that color, silver-embroidered boots and gloves, and a black hood edged with silver bells that do not tinkle. He carries a scepter topped with a small death's-head that wears a black hood like his own edged with tinier silver bells, soundless as the larger ones.*)

THE BLACK JESTER (*suddenly rearing up like a cobra from behind the sofa and speaking to the Man in the Black*

Flannel Suit over the latter's shoulder): Ho! So you're still teasing his rickety hopes with that shit about the Inner Circle? Good sport, brother!—you play your fish skillfully.

GOTT (*immensely startled, but controlling himself with some courage*): Who are you? How dare you bring your brabblement into my court?

THE BLACK JESTER: Listen to the old cock crow innocent! As if he didn't know he'd himself created both of us, time and again, to stave off boredom, madness, or suicide.

GOTT (*firmly*): I never created *you*.

THE BLACK JESTER: Oh, yes, you did, old cock. Truly your mind has never birthed anything but twins—for every good, a bad; for every breath, a fart; and for every white, a black.

GOTT (*flares his nostrils and glares a death-spell which hums toward the newcomer like a lazy invisible bee*).

THE BLACK JESTER (*pales and staggers backward as the death-spell strikes, but shakes it off with an effort and glares back murderously at Gott*): Old cockfather, I'm beginning to hate you at last.

Just then the refrigerator motor went on in the kitchen, and its loud rapid rocking sound seemed to Jane to be a voice saying, "Watch your children, they're in danger. Watch your children, they're in danger."

"I'm no ladybug," Jane retorted tartly in her thoughts, irked at the worrisome interruption now that her pencil was rapidly developing the outlines of the Clubhouse in the Tree with the moon risen across the ravine between clouds in the late afternoon sky. Nevertheless she looked at Heinie. He hadn't moved. She could see how the plastic helmet was open at neck and top, but it made her think of suffocation just the same.

"Heinie, are you still in the stars?" she asked.

"No, now I'm landing on a moon," he called back. "Don't talk to me, Mama, I've got to watch the road."

Jane at once wanted to imagine what roads in space might look like, but the refrigerator motor had said "children," not "child," and she knew that the language of machinery is studded with tropes. She looked at Gott. He was curled comfortably over his book, and as she watched, he turned

154

a page and touched his lips to the martini water. Nevertheless, she decided to test him.

"Gott, do you think this family is getting too ingrown?" she said. "We used to have more people around."

"Oh, I think we have quite a few as it is," he replied, looking up at the empty sofa, beyond it, and then around at her expectantly, as if ready to join in any conversation she cared to start. But she simply smiled at him and returned relieved to her thoughts and her picture. He smiled back and bowed his head again to his book.

BLACK FLANNEL (*ignoring the Black Jester*): My chief purpose in coming here tonight, Mr. Adler, is to inform you that the Inner Circle has begun a serious study of your qualifications for membership.

THE BLACK JESTER: At *his* age? After *his* failures? Now we curtsy forward toward the Big Lie!

BLACK FLANNEL (*in a pained voice*): Really! (*Then once more to Gott*) Point One: you have gained for yourself the reputation of a man of strong patriotism, deep company loyalty, and realistic self-interest, sternly contemptuous of all youthful idealism and rebelliousness. Point Two: you have cultivated constructive hatreds in your business life, deliberately knifing colleagues when you could, but allying yourself to those on the rise. Point Three and most important: you have gone some distance toward creating the master illusion of a man who has secret sources of information, secret new techniques for thinking more swiftly and acting more decisively than others, secret superior connections and contacts—in short, a dark new strength which all others envy even as they cringe from it.

THE BLACK JESTER (*in a kind of counterpoint as he advances around the sofa*): But he's come down in the world since he lost his big job. National Motors was at least a step in the right direction, but Hagbolt-Vincent has no company planes, no company apartments, no company shooting lodges, no company call girls! Besides, he drinks too much. The Inner Circle is not for drunks on the downgrade.

BLACK FLANNEL: Please! You're spoiling things.

THE BLACK JESTER: *He's* spoiled. (*Closing in on Gott*) Just look at him now. Eyes that need crutches for near and far. Ears that mis-hear the simplest remark.

GOTT: Keep off me, I tell you.

THE BLACK JESTER (*ignoring the warning*): Fat belly, flaccid sex, swollen ankles. And a mouthful of stinking cavities!—did you know he hasn't dared visit his dentist for five years? Here, open up and show them! (*Thrusts black-gloved hand toward Gott's face.*)

Gott, provoked beyond endurance, snarled aloud, "Keep off, damn you!" and shot out the heavy book in his left hand and snapped it shut on the Black Jester's nose. Both black figures collapsed instantly.

Jane lifted her pencil a foot from the pad, turned quickly, and demanded, "My God, Gott, what was that?"

"Only a winter fly, my dear," he told her soothingly. "One of the fat ones that hide in December and breed all the black clouds of spring." He found his place in Plutarch and dipped his face close to study both pages and the trough between them. He looked around slyly at Jane and said, "I didn't squush her."

The chair in the spaceship rutched. Jane asked, "What is it, Heinie?"

"A meteor exploded, Mama. I'm all right. I'm out in space again, in the middle of the road."

Jane was impressed by the time it had taken the sound of Gott's book clapping shut to reach the spaceship. She began lightly to sketch blob-children in swings hanging from high limbs in the Tree, swinging far out over the ravine into the stars.

Gott took a pull of martini water, but he felt lonely and impotent. He peeped over the edge of his Plutarch at the darkness below the sofa and grinned with new hope as he saw the huge flat blob of black putty the Jester and Flannel had collapsed into. *I'm on a black kick,* he thought, *why black?*—choosing to forget that he had first started to sculpt figures of the imagination from the star-specked blackness that pulsed under his eyelids while he lay in the dark abed: tiny black heads like wrinkled peas on which any three points of light made two eyes and a mouth. He'd come a long way since then. Now with strong rays from his eyes he rolled all the black putty he could see into a woman-long bolster and hoisted it onto the sofa. The bolster helped with blind sensuous hitching movements, especially where it bent at the middle. When it was lying full length on the sofa he began with cruel strength to sculpt it into the figure of a high-breasted exaggeratedly sexual girl.

Jane found she'd sketched some flies into the picture, buzzing around the swingers. She rubbed them out and put in more stars instead. But there would be flies in the ravine, she told herself, because people dumped garbage down the other side; so she drew one large fly in the lower left-hand corner of the picture. He could be the observer. She said to herself firmly, *No black clouds of spring in this picture* and changed them to hints of Roads in Space.

Gott finished the Black Girl with two twisting tweaks to point her nipples. Her waist was barely thick enough not to suggest an actual wasp or a giant amazon ant. Then he gulped martini water and leaned forward just a little and silently but very strongly blew the breath of life into her across the eight feet of living-room air between them.

The phrase "black clouds of spring" made Jane think of dead hopes and drowned talents. She said out loud, "I wish you'd start writing in the evenings again, Gott. Then I wouldn't feel so guilty."

"These days, my dear, I'm just a dull businessman, happy to relax in the heart of his family. There's not an atom of art in me," Gott informed her with quiet conviction, watching the Black Girl quiver and writhe as the creativity-wind from his lips hit her. With a sharp twinge of fear it occurred to him that the edges of the wind might leak over to Jane and Heinie, distorting them like heat shimmers, changing them nastily. Heinie especially was sitting so still in his little chair light-years away. Gott wanted to call to him, but he couldn't think of the right bit of spaceman's lingo.

THE BLACK GIRL (*sitting up and dropping her hand coquettishly to her crotch*): He-he! Now ain't this something, Mr. Adler! First time you've ever had me in your home.

GOTT (*eyeing her savagely over Plutarch*): Shut up!

THE BLACK GIRL (*unperturbed*): Before this it was only when you were away on trips or, once or twice lately, at the office.

GOTT (*flaring his nostrils*): Shut up, I say! You're less than dirt.

THE BLACK GIRL (*smirking*): But I'm interesting dirt,

ain't I? You want we should do it in front of her? I could come over and flow inside your clothes and—

GOTT: One more word and I uncreate you! I'll tear you apart like a boiled crow. I'll squunch you back to putty.

THE BLACK GIRL (*still serene, preening her nakedness*): Yes, and you'll enjoy every red-hot second of it, won't you?

Affronted beyond bearing, Gott sent chopping rays at her over the Plutarch parapet, but at that instant a black figure, thin as a spider, shot up behind the sofa and reaching over the Black Girl's shoulder brushed aside the chopping rays with one flick of a whiplike arm. Grown from the black putty Gott had overlooked under the sofa, the figure was that of an old conjure woman, stick-thin with limbs like wires and breasts like dangling ropes, face that was a pack of spearheads with black ostrich plumes a-quiver above it.

THE BLACK CRONE (*in a whistling voice like a hungry wind*): Injure one of the girls, Mister Adler, and I'll castrate you, I'll shrivel you with spells. You'll never be able to call them up again, no matter how far a trip you go on, or even pleasure your wife.

GOTT (*frightened, but not showing it*): Keep your arms and legs on, Mother. Flossie and I were only teasing each other. Vicious play is a specialty of your house, isn't it?

With a deep groaning cry the furnace fan switched on in the basement and began to say over and over again in a low rapid rumble, "Oh, my God, my God, my God. Demons, demons, demons, demons." Jane heard the warning very clearly, but she didn't want to lose the glow of her feelings. She asked, "Are you all right out there in space, Heinie?" and thought he nodded "Yes." She began to color the Clubhouse in the Tree—blue roof, red walls, a little like Chagall.

THE BLACK CRONE (*continuing a tirade*): Understand this, Mr. Adler, you don't own us, we own you. Because you gotta have the girls to live, you're the girls' slave.

THE BLACK GIRL: He-he! Shall I call Susie and Belle? They've never been here either, and they'd enjoy this.

THE BLACK CRONE: Later, if he's humble. You understand me, Slave? If I tell you have your wife cook dinner for the girls or wash their feet or watch you snuggle with them, then you gotta do it. And your boy gotta run our errands. Come over here now and sit by Flossie while I brand you with dry ice.

Gott quaked, for the Crone's arms were lengthening toward him like snakes, and he began to sweat, and he murmured, "God in Heaven," and the smell of fear went out of him to the walls—millions of stinking molecules.

A cold wind blew over the fence of Heinie's space road and the stars wavered and then fled before it like diamond leaves.

Jane caught the murmur and the fear-whiff too, but she was coloring the Clubhouse windows a warm rich yellow; so what she said in a rather loud, rapt, happy voice was: "I think Heaven is like a children's clubhouse. The only people there are the ones you remember from childhood—either because you were in childhood with them or they told you about their childhood honestly. The *real* people."

At the word *real* the Black Crone and the Black Girl strangled and began to bend and melt like a thin candle and a thicker one over a roaring fire.

Heinie turned his spaceship around and began to drive it bravely homeward through the unspeckled dark, following the ghostly white line that marked the center of the road. He thought of himself as the cat they'd had. Papa had told him stories of the cat coming back—from downtown, from Pittsburgh, from Los Angeles, from the moon. Cats could do that. He was the cat coming back.

Jane put down her brush and took up her pencil once more. She'd noticed that the two children swinging out farthest weren't attached yet to their swings. She started to hook them up, then hesitated. Wasn't it all right for some of the children to go sailing out to the stars? Wouldn't it be nice for some evening world—maybe the late-afternoon moon —to have a shower of babies? She wished a plane would crawl over the roof of the house and drone out an answer to her question. She didn't like to have to do all the wondering by herself. It made her feel guilty.

"Gott," she said, "why don't you at least finish the last story you were writing? The one about the Elephants' Graveyard." Then she wished she hadn't mentioned it, because it was an idea that had scared Heinie.

"Some day," her husband murmured, Jane thought.

Gott felt weak with relief, though he was forgetting why. Balancing his head carefully over his book, he drained the next to the last of the martini water. It always got stronger toward the bottom. He looked at the page through the lower halves of his executive bifocals and for a moment the word "Caesar" came up in letters an inch high, each jet serif showing its tatters and the white paper its ridgy fibers. Then, still never moving his head, he looked through the upper halves and saw the long thick blob of dull black putty on the wavering blue couch and automatically gathered the putty together and with thumb-and-palm rays swiftly shaped the Old Philosopher in the Black Toga, always an easy figure to sculpt since he was never finished, but rough-hewn in the style of Rodin or Daumier. It was always good to finish up an evening with the Old Philosopher.

The white line in space tried to fade. Heinie steered his ship closer to it. He remembered that in spite of Papa's stories, the cat had never come back.

Jane held her pencil poised over the detached children swinging out from the Clubhouse. One of them had a leg kicked over the moon.

THE PHILOSOPHER (*adjusting his craggy toga and yawning*): The topic for tonight's symposium is that vast container of all, the Void.

GOTT (*condescendingly*): The Void? That's interesting. Lately I've wished to merge with it. Life wearies me.

A smiling dull black skull, as crudely shaped as the Philosopher, looked over the latter's shoulder and then rose higher on a rickety black bone framework.

DEATH (*quietly, to Gott*): Really?

GOTT (*greatly shaken, but keeping up a front*): I *am* on a black kick tonight. Can't even do a white skeleton. Disintegrate, you two. You bore me almost as much as life.

DEATH: Really? If you did not cling to life like a limpet, you would have crashed your car, to give your wife and son the insurance, when National Motors fired you. You planned to do that. Remember?

GOTT (*with hysterical coolness*): Maybe I should have cast you in brass or aluminum. Then you'd at least have brightened things up. But it's too late now. Disintegrate quickly and don't leave any scraps around.

DEATH: Much too late. Yes, you planned to crash your car and doubly indemnify your dear ones. You had the spot picked, but your courage failed you.

GOTT (*blustering*): I'll have you know I am not only Gottfried but also Helmuth—Hell's Courage Adler!

THE PHILOSOPHER (*confused but trying to keep in the conversation*): A most swashbuckling sobriquet.

DEATH: Hell's courage failed you on the edge of the ravine. (*Pointing at Gott a three-fingered thumbless hand like a black winter branch*) Do you wish to die now?

GOTT (*blacking out visually*): Cowards die many times. (*Draining the last of the martini water in absolute darkness*) The valiant taste death once. Caesar.

DEATH (*a voice in darkness*): Coward. Yet you summoned me—and even though you fashioned me poorly, I am indeed Death—and there are others besides yourself take long trips. Even longer ones. Trips in the Void.

THE PHILOSOPHER (*another voice*): Ah, yes, the Void. Imprimis—

DEATH: Silence.

In the great obedient silence Gott heard the unhurried click of Death's feet as he stepped from behind the sofa across the bare floor toward Heinie's spaceship. Gott reached up in the dark and clung to his mind.

Jane heard the slow clicks too. They were the kitchen clock ticking out, "Now. Now. Now. Now. Now."

Suddenly Heinie called out, "The line's gone. Papa, Mama, I'm lost."

Jane said sharply, "No, you're not, Heinie. Come out of space at once."

"I'm not in space now. I'm in the Cats' Graveyard."

Jane told herself it was insane to feel suddenly so frightened. "Come back from wherever you are, Heinie," she said calmly. "It's time for bed."

"I'm lost, Papa," Heinie cried. "I can't hear Mama any more."

"Listen to your mother, Son," Gott said thickly, groping in the blackness for other words.

"All the Mamas and Papas in the world are dying," Heinie wailed.

Then the words came to Gott, and when he spoke his voice flowed. Are your atomic generators turning over, Heinie? Is your space-warp lever free?"

"Yes, Papa, but the line's gone."

"Forget it. I've got a fix on you through subspace and I'll coach you home. Swing her two units to the right and three up. Fire when I give the signal. Are you ready?"

"Yes, Papa."

"Roger. Three, two, one, fire and away! Dodge that comet! Swing left around that planet! Never mind the big dust cloud! Home on the third beacon. Now! Now! Now!"

Gott had dropped his Plutarch and come lurching blindly across the room, and as he uttered the last *Now!* the darkness cleared, and he caught Heinie up from his spacechair and staggered with him against Jane and steadied himself there without upsetting her paints, and she accused him laughingly, "You beefed up the martini water again," and Heinie pulled off his helmet and crowed, "Make a big hug," and they clung to each other and looked down at the half-colored picture where a children's clubhouse sat in a tree over a deep ravine and blob children swung out from it against the cool pearly moon and the winding roads in space and the next to the last child hooked onto his swing with one hand and with the other caught the last child of all, while from the picture's lower left-hand corner a fat, black fly looked on enviously.

Searching with his eyes as the room swung toward equilibrium, Gottfried Helmuth Adler saw Death peering at him through the crack between the hinges of the open kitchen door.

Laboriously, half passing out again, Gott sneered his face at him.

The future vitality of science fiction is almost entirely dependent upon the talented young writers who are using the genre, among them Thomas M. Disch, whose work has generated an intense reaction on both sides of the critical fence. Here, Mr. Disch offers an uncommonly strong (and grim) picture of youth in the 21st Century.

PROBLEMS OF CREATIVENESS

by Thomas M. Disch

There was a dull ache, a kind of hollowness, in the general area of his liver, the seat of the intelligence according to the *Psychology* of Aristotle—a feeling that there was someone inside his chest blowing up a balloon, or that the balloon was his body. Sometimes he could ignore it, but sometimes he could not ignore it. It was like a swollen gum that he must incessantly probe with his tongue or finger. Perhaps it was filled with pus. It was like being sick, but it was different too. His legs ached from sitting.

Professor Offengeld was telling them about Dante. Dante was born in 1265. 1265, he wrote in his notebook.

He might have felt the same way even if it weren't for Milly's coldness, but that made it worse. Milly was his girl, and they were in love, but for the last three nights she had been putting him off, telling him he should study or some other dumb excuse.

Professor Offengeld made a joke, and the other students in the auditorium laughed. Birdie ostentatiously stretched his legs out into the aisle and yawned.

"The hell that Dante describes is the hell that each of

us holds inside his own, most secret soul," Offengeld said solemnly.

Shit, he thought to himself. It's all a pile of shit. He wrote *Shit* in his notebook, then made the letters look three dimensional and shaded their sides carefully.

Offengeld was telling them about Florence now, and about the Popes and things. "What is simony?" Offengeld asked.

He was listening, but it didn't make any sense. Actually he wasn't listening. He was trying to draw Milly's face in his notebook, but he couldn't draw very well. Except skulls. He could draw very convincing skulls. Maybe he should have gone to art school. He turned Milly's face into a skull with long blonde hair. He felt sick.

He felt sick to his stomach. Maybe it was the Synthamon bar he had had in place of a hot lunch. He didn't eat a balanced diet. That was a mistake. For over two years he had been eating in cafeterias and sleeping in dorms. Ever since high school graduation in fact. It was a hell of a way to live. He needed a home life, regularity. He needed to get laid. When he married Milly they were going to have twin beds. They'd have a two-room apartment all their own, and one room would just have beds in it. Nothing but two beds. He imagined Milly in her spiffy little hostess uniform, and then he began undressing her in his imagination. He closed his eyes. First he took off her jacket with the Pan-Am monogram over the right breast. Then he popped open the snap at her waist and unzipped the zipper. He slid the skirt down over the smooth Antron slip. The slip was the old-fashioned kind with lace along the hem. Her blouse was the old-fashioned kind with buttons. It was hard to imagine unbuttoning all those buttons. He lost interest.

The carnal were in the first circle, because their sin was least. Francesca da Rimini, Cleopatra. Elizabeth Taylor. The class laughed at Offengeld's little joke. They all knew Elizabeth Taylor from the junior year course in the History of Cinema.

Rimini was a town in Italy.

What the hell was he supposed to care about this kind of crap? Who *cares* when Dante was born? Maybe he was *never* born. What difference did it make to *him*, to Birdie Ludd?

None.

Why didn't he come right out and ask Offengeld a question like that? Lay it on the line. Put it to him straight. Cut out the crap.

One good reason was because Offengeld wasn't there. What seemed to be Offengeld was in fact a flux of photons inside a large synthetic crystal. The real flesh-and-blood Offengeld had died two years ago. During his lifetime Offengeld had been considered the world's leading Dantean, which was why the National Educational Council was still using his tapes.

It was ridiculous: Dante, Florence, the Simoniac Popes. This wasn't the goddamn Middle Ages. This was the goddamn 21st Century, and he was Birdie Ludd, and he was in love, and he was lonely, and he was unemployed, and there wasn't a thing he could do, not a goddamn thing, or a single place to turn in the whole goddamn stinking country.

The hollow feeling inside his chest swelled, and he tried to think about the buttons on Milly's imaginary blouse and the warm, familiar flesh beneath. He did feel sick. He ripped the sheet with the skull on it out of his notebook, not without a guilty glance at the sign that hung above the stage of the auditorium: PAPER IS VALUABLE. DON'T WASTE IT. He folded it in half and tore it neatly down the seam. He repeated this process until the pieces were too small to tear any further, then he put them in his shirt pocket.

The girl sitting beside him was giving him a dirty look for wasting paper. Like most homely girls, she was a militant Conservationist, but she kept a good notebook, and Birdie was counting on her to get him through the Finals. One way or another. So he smiled at her. He had a real nice smile. Everybody was always pointing out what a nice smile he had. His only real problem was his nose, which was short.

Professor Offengeld said: "And now we will have a short comprehension test. Please close your notebooks and put them under your seats." Then he faded away, and the auditorium lights came on. A taped voice automatically boomed out: *No talking please!* Four old Negro monitors began distributing the little answer sheets to the five hundred students in the auditorium.

The lights dimmed, and the first Multiple Choice appeared on the screen:

1. *Dante Alighieri was born in* (*a*) *1300* (*b*) *1265* (*c*) *1625* (*d*) *Date unknown.*

As far as Birdie was concerned the date was unknown. The dog in the seat beside him was covering up her answers. So, when was Dante born? He'd written the date in his notebook, but he didn't remember now. He looked back at the four choices, but the second question was on the screen already. He scratched a mark in the (c) space and then erased it, feeling an obscure sense of unluckiness in the choice, but finally he checked that space anyhow. When he looked up the fourth question was on the screen.

The answers he had to choose from were all wop names he'd never heard of. The goddamn test didn't make any sense. Disgusted, he marked (*c*) for every question and carried his test paper to the monitor at the front of the room. The monitor told him he couldn't leave the room until the test was over. He sat in the dark and tried to think of Milly. Something was all wrong, but he didn't know what. The bell rang. Everyone breathed a sigh of relief.

334 East 11th Street was one of twenty identical buildings built in the early 1980's under the Federal Government's first MODICUM program. Each building was 21 stories high (one floor for shops, the rest for apartments); each floor was swastika-shaped; each of the arms of the swastikas opened onto four 3-room apartments (for couples with children) and six 2-room apartments (for childless couples). Thus each building was able to accommodate 2,240 occupants without overcrowding. The entire development, occupying an area of less than six city blocks, housed a population of 44,800. It had been an incredible accomplishment for its time.

SHADDUP, someone, a man, was yelling into the airshaft of 334 East 11th Street. WHY CAN'T YOU ALL SHADDUP? It was half past seven, and the man had been yelling into the airshaft for forty-five minutes already, ever since returning from his day's work (three hours' bussing dishes at a cafeteria). It was difficult to tell whom precisely he was yelling at. In one apartment a woman was yelling at a man, WHADAYA MEAN, TWENTY DOLLARS? And the man would yell back, TWENTY DOLLARS, THAT'S WHAT I MEAN! Numerous babies made noises of dissatisfaction, and older children made louder noises as they played guerrilla warfare in the corridors. Birdie, sitting on the steps of the stairwell, could see, on the floor below, a thirteen-year-old Negro girl dancing in place in front of a dresser mirror, singing along with the transistor radio that she pressed into the shallow declivity of her pubescent breasts. I CAN'T TELL YOU HOW *MUCH* I LOVE HIM, the radio sang at full volume. It was not a song that Birdie Ludd greatly admired, though it *was* Number Three in the Nation, and that meant something. She had a pretty little ass, and Birdie thought she was going to shake the tinselly fringes right off her street shorts. He tried to open the narrow window that looked from the stairwell out into the airshaft, but it was stuck tight. His hands came away covered with soot. He cursed mildly. I CAN'T HEAR MYSELF THINK, the man yelled into the airshaft.

Hearing someone coming up the steps, Birdie sat back down and pretended to read his schoolbook. He thought it might be Milly (whoever it was was wearing heels), and a lump began to form in his throat. If it were Milly, what would he say to her?

It wasn't Milly. It was just some old lady lugging a bag of groceries. She stopped at the landing below him, leaning against the handrail for support, sighed, and set down her grocery bag. She stuck a pink stick of Oraline between her flaccid lips, and after a few seconds it got to her and she smiled at Birdie. Birdie scowled down at the bad reproduction of David's *Death of Socrates* in his test.

"Studying?" the old woman asked.

"Yeah, that's what I'm doing all right. I'm studying."

"That's good." She took the tranquilizer out of her mouth, holding it like a cigarette between her index and middle fingers. Her smile broadened, as though she were elaborating some joke, honing it to a fine edge.

167

"It's good for a young man to study," she said at last, almost chuckling.

The tune on the radio changed to the new Ford commercial. It was one of Birdie's favorite commercials, and he wished the old bag would shut up so he could hear it.

"You can't get anywheres these days without studying."

Birdie made no reply. The old woman took a different tack. "These stairs," she said.

Birdie looked up from his book, peeved. "What about them?"

"What about them! The elevators have been out of commission for three weeks. That's what about them—three weeks!"

"So?"

"So, why don't they fix the elevators? But you just try to call up the MODICUM office and get an answer to a question like that and see what happens. Nothing—that's what happens!"

He wanted to tell her to can it. She was spoiling the commercial. Besides, she talked like she'd spent all her life in a private building instead of some crummy MODICUM slum. It had probably been years, not weeks, since the elevators in this building had been working.

With a look of disgust, he slid over to one side of the step so the old lady could get past him. She walked up three steps till her face was just level with his. She smelled of beer and Synthamon and old age. He hated old people. He hated their wrinkled faces and the touch of their cold dry flesh. It was because there were so many *old* people that Birdie Ludd couldn't get married to the girl he loved and have a baby. It was a goddamned shame.

"What are you studying about?"

Birdie glanced down at the painting. He read the caption, which he had not read before. "That's Socrates," he said, remembering dimly something his Art History teacher had said about Socrates. "It's a painting," he explained, "a Greek painting."

"You going to be an artist? Or what?"

"What," Birdie replied curtly.

"You're Milly Holt's steady boy, aren't you?" He didn't reply. "You waiting for Milly tonight?"

"Is there any law against waiting for someone?"

The old lady laughed right in his face. Then she made her way from step to step up to the next landing. Birdie tried not to turn around to look after her, but he couldn't help himself. They looked into each other's eyes, and she laughed again. Finally he had to ask her what she was laughing about. "Is there a law against laughing?" she asked right back. Her laughing grew harsher and turned into a hacking cough, like in a Health Education movie about the dangers of smoking. He wondered if maybe she was an addict. Birdie knew lots of men who used tobacco, but somehow it seemed disgusting in a woman.

Several floors below there was the sound of glass shattering. Birdie looked down the abyss of the stairwell. He could see a hand moving up the railing. Maybe it was Milly's hand. The fingers were slim, as Milly's fingers would be, and the nails seemed to be painted gold. In the dim light of the stairwell, at this distance, it was difficult to tell. A sudden ache of unbelieving hope made him forget the woman's laughter, the stench of garbage, the screaming. The stairwell became a scene of romance, like a show on television.

People had always told him Milly was pretty enough to be an actress. He wouldn't have been so bad-looking himself, if it weren't for his nose. He imagined how she would cry out "Birdie!" when she saw him waiting for her, how they would kiss, how she would take him into her mother's apartment . . .

At the eleventh or twelfth floor the hand left the railing and did not reappear. It hadn't been Milly after all.

He looked at his guaranteed Timex watch. It was eight o'clock. He could afford to wait two more hours for Milly. Then he would have to take the subway back to his dorm, an hour's ride. If he hadn't been put on probation because of his grades, he would have waited all night long.

He sat down to study Art History. He stared at the picture of Socrates in the bad light. With one hand he was holding a big cup; with the other he was giving somebody the finger. He didn't seem to be dying at all. His Midterm in Art History was going to be tomorrow afternoon at two o'clock. He really had to study. He stared at the picture more intently. Why did people paint pictures anyhow? He stared until his eyes hurt.

Somewhere a baby was crying. SHADDUP, WHY DON'T YA SHADDUP? ARE YA CRAZY OR SOMETHIN? A gang of kids impersonating Burmese nationals ran down the stairs, and a minute later another gang (U.S. guerrillas) ran down after them, screaming obscenities.

Staring at the picture in the bad light, he began to cry. He was certain, though he would not yet admit it in words, that Milly was cheating on him. He loved Milly so much; she was so beautiful. The last time he had seen her she'd called him stupid. "You're so stupid," she said, "you make me sick." But she was so beautiful.

A tear fell into Socrates' cup and was absorbed by the cheap paper of the text. The radio started to play a new commercial. Gradually he got hold of himself again. He had to buckle down and study, goddamnit!

Who in hell was Socrates?

Birdie Ludd's father was a fat man with a small chin and a short nose like Birdie's. Since his wife's death he'd lived by himself in a MODICUM dorm for elderly gentlemen, where Birdie visited him once a month. They never had anything to talk about, but the MODICUM people insisted that families should stick together. Family life was the single greatest cohesive force in any society. They'd meet in the Visitor's Room, and if either of them had gotten letters from Birdie's brothers or sisters they'd talk about that, and then they might watch some television (especially if there was baseball, for Mr. Ludd was a Yankee fan), and then right before he left, Birdie's father would hit him for five or ten dollars, since the allowance he got from MODICUM wasn't enough to keep him supplied with Thorazine. Birdie, of course, never had anything to spare.

Whenever Birdie visited his father, he was reminded of Mr. Mack. Mr. Mack had been Birdie's guidance counsellor in senior year at P.S. 125, and as such he had played a much more central role in Birdie's life than his father had. He was a balding, middle-aged man with a belly as big as Mr. Ludd's and a Jewish-type nose. Birdie had always had the feeling that the counsellor was toying with him,

that his professional blandness was a disguise for an un-
bounded contempt, that all his good advice was a snare.
The pity was that Birdie could not, in his very nature, help
but be caught up in it. It was Mr. Mack's game and had
to be played by his rules.

Actually Mr. Mack had felt a certain cool sympathy for
Birdie Ludd. Of the various students who'd failed their
REGENTS, Birdie was certainly the most attractive. He
never became violent or rude in interviews, and he always
seemed to want so hard to *try*. "In fact," Mr. Mack had told
his wife in confidence one evening (she was an educational
counsellor herself), "I think this is a splendid example of
the basic inequity of the system. Because that boy is *basically*
decent."

"Oh *you*," she'd replied. "Basically, you're just an old
softie."

And, in fact, Birdie's case was not that exceptional. Congress had passed the Revised Genetic Testing Act (or
REGENTS, as they were known popularly) in 2011, seven
years before Birdie turned eighteen and had to take them.
By that time the agitation and protests were over, and the
system seemed to be running smoothly. Population figures
had held steady since 2014.

By contrast, the first Genetic Testing Act (of 1998) had
altogether failed its hoped for effect. This act had merely
specified that such obvious genetic undesirables as diabetics,
the criminally insane, and morons were not to be allowed
the privilege of reproducing their kind. They were also
denied suffrage. The act of 1998 had met virtually no opposition, and it had been easy to implement, since by that
time civic contraception techniques were practiced everywhere but in the most benightedly rural areas. The chief,
though unstated, purpose of the Act of 1998 had been to
pave the way for the REGENTS system.

The REGENTS were tripartite: there was the familiar
Stanford-Binet intelligence test (short form); the Skinner-
Waxman Test for Creative Potential (which consisted in
large part of picking the punch lines for jokes on a multiple choice test); and the O'Ryan-Army physical performance and metabolism test. Candidates failed if they received scores that fell below one standard deviation in two

of the three tests. Birdie Ludd had been nervous on the day of his REGENTS (it was Friday the 13th, for Christ's sake!), and right in the middle of the Skinner-Waxman a sparrow flew into the auditorium and made a hell of a racket so that Birdie couldn't concentrate. He hadn't been at all surprised to find that he'd failed the I.Q. test and the Skinner-Waxman. On the physical Birdie got a score of 100 (the modal point, or peak, of the normal curve), which made him feel pretty proud.

Birdie didn't really believe in failure, not as a permanent condition. He had failed third grade, but had that kept him from graduating high school? The important thing to remember, as Mr. Mack had pointed out to Birdie and the 107 other failed candidates at a special assembly, was that failure was just a point-of-view. A positive point-of-view and self-confidence would solve most problems. Birdie had really believed him then, and he'd signed up to be retested at the big downtown office of the Health, Education, and Welfare Agency. This time he really crammed. He bought *How You Can Add 20 Points to Your I.Q.* by L. C. Wedgewood, Ph.D. (who appeared on the bookjacket in an old-fashioned suit with lapels and buttons) and *Your REGENTS Exams*, prepared by the National Educational Council. The latter book had a dozen sample tests, and Birdie worked all the easy problems in each test (the only part that really counted, the book explained, were the first thirty questions; the last thirty were strictly for the junior geniuses). By the day of the retesting, Birdie had a positive point-of-view and lots of self-confidence.

But the tests were all wrong. They weren't at all what he'd studied up on. For the I.Q. part of the test he sat in a stuffy cubicle with some old lady with a black dress and repeated telephone numbers after her, forward and backward. With the Area Code! Then she showed him different pictures, and he had to tell her what was wrong with them. Usually nothing was wrong. It went on like that for over an hour.

The creativity test was even weirder. They gave him a pair of pliers and took him into an empty room. Two pieces of string were hanging down from the ceiling. Birdie was supposed to tie the two strings together.

It was impossible. If you held the very end of one string in one hand, it was still too short, by a couple of feet, to reach the other string. Even if you held the tip of the string in the pliers, it was too short. He tried it a dozen times, and it never worked. He was about ready to scream when he left that room. There were three more crazy problems like that, but he hardly even tried to solve them. It was impossible.

Afterwards somebody told him he should have tied the pliers to the end of the string and set it swinging like a pendulum. Then he could have gone over and got the string, come back with it, and *caught* the string that was swinging like a pendulum. But then why had they given him *pliers!*

That bit with the pliers really made him angry. But what could he do about it? Nothing. Who could he complain to? Nobody. He complained to Mr. Mack, who promised to do everything in his power to help Birdie be reclassified. The important thing to remember was that failure was just a negative attitude. Birdie had to think positively and learn to help himself. Mr. Mack suggested that Birdie go to college.

At that time college had been the last thing Birdie Ludd had in mind for himself. He wanted to *relax* after the strains of P.S. 125. Birdie wasn't the college *type*. He wasn't anybody's fool, but on the other hand he didn't pretend to be some goddamn brain. Mr. Mack had pointed out that 73% of all high school graduates went on to college and that three-quarters of all college freshmen went on to take their degrees.

Birdie's reply had been, "Yeah, but . . ." He couldn't say what he was thinking; that Mack himself was just another goddamn brain and that of course *he* couldn't understand the way Birdie felt about college.

"You must remember, Birdie, that this is more now than a question of your educational goals. If you'd received high enough scores on the REGENTS you could drop out of school right now and get married and sign up for a MODICUM salary. Assuming that you had no more ambition than that . . ."

After a glum and weighty silence, Mr. Mack switched

THOMAS M. DISCH

from scolding to cajoling: "You do want to get married don't you?"

"Yeah, but . . ."

"And have children?"

"Yeah, of course, but . . ."

"Then it seems to *me* that college is your best bet, Birdie. You've taken your REGENTS and failed. You've taken the reclassification tests and gotten *lower* scores there than on the REGENTS. There are only three possibilities open after that. Either you perform an exceptional service for the country or the national economy, which is hardly something one can count on doing. Or else you demonstrate physical, intellectual, or creative abilities markedly above the level shown in the REGENTS test or tests you failed, which again poses certain problems. Or *else* you get a B.A. That certainly seems to be the easiest way, Birdie. Perhaps the only way."

"I suppose you're right."

Mr. Mack smiled a smile of greasy satisfaction and adjusted his massive stomach above his too-tight belt. Birdie wondered spitefully what sort of score Mack would have got on the O'Ryan-Army fitness test. Probably not 100.

"Now as far as money goes," Mack went on, opening Birdie's career file, "you won't have to be concerned over that. As long as you keep a C average, you can get a New York State Loan, at the very least. I assume your parents will be unable to help out?"

Birdie nodded. Mr. Mack handed him the loan application form.

"A college education is the right of every United States citizen, Birdie. But if we fail to exercise our rights, we have only ourselves to blame. There's no excuse today for not going to college."

So Birdie Ludd, lacking an excuse, had gone to college. From the very first, he had felt as though it were all a trap. A puzzle with a trick solution, and everyone had been shown the trick except Birdie. A labyrinth that others could enter and depart from at will, but whenever Birdie tried to get out, no matter which way he turned, it always led him back to the same dead end.

But what choice did he have? He was in love.

174

On the morning of the day of his Art History test Birdie lay in bed in the empty dorm, drowsing and thinking of his truelove. He couldn't quite sleep, but he didn't want to get up yet either. His body was bursting with untapped energies, it overflowed with the wine of youth, but those energies could not be spent brushing his teeth and going down to breakfast. Come to think of it, it was too late for breakfast. He was happy right here.

Sunlight spilled in through the south window. A breeze rustled the curtain. Birdie laughed from a sense of his own fullness. He turned over onto his left side and looked out the window at a perfect blue rectangle of sky. Beautiful. It was March, but it seemed more like April or May. It was going to be a wonderful day. He could feel it in his bones.

The way the breeze blew the curtain made him think of last summer, the lake breezes in Milly's hair. They had gone away for a weekend to Lake Hopatcong in New Jersey. They found a grassy spot not far from the shore but screened from the view of bathers by a windbreak of trees, and there they had made love almost the entire afternoon. Afterwards they just lay side by side, their heads reclining in the prickly grass, looking into each other's eyes. Milly's eyes were hazel flecked with gold. His were the blue of a cloudless sky. Wisps of her hair, soft and unmanageable after the morning swim, blew across her face. Birdie thought she was the most beautiful girl in the world. When he told her that she just smiled. Her lips had been so soft. She had not said one cruel thing.

He remembered kissing her. Her lips. He closed his eyes, to remember better.

"I love you so much, Birdie, so terribly *much*." She had said that to him. And he loved her too. More than anything in the world. Didn't she know that? Had she forgotten?

"I'll do anything for you," he said aloud in the empty dorm.

She smiled. She whispered into his ear, and he could feel her lips against his earlobe. "Just one thing, Birdie. I only ask one thing. You know what that is."

"I know, I know." He tried to twist his head around to

silence her with a kiss, but she held it firmly between her two hands.

"Get reclassified." It sounded almost cruel, but then she had let him go, and when he looked into her golden eyes again he could see no cruelty, only love.

"I want to have a baby, darling. Yours and mine. I want us to be married and have our own apartment and a baby. I'm sick of living with my mother. I want to be your wife. I'm sick of my job. I only want what every woman wants. Birdie, please."

"I'm trying. Aren't I trying? I'm going to school. Next year I'll be a junior. The year after that I'll be a senior. Then I'll have my degree. And then I'll be reclassified. We'll get married the same day." He looked at her with his wounded-puppydog look, which usually stopped all her arguments.

The clock on the wall of the dorm said it was 11:07. *This will be my lucky day*, Birdie promised himself. He threw himself out of bed and did ten pushups on the linoleum floor, which somehow never seemed to get dirty, though Birdie had never seen anyone cleaning it. Birdie couldn't push himself up from the last pushup, so he just rested there on the floor, his lips pressed against the cool linoleum.

He got up and sat on the edge of the unmade bed, watching the white curtain blow in the wind. He thought of Milly, his own dear beautiful lovely Milly. He wanted to marry her *now*. No matter what his genetic classification was. If she really loved him, that shouldn't make any difference. But he knew he was doing the right thing by waiting. He knew that haste was foolish. He knew, certainly, that Milly would have it no other way. Immediately after he'd failed the reclassification test, he had tried to persuade her to take a refertility pill that he had bought on the black market for twenty dollars. The pill counteracted the contraceptive agent in the city water.

"Are you crazy?" she shouted at him. "Are you off your rocker?"

"I just want a baby, that's all. Goddamnit, if they won't

let us have a baby legal, then we'll have a baby our own way."

"And what do you think will happen if *I* have an illegal pregnancy?"

Birdie remained stolidly silent. He *hadn't* thought, he didn't, he wouldn't.

"They'll give me a therapeutic abortion and I'll have a black mark against my record for the rest of my life as a sex offender. My God, Birdie, sometimes you can be positively dumb!"

"We could go to Mexico . . ."

"And what would we do there? Die? Or commit suicide? Haven't you read any newspapers in the last ten years?"

"Well, other women have done it. I've read stories in the papers *this* year. There was a protest. Civil rights and stuff."

"And what happened then? All those babies were put in federal orphanages, and the parents were put in prison. *And* sterilized. God, Birdie, you really didn't know that, did you?"

"Yeah, I knew that, but . . ."

"But what, stupid?"

"I just thought—"

"You *didn't* think. That's your problem. You never think. I have to do the thinking for both of us. It's a good thing I've got more brains than I need."

"Uh-huh," he said mockingly, smiling his special movie-star smile. She could never resist that smile. She shrugged her shoulders and, laughing, kissed him. She couldn't stay angry with Birdie ten minutes at a time. He'd make her laugh and forget everything but how much she loved him. In that way Milly was like his mother. In that way Birdie was like her son.

11:35. The Art History test was at two o'clock. He'd already missed a ten o'clock class in Consumer Skills. Tough.

He went to the bathroom to brush his teeth and shave. The Muzak started when he opened the door. It played WHAM-O, WHAM-O, WHY AM I SO HAPPY? Birdie could have asked himself the same question.

Back in the dorm he tried to telephone Milly at work, but there was only one phone on each Pan-Am second-class jet, and it was busy all through the flight. He left a message for her to call him, knowing perfectly well she wouldn't.

He decided to wear his white sweater with white Levis and white sneakers. He brushed whitening agent into his hair. He looked at himself in front of the bathroom mirror. He smiled. The Muzak started to play his favorite Ford commercial. Alone in the empty space before the urinals he danced with himself, singing the words of the commercial.

It was only a fifteen minute subway ride to Battery Park. He bought a bag of peanuts to feed to the pigeons in the aviary. When they were all gone, he walked along the rows of benches where the old people came to sit every day to look out at the sea and wait to die. But Birdie didn't feel the same hatred for old people this morning that he had felt last night. Lined up in rows, in the full glare of the afternoon sun, they seemed remote. They did not pose any threat.

The breeze coming in off the harbor smelled of salt, oil, and decay. but it wasn't a bad smell at all. It was sort of invigorating. Maybe if Birdie had lived centuries ago, he might have been a sailor. He ate two large bars of Synthamon and drank a container of Fun.

The sky was full of jets. Milly could have been on any one of them. A week ago, only a week ago, she'd told him, "I'll love you forever and a day. There'll never be anyone but you for me."

Birdie felt just great. Absolutely.

An old man in an old-fashioned suit with lapels shuffled along the walk, holding on to the sea-railing. His face was covered with a funny white beard, thick and curly, although his head was as bare as a police helmet. He asked Birdie for a quarter. He spoke with a strange accent, neither Spanish nor French. He reminded Birdie of something.

Birdie wrinkled his nose. "Sorry. I'm on the dole myself." Which was not, strictly speaking, true.

The bearded man gave him the finger, and then Birdie remembered who the old man looked like. Socrates!

He glanced down at his wrist, but he'd forgotten to wear his watch. He spun around. The gigantic advertising clock on the facade of the First National Citibank said it was fifteen after two. That wasn't possible. Birdie asked two of the old people on the benches if that was the right time. Their watches agreed.

There wasn't any use trying to get to the test. Without quite knowing why, Birdie Ludd smiled to himself.

He breathed a sigh of relief and sat down to watch the ocean.

"The basic point I'm trying to make, Birdie, if you'll let me finish, is that there are people more qualified than I to advise you. It's been years since I've seen your file. I've no idea of the progress you've made, the goals you're striving for. Certainly there's a psychologist at the college. . . ."

Birdie squirmed in the plastic shell of his seat, and the look of accusation in his guileless blue eyes communicated so successfully to the counsellor that he began to squirm slightly himself. Birdie had always had the power to make Mr. Mack feel in the wrong.

". . . and there are other students waiting to see me, Birdie. You managed to pick my busiest time of day." He gestured pathetically at the tiny foyer outside his office where a fourth student had just taken a seat to wait his three o'clock appointment.

"Well, if you don't *want* to help me, I guess I can go."

"Whether I want to or not, what can *I* possibly do? I still fail to see the reason you missed those tests. You were holding down a good C-average. If you'd just kept plugging away . . ." Mr. Mack smiled weakly. He was about to launch into a set-piece on the value of a positive attitude, but decided on second thought that Birdie would require a tougher approach. "If reclassification means as much to you as you say, then you should be willing to work for it, to make sacrifices."

"I *said* it was a mistake, didn't I? Is it my fault they won't let me take make-ups?"

"Two weeks, Birdie! Two weeks without going to a single class, without even calling in to the dorm. Where were you? And all those midterms! Really, it does look as though you were *trying* to be expelled."

"I said I'm *sorry!*"

"You prove nothing by becoming angry with me, Birdie Ludd. There's nothing I can do about it any more—nothing." Mr. Mack pushed his chair back from the desk, preparing to rise.

"But . . . before, when I failed my reclassification test, you talked about other ways to get reclassified besides college. What were they?"

"Exceptional service. You might want to try that."

"What's it mean?"

"In practical terms, for you, it would mean joining the Army and performing an action in combat of extraordinary heroism. And living to tell about it."

"A guerrilla?" Birdie laughed nervously. "Not this boy, not Birdie Ludd. Who ever heard of a guerrilla getting reclassified?"

"Admittedly, it's unusual. That's why I recommended college initially."

"The *third* way, what was that?"

"A demonstration of markedly superior abilities." Mr. Mack smiled, not without a certain irony. "Abilities that wouldn't be shown on the tests."

"How would I do that?"

"You must file intention with the Health, Education, and Welfare Agency three months in advance of the date of demonstration."

"But what is the demonstration? What do I do?"

"It's entirely up to you. Some people submit paintings, others might play a piece of music. The majority, I suppose, give a sample of their writing. As a matter of fact, I think there's a book published of stories and essays and such that have all achieved their purpose. Gotten their authors reclassified, that is. The great majority don't, of course. Those who make it are usually nonconformist types to begin with, the kind that are always bucking the system. I wouldn't advise—"

"Where can I get that book?"

"At the library, I suppose. But—"

"Will they let anyone try?"

"Yes. Once."

Birdie jumped out of his seat so quickly that for an unconsidered moment Mr. Mack feared the boy was going to strike him. But he was only holding his hand out to be shaken. "Thanks, Mr. Mack, thanks a lot. I knew *you'd* still find a way to help me. Thanks."

The Health, Education, and Welfare people were more helpful than he could have hoped. They arranged for him to receive a federal stipend of $500 to help him through the three-month "developmental period." They gave him a metal ID tab for his own desk at the Nassau branch of the National Library. They recommended several bona fide literary advisors, at various hourly consultation rates. They even gave him a free copy of the book Mr. Mack had told him about. *By Their Bootstraps* had an introduction by Lucille Mortimer Randolphe-Clapp, the architect of the REGENTS system, which Birdie found very encouraging though he didn't understand all of it too clearly.

Birdie didn't think much of the first essay in the book, "The Bottom of the Heap, an Account of a Lousy Modicum Childhood." It was written by 19-year-old Jack Ch——. Birdie could have written the same thing himself; there wasn't a single thing in it that he didn't know without being told. And even Birdie could see that the language was vulgar and ungrammatical. Next was a story that didn't have any point, and then a poem that didn't make any sense. Birdie read through the whole book in one day, something he had never done before, and he did find a few things he liked: there was a crazy story about a boy who'd dropped out of high school to work in an alligator preserve, and an eminently sensible essay on the difficulties of budgeting a MODICUM income. The best piece of the lot was called "The Consolations of Philosophy," which was written by a girl who was both blind and crippled! Aside from the textbook for his ethics course, Birdie had never read philosophy, and he thought it might be a good idea, during the three-month developmental period, to try some. Maybe it would give him an idea for something to write about of his own.

For the next three or four days, however, Birdie spent all his time just trying to find a room. He'd have to keep his expenses to a bare minimum if he was going to get along those three months on only $500. Eventually he found a room in a privately-owned building in Brooklyn that must have been built a century ago or longer. The room cost $30 a week, which was a real bargain spacewise, since it measured fully ten feet square. It contained a bed, an armchair, two floor lamps, a wooden table and chair, a rickety cardboard chest-of-drawers, and a rug made of genuine wool. He had his own private bathroom. His first night there he just walked around barefoot on the woolen rug with the radio up full volume. Twice he went down to the phone booth in the lobby in order to call up Milly and maybe invite her over for a little house-warming party, but then he would have had to explain why he wasn't living at the dorm, and (for she certainly must be wondering) why he hadn't called her since the day of the Art History test. The second time he came down to the lobby he got into a conversation with a girl who was waiting for a phone call. She said her name was Fran. She wore a tight dress of peekaboo plastic, but on her body it wasn't especially provocative since she was too scrawny. It was fun to talk to her though, because she wasn't stuck up like most girls. She lived right across the hall from Birdie, so it was the most natural thing in the world that he should go into her room for a carton of beer. Before they'd killed it, he'd told her his entire situation. Even about Milly. Fran started crying. It turned out that she'd failed the REGENTS herself—all three parts. Birdie was just starting to make out with her when her phone call came and she had to leave.

Next morning Birdie made his first visit (ever) to the National Library. The Nassau branch was housed in an old glass building a little to the west of the central Wall Street area. Each floor was a honeycomb of auditing and microviewing booths, except for 28, the topmost floor, which was given over to the electronic equipment that connected this branch with the midtown Morgan Library and, by relays, with the Library of Congress, the British Museum Library, and the Osterreichische National-bibliothek in Vienna. A page, who couldn't have been much older than Birdie, showed him how to use the dial-and-punch system in his booth. A researcher could call up almost any book in the world or listen to any tape without needing to employ more than a twelve-figure call-code. When the page was gone,

Birdie stared down glumly at the blank viewing screen. The only thing he could think of was the satisfaction it would give him to smash in the screen with his fist.

After a good hot lunch Birdie felt better. He recalled Socrates and the blind girl's essay on "The Consolations of Philosophy." So he put out a call for all the books on Socrates at senior high school level and began reading them at random.

At eleven o'clock that night Birdie finished reading the chapter in Plato's *Republic* that contains the famous Parable of the Cave. He left the library in a daze and wandered hours-long in the brilliantly illuminated Wall Street area. Even after midnight it was teeming with workers. Birdie watched them with amazement. Were any of them aware of the great truths that had transfigured Birdie's being that night? Or were they, like the poor prisoners of the cave, turned to the rockface, watching shadows and never suspecting the existence of the sun?

There was so much *beauty* in the world that Birdie had not so much as dreamt of! Beauty was more than a patch of blue sky or the curve of Milly's breasts. It penetrated everywhere. The city itself, hitherto that cruel machine whose special function it had been to thwart Birdie's natural desires, seemed now to glow from within, like a diamond struck by the light. Every passer-by's face was rife with ineffable significances.

Birdie remembered the vote of the Athenian Senate to put Socrates to death. For corrupting the youth! He hated the Athenian Senate, but it was a different sort of hate from the kind he was used to. He hated Athens for a *reason*. Justice!

Beauty, truth, justice. Love, too. Somewhere, Birdie realized, there was an explanation for everything! A meaning. *It all made sense.*

Emotions passed over him faster than he could take account of them. One moment, looking at his face reflected in a dark shopwindow, he wanted to laugh aloud. The next, remembering Fran sprawled out on her shabby bed in a cheap plastic dress, he wanted to cry. For he realized now, as he had not on the night before, that Fran was a prostitute, and that she could never hope to be anything else. While Birdie might hope for anything, anything at all in the (now suddenly so much wider) world.

He found himself alone in Battery Park. It was darker there, less busy. He stood alone beside the sea-railing and looked down at the dark waves lapping at the concrete shore. Red signal lights blinked on and off as they proceeded across the night sky to and from the Central Park Airport. And even this scene, though it chilled him in ways that he could not explain, he found exhilarating, in ways that he could not explain.

There was a *principle* involved in all this. It was important for Birdie to communicate this principle to the other people who didn't know of it, but he could not, quite, put his finger on just what principle it was. In his newly-awakened soul he fought a battle to try to bring it to words, but each time, just as he thought he had it, it eluded him. Finally, towards dawn, he went home, temporarily defeated.

Just as he went in the door of his own room, a guerrilla, wearing the opaque and featureless mask of his calling (with the ID number stenciled on the brow), came out of Fran's room. Birdie felt a brief impulse of hatred for him, followed by a wave of compassion and tenderness for the unfortunate girl. But he did not have the time, that night, to try and help her; he had his own problems.

He slept unsoundly and woke at eleven o'clock from a dream that stopped just short of being a nightmare. He had been in a room in which two ropes hung down from a raftered ceiling. He had stood between the ropes, trying to grasp them, but just as he thought he had one in his grasp, it would swing away wildly, like a berserk pendulum.

He knew what the dream meant. The ropes were a test of his *creativeness*. That was the principle he had sought so desperately the night before. Creativeness was the key to everything. If he could only learn about it, analyze it, he would be able to solve his problems.

The idea was still hazy in his mind, but he knew he was on the right track. He had some cultured eggs and a cup of coffee for breakfast and went straight to his booth at the library to study. Though he had a slight fever, he seemed to feel better than he had ever felt in his whole life. He was free. Or was it something else? One thing he was sure of: nothing in the past was worth shit. But the future was radiant with promise.

He didn't begin work on his essay until the very last week of the developmental period. There was so *much* that he had had to learn first. Literature, painting, philosophy, everything he had never understood before. There were still many things, he realized, that he couldn't understand, but now he firmly believed that eventually he would. Because he *wanted* to.

When he did begin working on his essay, he found it a more difficult task than he had anticipated. He paid ten dollars for an hour's consultation with a licensed literary advisor, who advised him to cut it. He was trying to cram in too many things. Lucille Mortimer Randolphe-Clapp had given more or less the same advice in *By Their Bootstraps*. She said that the best essays were often no more than 200 words long. Birdie wondered if future editions of *By Their Bootstraps* would contain his essay.

He went through four complete drafts before he was satisfied. Then he read it aloud to Fran. She said it made her want to cry. He did one more draft of it on June 8th, which was his 21st birthday, just for good luck, and then he sent it off to the Health, Education, and Welfare Agency.

This is the essay Birdie Ludd submitted:

PROBLEMS OF CREATIVENESS

By Berthold Anthony Ludd

"The conditions of beauty are three: wholeness, harmony, and radiance."

Aristotle

From ancient times to today we have learned that there is more than one criteria by which the critic analyzes the products of Creativeness. Can we know which of these measures to use. Shall we deal directly with the subject? Or, "by indirection find direction out."

We are all familiar with the great drama of Wolfgang Amadeus Goethe—"The Faust." It is not possible to deny it the undisputed literary pinnacle, a "Masterpiece." Yet what motivation can have drawn him to describe "heaven" and "hell" in this strange way? Who is Faust if not ourselves. Does this not show a genuine need to achieve communication? Our only answer can be "Yes!"

Thus once more we are led to the problem of Creativeness. All beauty has three conditions: 1, The subject shall be of literary format. 2, All parts are contained within the whole. And 3, the meaning is radiantly clear. True creativeness is only present when it can be observed in the work of art. This too is the philosophy of Aristotle.

The criteria of Creativeness is not alone sought in the domain of "literature." Does not the scientist, the prophet, the painter offer his own criteria of judgment toward the same general purpose? Which road shall we choose, in this event?

Another criteria of Creativeness was made by Socrates, so cruelly put to death by his own people, and I quote: "To know nothing is the first condition of all knowledge." From the wisdom of Socrates may we not draw our own conclusions concerning these problems? Creativeness is the ability to see relationships where none exist.

The machine that did the preliminary grading gave Berthold Anthony Ludd a score of 12 and fed the paper into the Automatic Reject file, where the essay was photostated and routed to the OUTMAIL room. The OUTMAIL sorter clipped Birdie's essay to a letter explaining the causes which made reclassification impossible at this time and advised him of his right to seek reclassification again 365 days from the day on which his essay had been notarized.

Birdie was waiting in the lobby when the mail came. He was so eager to open the envelope that he tore his essay in two getting it out. The same afternoon, without even bothering to get drunk, Birdie enlisted in the U. S. Marines to go defend democracy in Burma.

Immediately after his swearing in, the sergeant came forward and slipped the black mask with his ID number stenciled on the brow over Birdie's sullen face. His number was USMC100-7011-D07. He was a guerrilla now.

Robert Nathan is the author of fifty volumes of poetry and prose, including PORTRAIT OF JENNIE, SO LOVE RETURNS, THE WEANS, *and, most recently,* STONECLIFF, *a novel about an eminent writer who has shrouded himself with mystery. From this body of work he has acquired a reputation as a master of the improbable, as demonstrated below, in one of Mr. Nathan's rare short story appearances.*

ENCOUNTER IN THE PAST

by Robert Nathan

I remember that afternoon very well. I had stopped in at the Faculty Club to pass an hour or two between classes, and had found Maitland, the Anthropologist, standing at the window, looking out at the campus with its lozenges of green grass and sun-dusted trees. He beckoned me over. "Look here," he said.

I saw only a group of students on their way from one class to another. "They're in their usual Spring foliage," I said. "They do it every year."

He seemed curiously depressed. "It's sad," he said. "Down the old garden path."

I shrugged, and turned away, but he stopped me. "You don't know what I mean, do you?" he said. It was more of a statement than a question.

He took my silence for a negative answer. "They are here to acquire knowledge," he said. "And we are here to give it to them."

"So?" I asked.

He stared out at the campus again, and sighed. "Knowledge

is evil," he said. "Have you ever stopped to think about that? It says so in the Bible."

"Oh, that! I said, and smiled. "The myth of Eden and the Tree."

I rather expected him to smile with me, but he remained grave. "Ah," he said, "the myth. But we are beginning to find out that what we took for myths are based upon fact."

I realized that he was serious, and decided to humor him. He was naturally a mournful fellow, but I liked him; as far as I knew, he had never done anybody any harm. "Well, of course," I said carefully, "a great deal of the Bible has turned out to be historically correct. There really was a Flood; and Sodom was built over subterranean sulphur springs . . ."

He stopped me with an impatient movement of his hand. "Don't you find anything strange about Genesis 2:17?" he asked.

I had to think for a moment before I could pin-point it. "That's the one about the apple, isn't it?"

He nodded. "But of the tree of the knowledge of good and evil thou shalt not eat of it," he said.

"Well, yes," I said. "It makes sense, I suppose . . . of a sort. I mean. Innocence . . ."

"What is strange," said Maitland, "is the moment in time when man was first told to beware of knowledge. Or, at least, that moment when it was first mentioned in our history. It was a moment in the Bronze Age, midway between Neolithic times, and our own period; a moment when there actually was very little knowledge in the world—technologically speaking. Why then, one wonders?"

"Yes, of course," I murmured vaguely. I didn't see what he was getting at.

"On the other hand," he went on almost as though he were talking to himself, "if the myth of Eden and the Tree were actually a faroff memory of distant and more knowledgeable times . . ."

But I shook my head. After all, I know something about anthropology, myself. "They would have to be very distant indeed," I said. "We've dug our way through millions of years, and found only the bones of reptiles. And *they* were there for millions of years. There was no room for man in that world."

"Ah," he said. "But the world was already old then. More than three billion years old. Perhaps four. There could have been other ice ages."

He turned from the window, and fixed me with a strangely troubled gaze. "Let's take it from the beginning," he said. "Suppose we put aside a billion years for earth to cool and to acquire its atmosphere. And another billion for the first organic cells to appear, to divide, to turn into complex organisms, to move from trilobite to some sort of sea-creature. And another billion for that sea-creature to turn into fish and mammal, and try the land—and perhaps the air. Meanwhile, of course, the flora have proliferated, and the insects have made an appearance, for RNA and DNA, the ribonucleic acids work fast. So, what have we left? Almost a billion years . . . of empty time."

"I see," I said gravely, humoring him. "You obviously think that there was something going on?"

"I do," said Maitland.

"We've never found any trace of it," I said.

"Tell me," said Maitland, "if your own world were to be wiped out by fission tomorrow, what would be left? The atomic clouds would hide the sun, and bring about another ice age; whatever had survived would be churned up and ground to a powder . . . except the fossils in the deepest rocks. In a hundred million years, what would there be left to find?"

Despite myself, I was a bit shaken; it was an unpleasant thought. "Then you think," I said, "that somewhere in the past there may have been a world like our own?"

"With too much knowledge," said Maitland.

It was some time before I saw him again. I was obliged to leave on a lecture tour, and on my return I heard that he had gone off on an archaeological expedition to the north.

It must have been a good three years later that I bumped into him at the club. He looked a lot older, and I noticed that he'd developed a sort of tic on one side of his face. We exchanged the usual greetings, and then something—I don't know what—made me ask, half jokingly, "Well, did you find that other ice age?"

"Yes," he said.

"The devil you say!"

"It was just as I thought," said Maitland.

He said no more and turned away, but a few days later he asked me to visit him in his quarters. "You're a student of languages," he said. "I have something to show you."

Although I do speak a number of modern dialects, my studies have been mostly in the roots of language. "What I have," he said, "seems to be in some kind of English."

So saying, he brought out of a drawer in his desk, a flat object which on examination proved to be a notebook encased in a sort of plastic cover. "I found this," he said, "in the middle of a block of lava, one hundred feet below the surface, on the south slope of the eastern range of the Canadian Rocky Mountains."

His voice trembled a little. "As far as I know," he said, "there has been no volcanic activity in that region since the Pleistocene."

I looked at him incredulously. "Then," I said, unbelieving, "this would have been laid down before the first ice age!"

"Before *our* first ice age," said Maitland.

I opened the package, and extracted the notebook, which was of some material with which I was not familiar. The plastic case, also, struck me as strange; by way of experimentation, I touched a match to it, but nothing happened. It was, apparently, fireproof; as a matter of fact, later tests proved it to be proof against any heat whatever.

Inside the notebook, written in ink on heavy paper, were words in a language which, at first glance, I also took to be English. But with a difference. "I have to tell you," said Maitland, "it is not reassuring."

"But why don't you publish it, man!" I exclaimed. "A find like this . . . !"

"I want to be quite sure," said Maitland. "For I shall have every archaeologist, anthropologist, and Jesuit on my neck at once. If it's what I think it is, it blows everything sky-high."

My state of mind can be imagined; I was as excited as Maitland and set myself to study the notebook. It was, as he had said, written in English, both familiar and unfamiliar. Many words appeared to have ancient Celtic roots, while others seemed vaguely Semitic. But the strangest thing about it was the suggestion that whoever had written it had experienced a dislocation of some sort, a sudden "flap" of time (as he said) from one age to another. I was unable to offer any explanation of this (and am still unable to do so).

"He seems to have been a man not unlike ourselves," I said to Maitland, "but in a slightly different history. I should like to make a translation of it, if you do not mind."

"Please do," said Maitland. I thought then that he was in ill health, and did my best to hurry.

But I was too late; Maitland died a few days later of a heart attack. With him went whatever proof he had of the notebook having been found actually imbedded in a block of pre-Mesozoic lava.

I append the translation herewith. The last thing Maitland said to me was: "No one will believe it." I offer it as fiction, since I, too, am of the opinion that no one will believe it.

As Maitland said, it is not reassuring.

I call it "Tyrannosaurus Rex."

TYRANNOSAURUS REX

There was simply a moment that was like the flap of a camera's eye: a lightning-fast *click*, unheard, but heart-stopping, and then everything was the same as before. It was like a crack in the day, between one minute and another: a curious moment, nothing you could explain or even find words for. Just a flap, like a camera, or like a page turning, except that it was still the same page; nothing had changed. I was standing on the lawn in front of my house, on a bright spring day, the sky blue and clear and wind-washed overhead, and the leaves stirring. It seemed a little warmer than I had thought, and I noticed that my neighbor, Connover, who had been mowing the grass of his lawn, had taken off his jacket. "It's really quite a lovely day," I said.

He came over to the hedge, and took out his handkerchief to mop his face. "I didn't see you," he said. "How are you, Alfred?"

"Fine," I said. I must admit, it struck me as a little odd, his asking me how I was, since I'd seen him only the day before, but I didn't think much about it.

"That's good," he said. "I heard you had a cold."

"Why no," I said. "I did have a cold last week, but I'm over it."

"Well, that's it, then," he said. He must have lost track of time, I thought. But that wasn't so strange when you come right down to it; I do it myself sometimes, everybody does. The days go by before you know it. The years too, I guess.

A jet went over high above us, ahead of its own sound, and we both looked up. "You know," he said, "sometimes at night they drown out the television. Can you imagine what it will be like when the sky is full of them? And those new, two-thousand-miles-an-hour jobs . . ."

It was true, they were a nuisance; they'd block out half a symphony on the hi-fi, but I was used to them, and anyway, what could you do? "Did you see the satellite go over last night?" I asked.

But Connover hadn't seen it. Not that there was anything unusual about the satellites, but watching them swimming by overhead (they seem to move so slowly) always gives me a strange feeling. Those little star-like lights floating along far up there in the black sky bring home to me the mystery in which we live . . . the sense of endless time and endless space just out beyond earth's little crust of light and air and *now*.

"Do you think we'll ever get to Mars?" I asked, and Connover shrugged his shoulders. "I don't think much about things like that," he said. "They don't help pay the bills."

He was right, of course. As a matter of fact, I found it very hard to think ahead toward a future of some kind for man; I couldn't imagine what it would be like. The past was mysterious enough, what with the new discoveries in archaeology . . . but the future? "How's your wife?" I asked.

"Fine," he said, putting away his handkerchief. She's gone to a PTA meeting."

I thought: of course, I knew that; so had mine. After

all, schools were the real problem, not jets. "Children grow up so fast nowadays," I said.

Leaning on his lawnmower, he took out his tobacco pouch and started to fill his pipe. "You can say that again," he said. "By the time they're fourteen, they figure they're adults, and they want everything. You tell them no and they pay no attention to you."

He sighed, and touched a match to the tobacco. "There's no authority any more," he said. "I mean, nobody listens."

"I know," I said. "It's as though there wasn't anything to listen to."

We both smiled at that. But I had a feeling that I'd said it all before somewhere, and that it wasn't funny at all, but sad, and somehow frightening.

"Yes," said Connover, "they want everything while they can get it. The way they say it, it's now or maybe never. With the bomb, that is, and not knowing will anything be left tomorrow.

"Not that I worry, myself," he added. "I don't believe we'll ever use it."

"Of course not," I agreed. "But *They* might. Now that They have it. There's almost a billion of them; life is pretty cheap over there, the way They look at it."

"Well," he said, "They've forgot to figure something. It isn't the blowing-up of everything; it's the fallout, the radiation; it would wipe Them out just as easy as it would us. It would be maybe a million years before there'd be any kind of life again on this planet . . . if there ever *was* life again, which is doubtful. That's what gets me: not so much dying myself, on account of, hell, everybody's got to die sooner or later—but seeing earth as a kind of burnt-out cinder drifting through space . . ."

"Something would survive," I said hopefully. "Some pattern of ribonucleic acids . . ."

He nodded. "I suppose so," he said. "Under the sea, maybe; trilobites, like there used to be. But you have to think of the mutations; whatever survived would be changed. I mean, you take something like a beetle. You might have a monster."

"You might," I said. "Like in the horror films."

It seemed like a silly sort of conversation, and I turned

to go back into the house. But then I stopped, and looked back across the lawn. "What's the matter?" asked Connover.

"It's nothing," I said. "Only that I never seem to have noticed that tree-fern before."

He looked at me curiously. "You didn't?" he said. "It's always been there; it's just an ordinary eoptolis."

"Yes," I said, "of course." But why did I have a feeling that I'd never seen an eoptolis before?

I went inside and poured myself a Scotch, and I thought about the flap, and wondered if maybe it was me, and whether I ought to worry about it. But my pulse was all right, and the drink tasted fine, and I felt fine. I could hear a jet flying by overhead, and my wife was at the PTA along with Connover's wife. Everything was in order.

I turned the radio on for the afternoon news, and that was in order too. The winter had been cold; crime had more than doubled; the usual number of young hoodlums were stealing cars and beating people on the streets, for which they were being given the usual probation. The usual number of murderers were being let out on parole; anti-segregationists were being jailed, banks were being robbed; the stock market was soaring. New apartment houses were going up in every part of the city, children were dancing, purveyors of drugs and pornography were getting rich, and men were planning to land on the moon. My daughter, aged twelve, was "going-steady" . . . What was there to worry about?

Perhaps the bomb would be dropped some day, and we'd all be wiped out, or changed into "something wild and strange," like the poet said. But it seemed unlikely. Even "They" would hesitate to fill the earth with monster beetles!

I remembered that I had a date to meet my wife at the Zoo. We often met there in the late afternoon, to feed the animals—in particular those cunning little creatures called dinosaurs. There was one who never failed to come to the front of his cage to greet us; he was a clown, he had two tiny forelegs with which he would beg for peanuts or whatever we would give him, powerful haunches (that is, for his size which must have been all of a foot and a half) and a long snout with wicked little possum-like teeth.

For some reason we called him Tyrannosaurus Rex. I don't know why; I guess it amused us. We often laughed and joked about what the world would be like if this little fellow were to increase in size.

This is the second of two stories Mr. (Arthur) Jean Cox has written for F&SF. The first appeared seventeen years ago, and Anthony Boucher called it "an example of perfectly sustained mood." We intend to make every effort to reduce the inordinately long lapses between his stories, for, while Mr. Cox may not be a prolific writer, he is certainly a very good one—as evidenced by the haunting and moving tale you are about to read.

THE SEA CHANGE

by Jean Cox

He left his car parked at the top of the bluff, the face of which fell a sheer two hundred feet to the water. He stood on the verge, looking down. Just a step would do it. He would go twisting through the air in a slow somersault (so he imagined) and strike the sand directly below with a resounding and sickening blow—the only blow that it was in his power to strike.

But, no, he hadn't come here for that. Not exactly. He would have to find a slower way down to the water. He did, working his way cautiously (so as not to fall and hurt himself) down a scraggly, ankle-twisting path, dirt spilling into the sides of his shoes, to the beach. He stood in the sand at the water's edge and looked about. Yes, this was the place. His father had come here ten years ago and drowned himself. James Gordon had been happily married and popular with women; he had had money, health and wide social respect, and was famous in more than one line of scientific research: marine biology and biochemistry, most prominently. Everything he did was a success, and he did a great many

· 197

things. And yet he had come to this lonely beach one early morning, bringing with him certain glass jars and bottles, the visible evidence of a life's work. He had unscrewed the caps from the bottles and jars, and, cradling them gently in his arms, had waded out into the water, returning their contents and himself to the sea. His body had never been found.

And now that man's son and namesake had come to follow in his footsteps. The second James Gordon had not been so fortunate as the first, neither in love nor work. Certainly, not in the former. And although he had carefully not followed his father's line (he was a social worker, but somehow hadn't done anyone much good), he had nevertheless been overshadowed by him. Everyone had drawn the inevitable comparison between his lack of distinction and his father's brilliant career—a career which was qualified, it is true, by that shadowy interrogation mark with which it terminated, but which seemed only to make it all the more interesting and worthy of comment. And he, himself, had drawn the contrast more frequently than anyone else. At least, he had until recently, when he had run for election to the city council and had been ignominiously defeated by an older opponent who, in addition to mocking his youthful idealism—his lofty ideals of social co-operation, his hatred of the loneliness and isolation of modern society, the indifference which everyone feels towards his fellow man—had popularized that comparison which had been confined to his small circle of friends and associates. The public had shown their approval of his opponent's scorn by giving him the lowest number of votes received by any candidate in the history of the town. They had shown him what indifference was, and what loneliness and isolation could be. Well, he would show them that he could do one thing at least that his father had done, and do it just as well.

These thoughts he scanned without examining—they were very familiar—as he stood looking out over the water, which was slate-colored, chalk-streaked, but without anything written ten there that he could read. A bird scudded across the waste. He followed it with his eye and saw a white speck of a sail on the horizon, poignant against the mixed gloom and brightness of the sea-scape. He watched it with an aching wistfulness. It dipped suddenly and was gone, as if it had vanished beneath the waves, and he was alone again. A cold wind came off the water and he shivered, hands shoved deep into his pockets, like a little boy. But time must be passing . . . for the crescent of pale sand upon which he stood was slowly being eclipsed by the dark body of water.

He began plucking at his clothes, stripped himself naked—why not?—and dropped the clothes into a rather pathetic, lifeless-looking heap on the sand. He waded out into the water, which was not as cold as he had feared, and continued out until it was up to his waist, then lay forward and began to swim. He swam well enough, ducking his face and raising it with every stroke, being careful not to swallow too much water. His plan was to swim out until he reached the limit of his strength, and then . . . then that would be it. He glanced back once or twice and saw his car high on the cliff. How friendly it looked! But that was weakness. He swam on.

It took him a shorter time than he had expected to become tired. He was not far enough out yet. He wanted to make sure that his body, also, was never found. He swam on, resolutely. The tiredness of his arms and legs increased, dully at first. His chest ached. He gasped for breath. The waves broke over his head. He spewed water from his mouth. But still he swam. Soon, his arms were almost too sluggish to move, too heavy to lift. He could no longer swim, the best he could do would be to stay afloat. He did for a while, then sank. He reached the air, sucked it in, sank again—and again, convulsively trying to reach the surface. He was not conscious of any desperate will to live asserting itself, as it supposedly always did, at this last moment. He wished only to escape the pain and the immediate horror of suffocation. And he wished to escape the panic. But none of that was possible. His lungs burned, his limbs were tortured by the racking waves. He was gulping in the water now. It was very painful, like swallowing pebbles. The panic grew and as it did, that part of his consciousness which was detached became more distinctly so. It looked on with a disinterested clarity as he struggled in the close darkness, observing remotely that this was the end of his life-story. He had written *finis* to his autobiography.

He stirred, smiled and looked around, like an awakened Adam. It was morning—a beautiful morning, with the light streaming through the water and rippling and wavering on the surface not far above his head—and he was lying nakedly but comfortably enough on a kind of stone couch on the floor of the sea. He moved and stretched and found with a complacent sort of surprise that he needed to draw no breath. And in moving, he twisted easily about in the water and made a further discovery. Something was attached to his back, between the shoulder blades: a dark brown, leathery-looking flap, a foot and a half across; something like a ray-fish, he thought, from what he could see of it. The thing was fastened to him securely—he could feel a tightness back there—and yet, somehow, he felt no disgust or fear. He could see that it was swelling and falling slowly, as if it were breathing— breathing for him, of course. This thought seemed to have the authority of a perception. It was extracting oxygen from the water and passing it directly into his bloodstream. That was marvelous, no doubt, but not a very exciting marvel. Rather, he felt calm, deeply calm, as if he had taken a particularly potent tranquilizer. He felt . . . yes, he even felt a kind of gratitude for his friend. But he wondered, somewhat distantly, what it expected of *him*—for this must be one of those symbiotic relationships one sometimes read about. He supposed he would soon find out.

He stepped forward from his couch, floated, swam in a graceful circle. This underwater Eden was very beautiful. The landscape was dominated by rocks of many sizes and shapes, mottled and striated with subdued and pastel tints, their hard contours softened by an uneven but lush growth of plants and by the drifting lights and shadows which played across them. Many kinds of fish, none of which he could identify, swam everywhere, some very close to him, as if unafraid. Like Adam, he would have to name them. He felt wonderfully buoyant, confident and expectant, as if it were the beginning of the world.

He noticed some odd objects here and there, like small moons scattered among the constellations of starfish. They were clams of various sizes; some very large and others even larger: one foot, two, even three or four feet, in diameter. He went from each to each, tapping curiously on their shells.

Surely, they were not a standard feature of marine life? Not far away, propped almost upright against an outcropping of rock was what at first looked like a great circular stone, but which he found, on moving closer, to be a clam even larger than the others—as much as eight feet across the face, and encrusted with coral and garnished with sensuous sea-anemones. What sort of pearl could *it* contain? He touched the crack at the edge, ran his finger down it and felt an anticipatory thrill—of awe? of fear that the shell might open? or what?—tingling through him. He snatched his hand away and stepped back, contemplating the ponderous shell. Here was a mystery, indeed. What could it mean?

As he wondered, a fish, slender, and long as an arrow, came sailing by between him and the great clam. His startled eye followed its flight and saw it pause, as if pointing—at a spot not far from him where the skeleton of a man sat on a kind of natural throne. The skeleton of a drowned man, most likely. Strange that he hadn't seen it before, as he must have moved by it very closely once or twice. The arrow-shaped fish darted forward suddenly, touched the skeleton and swam away. And he saw that other fish were swimming to it, nudging it and moving away, and that a liquid light, through some movement of the water overhead, played about it. He swam to it, himself, and as he approached it, knew what it was. The skeleton of his father. The thought presented itself to him so easily and naturally that it seemed self-evident, like a recognition. He crouched before the skeleton, in a posture made easy by the water, and examined it.

"Full fathoms five, my father lies." Well, not quite. "Of his bones is coral made." Not quite that, either, although there were, here and there, many little bumps—molluscs, or barnacles, he supposed; he wasn't sure. "These are pearls that were his eyes." Certainly not that, although, peering closely, there *was* something . . . something in the skull, almost like eyes. Perhaps they were. The eyes, say, of some kind of fish that had claimed the hollow shell as a lodging.

> There is nothing about him that
>   doth fade,
> But doth suffer a sea-change,
> Into something rare and strange.

This was certainly true, for he began to make out that the skeleton was alive with sea-creatures. That was to be expected, no doubt, a thing of nature to which he could hardly take exception. They had taken up residence in its skull, rib-cage and loins. A beard-like fringe, of seaweed and perhaps of that netting which hangs beneath a jellyfish, cascaded down from inside the skull and partly over the chest, giving the skeleton a patriarchal appearance. It was quite a collage. Fish came as he studied it and gave it inquisitive and curious nudges.

He saw too that a network of fibres ran from, or into, the skull and from, or into, the chest cavity and pelvic region; and he saw that these pale or white fibres, whether of vegetative or animal matter he didn't know, ran the lengths of the arms and legs, to the feet and hands. One of the hands, the left, rested on the sea of the throne-like rock near him. He experimentally touched it, lifted it. The hand and arm remained intact. The bony fingers, which had been splayed out, drooped somewhat about his fleshy fingers, with the slightest possible pressure. An action of gravity, of course, but rather unpleasant. He stepped away, his hand still in the white fingers, pulling on them. The hand and arm remained intact still as the skeleton leaned forward and shifted position with this tug. He went back several steps and the skeleton was pulled forward and into an upright position. He disengaged his fingers then and snatched his hand away, but the effigy remained standing, with the arm still languidly outstretched. And it even took one or two steps forward, as if from sheer inertia, or to balance itself.

He and the skeleton stood confronting each other in a motionless tableau. Something beat within the rib-cage of the skeleton—and he felt something beating within his own rib-cage, frantically, as if trying to get out. His heart. The skeleton's hand moved, the palm extended towards him, as if in appeal, as if to say, Be not afraid. And he wasn't afraid. His heart quieted, as if touched by something soothing and calming.

The skeleton faced him from about five feet away. He saw that he had been right; it *was* alive with sea-creatures. He could see them moving, wiggling, gently stirring the water and maintaining the structure in an upright position. Perhaps, too, the fibres had relaxed or contracted. The white arm moved again, in a gesture which would have had, if Gordon had made it, the crude significance of a semaphoric signal, but which was now almost overbearingly expressive: When he whose shell? shape? whose shape we bear came, he brought with him the seeds and spores, the life-giving juices. These words sounded in Gordon's own inner voice, but hesitantly, as if he were reading aloud, or translating from a foreign text. His inner voice added, in a quieter, more familiar and fluent tone: He? When he came? It must mean my father. I wonder if it knows . . . A fish swam by, eyeing him: We recognize you. The skeleton spread both arms, indicating the surrounding . . . terrain? No, the tribes of floating and darting fish, the teeming sea-life—which suddenly effloresced, rose up in an aquatic display of its numbers and diversity and wheeled and swirled in concert a moment about the little place in which they stood, then subsided and dispersed. And there came to be, conveyed the skeleton, that which you see, the harmonious thing, the hive.

The white hand made the slightest gesture, and he was conscious of the flap on his back. A claim was being made on him, as if to say, We gave you life. They needed him. But for what? The skeleton lifted a hand, spread its fingers. Your hands are needed, your supple strength and easy skill. The skeleton moved nearer and, reaching out, touched him lightly on the chest. Your warm blood is needed. His blood? That must be because . . . Because its steady warmth makes possible your . . . His what? Your individual mobile intelligence. Was that all? Gordon sensed more, something left unsaid, like a great blank. But he could glean no hint of what it could be, though he searched for it in the skeleton's posture, gesture and surroundings.

The hand moved again, Come and you shall see.

They swam together, the skeleton with a spectral elegance, and he was shown the hive. As they swam, Gordon studied the other, the *pastiche*. It wasn't his father, of course; he hadn't thought of it as being that. In fact, it wasn't a person at all, but a kind of committee; a committee which, oddly enough, was consulted every now and then by the other citizens of the community. Or were they merely giving it helpful nudges along its line of swim? Such thoughts as these, and others, skirted the edges of his mind, but there was too much to see and to feel to attend to them.

It was borne in upon him, by a thousand bits of fresh evidence, that the terrain, with its grottoes and lush plant-life, was beautiful. And that the swarming species of fish were also beautiful, each in its appropriate way. He noted with surprise that fish of different kinds were swimming together and wondered what his father would have thought of that, for he sympathized now with his father's noble fascination with the sea. He, himself, could spend his life here studying the many forms which life had taken and never exhaust the treasures of the hive. What would his father have thought on seeing fish engaged in communal activities, such as gathering, storing and distributing plant food? And what would he have made of those flocks of tame-looking, uniform fish tended and herded by a few other more authoritative and varied fish? But through some subtle alchemy of sympathy, that same silent process which enabled him to respond so fully to the expressive gestures of his host, he saw what his father, peering down from the other side of that wavering curtain above, could never have seen. That to the fish, separated only by a thin film from their wild state, nearly every movement was a pleasure. That the molluscs and other fixed creatures, though likewise filmed over with the pale cast of community belonging, were enjoying lives of gratified palates and reproductive rapture. He wondered if that defined the boundaries of their lives; if they ever felt fear, for instance, or if there was ever anything of which to be afraid.

He had appetites, too, and food was brought to him on a half-shell by toddling crabs. There was a variety of meats which he could not identify, but which tasted absolutely delicious, despite their being eaten in a solution of salt water. He half-suspected that they were synthetic, and that his appetite was being adjusted. There were greens and something sweet, a pastille which he named manna. He ate voraciously enjoying it all. Swallowing was at once natural and strange, as if the mechanism had been altered, or as if his windpipe were closed. Perhaps it was. And his lungs didn't feel as if they were filled with water. Perhaps they weren't. The hive had evolved a strange art and science of the flesh.

THE SEA CHANGE

He had finished his meal and was licking his fingers when he received an answer of sorts to the question he had lately asked himself. He couldn't tell how he first became aware of the danger. It was like some change in the tempo of movement around him, or like the introduction of a sinister anticipatory *motif* in the musical score of a melodrama; but he *was* aware before he saw the supple shadow gliding swiftly across the uneven terrain. This was a fish of which he knew the name. The fear which shook him and took his mentors by surprise was again smoothly quieted. Calm washed through him. But though the physical fear vanished, a kind of disembodied fear was left behind; almost an aesthetic fear, which permitted him to admire the chilling effect of the predator, with its white underbelly and gnashing crescent of a mouth, its effortless strength and easy cruising speed. There seemed to be some danger, judging by the behavior of the hive, but nothing with which it couldn't cope. The myriad drifting fish were sinking quietly into and among the vegetation and the rocks, but the posture of the skeletal structure at his side suggested caution more than fear.

As he watched, he saw two forms rise from the bottom and approach the shark from opposite directions. A nondescript-looking fish swam towards it boldly from the front, while a leathery-flap of a fish, very much like the one on his back, came upon it swiftly, stealthily, from the rear. The shark turned aside toward the heroic commonplace citizen of the hive and flickered upon it. The smaller fish was suddenly impaled in the murderous jaws, its tail protruding gruesomely; a gnash or two, and the tail had folded out of sight and there was a murky, staining, vaporous clot of red. The shark sailed on, directly over head. Its shadow fell across Gordon and the skeleton. And Gordon saw, as it went by, that it had a passenger. The flap was attached to its back. The killer turned to one side, hesitated dangerously—for a shark, quickly exhausting the oxygen from the water around it, must move to live—lashed forward a few yards and then poised again, this time too long. It sank downward and out of sight. As it did so, the population of the hive flushed up out of the undergrowth. Gordon saw many of its members converging quickly upon the spot where the great fish had gone down, while the others resumed their accustomed ways.

The friendly skeleton beckoned and they moved on, convoyed by fish, to explore the little community. Gordon found that the hive was held in a shallow bowl about a quarter of a mile across. It was, he discovered, a bowl on a shelf—for there was a steep drop-off a few yards beyond the outer margin, a drop which went down, down into impenetrable gloom. They, his host and himself and company, swam around the perimeter of the hive. Pausing once or twice, Gordon became aware of something. Coming from outside the pale, there was a cacophony of voices, sounds, vibrations: muffled boots, screechings, bubblings, diffused and deadened slaps—such sounds as one might imagine the drowning to make. But from inside the charmed circle there was a harmony. He could hear it now. He had been dimly and fragmentarily aware of it from the first. He had heard melodious noises from various points of the compass, almost like echoes of a watchman's call, "All's well! All's well!" But now he could tell that there were a great many voices and that they might be likened to a choir, each distinct and distinctive voice singing only its part, but all fitting together in harmony. It was beautiful, extraordinarily comforting and right. He paused a long while, listening to it, and was surprised by an upwelling of tender sympathy. The salt water swam before his eyes like tears. Here, in this little place, was being realized that soft dream of peace, of brotherhood, of community-living free from all harsh strife and competition, which had been one of the great dreams of mankind. All these multitudinous creatures were living together in something like love, exchanging . . . exchanging . . . juices of certain kinds, probably: chemicals, hormones, homeopathic substances. That was why the fish so frequently "nudged" the skeleton, no doubt—just as the ants and bees, living together in their communities, touchingly exchange tiny droplets with each other and with the queen, which bind them together chemically and without which they cannot live. For if the queen bee should die without a replacement—

Fish scattered from him, explosively, in all directions. He paused in surprise, then watched in admiration as they regrouped in swirling loose formations, their sides turning and flashing in the moving water, like a forest of silver leaves.

His guide conducted him back towards the center of the hive and they came to that crop of large clams he had seen on awakening. The skeleton indicated them and, in a comprehensive gesture, Gordon and himself. We have desired to create a form like yours. The hand drooped, conveying disappointment, which Gordon put into words as, But without success. His host bent over one of the clams, a foot in diameter. Here is one such failure. We grieve for it. A chalk-white finger lightly tapped the face of the clam, which responsively opened. Inside, embedded in the milky white flesh, was a red and pink splotch, like the yolk of an egg that had gone bad, and which Gordon found, on closer examination, to be a curled human foetus. It seemed imperfect to his unpracticed eye, even in that early stage of development. But, still, such near success was a marvel. What could the hive have used as a model? Probably, he surmised, the cells, the chromosomes and genes of his father, poor unwitting Prometheus.

The inclination in the form of the skeleton suggested a deep sadness. We cannot suffer this imperfect thing to grow. And there was a gesture, a poignant appeal. Gordon understood. His fingers fortuitously touched upon a sharp stone, like a chiselled arrowhead, which lay nearby. He picked it up, poised it . . . and paused. Strange. He looked around, trying to place what was wrong. It was as if someone were holding his breath, but there was no breath to be held. Everything was as usual. Fish floated silently by. From beyond the pale there came random cacophonous noises, faint and thin in the distance. The skeleton was crouched at his side, face downward, patiently waiting. Nothing wrong. He brought the stone down sharply, performed the abortion by removing the detachable mess. It was over. The clam shut. The skeleton moved. The harmonious hum of the hive sounded all around.

He glanced towards the great clam eight feet across the face and wondered if his host would show him what *that* contained. But not yet, apparently, for he was taken in another direction and for some distance, till they came to a place on the perimeter of the hive. It was a circle of white sand, like an arena, unevenly bordered by rocks. The skeleton drifted downward and stood upright on the margin of the

sand. Gordon imitated the action. The skeleton's attitude
expressed expectancy. We will show you something else.
The hand lifted again in a gesture of sadness and of appeal
to him, that very same appeal as of a moment ago. Another failure to be dispensed with? puzzled Gordon, looking
around. The water was so clear that he could see for hundreds of yards. The touch of a bony finger recalled him
to his companion, the touch somehow also reminding him
of their previous conversation. We have brought forth a
thing-like-you (man-form, emended Gordon), but—The
skeleton struggled to express something, and failed. It fell
back, its limbs moved haphazardly and without relation to
each other, as if it were about to fly apart. The action
was ugly and grotesque, the contrast to his usual uncanny expressiveness disconcerting. There was something which
could not be conveyed, something too horrible and men-
acing. Treachery. Cannibalism. Incest. Fratricide. These
were the ideas among which Gordon groped. Whatever it
was, it was far more terrifying than the shark. Perhaps,
he thought, they had bred something peculiarly dangerous
to the hive. The skeleton stilled its motions, became coherent again and stood upright. It pointed, Look.

And Gordon looked. Something was swimming towards
them from the distance, arms and legs working. A man-form,
indeed. He watched, fascinated, and as he watched, he became aware that the whole area of the hive was somehow
darkening, so that the white arena stood out in brilliant, inviting contrast. The man-creature corrected its course slightly, so that it approached more directly. It grew larger, stilled
its vigorous motions and came gliding easily to the far edge
of the arena, where it touched the sandy bottom and likewise stood regarding them—or him, more likely—across a
distance of some twenty feet. It seemed large for a man, but
was perhaps no more than six feet tall. It was very thick,
with a flat chest, and its limbs were disproportionately heavy,
as if fashioned by a bad sculptor. It was as white as the
belly of the shark, but had a large crop of jet black hair,
from beneath which its eyes, which seemed to be grey,
watched. Its eyes were the most human thing about it, so
successfully human that they might have passed for Gordon's

own; but its sexual organs—Gordon averted *his* eyes—were a failure, being incomplete.

Both he and the creature stood looking on for some time, and then approached each other. That is, the man-thing moved forward towards him, slowly and hesitantly, and Gordon, so as not to appear afraid, even with some idea of facing down the creature, although he was unsure of what was expected of him, stepped forward also. They stopped about eight feet from each other, both upright, with their toes trailing in the white sand. The sounds of the ocean washed around and over them, sounds from beyond the pale of the hive. And again something was strange. Gordon sensed that lapse, that curious suspension, as of a held breath. And he knew what it was—it must be that. He was alone. Alone. Alone, except for the hooded flap on his back, which was breathing heavily but easily, as if asleep. Alone, because the skeleton had moved back, had faded completely into the shadows of the dark ferns and rocks, and no other fish were visible. The hive was no longer holding converse with him. He could hear no harmonious music. He was alone, except for the dead white thing which faced him.

Of course. This is why they needed him. *They*—it, the hive—cannot kill this thing. They cannot kill what is of themselves, what they have brought forth. Some biological inhibition prevents them, one of those hidden feelings, obscure but absolutely peremptory. Such things were not unknown in the animal world; he had read of them. The most ferocious species were unable to kill their own kind; or, fighting, were unable to deliver the *coup de grace* to a fallen, related foe. Such must be the case here. They could plan, but couldn't execute. He remembered the horror the skeleton had been unable to express. What had occasioned it, but the fact that this thing they had created did not share those inhibitions: It must be killing, eating members of the hive. That's why they needed *him*. His teeth were blunt, his hands were weak, but he could kill what they couldn't. Human beings can kill anything. Mothers, fathers, brothers—none are safe. Kinship is of the human mind, not the human body. Incest, parricide, these things arouse a horror, a revulsion so deep that it seems to be physical, but it is of the mind, not the blood. If it had been of the blood, then Oedipus could never have slain Laius and wedded Jocasta . . . These thoughts brushed across his mind. He recognized them mostly by touch, for his eyes were all for the poor failure before him.

The creature came closer. Gordon backed away. On that white face were emotions which he couldn't read. And he was repelled. It was pity he felt mostly; but pity so deep, so helpless and hopeless, that it was sickening. This thing, this freak, this loathsome parody of a man, which should never have come into existence, offended him. It was like an affront. And what did that trembling working of its features mean?

He backed away and the other moved closer. It was now hardly more than a yard from him. Gordon found himself stopped, backed against a large rock. Again, his fortunate fingers touched something lying on a flat surface of the rock: a long thick shard of glass. A broken fragment of a glass jar—and he knew whose jar it had been. His fingers closed upon it. The poor white thing facing him reached out a trembling arm and touched him on the shoulder. Gordon's hand struck out, brutally stabbing the jagged glass deep into the white chest.

The other was at first surprised. Then it made a sound, a cry of anguish—anguish mingled with a rage and despair which turned Gordon faint and weak. Blood curled from the wound and streamed through the water like a scarf. Still the creature cried, features working convulsively. It slumped backwards, kicked, struggled, swam off into the distance. Gordon, tremblingly supporting himself against the rock, watched as it, twitching spasmodically, grew smaller with the distance. Very likely, that wound was mortal. He saw his unlucky foe, at the outer range of vision, cease its struggles and for a short while float listlessly. And he saw the body, now very still, sink downward out of sight, very likely over the edge of that steep cliff, or shelf, into the dark depths below.

And he was no longer alone, for he heard again the harmonious music of the hive, breathing freely with a solemn lilt, a sad strain in it growing ever fainter. The undesirable element had been rejected from the body politic. The weakness ebbed from his limbs and he was tranquil again, even happy.

His spectral guide reappeared and beckoned. Together, the skeleton slightly in the lead, they swam towards the heart of the hive, which throbbed with sound. You will live here forever in happiness. Forever? Yes. Never to cease, for the community is safe. Gordon amplified that for himself, for he had heard that fish never die of old age. It was, he recalled, the fascinating subject of his father's last researches, before he had hit upon the certain means of insuring that he too would never die of old age. He would go his father one better, for this wonderful fringe benefit—now that he was no longer subject to bone-jarring locomotion over dry land and was accessible to the hormonal wizardry of the hive—was to be extended to him. He was never to die, but to live here forever in this underwater Beulah, this submarine Eden.

The skeleton came to a rest and faced him, significantly. There was more. He was to receive something: that much he inferred. A reward? A privilege? An obligation? Perhaps all three were one. They were again at the spot where he had first awakened. Here was the throne on which the patriarchal skeleton had sat so magisterially. And there was the giant clam. It was to the clam that he was conducted. Again, he felt a stirring in his pulse, unaccountable, but like a promise. It was late afternoon. Shadows streamed through the water and touched the face of the shell. The music of the hive rose in a muted crescendo. And there was another manifestation: a fluorescent glow, a pale shimmer or halo, arose and played about the shell, a phosphorescence coming from millions of floating miniscule plants or plant-animals. They bathed it in their soft effulgent light. And the shell opened. Slowly, like a door, as the music thrilled. And he could see that there was something inside, something bedded in the soft flesh. Wider moved the ponderous door, still wider, and he could see the entire form. It was that of a girl. A mammal, beautifully formed.

And as he hovered there, she opened her eyes, which were grey, and lay looking at nothing. He contemplated that silent gaze. It seemed to him to have the blank comprehensiveness of the sea and the sky and the weather . . . and yet, he saw in it something oddly familiar. For he was reminded of those warm lazy summer days, when the stillness and the gently vibrating haze give to our impressions a kind of finality, as if nothing again were ever going to happen, or should.

Summer days? Perhaps it was from his memories of those days, memories unshared by the multi-formed life around him and the pale effigy at his side, that the inspiration and the resource came. *Here? Under the thumb of this giant, for ever?* He turned and took a step towards the skeleton. He grasped its chest with both hands and, heaving, broke the rib-cage, savagely shattering it and tearing the white connecting fibres. And with one other reflex movement, he wrenched the skull from the backbone and sent it tumbling through the water to the sand. He broke the pelvis with a kick, and the thin white legs, left standing separately, toppled in opposite directions. And those creatures which had animated and vivified the structure dispersed and scattered in confusion—squidbit, eelportion, musselpart, codpiece, crabmember. All this was the work of one moment. In the next he felt fear, a spasm of fear such as he had never known before. But it didn't destroy him, for attached to the fear, like a rider, was exultation—*his* exultation, for he knew that the fear was the fear of the thing fastened to his back and which was flooding his body with its artful hormones.

He turned, his muscular legs and feet twisting about in the swirling sand and, reaching back, grasped the brown flap with strong prying fingers. As he did so, he saw the pale grey light die in the eyes of the newborn girl, saw the soft effulgent glow which bathed her and her soft couch die away, saw the heavy door close slowly down and shut as the music died, brokenly. And he wrenched, tore the thing from his bloody back. It flapped frantically away. In the next instant he was struggling with his own panic and despair, for there was not only the pain of his lacerated back, but that inserted blockage in his throat. He gasped, gaped, strangled. Something tore in his throat and suddenly he was choking on water. He expelled the water, held his breath, and climbed hand over hand to the ceiling. But even as he broke the surface and greeted the glorious light and air of the outer world, he knew that he was lost. He could never make it. He was too far from the shore.

But he struggled, struggled for a long time . . . struggled for air, found something over his mouth, something like a leathery flap, and pawed at it with a nightmarish heaviness and a horrible comprehension. The flap, whatever it was, came loose. He lay for a moment, profoundly exhausted. Sweet, clean pure air flowed into his mouth and over his face. He heard voices and felt hands and opened his eyes. He was lying on wet sand and was peering closely—it took him a long moment to make it out—at the mouth-piece and hose of a pulmotor.

"He's conscious. Wait a minute! Wait a minute, there, fellow—you can't get up without help."

But he struggled, anyway, against their ministering hands. "I'll stand on my own feet," he said. And succeeded in doing so.

He heard a gasp, "He's naked!" and saw a pretty girl in white shorts and a striped blouse turn away, giggling.

The man who had spoken, a life-guard possibly, and who was still saying, "Whoa, there, fellow! You're going to the hospital!" threw a beach-robe over him. He almost shook it off. Once he had deplored all separateness from his fellow man, but now he didn't want help or guidance from anyone. Not ever again. His individual resources would be enough for him, who had broken the bonds of the hive and escaped by his own strength.

But at the moment he was very weak. He looked around, unsteadily: at the ocean, the rugged cliff (his car was still up there, he supposed) and at the white houses in the distance—each thing separately and uniquely itself in the clear sunlight. A world worth living in.

"I'm sorry," said another man, sunburnt and dry, who was lending him support from the other side, "we weren't able to save your friend."

"My friend?"

"Yes. Must have been a powerful swimmer. He got you to shore—or, anyway, out to those rocks out there—but couldn't save himself. You were pretty far away, but I could see that you were both hurt. Dashed against the rocks, I guess. Good thing we were looking for you—we found some clothes here. This is no place to go swimming, you know. I saw your friend, large fellow, disappear. He just sank from sight. You see over there, in the boats—they're searching for his body now."

So, mused Gordon, he hadn't done it all by himself, after all? There was something in that to think about.

The two men, holding him above the elbow on each side, conducted him through the crowd of solicitous onlookers—his community of peers: Gordon gratefully, proudly, bestowed that title on them—and from the beach towards a waiting ambulance. The man whose robe he was wearing said, in a tone in which was mingled not only an attempt at consolation but admiration and even envy, "He must have been quite a friend."

Gordon looked out across the bleak ocean. "No," and his reply would have astonished his questioner, if he had heard it. "He was no friend of mine. He was my brother." But he didn't hear it, for Gordon's voice was as faint as the breeze which sighed off the water.

What with the established power of organized labor and the influence of various other protest movements, it may one day become difficult to isolate a reliable case of oppression. But there's always one Place where we can count on finding a vast army of downtrodden. Here, Brian Cleeve spins a fanciful tale of unionization against the blackest Boss of all, with some uncertain, but extremely funny results. Mr. Cleeve has written for British television, American magazines, and is the author of four novels. He is a citizen of the Irish Republic.

THE DEVIL AND DEMOCRACY

by Brian Cleeve

"Your lowness is always Left," said Belphagor, absent-mindedly taking the needle-sharp little soul of a TV producer out of his lapel and starting to pick his fangs. "But I think you ought to see them."

"I will not," snarled the Devil. "I've been master here since before the Creation. D'you think I'm going to let this crawling little worm of a fifth-class sinner come down here and unionise Hell? I will not see them. I will not deal with them. I will not recognise them. And if that picket isn't off Hell's Gates inside ten minutes I'm going to—" and he lashed his tail so violently that he swept half a hundred weight of Kitchen Cob Souls straight out of the soul scuttle into the fire. They sputtered damply and began to smoulder with a rather nasty smell.

"I asked you for Bright Household Nuts," said the Devil in a low, dangerous voice.

Belphagor shrugged.

"That's all there is. And when they're gone—" He shrugged again. "It's going to be extremely cold." He stuck the TV producer in the corner of his mouth in a rather vulgar manner and spread out his hands in front of the smoky mass of bankers, politicans and armchair generals. "If the electricians join in—" As he said it the bulbs began to dim and fade in the great crystal chandeliers. The photographers' models, boutique owners, cardsharps and motorcar salesmen inside the bulbs stopped glowing white, turned dull red, faded and vanished in the general gloom. Only the fire still burned an unhealthy blue at one end of the vast throne room. "I really think you ought to see them," Belphagor said. "After all, just seeing them needn't commit you to anything. And it might get the lights back."

Three hours later they were facing the union organisers across the black basalt conference table in the Third Circle of the Executive Suite. And a nastier group, thought the Devil, he had never seen since the Fall. Imps, trolls, fiends, illiterate demons; not a decently educated devil in the whole pompous bunch. Bad breath and worse manners, picking their noses with their tails, belching and scratching and trying to look as if they were used to sitting in leather armchairs instead of squatting on red hot buckets. "Why am I doing it?" the Devil thought. "Why don't I just retire to the country and forget all this? Lilith would love it. She's been at me for centuries—"

But Belphagor was knocking on the table. "We are delighted to welcome you, gentlemen. If you have a spokesman?"

From the depths of an armchair upholstered in genuine Storm Trooper, a fat, slubberly, oily-faced imp wearing a dirty boiler suit clambered to his hind paws, and wiping the back of a thick, hairy front paw across his snout said in an atrocious accent, "Our spokesman is Brother Grunge," and sticking his paw into the pocket of his boiler suit pulled out a raucous, shouting, gesticulating little soul carrying a picket's banner in one fist and a red bandana handkerchief in the other.

"Brothers!" screamed Grunge, obviously continuing from the point where he had been stuffed into the imp's pocket a few minutes earlier. "I've been fighting the employer-class for forty-seven years, and I know them like a dog knows fleas. They're yellow, I tell you, yellow all through—"

The slubbery imp tapped Grunge on top of his head with a horny claw. "That *is* the employer." He himself had the decency to blush a dark shade of black, but Grunge was unabashed. "An exploiter if ever I saw one," he shouted. "We haven't come here to bargain. We've come here to tell you. We've got solidarity! We've got brotherhood! And we're going to stick this out till Hell freezes over. You can lock us out. You can starve us. But you'll never beat us. We're going to have justice here or you can sell this plant for a pig farm. Isn't that right, brothers? Am I speaking for us all?"

The row of ungainly imps nodded and growled agreement.

The Devil lurched unsteadily to his feet. From the moment that Grunge had first appeared, bilious green and sweating out of the dirty pocket of the leading imp's boiler suit, the Devil had begun to look extremely reactionary, and the effect of Grunge's opening remarks had been far from beneficial. He had begun to swell and change colour in a marked manner, and by the time the imps had signified their agreement with Grunge, the Devil looked dangerously near having a stroke.

"Tell them to go away," he whispered, clawing at the collar of his reptile green suit, which had grown extremely tight. "The meeting is over. Get me my pills."

"But you can't!" screamed the leading imp. "We have to discuss—"

"I don't," said the Devil, holding on to the gold dragon's head door handle for support.

"Fascist!" screamed Grunge. "Close the plant! Pull out the maintenance men! One for all and all for one, eh, brothers?"

The Devil felt his way out of the room, and as Belphagor followed him, Grunge began leading the imps in the first bars of the Red Flag. Five seconds later all the lights went out. Outside the Palace crowds of working-class imps were standing about in sullen idleness, staring up at the now darkened windows of the conference room. Grunge, waving his red bandana, appeared on a window sill, put there by the leader-imp. "Brothers!" screamed Grunge. "Lay down your forks! The day has come! Justice! Liberty! Freedom! Let imps and sinners stand shoulder to shoulder in the fight for democracy! The bosses have divided us! Exploited us! Told us our interests are opposed! Give them the lie brothers! Let sinner and imp clasp hands in deathless brotherhood. Let the fires go out. Unity! Equality! I proclaim the Eternal Liberty of the Imps and Sinners Soviet Republic. This isn't a strike any longer, comrades, this is War, this is Revolution, this is the March of History!"

An ugly roar of approval rose from several thousand scaly throats, counterpointed by the shrill piping of an even larger number of souls just liberated from the furnaces.

"It's the end of everything," whimpered Belphagor. "If only you'd given them the ninety-six-hour week when they first asked for it—"

"Rubbish," said the Devil, who had taken three of his heart pills in a glass of blood and was both looking and feeling very much stronger. "All we need is strategy. Inside a week I'll have them begging for mercy."

They slipped out of the back door of the Palace disguised as scullery imps. Grunge was still shouting. Belphagor shuddered. Sinners were lolling around at their ease. Younger imps were playing hopscotch or blindman's bluff. Older imps were playing cards on top of the cooling gridirons or lying asleep in the still warm ashes of the furnaces. Not a punishment was in progress. Not a sinner was screaming. The chute from the upper regions gaped over its empty bin. "Look," whispered Belphagor, awed by a sight that no devil had been since Eve bit the apple. "It's empty. The top-side staff have struck as well!" A cold shiver of fear ran through his tail.

"We're going to fix Grunge," said the Devil, restraining himself with super-devilish control from kicking the night-lights out of an unwholesome looking stoker-imp who was playing three-handed stud with two souls from the Fourth Circle. "We're going to send him back. Up Top."

Belphagor stared at his Master open-mouthed. "Up Top! Back? But you can't! Why—"

The First Law of Damnation learned by every imp and juvenile devil in third grade forbade it. It was unthinkable. "What comes down can't go up." Q.E.D. Quod est Damnatum.

"Watch Me," said the Devil. "I haven't built this place

down to see it taken over by a bunch of stokers. Stick close behind me and shut your snout."

They threaded their way through the crowd toward one of the lesser Gates. Already things were taking an even uglier turn. In the distance they saw a senior devil surrounded by jeering imps, who were forcing him to sing the Red Flag. On the far side of the Palace there was a sound of breaking glass as if windows were being smashed. "They'll be looting soon," whispered Belphagor. "Oughtn't we—"

"Let them," snarled the Devil. "Tomorrow is another century." They slipped out of the unguarded Gate, threw off their repulsive and humiliating disguises behind a convenient bush, and spread their wings.

"Where are we going?" Belphagor said timidly.

"Belmuck," said the Devil. "Rapesprocket's parish."

An instant later, if you calculate such things by earthly time, the Devil and his henchman landed in a small cave in the fair and wholesome parish of Belmuck. As you'll know, if you are at all versed in Infernal Theology, every Christian parish—and for all I know to the contrary, every pagan parish as well—has a Devil's Hole, through which, a moment or so after death, the souls of the unhappy damned are tipped to their eternal doom by the Resident Imp of the parish, the infernal counterpart of the parish priest. The Resident Imp of Belmuck was Rapesprocket, and a lazier, more unsatisfactory, more inefficient R.I. it would be hard to find in the length and breadth of Christendom. In centuries no parishioner of Belmuck had been tipped down the Hole. Even on the infamous occasion when the two O'Shaughnessys had killed each other over the widow Hegarty's cow, Rapesprocket had let them both slip out of his hands simply by being asleep at the crucial moment. Only family connections and the almost feudal conservatism of Hell had allowed Rapesprocket to retain his Care of Souls. Now, the Devil was extremely glad of it.

"Look at him," he said to Belphagor with grim satisfaction. "As usual." And indeed, Rapesprocket's condition was all too usual, disgraceful as it was. An empty poteen jar lay under his head in the guise of a pillow. Another, almost as empty, lay in the crook of his fat and hairy arm. A clay pipe drooped from the slack and rubbery lips of his sack-like mouth, and out of the black vents of his snout came the soft snores of a far too contented sleep. Rapesprocket was both drunk and incapable.

"Shall I kick his head in?" Belphagor said hopefully. The Devil restrained him.

"Not yet. Not for another twenty-four hours. First we want a soul. Any one will do, so long as we get it in a nice state of mortal sin at the appropriate moment. Then we get Rapesprocket to throw it down the Hole." He was clearing away a thick tangle of cobwebs from the mouth of the Hole as he was talking. "Even Rapesprocket ought to be able to do that if we put it into his hand first."

Belphagor gaped at him. "What good will that do?"

"My dear Belphagor," said the Devil wearily, "there is a strike on at the bottom? Agreed? No souls are going down. No Resident Imp will agree to send one down because of the strike. Am I making myself clear? Except Rapesprocket, who as you see is obviously incapable of having heard of the strike, let alone joining it. Therefore, if we can induce Rapesprocket to send down a soul, this will be whitelegging? Am I going too fast for you? Down below they will refuse to process the soul, or even to receive it, and there will therefore be a discrepancy in the books between us below, and—" He coughed gently as he always did when he mentioned the Opposition—"and Them above."

Belphagor still gaped. The Devil closed his eyes, and thoroughly unpleasant sparks came out of his ears and turned into fireflies. "Someone give me patience," he murmured. "We go back down and negotiate. We agree to absolutely anything they want. And at a certain moment this matter of Rapesprocket's whitelegging is bound to come up. They'll demand the scab-production soul be sent back up Top. And—" He coughed gently—"the Opposition will have to agree in principle that we be permitted to send one soul back up the chute. *They* don't want to see us close down any more than we do. And when I've got that permission—" His eyes glittered ferociously, and he swelled so large that he suddenly filled the cave and bruised himself badly on a knob of rock— "then I send one soul back up the chute the very next instant. But it won't be Rapesprocket's little capture. It will be Grunge." He clicked two clawed fingers together like a

220

pistol shot. "Let's see how long the strike lasts without *him.*"

And followed by Belphagor in an admiring silence, he set off down the hillside toward the innocently sleeping village of Belmuck.

Unfortunately for our two fiends Belmuck believed in "early to bed" if not in "early to rise," and on reaching the village the Devil found not a light lighting nor a soul stirring nor even a mouse nibbling cheese, and he and Belphagor had to occupy the next nine hours by disturbing and tormenting the sleep of any sleeper who caught their impatient and devilish fancy. Even old Concepta Hennigan, who was a hundred and six, had such dreams as startled her out of her white woolly bedsocks, and she woke up with such an appetite for breakfast and such a bright, hopeful eye as astonished her great-granddaughter, Rose Ann McCarthy, into nearly spilling the tea on her great-grandmother's coverlet. "Watch what you're doing, gerrul," quavered the old crone, but instead of telling her to be glad of any class of breakfast at all, even with tea in the saucer, Rose Ann simply smiled delightfully and emptied the spilled drops into the geranium pot on the window sill. "Yer'll kill me geramium!" screeched Concepta, and Rose Ann merey patted the white pillow into its proper shape behind her great-grandmother's nearly bald head, set the tray on her lap, and buttered the homemade bread for her before cutting it into little, delicious morsels for the old woman's convenience. The Devil, who was watching all this sickening display of virtuous patience in the guise of a bluebottle perched on the geranium, ground his front feelers together and obliterated a small, innocent fruit fly which got in the way.

To see virtue in daily use was bad enough, but to see it in such a toothsome shape as Rose Ann McCarthy was infinitely worse. In fact it was intolerable, and then and there, almost forgetting the main purpose of the visit, the Devil determined that the soul he had come for should be the soul of Rose Ann and no other. "I'll have her," he snarled, gnashing his saw-edge proboscis over the mangled remains of the fruit fly. "I'll have her inside the day." And taking off from the geranium he buzzed round her dark and luscious head like an undertaker measuring a prospective customer. Although such a customer would surely have melted the heart of any undertaker and made him regret his mournful calling.

Her hair shone like brown silk of the darkest shade, thick and curling, with the warmth of the sun and the beauty of the moon in its deepest shadows. Her teeth were like white hawthorn flowers behind the red promise of her mouth, and the blush and flush on her cheeks was like the warm down of a ripe peach. And this would be only the beginning of the short description of the heads and chapters of her beauty. The soft throat of her, with hollows under the rounded chin where a bird could nestle; the sweet breast like modesty itself under the starched and pleated linen of her blouse—for what so beautiful as modesty in a young girl?—the supple promise of her waist that would scarcely fill a man's two hands unless he squeezed them tight—and who wouldn't, unless he was a Carmelite?—all this that I'm bashfully describing was merely the outermost revelations of her charm.

Let you watch her walking and guess at the hidden mechanism of her beauty, and I warrant that if you hadn't already, why then you'd fall down in the same fit of passionate attachment as had taken half the boys in the village, the other half being freed from it only by emigration. But however passionate your attachment was, it wouldn't be likely to be half so passionate as that of Desmond Sorley Boy O'Shaughnessy, the postman's son. He had only to think of her to go into cantrips and calamities of passion, and if he got more than two glimpses of her in any one day he had to steady himself that night with enough poteen to slaughter an ox or he couldn't have slept. Indeed it was in a slightly poteen-induced sleep that the Devil had found him, and through his tortured dreams of longing and love had got wind of the apparently impregnable state of Rose Ann's virtue.

"Get rid of that nasty fly!" screeched Concepta, and obediently Rose Ann picked up a tightly rolled copy of the *Cork Examiner* kept precisely for such purposes, and caught the Devil a terrible smack on the left side of the head. Thirty seconds later, and about thirty feet from Concepta's open window, the Devil came to his senses in the middle of the road and narrowly avoided being obliterated by a passing donkey.

"Yerrah damn," said Belphagor in the shape of a wasp, alighting beside his master on a convenient lump of the donkey's droppings. "That was a formidable belt you got from that lassie. I'd leave her alone if I were you."

Most of what the Devil said in reply is completely unprintable, even with stars and asterisks, and all that can be safely repeated here are the last two words, "follow me," as the noisome pair flew off to meditate and scheme in the little shed behind Concepta's cottage. "Now," said the Devil, when they were comfortably settled, "I mean to have that girl if it takes me till Doomsday, or at least till this midnight, and if you're unable to assist in bringing about this simple consummation, I suggest that you don't bother to return below with me, because if you do, by the red hot horns of my Throne I'll make you wish you'd stayed bleating and harping with the—ahem—Opposition."

Belphagor polished his sting on the wooden seat in a rebellious manner, and eyed his Master with something close to exasperation. "Why do you always want things the difficult way? Why not the old woman? Why not Shoneen James, the publican down the road? I've been watching him water the whiskey. He'd be a pushover."

"It's Rose Ann I want," buzzed the Devil, "and Rose Ann I'll have. And I think I know how. Come back out to the road." And back they flew, and a mile out of the village, where down a quiet boreen they transformed themselves in less than an instant into two of the sleekest, most persuasive travelling salesmen that had ever travelled the quiet roads of West Cork. And if you don't know the district, then you must merely accept my word for it that that's saying a great deal. Belphagor wore a camel's hair overcoat in spite of the warm June weather, and a green velours hat with a narrow, curly brim, and a pink bow tie with chocolate stripes, and a shirt to match, and a pearl cuff link just peeping out of the sleeve of his tasteful green suit. A pair of pink fluorescent socks and dark blue suede shoes completed the genteel ensemble.

But if Belphagor knocked the eye out of the day with his tasteful splendour, the Devil put it back again. A pale yellow suit with the faintest white checks in it would have made any onlooker realise at once that whatever else He was, He was a gentleman, by the sheer masterful cut of his double-breasted waistcoat with its sharp lapels and little gilt buttons. His socks were lavender blue, and his shoes were black and white, glistening like a wet heifer in the June sunlight.

His jacket was of the Italian cut, with cuffs to the sleeves and four buttons down the front. He wore a pink rosebud in his lapel and a four-in-hand tie of purple silk with a large gold stickpin to match his waistcoat buttons. His hat was purple to match his cravat and surrounded with a narrow white silk ribbon with a gold buckle. You might well have described him as dripping with splendour, and an ugly glisten of jealousy crept into Belphagor's eye at the sight of him.

"Now for a motorcar," said the Devil, rubbing his hands, and there, shining with chromium plate and glory, was a new American roadster of the most opulent appearance: white leather upholstery, salmon pink body work, radio aerials, fog lights, automatic transmission, power steering, 384 brake horse power, a cruising speed of ninety-seven m.p.h., a built-in cocktail bar, a record player with stereophonic sound, and a collapsible rubber dinghy in the boot, not that the Devil cared about that.

In our villains got, with the Devil driving, up the boreen with them, round into the main road—main is it, God help it, nineteen-feet wide at the best, but yerrah, who'd pay the rates to widen it?—up the main road then, and coming to a whispering rest outside old Concepta's cottage. Out hops the Devil and knocks on the little rose-covered door. "Musha," says he when Rose Ann comes to the door, "glad I am to be the bearer of such good tidings to the like of you, Rose Ann McCarthy asthorre." For he was under the impression that this was how everyone in Ireland talked, no real Irishman having condescended to go below to him for some considerable time.

Rose Ann gapes at him, as well she might, what with his language, and his Dublin accent, and his grandeur, and the sight of Belphagor lifting his green velours hat and grimacing politely at her over the Devil's shoulder. "It *is* Miss Rose Ann that I have the honour and pleasure of addressing, isn't it?" said the Devil anxiously.

"Why yes, sir," trembles Rose, "but—"

"Say no more," says the Devil. "Am I right in thinking that you are a constant user of Sinko soap"—a question to which he already knew the answer, having flown through the kitchen that morning—"and have you by a lucky chance an open packet of that incomparable soap powder in your kitchen at this moment? For if you have—"

"Why yes," said Rose, a tiny flutter of cupidity disturbing the innocence of her mind. "As a matter of fact, I have." And on twinkling feet and dazzling ankles she flew to get it. Little and slight the start of the slope! So back she comes with her bright blue packet of Sinko Powder, and the Devil throws up his hands in delight. "Now for our question," he cried. "Tell me, what is the name of the capital city of England?"

A faint shadow crossed the perfect surface of Rose Ann's forehead as she strained to think. "L-o-n-d-" whispered Belphagor, mouthing and eyeing her from behind his Master's back.

"Why—London!" cried Rose Ann as if she had immediately thought of it herself. Oh sorrow! Oh alas, alas, that second step, that steepening of the slipperty path! Oh poor lost innocence!

"Brains as well as beauty," cried both the Devil and Belphagor, "what a happy combination!" And the Devil snapped his fingers. "Belphy, my dear chap, get Miss Rose Ann McCarthy her splendid Sinko Summer Dress with ruched pleats and pannier pockets and don't forget to slip that crisp new five pound note into one of them."

Back to the car sped Belphagor, where lying on the back seat in its transparent plastic-wardrobe-carrying-bag lay the beautiful dress, little embroidered flowers on the hem, and the crispest, most wearable blue and white linen bodice and skirt that a girl could desire. "Here, my dear!" cried the Devil, lifting his hat once more. "Well may you wear it, and if a stranger may make so bold, may you soon wear it in"— he dropped his musical voice an octave—"in agreeable company. At the dance tonight in the next parish, perhaps? A little of that five pounds expended on potable enjoyments for your aged great-grandmother would make her sleep so soundly that she would never note your absence, why not even if it was prolonged until midnight." But whether he said that aloud or

225

merely whispered it into Rose Ann's receptive mind it would beyond the wit of man to say.

Suffice it that tripping down later that morning to Shoneen James's Public House, Rose Ann bought her great-grandmother a medicine bottle full of watered whiskey and allowed it to transpire in passing that she had a new dress and that if anyone was of a mind to ask her she might even consider accompanying him to the dance in the next parish that same night.

And all this she said over the counter to Shoneen James in the full knowledge that, as she could see by the mirror behind and to one side of Shoneen James's head, Desmond Sorley Boy O'Shaughnessy was drowning his desires in the public bar next door to the Off-License department where she was transacting her business. Oh wirra, how far and fast the innocent can fall when once they lose their footing. Deception on deception. Oh alas. The Devil, again in the unsightly guise of a bluebottle sipping spilt beer on the counter, almost choked with satisfaction. "I'll have her," he spluttered, "I'll have her surely."

And round the corner he buzzed to fill the mind of Desmond Sorley Boy with unspeakable thoughts. And all the rest of that day till nightfall he and Belphagor left neither of those two unfortunates in peace or tranquillity, but first one and then the other had displayed to them the fruits of vice and the shameful joys of dalliance, until putting the two of them together on the same yard of road leading to the dance hall that night was like putting a magnet against a needle. They weren't two steps up the road but they were holding hands.

And they weren't ten steps further again but Desmond Sorley Boy was slyly and covetously slipping his arm round Rose Ann's waist, and finding the resistance to it no more than the merest formality. While at the same time his mind and mouth were filled with words of a passionate persuasiveness such as Rose Ann had never heard in her life and he himself was unaware that he was capable of framing. As no more he was, the poor thick, the Devil sitting on his shoulder all the while and whispering them into his ear one after the other, blarney upon blarney, enough to melt stone let alone the heart of a girl in a new summer dress with flowers on the hem and the change of a five pound note tucked safely in the Post Office Savings account.

And all the while wasn't Belphagor perched on her warm and delicately rounded shoulder in the shape and form of a moneyspider, whispering to *her*? "What's an arm round the waist after what you see in the films and on the television," he was whispering—and then, as they came to the shady trees hanging over the road a quarter mile further on—"Suppose he was to try and kiss you?"—and the hot flushes and blushes nearly scalded his spidery foot as he trod on her bending neck. And Rose Ann near fainting with the persuasion she was receiving from two sides, and Desmond Sorley Boy nearly losing his footing on the stones of the road with unbridled passion—yerrah, damn is it any wonder that inside another ten steps he was kissing her like a starving man with a dish of pig's feet, and she—oh, how can a decent man write down the whole of it, she wasn't resisting him at all?

Everything she'd ever been told by her great-grandmother, and by her grandmother on her father's side (her grandmother on her mother's side being nothing much and dying at sixty-three of an accident), and by her mother, and by her aunt the good nun Mother Mary of the Angels, and by Father O'Byrne in Confessions and Retreats, and by the good Bishop of Cork at her Confirmation, all, all of it might have been so much smoke on the wind for all it did for her, and they weren't half way to the dance—Holy Heaven, if it had been coming *back* from the dance it might have been another thing, but going *to* the dance, not even getting there—where in the world are girls coming to at all, I ask you?— they weren't half nor a quarter of the way to that unhappy occasion of sin, the Belcladder Parish Friday night dance with a late extension till two a.m. of a Saturday morning, when their feet inclined of their own accord it seemed down a little side turning, and from the side turning into a gateway, and from the gateway into a field full of the softest meadow grass and the most fragrant daisies and buttercups and cowslips, and from walking slower and slower, with their arms entwined and their lips meeting, didn't they—

But human pen refuses to continue. Let the Devil watch —as indeed he did—you and I can only avert our shocked eyes and withdraw into some more decent place. And having withdrawn, neither you nor I can know or say exactly what happened during the next hour or so in that misfortunate meadow, or why at the end of the time the pair of them came out looking shame-faced and down cast and brushing grass and cowslips off of their crumpled garments. But I fear the worst. And the Devil was sure of it.

"We have her," he cried to Belphagor, the pair of them resuming their disguise as salesmen, behind the wheel of their powerful car. "Not a second to lose." And throwing the car into one of its powerful gears, the Devil hurtled down the boreen at seventy miles an hour with the lights out, or at least out until the second. The unhappy lovers stumbled into the little lane through the gateway to be suddenly blinded as the ferocious headlights pierced the dark. A scream, a shadow, the thump of a bumper against yielding humanity, and all was done. Leaving Belphagor to park the car, the Devil leapt out of his seat, and his human shape, grasped the fluttering soul of the just-murdered Rose Ann McCarthy, and crushing her in his cruel grip, flew off to where Rapesprocket still lay stretched and snoring beside the long-unused Devil's Hole.

"Let me go!" cried poor Rose Ann, or rather her poor tarnished but still beautiful soul. "Let me go! I am innocent!" But alas she lied, or the Devil Himself for all his dreadful powers could never have matched his noisome strength against her weak innocence. She lied indeed, and with a swift swing of his long arm the Devil pitched her like a baseball into the gaped and snoring mouth of Rapesprocket, waking him up in a choking paroxysm of coughing.

"Garrh, Wugggh, Grummppff," Rapesprocket gargled, and poor Rose Ann all but disappeared down his black throat into his unspeakable interior. But he coughed her out onto the palm of his paw and stared at her as if he had never seen a condemned soul before. Which as a matter of fact he hadn't, at least for several hundred years. "Whar? Who? Wharramarrer?" he said, breathing poteen fumes all over the poor trembling sinner.

"Throw her down the Hole," shouted the Devil impatiently.

"The Hole?" gaped Rapesprocket, staring round in alcoholic

befuddlement. "Wha' Hole? Whug? Oh, the Hole?" And then, even more befuddled, "Who said tha'?"

The Devil began to dance with frustration. "Throw her down!" he screamed, for to achieve his full and ultimate purpose against Grunge it was not enough that Rose Ann, or any other sinner, should merely descend the chute into the waiting bin Below. She must be sent down by an officially accredited Resident Imp, holding his Residence and Parish by feudal enfeoffment from His Satanic Majesty, and now, by the progress of Democracy, unionised by Grunge. In other words, by an Imp who ought to be on strike, but wasn't. In short a whiteleg.

"Throw her down," mumbled Rapesprocket dizzily. "Umm, ahh." He peered round him, lumbering unsteadily to his webbed feet, searching for the black and gaping Hole beside him. So unsteadily in fact that he nearly fell down it himself.

"Help!" cried Rose Ann to the surely not indifferent but still helpless sky. "Save me!"

Rapesprocket sniggered, belched, pawed her in a most indecent manner while folding her into a convenient shape for throwing, and prepared to fling her down the chute. The Devil smiled. Belphagor, who had joined him, clasped his dreadful claws in triumph. Up went Rapesprocket's unsteady arm. One white hand struggled between his gripping claws to appeal uselessly to the lost world of life and hope. "Down she goes," snarled the Devil.

"In with you," cried Rapesprocket, and hurled her into the entrance of the Pit. When out of the Pit came pouring imps and demons, trolls and greasy, unshaven fiends, carrying banners with clumsily written messages scrawled on them: DOWN WITH THE DEVIL-CLASS; DEATH TO THE FASCIST MONSTER SATAN; ANGELS GO HOME; TO HELL WITH SANCTITY; UNIVERSAL FRATERNITY OF IMPS AND SINNERS; SINNERS OF THE WORLD UNITE! YOU HAVE NOTHING TO LOSE BUT YOUR PAINS; and similarly subversive slogans.

One of the upsurging marchers saw Rose Ann's poor soul flying toward him in a downward curve, swung his banner with a practised ease that told of far too many hours wasted playing baseball behind the furnaces when he ought to have been tormenting sinners in front of them, and batted her straight back over Rapesprocket's head, over the Devil's head, over Belphagor's head, and although that was no part of his impish intention, right back into the boreen where a minute or so before she had been knocked senseless and apparently lifeless by the Devil's motorcar.

She opened her eyes to find Desmond Sorley Boy bending over her and murmuring the most extraordinary promises of future virtue and abstention from alcohol and other matters if only she would open them, and it is amazing proof of the resilient qualities of the human frame, and particularly of the young female human frame, that apart from extensive bruising in an indelicate (but given the full circumstances, perhaps an appropriate) place, and a resultant lameness that confined her to her bed for a penitential month, she suffered no lasting ill effects from the night's adventures. Unless her eventual and in fact somewhat hastily arranged marriage with Sorley Boy could be considered an ill-effect. She certainly seemed quite reasonably contented the last time I saw her.

As for the Devil and Belphagor, I am really not at liberty to say what has happened to them, these matters being *sub judice* and even *sub rosa* and *sub sigillum.* But I would advise you that if two extremely well-dressed men should come to your door asking if you by any chance have a packet of Sinko soap in your kitchen, you should close the door sharply in their ingratiating faces and have nothing whatsoever to do with them. Nothing.

Our grandchildren will be part of a civilization bursting at the seams. And their children? It will be a time for drastic action, though not, we hope, as drastic as this astonishing projection.

RANDY'S SYNDROME

by Brian W. Aldiss

Gordana stood in the foyer of the Maternity Hospital, idly watching cubision as she waited for Sonia Greenslade. A university program was showing, shots of fleas of the cliff swallow climbing up a cliff swallow's legs alternating with close-ups of a cadaverous professor delivering himself at length on the subject of parasitology.

When Sonia came up, her face crimson, she took Gordana's arm and tried to hustle her away.

"Just a moment," Gordana said. A line of fleas was working its way steadily up a sheet of damp laboratory glass. "Negative geotropism!"

"Let's get out of here, honey!" Sonia begged. She turned Gordana towards the stride-strip entrance of the hospital, looking rather like a mouse towing a golden hamster—for she was only five months on the way against the blonde Gordana's nine-month season. "Let's get home—you can watch CB in my place if you like. I just can't bear to stay here one moment longer. I was brought up modest. The things that doctor does to a woman without turning a hair!— Makes me want to die!"

The high color disappeared from her cheeks as they sped homewards along the strip. This was the quietest time of day in their level, midmorning, when most of the millions

231

of the city's inhabitants were swallowed into offices and factories. For all that, the moving streets with their turntable intersections were spilling over with people, the monoducts hissed overhead, and beneath their feet they could feel and hear the snarl of the sub-walk supply lanes. Both women were glad to get into Block 661.

"Maybe we'd better go into the canteen," Sonia suggested, as they swept into the porch. "John was on night duty last night, and he's bound to be writing now. He'll get all neurotic if we disturb him.

"He sure works hard," Sonia said. "He's nearly finished the eighteenth chapter."

"Good." Although the Greenslades happened to live in a flat on the same floor as Gordana and Randy, Gordana doubted whether they would ever have become friends but for the chance of their pregnancies coinciding. Randy was a simple guy who worked on an assembly line in the day and watched cubision and cuddled his wife in the evening; John was a scholar who packaged dinner cereals all night and wrote a book on The Effect of the Bible on Western Civilization, 1611-2005, during the day. Gordana was large and content. Sonia was small and nervous. The more Sonia talked, the more Gordana retreated into her little world dominated by her loving husband and, increasingly, her unborn child.

Together, the two girls scanned the canteen menu. Rodent's meat was in fashion this week; the man at the next table was eating chinchilla con carne. Sonia ordered a beaverberger. Gordana settled for a cup of coffeemix.

"Go on and eat if you want to; it's all the same to me."

She looked round nervously. The voice sounded so terribly loud to her, a shout that filled her being, yet nobody else noticed a thing. "Just coffeemix," she sub-vocalised. Mercifully, silence then; it had gone back into its mysterious slumbers, but she knew it would soon rouse completely and wanted to be alone with it when that happened.

". . . Still and all, I mustn't keep on about John," Sonia said. "It's just—well, you know, he works such long hours and I don't get enough sleep and he will play back what he's written so loud. Some of it is very interesting, especially the bit he's got to now about the Bible and evolution.

John says that even if the Bible was wrong about evolution and society, that's no reason for it to have been banned by the government in 2005, and that it doesn't have the harmful effects that they claim. . . . Say, honey, what did the medics say about you back at the hospital? Didn't they say you were overdue?"

"Yes, ten days overdue. My gynaecologist wants to induce it next week, but I'm not going to let him. Men never have any faith in nature. I want my baby born when it wants to be born and not before."

Sonia tilted her little head to one side and fluttered her eyes in admiration. "My, you're so good at sticking up for yourself, Gordana Hicks, I just wish I were that brave. But suppose they grab you next week and *force* you to go through with it?"

"I'm not going back there next week, Sonia."

Gordana kept their flat very tidy and clean, or had done until the languors of this last month. Not that there was much to keep clean. She and Randy had a single room in which to live, ten feet by twelve, with a bed that swung ingeniously down from the ceiling. Their one unopening window looked onto the hissing monoduct, so that they generally kept it opaqued.

They were six levels below ground level. Their building, a low avant-garde one situated in the suburbs, had thirty-two stories, twenty-four of them above ground. With luck, and not too many kids, they might expect to rise, on Randy's pay scale, to the twenty-eighth floor in successful middle age, only to sink back underground, layer by layer, year by year, like sediment, as they grew older and less able to earn. Unless something awful happened, like civilization falling or bursting apart at the seams, as it threatened to do.

Having left Sonia at her flat door, tiptoeing in to see if John was working or sleeping, Gordana put her feet up in her own room and massaged her ankles. Listlessly, she switched on the wall taper, to listen to the daily news that had just popped through the slot.

It had nothing to offer by way of refreshment. The project for levelling the Rocky Mountains was meeting trouble; the plagues of mutated fish was still climbing out of the sea near Atlantic City, covering sidewalks a foot deep; the birth rate had doubled in the last ten years, the suicide rate in the last five; Jackie "Knees" Norris, famed CB star, was unconscious from a stroke. Abroad, there was a rash of troubles. Europe was about to blow itself up, as Indonesia had done. Gordana switched off before the catalogue was complete.

A vague claustrophobia seized her. She just wished Randy earned enough to let them live up in the daylight. She wanted her baby brought up in daylight.

"Then why doesn't Randy study for a better job?"

"Negative geotropism," she answered aloud. "We work our way up towards the sun like the fleas working their way up the swallows' legs."

The foetus made no attempt to understand that, perhaps guessing that it was never likely to meet either swallows or fleas in the flesh. Indeed, it repeated its question in the non-voice that roared through Gordana's being. *"Why doesn't Randy study for a better job?"*

"Do try to call him Daddy, or Pop, not Randy. It makes it sound as if I wasn't married to him for the next five years."

"Why doesn't he try and get a better job?"

"Darling, you are about to emerge into a suffocatingly overcrowded world. There's no room for *anything* any longer, not even for success. But your dad and me are happy as things are, and I don't want him worrying. Look at that John Greenslade! He spent five years working at the CB University course, doubling up on History and Religion and Literature streams, and where'd it get him when he took his diploma? Why, nowhere—all places were filled. So he drives himself and his wife mad, working all his spare hours, trying to pump all that education back out of his system into some magnabook that nobody is going to publish. No, my boy, we're just fine as we are. You'll see as soon as you arrive!"

"I don't want to arrive!"

"So you keep saying—it was the first thing you ever said to me, three months ago. But nature must take its course."

Ironically, his voice echoed hers: *"Nature must take its course."*

He had heard her say it often enough, or listened to it echo round her thoughts since the time he had first made her aware that his intelligence was no longer dormant. Gordana had never been scared. The embryo was a part of her, its booming and soundless voice—produced, she suspected, as much in her own head as in his little cranium that was fed by her bloodstream—seemed as much part of her as the weight she carried before her.

Randy had been hostile when she told him about the conversations at first. She still wondered what he really thought, but was grateful that he seemed resigned to the situation; she wanted no trouble. Perhaps he still did not fully believe, just because he could not hear that monstrous tiny voice himself. However he had managed it, he seemed content with things as they were.

But when Randy returned that evening, he had a nasty surprise for her.

"We're in trouble, old pet," he said. He was pale, small, squat—The Packaged Modern Man, she thought, with nothing but affection—and tonight the genial look about his eyes was extinguished. "I've notice to quit at the end of the week."

"Oh, sweetie, why? They can't do this to you, you know they can't! You were so good at the job, I'm sure!"

After the usual protestations, he broke off and tried to explain.

"It's this World Reallocation of Labor Act—they're closing the factory down. Everyone's been fired."

"They can't do that!" she wailed. "People will always need wristcomputers!"

"Surely they will, but we manufacture for the Mid-European block. Now we've set up a factory in Prague, Czechoslovakia, that is going to turn out all parts on the spot, cut distribution costs, give employment to a million Mid-Europeans."

"What about a million Mid-Americans!"

"Hon, you think we got over-population problems, you should see Europe!"

"But we're at *war* with Czechoslovakia!"

He sighed. You couldn't explain these things to women. "That's just a political war," he said, "like our contained war with Mongolia, but a degree less hot. Don't forget that the Czechs are not only in the Comblok politically, they are now in the Eurcom economically, not to mention Natforce strategically. We have to help those goddamned Czechs, or bust."

"So you're bust," she sighed.

Randy was annoyed. "I could have broken this news better if you could still manage to sit on my knee. When are you going to give birth, I want to know? What are they going to do about it down at that goddamned hospital?"

"Randy Hicks, I will give birth when I am good and ready and not before."

"It's all very well for you, but how do you think a man feels? I want you with your figure back again, sweetie pie." He sank to his knees against her, whispering, "I want to love you again, sugar, show you how much I love you."

"Oh, no, you don't!" she exclaimed. "We've only been married ten months yet! We're just not going to have a whole brood of kids—I want to see daylight through my window before I die—I—"

"Daylight! All you think of is daylight!"

"Tell him I won't be born until the world is a fit place to be born into!"

The sound of that interior voice recalled Gordana to realities. She laughed and said, "Randy Junior says he is not appearing on the world scene until the world scene looks rosier. We'd better try to fix you up with a job, pet, instead of quarreling."

The days that followed were exhausting for both Gordana and Randy. Randy left the one-room flat early every morning to go looking for a job. Since private transport had long since been forbidden inside city areas, he was forced to use the crowded urban transports, often travelling miles to chase the rumour of a job. Once he took a job for three days pouring concrete, where the foundations of a new government building had pierced through the earth's crust into the Mohorovicic discontinuity below, creating a subterranean volcanic eruption; then he was on the hunt again, more exhausted than ever.

Gordana was left alone. She had Sonia Greenslade to visit with her once or twice, but Sonia was too busy worrying about John to be best company: John was under threat of dismissal at the packing plant if his work did not improve. On the next day that she was due to report to the hospital, Gordana went out instead and took a robowl up to the surface.

It was a fine sweet sunlit day with one white cloud shaped like a flea moving in a southwesterly direction over the city. This was summer as she remembered it; she had forgotten how sharply the summer breeze whistled between blocks and how chill the shadows of the giant buildings were. She had forgotten, too, that it was forbidden to walk on the surface. And she had forgotten that transport was for free only on one's own living-level. She paid out from her little stock of cash to get to the first green park.

The park was encased in glass and air-conditioned against the hazards of weather. It was tiled throughout and thronged with people at this hour of the afternoon. An old church stood in the middle of the crowded place, converted into a combined museum and fun house. She went in, past the turnstiles and swings and flashing machines and "Test-Your-Heterosexuality" girls, into a dim side arcade, where vestments were exhibited. People were pressed thick against the cases, but there was space in the middle of the aisle to stand still a minute without getting jostled. Gordana stood without getting jostled and, to her surprise, began to cry.

She did it very quietly, but was unable to stop. People began to gather round her, curious at the sight. Hooliganism one noticed in public, but never crying. Soon there was a big crowd around her. The men began to laugh uncomfortably and make remarks. Two gawky creatures with shaven heads and sidewhiskers, who could not be said to be either boys or men, began to mimic her for each other's delight. The blobby-nosed one gave a running commentary on Gordana's actions.

"New tear forming up in her left eye, folks. This one'll be a beaut, that's my guess, and I've seen tears. I'm World's

BRIAN W. ALDISS

Champion Tear Spotter Number One! Yeah, it's swelling up to the lid, yeah, gosh, there she tumbles, very pretty, very nice, nice delivery, she's infanticipating I should say, got no husband, just a good time girl having a bad time, and now another tear gathering strength in her right eye —no, no, tears in both eyes! Oh, this is really some performance here, and she's trying to catch them in a handkerchief, she's making quite a noise—"

"Help me!" Gordana said to her unborn child. It was the first time she had ever addressed it without waiting to hear it speak.

"I brought you here so that you could make public the latest development."

"You brought me here?"

"I can communicate to you on more than one conscious level, and some of your lower levels are very open to suggestion."

"I don't want to be here—I hate these people!"

"So do I! You expect me to be born into this world among these zombies? What do you think I am? I'm not arriving till the world improves. I'll stay where I am for ever, do you hear?"

That was the point at which Gordana had hysterics.

Eventually they got her out of the old church and into an ambulance. She was shot full of sedative and shipped down to her own living-level.

When she woke, she was in her own room, in her own bed, looking mountainous under the bed clothes. Randy was sitting by her, stroking her hand, and looking remarkably downcast. She thought perhaps he was reflecting on how long he had had to sleep on the floor because the bed was too full of her, but when he saw her eyes opening, he said bitterly, "This jaunt of yours has cost us ninety-eight smackers on the public services. How are we going to pay that?"

Then, seeing he had hurt her, he tried to make up to her. He was sorry to be snide but he thought she had run away. He could not find a job, they might have to leave the flat, and weren't things just hell? In the end, they were both crying. Arms round each other, they fell asleep.

But without knowing it, Gordana had already solved

238

their financial problems. The ambulance crew that shipped her home had reported her case to the Maternity Hospital, and now a thin stream of experts began to arrive at the flat—and not only gynaecologists, but a sociologist from Third Level University and a reporter from "Third Level News." They all wanted to investigate Gordana's statement that her baby would not be born till the world improved. Since they lived in a cash society, Randy had no trouble at screwing money out of them before they could get in to see his wife. In a short while, Gordana was news, and the interviewees doubled. The cash flowed in and Randy bought himself a doorman's cap and smiled again.

"It's all very well for you, darling," Gordana said one evening, as he strolled into the room and flung his hat into a corner. "I get so tired telling them the same things and posing for profile photos. When's it all going to end?"

"Cherub, I regret to say it's ending any moment now. We've had our day. You are news no longer! No longer are you a freak, but one of many."

She flung a cushion at him and stamped. "I am not a freak and I never was a freak and you are just a miserable horrible cheapskate little man to say I am!"

"I didn't mean it, hon, really, not that way, you know I didn't, you know I love you, even if you are ten months gone. But look at the papers!"

He held a couple of coloreds out at her.

The story was all over the front page. Gordana was by no means the only pebble on the beach. No babies were being born all the way across the country, and there were hundreds of thousands of pregnancies of almost ten months' duration. Gordana's hysterics had triggered off the whole fantastic story. The medical world and the government were baffled, or, as the headlines put it, STATE STALKS STORK STRIKE. One columnist was inclined to blame Comblok for the trouble, but that seemed hardly likely since a wave of un-births was reported from all capitals of the world.

Gordana read every word. Then she sprawled on the bed and looked her husband in the eye.

"Randy, there's no mention here of any woman being able to communicate with her unborn child the way I can."

"Like I told you, honey, you're unique—that was the word I was looking for—unique."

"I suspect all these mothers-to-be can talk with their babes same as I can. But you're the only person I told about that, and these women must feel as I do. It's a private thing. I want you to promise me you will not tell a soul I can talk to our baby. Promise?"

"Why, sure, hon, but what harm would it do? It wouldn't hurt you or junior."

"It's a woman's instinct, Randy, that's why, and that's reliable. People would only make capital out of it. Now, promise me you'll keep the secret."

"Sure, pet, I promise, but look, one of all these millions of expectant women is going to leak the secret, you know, and then it will not be a secret any more—"

"That's why it is essential to say nothing!"

"—But the guy—the gal who leaks it first could sure clean up a lot of dough if he leaked it to the right place!"

"Randy!"

"Why, we could even move up into the upper levels, with daylight and all, the way you always wanted."

"Randy, get out of my sight! Get out and don't come back! Haven't you made enough money already out of my misfortune without debasing us both? Get out and get yourself an honest job, and don't come back till you've got one."

Randy spent a dismal night in the canteen bar before he returned unhappily home.

A man was sitting on the bed beside Gordana.

"Hey! You're a fast worker, aren't you?" Randy exclaimed. The drinks were an effective tranquilizer.

His wife gave him a dazzling smile and held out a puffy hand to him. "Come along, darling! Where've you *been?* I thought things over and changed my mind about our little secret. This is Mr. Maurice Tenberg of CB 'Masterview,' who is going to handle me exclusively for the next month."

"For a considerable fee, Mr. Hicks," Tenberg said, rising and extending his hand. "Your wife is a perspicacious business woman."

The clutter of the cubision equipment in the hall was a

considerable obstruction to the occupants of the flats, particularly those unfortunates like Sonia and John Greenslade on the same floor as the Hickses. As they climbed over cables or skirted trollies and monitor banks and power-packs, they could see into the Hickses' room, which had lost the personality of its owners and was now a studio. Gordana's bed had given way to a fancy couch, and the cooking equipment and sink were shrouded behind a wall-length curtain from the Props Department.

Gordana herself was heavily made up and dressed in a new gown. She was the star turn in an hour long program showing at a peak period on national networks. A panel of famous men had discussed the Baby Drought, as it was called, and now Maurice Tenberg was interviewing Gordana.

Subtly, he stressed both the human and the sensational side of the problem, the woman loving her child despite its irregularity, the novelty of a world into which no child had been born for six weeks, and now this remarkable new development, where the mother could communicate sub-vocally with her infant. Finally, he turned to address the 3D cameras direct.

"And now we are going to do something that has never been done before. We are going to attempt to interview a human being while it is still in the womb. I am going to ask Randy Junior questions, which will be relayed to him by Gordana. She will speak out aloud to him, but I would like to emphasize that that is just for her convenience, not his. Randy Junior appears able to have access to all the thought processes going on in her brain."

Tenberg turned to Gordana and, addressing himself to her stomach, said, "Can you tell us what sort of world you are living in down there?"

Gordana repeated the question in a low voice. There was a long silence, and then she said, "He says he lives in a great universe. He says he is like a thousand fish."

"That's not a very clear answer. Ask him to answer more precisely. Is he aware of the difference between day and night?"

She put the question to him, and was aware of her child's answer growing like a tidal wave sweeping towards the shores of her understanding. Before it reached her, she knew it would overwhelm her.

The foetus within could vocalise thoughts no better than she could. But without words, it threw up at her a pictorial and sensory summary of its universe, a scalding hotchpotch of the environment in which it lived. Dark buildings from a thousand reveries, drowning faces, trees, household articles, landscapes that swelled grandly by like escaping oceans, an old ruined church, numberless, numberless people invaded her.

This was her son's world, gleaned from her, cast back— a world for him, floating in his cell without movement, which knew no dimensions of space. Everything, even the glimpses of widest desert or tallest building, came flattened in a strange two-dimensional effect, like the image dying in a cubision box when the tube blows. But if the embryo world had no space, it had its dimensions of time.

In its reverie-life, the embryo had been free to drift in the deep reaches of its mother's mind, hanging beyond time where its mother's consciousness was unable to reach. It had no space, but it had, as it claimed, a great universe indeed!

As the flow of images smothered her, driving her into a deep faint, Gordana saw—knew—her mother, grandmother, great-grandmother—they were all there, seemingly at once, her female line, back and back, the most vividly remembered experience of a human life, faces looking down smiling, oddly similar, smiling, fading slowly as they flickered by, lowly faces at last, far back in lapsed time, their eyes still full of gentleness but at last no longer human, only small and shrewd and scared.

And over those maternal faces raced great gouts of light and shadow, as the cardinal facts of existence made themselves felt not as abstracts but tangible things: birth and love and hunger and reproduction and warmth and cold and death. She was a mammal again, no longer a tiny unit in a grinding life machine whose dark days were enacted before a background of plastic and brick: she was the living thing, a clever mammal, running from cold to warmth among the thronging animal kingdom, an animated pipeline from the distant past of sunlight and blood. She tried to cry at the magnificence and terror of what she felt . . . her mouth opened, only a faint animal sound emerged.

Of course, it made highly viewable CB. A doctor hurried on to the set and revived her, and in no time Tenberg was pressing ahead with the interview.

"He gave you a shock, didn't he, Gordana? What did your baby show you?"

With eyes closed, she said, "The womb world. I saw the womb world. It is a universe. He is right . . . he has a freedom to live we have never known. Why should he want to be born from all that into this miserable cramped flat?"

"Your husband tells me you will be able to move up above ground soon," Tenberg said, firmly cheerful. Gordana could not be said to respond to his tone.

"He can roam . . . everywhere. I'm just an ignorant woman and yet he can find in me a sort of wisdom that our brick and plastic civilization has disqualified. . . . He's— oh, God!—he's more of a whole person than anyone I've—"

Observing that Gordana was on the brink of tears, Tenberg grasped her wrist and said firmly, "Now, Gordana, we are wandering a little, and it is time we put another question to your son. Ask him when he is going to be born?"

Dutifully, she pulled herself together and repeated the question. She knew by his reply that Randy Junior too was exhausted by the attempt to communicate. His reply came back pale and without emotional tone, and she was able to repeat it aloud as he sub-vocalised.

"He says that he and all babies like him have decided not to be born into our world. It is our world, and we have made it and must keep it. They don't want it. It is too unpleasant a place for them . . . I don't understand . . . oh, yes, he wishes us to pass on this message to all other babies, that they are to control their feeding so that they grow no more and do not incapacitate their mothers further. From now on, they will remain as a parasitical subrace. . . ."

Her voice faltered and died as she realised what was said. And it was this crucial statement on which everyone, almost throughout the world, dwelt next morning. This was the point, as an astute commentator was to remark, at which the Baby Drought developed from an amusing stunt to a national conspiracy—for Randy Junior had succeeded in communicating with all other unborn children through their watching mothers—and to a global disaster.

In the Hickses' flat, panic broke out, and the producer of the show ran forward to silence Gordana. But she had something else to convey to the world from her son. Eyes shut, she raised one hand imperiously for silence and said, "He says that to him and his kind, the foetuses, their life is the only life, the only complete life, the only life without isolation. The birth of a human being is the death of a foetus. In human religions which spoke of an afterlife, it was only a pale memory of the fore-life of the foetus. Hitherto, the human race has only survived by foeticide. Humans are dead foetuses walking. From now on, there will be only foetuses. . . ."

The crises, financial, political, national, ecumenical, educational, sociological, economic, and moral, through which the world was staggering, seemed as nothing after that. If the foetuses meant what they said, the human race was finished: there was a traitor literally within the gates.

In maternity hospitals, a series of emergency operations took place. Man could not bear to be defeated by mere unborn children. Everywhere, surgeons performed caesarean operations. Everywhere, the results were the same: the infants involved died. Frequently their mothers died. Within a few days, most countries had declared such operations illegal.

Gordana was immune from this wave of panic. She was too famous to be tampered with. She was made President of the Perpetually Pregnant, she was sent gifts and money and advice. Nevertheless, she remained downcast.

"Come on, hon, smile for Poppa!" Randy exclaimed, when he returned to the little flat a week after the momentous interview. Taking her in his arms, he said, "Know what, Gordy, you and I are going topside to see our new flat! It's all fixed—well, it's not fixed, but we can take possession, and then we'll get it decorated and move in as soon as we can."

"Darling Randy, you're so sweet to me!" she said sadly.

"Course I'm sweet to you, darling—who wouldn't be? But aren't you even going to ask me how many floors up we'll be? We're going to be fourteen floors above ground level! How do you like that? And we are going to have two rooms! How about that, hon?"

"It is wonderful, Randy."

"Smile when you say that!"

They went to see the flat. The tenants had just died—at least the old lady had died and her husband had submitted to euthanasia—and everything was in a mess. But the view from the windows was fine and real sunlight came through them. All the same, Gordana remained low in spirits. It was as if life was a burden that was becoming too much for her to bear.

What with legal delays and decorators' delays, it was a month before Randy and Gordana Hicks moved into their new flat. On the last day in the old one, Gordana went and said a tearful goodbye to Sonia Greenslade, whose pregnancy was now so well advanced that she and her child were communicating. She felt an unexpected reluctance to leave the old environment when the time came.

"You are happy here, Gordy?" Randy asked, when they had been installed for a week in their new home.

"Yes," she said. She was sitting on a new couch that converted into a bed at night—no more cots that folded up into the ceiling. Randy sat on the window sill, looking down at the teeming city. He did no work now and looked for none; money was in plentiful supply for once in their lives and he was making the most of the situation by doing no work, and eating and drinking too much.

"You don't sound very happy, I'd say."

"Well, I am. It's just—just that I feel we have sold ourselves, and the child."

"We got a good price, didn't we?"

She winced at his cynicism. Slowly she got up, looking steadily at him. "I'm going back down to the third level to see Sonia," she said. "We've got no friends on this level."

"Tell me if I'm boring you!"

"Randy, I only said I was going to see Sonia."

Sonia was delighted to see her old neighbor again. She

invited Gordana in and they sat painfully at one end of the little room, close together, while John Greenslade sat at the other end of the room wrestling with the Bible and Western Civilization. He was a small ragged man, not much taller than his wife and decidedly thinner. He sat in an old pair of slacks and a sweat shirt, peering through his contact lenses at his phototape, occasionally uttering a sentence or two into it, but mainly scratching his head and muttering and playing back references in the mountains and alps of magnabooks piled round him. He paid no attention to the women.

"Mine's going to be a little boy—that is, I mean mine *is* a little boy, I mean to say. A little boy foetus," Sonia confided, fluttering her eyelashes. "I don't make him any garments and we haven't prepared a creche or anything— you do sort of save money that way, don't you think? His thoughts are coming on nicely, he talks quite well now— and he's not eight months yet, fancy! It is rather exciting, isn't it?"

"I don't know. I feel kind of depressed all the time."

"My, that'll pass! Now you take me, I don't feel depressed at all, yet I'm much smaller than you, so I find Johnny heavy to carry. He seems to press down on my pelvis just *here*. Maybe when he's more responsive, I can get him to move round a bit. I get cramps, you know, can't sleep, get terrible restless, but no, I'm not a bit depressed. And you know what, Johnny already seems to take an interest in what John is writing. When John reads his stuff aloud, I can *feel* little Johnny drink it all in. I don't think it's just my imagination, I can feel him drink it all in. He's going to be quite a little scholar!"

Gordana broke in on what threatened to become a monologue. "Randy Junior doesn't talk much to me any more. I have a guilty feeling I lost his confidence when I let him be interviewed before all the world. But he's working away down there. Sometimes, I can't explain, but sometimes I feel he may be going to take me over and run me as if I were his—well, his automobile."

"But we *are* their automobiles in a way, bless their sweet little hearts!"

"Sonia, I am not an automobile!"

"No, I didn't mean personally naturally. But women—well, we women are used to being chattels, aren't we? Of men certainly, so why not of our babes?"

"You've been reading too much from the Bible."

"As John always says, there was a lot of sense in that old book," Sonia replied.

"Will you confounded women keep your confounded voices down!" John shrieked, scattering reference books.

The days went by, and the weeks and months. No babies were born live. The foetuses of the world had united. They preferred their vivid and safe pre-life to the hazards of human existence. The vast sums of money that the nations had hitherto devoted to defense were channeled increasingly into research on the birth problem.

Some of this money went to purchase the services of a noted psychiatrist, Mr. Herbert Herbinvore, an immense pastoral man with shrewd eyes, a hairy mole on one cheek, and a manner so gentle it made him look like a somnambulist. He was appointed to get what sense he could out of Gordana, and they met for an hour every day.

In these sessions, Herbinvore coaxed Gordana into going over all her past life and into the reverie-life of her unborn child. He made copious notes, nodded wisely, closed his eyes, and went away smiling each morning at eleven-thirty.

When this had been going on for some weeks with no noticeable result, Gordana asked him, "Are you coming to any conclusions yet, Herbert?"

He twinkled slightly at her. "Surprisingly enough, yes. My assumptions are based on the opinion I have reached that you are a woman."

"You don't say!"

"But I do say, my dear. It's something that mankind has never seriously taken into account—the femaleness of women, I mean. How did your foetus and every other foetus suddenly begin to communicate to you? Because that's what foetuses have always done with their mothers; that's why the months of pregnancy are such a dreamy time for most women. It has come to be a much more outward thing now because of the crisis, but women have always been in contact with the verities of life that little

Randy exposed to you. Man is cut off from that, and has to make the external world, without much aid from his womankind. It is, as they say, a man's world. More and more, these last centuries, the external world has ceased to resemble the reality that women know of sub-consciously. When the conflict between the two opposites became sharp enough, the foetuses were jerked into a state of wakefulness by it—with the results we are now experiencing."

Suddenly she was overcome with laughter. It seemed so silly, this fanciful stuff he was talking! As if he had any idea of what it was like to be a woman—yet he was telling her. "And does—and does—" she controlled herself, "—does what you are saying now resemble most reality or the external world?"

"Mrs. Hicks, you laugh like a sick woman! Man has adapted to his world, woman has failed to. Woman has stuck in the little reality-world. You take this matter too lightly. Unless you and all the other women like you pull yourselves together and deliver the goods, there isn't going to be any sort of reality to adjust to, because the human race will all be extinct."

"How dare you call my son 'goods'? He is an individual, and exists for his own self and not for any abstract like the human race. That's another man's notion if I ever heard one!"

He nodded so gently that it seemed he must rock himself to sleep. "You more than confirm my diagnosis."

They were both silent for a little while, and then Gordana asked, "Herbert, haven't you ever read the Bible?"

"The Bible? It was long ago debunked as a work of cosmology, while as a handbook of etiquette it is entirely out of date. No, I haven't read it. Why do you ask?"

"A friend told me it says 'Go forth and multiply.' I wondered if maybe a woman wrote it?" And she started to laugh again. The sound of her son's voice within cut off her giggles.

"Mom, what is it like to be a man? Why is it so different?"

She had forgotten, as so often she did, that every conversation she had was available to Randy Junior as soon as it registered in her mind. "Those are silly questions, darling. Go back to sleep," she said.

"What did he ask?" Herbinvore inquired, looking more relaxed than ever.

"Never mind," she muttered. Randy was repeating his questions. He repeated them after Herbinvore had left and throughout the afternoon, as though he could not believe there were things his omnipresent host did not know. He was only silenced when Sonia came to visit in the afternoon.

Sonia looked tear-stained and dishevelled. She clutched at Gordana and looked at her wild-eyed.

"Is your husband here?"

"No. Out as usual."

"Listen, Gordana, my poor little babykins has gone stark staring crazy! He wanted to know a whole lot of things I couldn't answer, and so I got John to answer, and then Johnny got interested in John's work, you know how they are. I just can't satisfy him. And now this morning—what do you think?—he ordered me to work at the phototaper when my husband was getting some sleep, and then he just took over my mind, and made me write the most utter nonsense!"

She waved a tape at Gordana. Gordana reached for it, but Sonia snatched it away.

"If you listen to it, you'll think my poor little baby has gone mad. He's digested everything from my husband's brain and scrambled it all up, and you'll think he's gone mad. As a matter of fact, *I* think he's gone mad. . . ."

As she broke into wails of misery, Gordana grabbed the tape and thrust it into the wall tapespeaker.

Sonia's voice filled the room—Sonia's voice, but barely recognisable as such, as it slowly pronounced its nonsense.

"Here no able, sow no able, spee no able, was the mogger of the three mogries, mescalin, feminine, and deuteronomy, and by their boots ye shall know them. And it came to pass water, and darkness was over the face of the land, so that the land hid its face and could not look itself in the I, as was prophesied even in the days of the lesser prophets, particularly those born of the linen of Bluff King Hal, Hal King Bluff and of course Bess Queen Good. Though she had the soul of a woman, she had the body of a man,

kept in her privy where none should see. Woe to women
who commit deuteronomy!

"The former treatise are shoter than the ones you are
wearing, O excellent Thuck; yet, yea verily and between
you and me and this megadeth, the royal lineage shall not
pass away nor the land of the Ambisaurs which devour the
sledded Polticians on the ice, nor the sun in the morning
nor the moon in June, and as long as rivers cease to run
this treaty shall stand between us though dynasties pass:
you, you, and your airs and assigns and all who inherit,
viz., your mother, your mother-in-law, daughter, female
servant, ass, cow, sister, governess, god-daughter, or any
other species of deuteronomous female, herinafter referred
to as The Publishers, shall not brew Liquor on the prem-
ises or allow anything to ferment or rot except on the third
Sunday after Sexagesima, Boadecia, or Cleopatra, unto the
third and fourth degeneration, for ever and ever, Amen."

The silence grew in the room until Sonia said in her
tiniest voice, "You see, it's utterly meaningless. . . ."

"It seemed to me to have lots of—" Gordana broke off.
The foetus within her was making a noise like laughter;
it said, *Now do you believe in Santa Claustrophobia!*

Urgently, Gordana said, "I'm sorry, Sonia, you must get
out of here, before you infect Randy Junior with the madness too. He is starting to talk nonsense as well."

Without ceremony, she hustled her little bulging friend
out of the door and leant against it, panting.

"You're going to try and scare us, aren't you?" she said
aloud.

*Do you suffer from negative geotropism? Remember the
fleas, climbing ever upward? You know what they were
doing.*

"Annoying the swallows! But you're not going to be a
flea, you're going to be a man."

*The fleas were climbing upwards towards the light.
Let there be light, let there be light!*

Whimpering softly, she crept over to the couch, lay down
on it, and began meekly to give birth.

Randy Hicks, Herbert Herbinvore, Maurice Tenberg, the
Mayor of the city, the Director of the Maternity Hospital,
a gynaecologist and her assistant, three nurses, and an in-

quisitive shoeshine boy who happened to be passing stood round Gordana's bed, admiring her and her baby as they slept the deep sleep that only sedation can bring.

"She'll be just fine," Herbinvore murmured to Randy, standing more relaxedly than most men sit. "Everything is working out as I predicted. Don't forget, I was consulting your friend Sonia Greenslade every morning from eleven-thirty till twelve-thirty, and I could see how these foetuses were feeling. They liked their little world, but they were getting past it. Remember what your son was supposed to have said about a foetus having to die for a human to be born?"

Randy nodded mutely.

"Then picture how a human would feel if his life were unnaturally protracted to two hundred years; he would long for death and for what our superstitious ancestors would have called the Light Beyond. Young Randy felt like that. The time came when he had to overcome the forces ranged against him and move forth to be born."

Randy pulled himself out of his daze. He longed to kneel and embrace his sleeping wife, but was cagey about the nurses who might laugh at him. "Wait a bit, Doc, how do you mean he had to overcome the forces ranged against him? What forces? It was his idea not to get born in the first place."

Only an old cow asleep in a meadow deep in grass could have shaken her head as gently as Herbinvore did now in contradiction.

"No, no, no, I fear not. Things were not as they might have seemed to laymen like you. As I shall be saying to the world over the CB later tonight, the foetuses really had no option in the matter. The world was at crisis—half a dozen crises—and the women just suddenly came out with a mass neurosis. You might even say that world tensions had paralysed women like Gordana, paralysed their uterine contractions so that labor could not take place. There are examples in the insect kingdom—among the flies, for instance—of creatures that can control their pregnancies until the moment is fit, so this incident is not entirely without precedent. It was the women that didn't want babies—nothing to do with what the babies felt at all."

"But you heard what my kid—what Randy Junior said."

"No, Mr. Hicks, I did not. I never heard him utter a word. Nor did you. Nor did anyone else. We have only the word of the reluctant mothers that their babes spoke. That idea is all nonsense. Telepathy is nonsense, hogwash! The whole idea was just part and parcel of the womanly mass neurosis. Now that it looks as if the world's on the upgrade again, the girls are all giving birth. I'll guarantee that by tomorrow there's not a delayed pregnancy left!"

Randy felt himself compelled to scratch his head, but the whirling thoughts there refused to come to heel. "Gosh!" he said.

"Precisely. I have it all diagnosed." The grass in the meadow was well up to the cow's hocks. "In fact, I will tell you something else."

But Randy had already heard too much. Breaking away from the hypnotic sight of Herbinvore pontificating, he braved the nurses and flung himself down beside Gordana. Rousing gently, she wrapped an arm about him. The baby opened its blue eyes and looked at its father with a knowing and intelligent air.

Unperturbed, the psychiatrist continued to hold forth for the good of the company. "I will tell you something else. When I had completed my diagnosis, I placed Mrs. Greenslade under light hypnosis to persuade her to write the nonsense she did. That was quite enough to scare the women into their senses again. I have the feeling that when this whole affair is written about in times to come, it may well be known as 'Herbinvore's Syndrome'. . . ."

The babe on the bed fixed him with a knowing eye.

"Nuts!" it said.